Lady of the Grave

F.S. AUTUMN

Copyright © 2024 by F.S. Autumn

All rights reserved.

No part of this book may be reproduced, in any form or by any electronic or mechanical means, including information storage and retrieval systems, without written permission, except for in the use of brief quotations embodied in articles, interviews, and reviews.

Without limiting the author's exclusive rights, any unauthorized use of this publication to train generative artificial intelligence (AI) technologies is expressly prohibited.

This is a work of fiction. All of the characters, events, and incidents portrayed in this novel are either the products of the author's imagination or used fictitiously. Any resemblance to actual persons, living or dead, or actual events is purely coincidental.

Cover and Map Design: Emily Kirk (IG: @ek.design.and.art)
Interior Formatting and Illustrations: FeelinStabby (IG: @feelinstabbyart)
Editing: Brit Corely (IG: @thisbitchreads_)

ISBNs: 9798990150508 (paperback) 9798990150515 (ebook)

CONTENT WARNINGS

Lady of the Grave is a piece of fiction that focuses on the effects of being in a cult and the trauma that comes with it. This dark fantasy is intended for audiences 18+ and contains content that may be triggering or inappropriate for some readers.

Lady of the Grave contains:
Cults, Abusive relationships (emotional and physical), Violence, Blood, Gore, Murder, Death, Hallucinations/Delusions/Dissociation, Human trafficking (mentioned), SA/Rape (mentioned), Transmisia, Self-harm, Sexually explicit scenes, Suicidal ideation and attempt, Torture, War

You can find the full list of trigger warnings-*with spoilers*-on my website: www.fsautumnbooks.com/content-warnings

For Ben,
For all the times you pulled me down from that conclusive ledge.
For protecting me from myself, even when I despised you for it. For embracing my darkness with the same ferocity you welcome my light.
This one's for you, my charming bard.

And for anyone battling psychosis, you're not alone.

"It is real for you. I know that doesn't erase the fear, but I'm here."
-Throwen

Pronunciation Guide

Regions
Theldea (thel-DEE-uh)

Ombra Lurra (OHM-brah LURR-uh)

Ozuria (oh-ZUR-ee-uh)

Luftor (LOOF-toor)

Volgsump (VOALG-sump)

Stranata (strah-NOT-a)

Furothia (FIR-oath-ee-uh)

Covens
Oxvein (OX-vayn)

Graygarde (GRAY-gaard)

Drybourne (DRY-born)

Fearmore (FEER-more)

Goldhaven (GOLD-hay-ven)

Starpass (STAR-pass)

Miren (MEER-in)

Blatock (BLA-taak)

Eldercombe (EL-der-comb)

Toffdank (TOFF-dangk)

Squalsend (SKWAALS-end)

Chapter 1

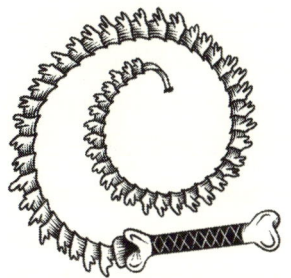

OCTAVIA

F or as long as I could remember, I had worn a crown like this.
A crown fit for a Lady.

It was light, a fabrication of slender bones with talon-like peaks intricately wrapped into delicate teardrops around my head. Lustrous gold filled any cracks produced from the warping.

I fidgeted with it until the inverted teardrop at the epicenter pointed down between my brows.

"How can you be so beautiful and light and weigh so heavily on my soul?" I asked the crown, as if it might reply.

It wasn't the weight of the crown or the black-laced monstrosity that was my Name Day dress I was carrying. It was the weight of responsibility. Only I could ensure my people were concealed from the war, inequality, and many other atrocities that plagued the rest of Theldea.

Excited shouts trickled through my open window from below, and I flicked my wrist, closing it with a burst of air. I walked over and clicked the lock into place then took a seat on the plush green cushion where I often read and admired the distant landscape.

A thick haze always wrapped Ombra Lurra in a tight embrace, as if the Goddess decided what lay in its depths wasn't worth remembering. Dark onyx rocks jutted out, forming the unnaturally sharp slopes that rose into peaks.

Unsettled, I marched to my bed and rubbed my aching chest. Closing my eyes, I fastened my unbearable, golden skeletal corset. Instead of the fabricated metal, I imagined what the snow on the peaks might feel like being squished between my fingers. It didn't snow in Ombra Lurra. It was one of the many things the rest of Theldea offered outside our boundaries that I longed to see.

Sitting, I weaved the golden straps of my heels up my calves. I tried to focus on the honor of protecting my people in the upcoming ceremony, but the mysterious book resting next to me begged for more of my attention. It'd shown up weeks ago, and I hadn't the slightest idea how it arrived in my room. Not just any book, but one that didn't have Malik's seal of approval. *Contraband.* The silver binding broke through my culpability like the dead bursting from their graves.

"The History of Broom Making." I scoffed and searched for my favorite page, skimming the beautiful sketches of brooms throughout.

"There you are." In delicate watercolor, almost completely faded, was a cloaked witch riding a broom. Their long hair undulated in the breeze in front of a massive red moon. They seemed unabashedly wild, and from the looseness of their posture, I could tell whoever this was lived with reckless abandon.

Slamming the book shut, I then tossed it aside. The witches of Theldea could manipulate the elements. But to sustain it long enough to make a journey on a broom? Utter nonsense. They would burn out and need rest to replenish their magic before they could cover any significant distance. And yet…

What if I could be free?

My flesh pebbled and the mark on the back of my neck grew hot. There was no mistaking that the mark was from a deity. It let off a steady, faint glow that changed intensity with my strong and ever-shifting moods. Put there by the Goddess to taunt me endlessly.

"Goddess-born." Frowning, I trailed my finger over my vertebrae, tracing the golden spiral at the center of my mark. Theldea was a chance to see the world, and find out why my creator abandoned me, leaving me alone, the only witch to hold a piece of her inside me. But I knew the answers wouldn't be found inside my coven's boundary.

My fingers clutched firmly around the thick gold-plated choker squeezing my neck, leaving imprints. My ribs constricted, forcing out an irritable, short exhale, and I pictured myself wearing it with a chain attached, a dog forever anchored to its master.

Boisterous scouts laughed on their way up the spiral stairs, and I jumped at my traitorous thoughts. I rushed to my closet, shoving the book under the long stretch of tiles where I hid the things I didn't want to be taken away.

"I don't need you. Tonight will be different." As I put the tiles back, I could taste it, the kernel of hope popping within my chest. I thrust the feeling deep down and rushed to my door. I slipped on my mask of carefully crafted indifference.

One knock sounded. I opened the door, and a young scout nearly punched my tit with her second knock. She recovered quickly, keeping her balance and then straightening her spine. Her cheeks were rosy and smooth. I lifted my hand to my mouth where frown lines pulled the corners of my lips down. Younger witches became a constant reminder that I was caught in this infuriating limbo between young and old.

"S-sorry L-lady!" she stammered.

I pursed my lips as she rolled her shoulders. She wore chainmail under overlapping pieces of bone melded together to cover her like armor. As if anyone in these boundaries would try to attack a scout, armor or not.

"All is forgiven." I kept my face stoic and slipped in front of her, two scouts marching ahead of me.

"This is my first Concealment Ceremony. Don't get me wrong, I love our monthly ceremonies but I've heard this one is remarkable. I'm thrilled to watch Malik bring us another year of safety," the naïve witch said. New members were always chatty before they learned how important every word uttered aloud here was. Words were weapons in our coven when wielded properly.

"Indeed," I replied, and my heels clicked against the hard obsidian floor, where amber flecks danced amongst the black like stars.

Without warning, my mind twisted the gold into a deep red, a coppery scent filling my nose. *One tragic, humiliating accident and you'd finally be free...*

Blinking rapidly, I attempted to banish the morbid hallucination. I couldn't abandon Malik or my coven. Aloof as I made myself appear, I cared for them more than myself.

With each step, I reminded myself of who Malik was. My mentor. I respected and loved him like a father. If I was to go beyond the boundary, it had to be done properly, and becoming a scout was the only option.

Black candles filled every golden sconce, casting the entrance of our castle in an eerie light. Malik's strong silhouette filled the open doorway.

My head pounded, an intense pressure building behind my eyes. I hoped to be as tenacious and powerful as Malik someday. Unfortunately, I was overly emotional, sensitive, and wild. Attributes that made for a traitor, not a coven figurehead.

The scouts parted, and I took my place beside him. "My Lord."

"Lady." Malik donned his classic black fitted suit. The lapels of his jacket and tie were embroidered elegantly with golden skulls and flourishes.

"It's a lovely night for my Name Day Ceremony." Twenty-nine years old and I still despised this day almost as much as I despised myself.

"Yes," he said. "Tonight we will provide and ensure our people's safety."

I reached for his hand, and he took it. "Of course, Lord! Your people will be overjoyed. Afterward, we can dance the night away." I squeezed Malik's hand and waited like a desperate child for him to return the sentiment.

"I hope you're not getting emotional, Lady. It is paramount that we stand strong and united for our people." His tone was light and brutal at the same time.

"Of course not, Lord. I'm just honored to do my part." I kept my voice even, locking down any further hints of emotion as sweat slithered down my spine.

We strode side-by-side down the long path leading from the castle to the glowering towers standing tall near the coven's boundary edge. Witches from every walk of life lined the illuminated path, keeping steady beats on their makeshift instruments as we walked through the gardens. The sweet-smelling lavender I had planted along the path calmed my nerves. Our people fell into two orderly lines behind us.

We walked over the ivy-covered bridge and water rushed loudly beneath. I counted my steps to distract from the silence between us, our people steadily increasing the tempo of their drumming.

Malik's eyes glowed, as if he drank in the happiness of his people, his posture perfectly strong. I steeled my nerves, holding my head high, and pushed my chest out like him.

As we neared the archway leading into the labyrinth, my gut twisted. The entire structure was composed of skulls in all shapes and sizes. Dozens of depthless hollow eyes pierced through me. The scouts surrounding us on either side started pounding their various weapons harshly on the ground.

I shakily maneuvered around the stacked rocks composing the labyrinth. Keeping my eyes on the ground, I fixated on the complicated network of white bone shards sprinkled throughout the rocks meant as a path to contemplate.

The lines undulated and my head felt light... too light. I couldn't find my way back, stuck in the maze. The white paths pooled with blood. Nausea threatened to cut through my carefully crafted tranquility.

It isn't real. It isn't real. Digging my nails into my palms to tether myself to reality, I said the mantra I had taught myself when the visions popped up, like my mind had a serious rat problem.

We stopped at the center, the same location where we held the Concealment Ceremony every year. The gnarled, black tree twisted up and out unnaturally, and the roots pulsed a deep glowing red, the heartbeat of a beast forever tethered to this place. It stood tall and stoic in the center of the labyrinth.

Scouts created a circle around their Lord and Lady while the rest of the coven made concentric circles around them. New members were added year after year as our coven evolved and grew like the rings of a mighty oak.

"Praise Malik!" The loud thumping was now accompanied by shouts. The sheer number of witches in such a small area made my skin crawl.

Beaming at his coven, wrinkles appeared at the sides of our fearless leader's red eyes. He raised both his arms high in the air, and the coven shouted as one. "Hail the Lord and Lady of the true Ether!"

The shouting stopped all at once, and I grew restless with the ominous silence that followed. Each face in the overwhelming sea of witches who once were desolate and lonely reminded me that Malik had saved all of them and I had to do my part to help keep them safe.

The deep red moon made her yearly appearance and peeked out over the mountains, bathing us in her eerie light.

Malik licked his lips and held a finger to his freshly shaved neck just under his sharp, bearded jaw, manipulating the air to carry his voice to the rest of the coven. "When I was a boy, I knew I was special. I could feel it deep in the *marrow of my bones.*"

A scout who held a large staff made of a spinal column with a skull at the top punched his friend in the shoulder, whooping loudly.

I didn't blame them for enjoying being Malik's chosen. It was their freedom I truly coveted, though I knew their status was just a different kind of chain. I tried to hate them for years unsuccessfully, but when you know your enemies by name, it's harder to feel hatred.

"For years, my mentor chastised me for my ideas." Malik's free hand moved wildly, along with his passionate speech. "I refused to accept that the Goddess was the only path to the Ether. What made her so special when the same essence was coursing through me?"

Malik's Ether gave us the opportunity to serve our people beyond this life. To come back when one of us was in need of help. The Goddess merely collected souls like trinkets, locking them away, their only purpose to worship her for eternity.

I was fatigued and my dress and corset weren't doing me any favors. But as Malik turned to face me, years of practice composing myself when necessary kicked in and I straightened, all my pain fading into the background.

"But worshiping her is not the only path. She is nothing but a glutton!" More shouts. "We must purge Theldea of the filth who continually worship the same cunt who left our Lady to die in the woods! Why would anyone follow a creator who discards one of her own, only a child?" His voice was soft as he pointed at me.

Heat poured from their gazes, lingering on me while Malik stayed silent.

Their pity burned so hot across my skin that I feared I would melt. I fought the urge to curl into a ball or flee. My leg shook, unable to bear the weight of attention the way Malik could.

He glowered at my leg and then back at me.

I froze. If I couldn't make it through this part of the ceremony, how was I supposed to get through the next?

A slow smile spread across Malik's face, his light brown skin wrinkling in certain places. "My mission has always been the same. I was a misfit, just like all of you. Here you will find community, belonging, and acceptance. Theldea has *none* of these things. The Coven of the Grave is where we belong. We know the power of *my* Ether—the *true* Ether!"

Praise erupted all around us from the circles of witches. Fireballs shot into the air from some particularly zealous members. A raucous thankfulness to Malik for the true Ether, for community and sanctuary.

Malik spun in a circle with both his arms up, as if savoring the praise. "We like to start this yearly Concealment Ceremony by first purging our coven of those who are nothing but a detriment to our community and what I created here. These witches have all signed confessions."

He gestured to a group of witches who were brought forward by scouts and forced to their knees in a line in front of us. Malik offered me the stack of papers.

Keeping my hands steady and my face cold, I walked up to the first witch. I made the mistake of considering her hazel eyes. Memories of helping her in the kitchen and washing the laundry near her. When I was a child, she showed me how to weave daisies into a chain while we were supposed to be gathering berries.

If this was the way to the true Ether, why did it always feel so wrong?

Emotion is weakness!

I stiffened further as Malik's familiar words slithered around me. My body was no longer my own, but a tool of the coven. These bodies were already filled with tainted souls. I was only helping relieve them of their fleshly forms, so they could be of full and proper use to the coven.

My voice came out low and thick as I read Malik's written words aloud. "Ellinor, you have confessed to slandering"—the blood drained from my face—"your Lady, for which the sentence is transformation."

Her crow's feet were prominent next to her pleading eyes, just like the doubts that had formed around my soul in recent years. She knew better than to speak. If she remained quiet, it would end quickly.

There was only one problem. Ellinor would've never slandered me.

Brows knitting together in confusion, my silent gaze pleaded with her for answers.

She merely mouthed "I'm sorry, Lady" with tear-stained cheeks.

Malik released his whip, made entirely of vertebrae, that he always kept at his hip. He flicked it, wrapping it around Ellinor's neck. Her hands instinctively went up, trying to pry it free. Heat burned behind my eyes, but I knew better than to show disrespect to Malik's decisions with tears.

"Traitor!" witches yelled out.

The tinny smell wafted around me weakly like a perverse blanket.

"Coward!" Another voice pierced my already aching eardrums.

The skin and underlying muscles in her neck were torn to shreds. Malik pulled on the whip and manipulated the air to tighten, forcing the minuscule sharp bones deeper. Her thin neck fought a losing battle, and it tore, opening further. Blood streamed down like a rushing red waterfall and the clinking of Malik's whip releasing and falling to the ground below echoed.

The crowd quieted. They watched in awe as Malik's eyes glowed red and he channeled our unique connection to his Ether, one not through the Goddess but through him and his guidance.

From the ground the lifeless body savagely contorted, bones cracking loudly. Her pale, mangled form rose stiffly. Her heart looked as if it was trying to burst from her chest, only a paper-thin layer of stretched gray skin covering it. It pulsed a glowing red, and I swallowed. It wasn't Ellinor's true life-force, not really. She was part of a collective now, their purpose to serve.

Red smoke poured from the sockets of her eyes and they locked on Malik, patiently waiting.

"You will work in the catacombs until your transformation is complete, then I will help you enter the Ether until we call upon you once more."

The mangled form gurgled and spewed black drool in mandatory agreement.

Two scouts pushed what remained of Ellinor toward the catacombs, where her body would be used until it decomposed. The tunnels under the Odraze Mountains were paramount to our mission. It's how Malik and the scouts got in and out of Theldea unnoticed.

Malik motioned for the next witch to be brought forward. Tears streamed down the scout's cheeks as he was forced to his knees.

I shuffled Ellinor's confession to the back of the pile and continued my duties. "Zolin, you will first be removed of your armor."

Scouts he fought beside for years ripped his armor off. He wheezed as they kicked him repeatedly. But I could only focus on his armor lying on the blood-soaked ground, hating myself for hoping it might become mine.

When they forced him to stand, the entire coven erupted with curses. Soaked in Ellinor's blood, he shook and soiled himself.

"This one is yours!" Malik shouted to the scouts.

They whooped and used the elements to eliminate him. Zolin's screams were piercing as rocks smashed his bones, water poured down his throat, and some scouts held flames against his legs. Once his body was pulverized beyond use, Malik sent him to the Ether. He didn't deserve the honor of serving in the catacombs or the title of scout.

It seemed cruel, but Malik was merciful and returned all of our misled and fallen to the Ether despite their crimes. They would be free of the Abyss; a place for the most devious of witches. Most Theldeans ended up there, too tarnished for the Goddess's precious hoard of souls. With Malik's help our people could be free of the Abyss forever and serve our coven without doubt or fear, living blissfully unaware in Malik's promised Ether.

I read the next names in a foggy daze. Their blood soaked through their shirts. Shouts of disdain for the guilty ringing throughout the crowd.

Crack! Crack! Crack!

Malik's whip shot out again and again.

After what seemed like an eternity, we reached the thirteenth and final witch. Her big blue eyes gleamed, and she shared a grin with Malik.

Malik walked up and crouched in front of her. The *drip drip drip* echoed beneath his whip, crashing to the ground with a final warning.

I leaned into my numbness, preparing for what I had convinced myself was the right thing to do.

"Each year our Lady spares one member because it is her Name Day." His voice boomed. "To remind us all of the mercy I showed her that day when I saved her in those wretched woods." Malik winked at her, then rose. "It's your lucky night, Oleander." He was a symbol of strength, mercy, and peace. All things I would never be.

The young girl's plump cheeks bloomed red. It paid to be one of Malik's favorite sexual partners.

"No." My blatant challenge came out steadier and louder than I expected.

Malik stiffened, then rounded on me with a predator-like posture. His nostrils flared, and his chin lifted, displaying his engorged neck vein. "No?"

Challenging Malik always resulted in punishment, but I hoped this time would be different.

"For my Name Day this year, I want to help this final witch transform, mix my blood with hers, and then touch the tree. I want to become a scout." The last 't' was so sharp I swore my mentor's eye twitched.

The act allowed witches a pathway to the spirits within the Ether and with it came powerful magic and the title of scout. Not only were their natural abilities enhanced but they could help witches transform. I already possessed this magic from touching the tree with my blood once a year. I only lacked the training and title. *And the freedom.*

"I understand the sacrifice needed and I'm willing." I had practiced this in my head so many times that it came out perfectly. Confident, charismatic, and dominant. Using all I had learned from years of studying Malik closely.

The rush of newfound strength caused my mark to glow brighter and burn hotter. I would do whatever it took to see the rest of our world. No longer slouching, I stood up to my full height, still laughable even in these heels, but I had never felt quite this tall before. Stoic and silent, I stood in anticipation of his response to my courage and boldness.

Some emotion I had never seen before flashed across his face. Shock wasn't quite right, it looked so foreign I couldn't place it. I had passed some sort of test. He was going to agree. He was *finally* proud of me.

Time slowed, and it was as if I watched his reactions through a foggy windowpane. He ran a hand through his slicked-back silver hair, chuckling as he pushed away the pieces that had fallen over his forehead. "You think I keep you here because I'm imperious?"

Reckless. Failure. Ungrateful. Child.

The memories of his words built up like armor all around me. I knew this tone of voice; it meant it was time for him to speak and for me to listen. I stayed silent, proficient from years of sitting through his lectures and punishments.

"You know *exactly* why I can't make you a scout, Octavia." He spat across us before invading my space and grabbed my chin forcefully, making me look directly into his eyes.

The crowd stayed as silent as the empty skeletal vessels scattered around us.

He pressed a finger to his throat. "The Goddess left you in that *cursed* lethal forest to perish." Spit flew from his mouth and he rounded the circle, making eye contact with as many coven members as he could.

"Leave this coven and that bitch will leave you to die again. And believe me, you *will* die if you leave. I was just out there, those witches who follow the Goddess would destroy you piece by piece."

He paced and grew louder. "They would rape you, torture you, use your abilities for their own gain, and maybe if they got bored with you, they would give you the courtesy of killing you."

His inflections were perfect, his tone coercing my conscience into a sense of security as he repeated words I had heard all my life.

Terrified murmurs sounded throughout the crowd. I lifted my shaking arm to wipe the sweat dripping down my jaw. I may have been Goddess-born, but I bled just like every other witch.

"You will get your wish and help her transform." Oleander's mouth fell open, her eyes bulging. "But you will *never* be a scout, Lady. It seems as if I will *yet again* have to figure out a creative way to subdue your hazardous fantasies."

I pulled out my golden dagger I kept strapped to my thigh. Kneeling before the witch I had just sentenced to death, with a monotone voice and cold stare, I said, "Oleander, you have confessed to attempting to flee."

She was sobbing. My lips pursed, and I gripped the stack of papers tightly, envisioning myself in her place.

Her soft skin was wet with sweat, and I gingerly raised her chin high. "Thank you for your service to our coven, may your transformation be bliss and your passage into Malik's Ether be swift."

I slit her throat efficiently with one swift cut, the sharpened dagger doing most of the work for me. Her gargles lasted only a moment before I called on my powers, connecting her spirit to her corpse. It only took seconds for her veiny heart to pulse and glow.

A gaunt witch named Devon bowed low, seemingly entranced by the floor. They shot water from their palms and washed away the gore, manipulating air and water in a strong spray.

Malik reached his ring-adorned hand down to me. It would have been a nice gesture, but I knew what this particular movement meant. His aim wasn't to comfort me.

He latched onto my wrist, and I hissed. My skin sizzled with the heat he used to burn me. Then he led me to the tree and forcefully sent me to my knees. I could barely register the scrapes and blood seeping from my kneecaps.

Malik still gripped me tightly, my arm in an unnatural curve. I grit my teeth, a new pain slicing through as his blade cut deeply across my palm.

Invisible chains shackled my wrists and ankles, a phantom of the cage I lived in. How could I be equally grateful and hateful at the same time?

The contradicting emotions reverberated off my skull so loudly that I squeezed my eyes shut, willing them to quiet so I could focus on what I had to do. *Don't get emotional. Don't get emotional.*

Malik grabbed my wrist and pressed my already swelling palm roughly against the tree. "Octavia. *Intent.*"

Gold light pulsed through my entire being. This magic was unique, something about my Goddess-born blood that even Malik didn't understand. I forced my eyes to stay open and looked around at the coven of witches who surrounded us, relied on us, on me. Panting, I centered myself, harnessing the intent to keep my people and Malik safe, to keep us hidden.

One final pulse of gold light streamed into the tree, entwining with the deep red. Our thin, smokey boundary thickened and became darker. Another year of protection for our people.

Weariness filled my limbs and my alertness faded from the colossal amount of magic I had just pumped into our lands, like a raisin that had sat in the sun for too long, deprived of all moisture and life.

The rest of the ceremony faded into a blur of initiations, praises, and testimonials of true devotion, all memories I could no longer access as I trapped them away in the deepest recesses of my mind.

The weight of my failure piled up as if each member of the coven were taking a turn placing a stone upon my chest. How I was still breathing and conscious was a miracle in and of itself.

Chapter 2

OCTAVIA

Ale splashed across the chests of Malik's chosen lovers for the night. Shouts of praise rippled through the dancers. "The Ether is ours!"

Black velvety petunias lined the wooden beams along the conservatory's roof, and roses bloomed from large pots. Deep red fabric draped over the wooden tables accompanied by onyx plates and cutlery. We stuck to red and black; the color palette Malik favored this month. We were meticulous when setting up for ceremonies so that we didn't face his disapproval.

Tempered night air crept in from the open windows. Everyone was singing, drinking, and fucking merrily. This was our biggest ceremony of the year, and the revelry went on for days. It was another year trapped inside this suffocating canopy of protection.

Watching the dancers was my favorite part of my Name Day. I could witness the echo of Theldea's regions through their movements.

The few witches from Ozuria rarely danced and huddled near the table full of food. Nausea washed through me just thinking about eating. I focused on the dancers instead.

Tessa moved like the lethal snakes that overpopulated Stranata. They hoarded their resources born of the richest soil that I often imagined sinking my toes into.

Magnolia danced like wet noodles, waving her limbs and letting gravity do the rest. The silly style must be from all the fire bugs that flew around Volgsump, destroying entire covens.

Luftor produced a more demanding style. Dancers stood in a wide circle while one witch in the middle lowered to the ground as far as they could, kicking their feet straight out in rapid succession. I couldn't imagine a group of happy witches like that slaughtering one another.

Laughing, I moved toward the exit. The noise dampened once I was within the thick castle walls. I allowed myself a final look at the merriment.

Finch and Marley were from a coven called Eldercombe and were rigid, creating little boxes as they moved.

Logan and Salane were smooth, floating happily along in my favorite style from the coven of Goldhaven. Both covens resided in Furothia but were still unique in their culture.

My stomach quivered, and I strode toward the stairs that led to my room. Theldea was dangerous, but it had to have pockets of happiness to produce witches that could dance so freely.

A couple stumbled over to where I sat on the bottom steps, dancing around me, completely unaware of my presence. I ignored them and started unlacing my heels. Tiny blisters had formed around the laces.

A satisfied sigh left my lips, and I was enthralled with how pleasing the uniform crisscross pattern sashayed across my skin. Guilt and pain would be my only dance partners tonight.

"Oh, Lady! Thank you!" The couple spotted me hiding in the shadows. Mercy's cheeks were flushed and her eyes narrowed. I threw on a fake smile to be polite.

The lovers danced back into the night. A huge weight crashed against my aching heart. Love was a desire of mine that would never be met. I thought I had it once, but it was a lie.

Tears threatened to unleash, and I stroked my tender blisters softly.

Stop being so sensitive! Too sensitive. Too sensitive.

My muscles tightened, and I leaned into the discomfort, my self-loathing demon a constant companion. I bit the inside of my cheek hard to distract from the burning in my eyes. Pain usually seemed to satiate the beast, and I had decided years ago that nobody would ever see me cry or overreact again.

I climbed the spiral steps with my heels thrown over my shoulder. Disorientation made me lightheaded as I trudged the long hallway back to my room.

Paintings of Malik's accomplishments lined the halls. One after the other. Each accomplishment was greater than the last. Dark oils mixed to form one of my favorites. It was of Malik breaking ground when he first established our coven. I was in the painting, maybe three, holding onto his pinky.

As I walked, the paintings shifted and contorted into ones of my imagination. Glimpses of depraved witches capturing me, raping me, and locking me in a cage. Draining me of my magic. The horrid images morphed into witches I'd grown up with, now being torn apart by Malik's whip or a scout's weapon of choice.

Gagging, I stumbled into my room and slammed the door shut. I was nothing but a selfish princess who was lucky to have a safe home.

I threw up an air shield before regurgitating all my pent-up emotions all over my favorite woven rug. My breaths came short and fast now. With the air shield still in place, I wiped my mouth roughly, smearing vomit and the glittering gold lipstick Malik had picked out for tonight all over my sleeve.

A guttural cry ripped free from somewhere deep inside of me. I lost track of how long I had screamed, but my throat was hot and burning. I pulled at my hair, desperate for it to stop, but ripping out follicles wasn't nearly enough.

In a moment of uncontrollable rage, I stood and stomped over to my vanity. I stared at my feet, refusing to face what I would see in that mirror. In a year, this cycle would start all over again. I would be right back here hallucinating and being lost in my mind until…

The Goddess left you to die out in those woods.

My fist collided with the glass. "*Fuck!*" More blood splattered across this ridiculous dress than was already there from the ceremony.

My air shield broke, and I shook my injured hand. I seethed at the sharp, jagged version of myself, though the sting across my knuckles brought me comfort.

Clutching tightly onto the train of my dress, I ripped a strip from the infuriating abomination and laughed at the destruction. I wrapped my bleeding knuckles, making sure sweet hot pain shot through my hand and up my arm at the tightness. Like a rabid dog, I used my teeth to give it a final pull.

Rage still seeped through me, soaking into my muscles and propelling me to my closet. I grimaced at the contents of the gaudy, uncomfortable clothing Malik gifted me.

The closet was long with a large, thin mirror on the far end. It always contorted my body as I walked toward it, confusing my perceptions about how I truly appeared. I knelt and removed the tiles.

"I wasn't supposed to need you." I reached into the hole, pulling out something I wasn't supposed to have. Something forbidden.

My broom.

I never thought of a broom as enchanting before, but that's exactly what the work of art resting in my hands was.

The shaft was a thick, blackened branch I had found by our tree and I had burned my name into it. I ran my fingers slowly along the smooth length that I had sanded into an almost straight shape and down to the bristles. They were wild but thinner twigs from the tree that I dipped in some reflective paint, making the tips iridescent. Sturdy black twine held the bristles to the shaft.

I had secretly been gathering materials and working on her every night since discovering the book.

My doubts about Malik's way of life had always been there, but over the past ten years, they had grown exponentially. He spouted a community of peace, yet always used violence to achieve it.

"It's the right thing to do," I said. I had promised myself that if I couldn't be a scout, I would try to fly to a peak and once I felt the snow, I would come back. Once I experienced something other than this coven, I could finally push this idea of freedom from my mind and be fully present for my people.

Securing the tiles back into place, I curled my fingers around my new creation and stood. I reached back, my mark warm and buzzing at my touch.

"Stealth… stealth…" I made precise movements up and down the closet and found the box I was searching for. Blowing the dust off the top, I then traced my finger across the smooth metal horse that was skillfully inlaid on the lid.

Galloping around the same perimeter year after year lost its appeal long ago. I used to dream of riding across all of Theldea, helping as many witches as I could along the way. My old riding leathers were black as the night sky with just a slight sheen.

I grabbed my knee-high, black lace-up boots and rushed back to my bed. My bones were vibrating, and despite the events of the night I was fully aware and awake, as if a switch within me had been flipped.

As my golden corpse corset fell to the floor, I took a full, deep breath and rubbed at my ribs. "*Goddess's tits* that was tighter than I thought."

I stepped out of my other clothing, opting to ditch my lingerie to try to fit in these old clothes. "You have to be kidding me. These are only a few years old!"

Grunting, I continued my odd jumps and struggled to pull up the tight leather pants. My thighs showed some mercy, and once they were on, I continued to see if they had any give. They didn't. They were just slightly too tight, but it was the most comfortable dark clothing I owned.

Quickly pulling on the oversized black shirt that I usually wore to bed, I moaned as the thin, worn fabric acted like a balm to my irritated skin. I retrieved my black cloak from the floor and flung it around my neck, fastening it with a bird skull broach I had made myself, the tip of the beak burned black.

I knew the mountains were capped in snow, but I had no idea what the temperatures would be like outside of our boundary. My loose ideas about what the rest of Theldea looked like were limited to our small collection of history books.

A single hot tear streamed down my cheek, and I retrieved my crown from the soiled rug.

A sob escaped me as I sat it gently on the center of my vanity. To do this, I had to be completely free of it all, of this place. My one moment of freedom. I couldn't risk destroying this gift from Malik. It was too precious.

If the Theldeans find you and see your mark, they will cage you.

But what Malik didn't take the time to see or comprehend was that I already lived inside a cage.

My legs wobbled and, to my surprise, a giggle escaped through my sobs. Exhilaration replaced overwhelming fear and guilt, like the sun breaking through the clouds.

A new determination pulled at my brows, and I allowed myself a rare, full view of myself in the mirror. I didn't recognize the woman I was seeing. I was... an absolute emotional mess. Makeup smeared, matted hair billowing out around my hood, and a crazed gleam in my eyes. But I was wild, free, *myself*.

The thrill of adventure filled me, and I grabbed my broom, rushing to the window. Flinging it open, I gripped her tightly. I had stood in this exact spot many nights, contemplating the fall.

I had studied the book meticulously between preparations for the ceremony, following it as best I could. There was no guarantee this would work.

Theldeans could slaughter me if I was spotted. Or they could cage me the moment my feet hit solid ground. It could all just be a fantasy on a page, but I adored those fantasies; they got me through each day.

Death by faith in fantasies. I was more than content with an ending like that.

Intent. I tightened my grip on my broom and recalled Malik's last words to me before the celebration began.

"Intent..." I let out an exhausted breath, the last molecule of self-control I had left gone. Closing my eyes, I wrapped my hands around the smooth wood, squeezing gently. The book claimed the intent had to go to the very root of the desire. This obsession went far beyond me wanting to touch some snow.

"I want to help witches throughout the entirety of Theldea, not just those inside our boundaries."

A pulse of gold light similar to the one at the tree wrapped around my broom.

"Well, that's a good sign." I couldn't stop the treasonable smile from spreading across my face, even if I wanted to.

My palms were sweating, and I stood up on the ledge. I had only stood this close a few times after some especially severe punishments. A cackle escaped me as I remembered finding the book. It would be my undoing one way or another.

This was selfish, irresponsible, and crazy, but there was no stopping it now.

I jumped.

Chapter 3

THROWEN

Red moonlight painted the forest in deep maroons as flecks of blood floated down the stream. I washed my knife in the cool water, and frowned, noticing a chip in the blade.

"Fucking necromancers." I dabbed the sweat from my brow and returned it to its sheath.

Lucky nickered and pranced in a small circle at the top of the small hill, her black shiny coat glistening in the night.

"You're right. No point living in the past. Let's go home." I took one last sip of crisp water and retrieved my songbook and bow.

Sighing, I trudged up the slope, tossing my bow over my head and letting it rest across my chest. I opened my songbook, tapping my finger against the parchment to a steady rhythm.

"Whether flesh or bone, I have touched it all"

The key wasn't right, and I drew an arrow pointing up to remind myself of the change I wanted to make. Humming, I buckled my songbook back to my thigh and patted Lucky's side.

I mounted Lucky, and we trotted steadily, her hooves splattering mud as we followed the path leading to Whynnie's hovel. A path I'd traveled thousands of times.

Squeezing my knees tighter, I urged Lucky to run faster. I squatted and leaned into her speed. I needed the monotony to be nothing but a blur, so I didn't have to dwell on the hollow feeling that had set up residence in my soul.

Once again, I would report on a successful assassination and be assigned another. I was grateful for my work and my ability to aid the Goddess through Whynnie's leadership. But I feared my days of true adventure were being ground by a pommel stone. Soon there would be only a powder of relived experiences.

Lights flickered in the distance as we neared my childhood home. Whynnie's hovel was inside an enormous sequoia tree on the outskirts of Goldhaven, our coven. She loved her coven, but preferred the privacy and seclusion the large trees provided.

I tugged on the reins, and Lucky slowed as I hopped off.

"And I suppose you expect two carrots for your speed?" Lucky snorted at my question, and I tied her to the post next to my sibling's horses.

I removed the bags from her back and pulled out three carrots. "Special treats since we are home." I winked and she chomped them from my hands. Switching from my weapon to my lute, I felt my muscles finally relax with the comfort of being home.

A thick indigo fabric waved in the breeze, and I rested a hand against one of the branches that wrapped around each other, framing the entrance.

As I entered, I took a deep breath, the smell of tea enveloping me. My childhood home perpetually had one of Whynnie's half-full teacups on every surface. She would always make a new cup, forgetting about her last.

I shed my thoughts of unending repetition, throwing on my flashing bard smile and flinging my arms wide. "I have arrived! We can start the celebration now."

"Little Miracle!" Whynnie shouted from the small kitchen table. Even sitting she looked stooped and plump. Her dark silver hair was pulled to one side, falling over her shoulders. A warm golden glow haloed around her neck.

Echo rushed over, picking me up like a ragdoll, and wrapped me in their arms. They spun us in a circle before lowering me back to the ground. "I missed you!" They smelled of sweet ale, a blend of fruits and spice. Their light brown skin had undertones of yellow and when they pulled away their cheeks were pink with the warmth of the ale.

Kallan sat at the table, his large muscles shifting as he rubbed his temples. Some of the short locks on the top of his head fell over his forehead and covered his dark eyes. "These two said thanking the Goddess for another year of safety, health, and happiness couldn't wait."

I followed Echo to the kitchen, their joy helping my burdens tumble off. The hovel had large wooden workbenches built into the sides of the tree, completely encircling the round room. Bottles, bowls, herbs, and ointments were strewn across them.

Whynnie's many grimoires were spread open amongst the chaos. I slid one aside, leaning against the kitchen island. Echo returned to their seat with a bowl of grapes, fanning their cards and focusing on their hand.

"Who's winning?" I smirked and waggled my eyebrows at Echo.

They squinted at me, taking another long swig from their mug.

"Echo wants to learn how to play poker." Kallan's controlled, deep voice penetrated the sound of Whynnie's gasping laugh.

Snorting, I grabbed a mug and poured myself some ale.

Echo slammed a card onto the table. "Hah!"

"Echo, I told you a million times, this is a game of chance. You can't rationalize your way to winning. You have to read your opponent, stay calm, be patient, and bluff wisely." Kallan sighed, crossing his dark arms that were littered with scars. His constant pursuit of balance and peace was disturbingly ironic, considering he often achieved those through violence.

Echo twisted a piece of teal hair around their little finger. "Well, *Abyss consume me* because I can only do two of those things. I have to figure out this joke of a card game before I visit Fennix. He will be much more malleable once I chisel away at his pride."

"You mean to tell me you aren't *elated* at the idea of a visit to Fennix?" I grabbed an apple from the table, biting into it with a huge grin.

Echo flicked their finger and manipulated the water in the pitcher next to me, squirting it right into my eyes.

"*Seriously*?" I rubbed at them with my tan sleeve. I hated it when they went right for my eyes.

Echo's lips curled into a devilish grin. "The *real* question is, do I feel like appeasing him this time or do I want to instigate him into one of his infamous temper tantrums? They truly are one of the most amusing things I get to experience."

"Concentrate, Peacock. Your communication skills are exceptional, but Stranatans have a hard time accepting outsiders into their culture. Winning could earn you respect," Whynnie said.

Echo shot up and spun in a circle, flicking their fingers to create a burst of wind that tickled my mustache. The cards flew up and to the floor.

Grunting, Kallan knelt to pick up his worn cards. "Just because you're losing doesn't mean you have to resort to dramatics."

Echo laughed while they spun, Whynnie laughing right along with them. Kallan mumbled from the floor, and I offered him a bemused smile. Echo hopped up onto the kitchen island and sat up tall. They slicked their teal hair back and crossed their ankles.

I choked on the apple between laughs. It was rare that we were all home together these days, and the laughter they brought me was cathartic.

I took a swig of ale and let it warm my throat and belly before striding over to where they sat.

"Let's try again tomorrow." Kallan flopped back into his seat and shuffled his cards before sliding them into the metal case he kept them in. He tapped the lid three times to ensure it was closed — a creature of habit.

Unable to contain myself any longer, I pulled my lute swiftly across my chest. I lifted my foot, resting it on the seat and leaned into a small comfortable lunge before picking.

"Captain Fennix so bold and so brash
If only he could keep his sheets clean
He might have avoided that rash!"

My playful words bounced off the walls, and everyone choked on their drinks.

Whynnie spoke loudly over my playing. "He always was a little shit. When he was a boy, I would catch him creeping outside my bathroom window. Now I don't blame him because back then my tits were *flawless* but still, I don't know why his unbearable joke of a father kept bringing him to our meetings." She shrugged and sipped her ale.

Echo burst out laughing, still swaying happily to my upbeat chords. This was a popular song at the taverns in the covens surrounding Fennix's.

"Let's get business out of the way so we can properly celebrate," Whynnie said.

I frowned, putting my lute away and joining everyone at the table instead of finishing my song.

"Do we have to?" Echo complained loudly, and Kallan and I groaned.

Whynnie pinched the bridge of her nose, using her other hand to flick little gusts of wind at each of us. She shook her head, but her smile was that of a proud mother dealing with her strong-willed children.

Whynnie folded her hands together, placing them on the table. "Kallan, let's start with you. How are things going in Graygarde?"

"As expected, Mayson's hunger to expand has caused two rockslides. They lost eight witches this month." My brother's neck vein pulsed. "Oliver is trying to clean up Mayson's mess. He helped me visit the families of those affected, and some of them will need our support."

"I'll send a bird and ask the surrounding covens to contribute some food until they can get back on their feet, and you can take them some more medical supplies." Whynnie wrote on a spare piece of ripped paper.

"Maybe it's time Kallan paid Mayson a visit." I suggested.

Kallan's eyes gleamed, and he cracked his knuckles. "He only cares about his legacy. I think I could *persuade* him to focus on his people."

"Mayson doesn't respond well to threats," Echo countered. "Let me talk to him."

"We need you in Fennix's Coven, Echo. Kallan can handle this without going overboard." Whynnie leveled a look at Kallan and spoke in an even tone.

"Got it. Not in the face." Kallan deadpanned.

I pressed my lips together, suppressing a laugh.

"Teddy Bear, use intimidation for now. You're scary enough to make him pause and think about his choices." Whynnie poked Kallan on the nose. He nodded in response.

"And what am I to do with Fennix? He refuses to step into the role. He cares more about his own coven than trying to unite the others." Echo pushed out their lips, releasing a long breath of air.

"It has to be him. We need him to see that it's the only way to stop the senseless killing. I've had many visions, and he is always present." Whynnie's milky white eyes looked to the ceiling.

The Goddess gifted Whynnie with the unique ability to get glimpses of the future, and despite their appearance, she could see as well as me. I loved her eyes. They made me feel less alone. Like I wasn't the only one wearing the Goddess's gift on the outside.

I looked at my pitch-black hands that the Goddess had bestowed upon me. Hands touched by an ancient magic. The supernatural color wandered up my arms, tapering out at my forearms in whisps. Every day I wished our creator would show me why she had chosen this for me.

"I'll keep trying. He knows the Goddess didn't create us just to hold grudges and kill for revenge." Echo's voice was steady, their jaw set.

"I'll send a bird tonight, so he knows you will be coming." Whynnie beamed at Echo.

"*My* mission was a success, not that any of you asked. Three more necromancers wiped off the map." I licked my finger and made a checkmark in the air.

Kallan popped a grape into his mouth, and I fidgeted, already perturbed by the thought of staying in Goldhaven too long.

"Where to next?" I asked.

"I got word from Nova last night. Some of her people were recently attacked just outside their coven by a large group of necromancers." Her wrinkled hands tightened around her mug; her knuckles white. "They were heading to Luftor to visit their families."

"How close were they to Oxvein?" Kallan forced out through gritted teeth, his large muscles tightening under his white shirt.

"One hour by horse. They left behind two bound and two witches are missing." Whynnie's voice cracked. My siblings' spines straightened, and I flexed my fingers.

I leaned forward, resting my arms on the table. The Lord of the Grave never left survivors. "They're getting bolder with their attacks."

Echo peered at the ceiling. "To be sent to the Abyss and be separated from the Goddess must be utter agony."

"We have to lure Malik out. Cut off the head and the others will follow," Kallan suggested.

"For now, all I can do is send aid to those in need." Whynnie noticeably deflated and her face became a stoic mask of indifference, the burden of leadership weighing heavy on her shrinking body.

"It's okay, Whynnie," Echo offered.

"It's not." Whynnie shook her head. "The Goddess makes the Goddess-born to keep Theldea safe. Lumin did that. And I just—" She pounded her fist on the table so hard, we jumped at the outburst. "It'll never be enough."

The steaming ale she had heated just moments ago spilled onto her before hitting the floor.

Kallan rushed to her side, taking her hands gently into his and drying them off with his white shirt. Echo walked calmly to fetch a rag and started cleaning up the mess.

I moved to grab my lute and strummed a low melancholic tune. The familiar purple smoke-like tendrils moved around my fingers in spirals. They spread up my arms until meeting with my pale biceps.

Calling on my magic, comforting spirits listened, curling and looping around me. I had written this song years ago, specifically for the grieving. For those that had lost loved ones to the cult. I often visited the taverns of those recently targeted to share this with them. To help them heal.

My family sat in silence and lavender tendrils wrapped around their bodies. I used the powers the spirits bestowed upon me to calm everyone down. The music slowed and faded, coercing their heartbeats into a steadier cadence.

A single tear rolled down Whynnie's cheek. I finished the song while Echo and Kallan tended to her, rubbing her back softly.

Eyes vacant, Whynnie stared into the distance. I preferred her fury to her sorrow. I couldn't stand seeing Whynnie sad. At least when she was angry, she would be productive, pouring her emotions into her work.

"We will figure it out. We just need to think of a new angle." Kallan threw a worried glance my way. Sometimes Whynnie would become bedridden, unable to function under the weight of the betterment of the entirety of Theldea.

Clouds covered the moon, bathing us in momentary darkness, the candles flickering in the wind. Whynnie's head tilted to the side like a curious cat.

"What's the plan, Whyn—"

Whynnie lurched across the table and clutched my wrist. "My mirror! Get my mirror!" Her voice was urgent, as if it was life or death.

The mark on her neck was brighter than I'd ever seen. Releasing my wrist, her wrinkled hands shook. Her eyes were less foggy, but tears pooled there.

"Whynnie, what is going on?" Echo cupped Whynnie's face in their hands.

I fell to my knees, deep purple coils wrapping around where I held her hand. Kallan sprinted back from Whynnie's room.

As soon as the melon-shaped mirror reached Whynnie's hands, a fuzzy image blurred across its surface.

Echo's mouth hung open, and Kallan ceased all movement. I was already back on my feet, overcome with a burning desire to get closer. This was the old magic of the Goddess-born. I could sense it as the spirits swirled happily in tiny tendrils across my knuckles.

In a single pulse of golden light, the image came into focus. I gasped, gripping the side of the mirror and staring at the most captivating witch I had ever laid eyes on. This enigmatic witch called to the thrill-seeker in me.

Perhaps this was the Goddess herself connecting with Whynnie.

"Um, she's riding a broom. Poorly? I think. I've never seen a witch ride a broom." Echo's perplexed voice was muffled, and I watched the mirror like a hawk, afraid that this might be my last glance at this enchantress.

Whynnie grabbed my chin, breaking the hold the witch had on me. "Can you tell where she is?"

I bristled at her harsh tone. The witch's hood flew back with the increasing force of the breeze, and I fell to my knees once more, the restless spirits bracing my fall.

Her hair looked dark brown, and it whipped fiercely around her face. Gold lipstick was smeared across her mouth and cheeks, stained with tears. I wished I could make out the color of her eyes in the crimson moonlight.

Her cloak was held together in the center of her neck by a delicate bird skull broach. I continued to analyze the image, hunting for anything recognizable around her.

"It's too dark to see. There's snow, so somewhere in Ozuria. It's too windy to—"

The image shifted perspectives again, this time from behind and *Goddess forgive me*, I had a new favorite view. I had traveled all over Theldea, the mountains of Luftor, the forests of Stranata, and nothing compared to what I was discovering now.

Her movements were chaotic, zigzagging in a generally straight trajectory, like a child learning how to ride a horse.

A gold light pulsed behind her hair and a gust of wind revealed her neck.

We gasped in unison.

Seven circles that represented the phases of the moon formed a v, two crescents ending just below her ears, in line with her jaw. The spiraled full moon formed the bottom, centered on her spine.

"She's Goddess-born..." Kallan's reverent voice penetrated the air delicately.

"Stop ogling her like a teenager and fucking *find her*, Throwen!" Whynnie sobbed.

It was hard to think when I was determined to remember every detail about her, not her surroundings. Her knuckles were wrapped poorly, blood soaking through the fabric. My chest burned. I wanted to keep this witch safe, to allow no one to spill even a drop of her precious Goddess-born blood again.

"She's somewhere in the Odraze Mountains." My stomach dropped, and the witch wobbled, sharp rocks almost touching her feet. There was no mistaking the reflective properties of the black mountains.

Energy coursed through me with unyielding determination. It had been some time since I climbed the perilous mountains. A climb to find a Goddess-born would make a fantastic song.

"Oh, no... she's preparing to land," Kallan said, voice tinged with panic.

My fearful heart thrashed against the inside of my chest. I could already tell this witch was going to be terrible for my health.

With wild jerking movements, the witch held onto the broom with one hand while manipulating the air around her with the other. She slipped, and I stopped breathing.

The witch gripped the broom, boots dangling far too high above her intended landing point—an open and fairly flat area of snow on the mountain's peak. I still couldn't place the exact peak she was on; the Odraze Mountains were too vast.

She let go, unable to fight the bitter winds pummeling her. My ears rang and it felt as if I was dying a second death.

The witch hurtled toward the ground, and just before the moment of impact, she thrust her hands in front of her. As she screamed, her air shield locked into place just long enough to break her fall.

Her shield flickered out before she could stand up and she fell face-first into the snow. Shaky laughter erupted, and I trembled. With excitement or anxiety, I couldn't tell. But whatever the feeling was, it was thrilling.

She peered up at her broom, snow-covered and in a state of panic. It slowly lowered, hovering too high for her to reach. She thrust both her middle fingers into the air, aggressively yelling at it.

"Feisty." Echo said.

The broom fell, and the witch reached her arms above her head too late, the broom hitting her directly in the face.

"Ouch." Kallan winced.

Just beyond the most endearing pile of snow and limbs I had ever seen was a recognizable glimmer of reflective crystals in the distance. "She's near Oxvein." The hairs on my arms rose to attention with the revelation.

"The Goddess answered my prayers." Whynnie panted, releasing the mirror and sunk heavily into the bench.

I ran a finger along its cool glass surface and the witch rubbed the welt already forming on her forehead. She kicked snow at her broom and cocked her head at the coven twinkling in the distance.

As her image flickered out, I swallowed hard, releasing the mirror. I sat on the floor and smoothed my mustache.

Echo fetched Whynnie a cup of chamomile tea and Kallan rubbed her back gently.

"The Goddess... answered." Whynnie's body shook, and her skin was pale. A sign that her magic was completely drained. "*Praise the Goddess* for her provision, the hope she reignites within us. We now ask for her guidance."

"Did you know?" Echo's voice was soft, always the first to break the tension in a room. They sat and Whynnie sipped her tea, color gradually returning to her face and limbs.

"I did," Whynnie whispered and sobbed, the sounds too bleak for our ears to handle.

"Why did you never mention her?" I asked, as a knife of betrayal pierced my heart. "You said the Goddess hadn't brought you a Goddess-born yet."

As Whynnie's tears flowed, her gasps prohibited any further insight. I made eye contact with my siblings, silently communicating our course of action. They nodded in agreement.

We swarmed Whynnie, Kallan and Echo on either side. I slid underneath the table and wrapped myself around her legs.

Eventually, the sobs subsided, and she grunted out between sniffs, "Not a hugger."

"We know. But we are." Echo kissed the top of Whynnie's head before we all sat around the table.

"I'll make this as simple as possible." Whynnie wiped her eyes with her sleeve. "Her name is Octavia. Malik abducted her from me twenty-six years ago."

"Why did you keep this from us?" Kallan sounded more hurt than confused.

Whynnie placed a small hand on his massive bicep. "I thought she was gone. I truly thought Malik had killed her."

My hackles were up, muscles tight, but I stayed silent, a soldier overly eager for his next assignment. The thought of that monster keeping her hidden all these years doing who knows what to her... I should have felt afraid, but I felt satiated. She could be our answer.

"She could be the key." My chest expanded; my new mission evident. "I'll go get her."

All heads turned to me, and Kallan snorted. "I haven't seen you this enthusiastic to work in years, brother."

"It makes perfect sense." I stood and paced. "She's integral. With her magic and knowledge, she could help us fight the necromancers."

"We don't even know what her magic does." Echo made a good point. Whynnie had sight and her mentor, Lumin could tell when he was being lied to. Some Goddess-born had relatively tame powers, like breathing underwater or camouflaging into their surroundings. But Octavia was a wildcard.

"Her powers could be limitless, we don't know until we go get her." I defended my logic. This was *my* quest. I knew it as plainly as I knew the sun would rise in the east and fall in the west.

"And why do you get the honor of retrieving her?" Kallan smirked, poking at my ego with a pointy stick.

Kallan's words heated my blood, and I placed my palms flat against the table, leaning into his cherished personal space. My magic rose to the surface and tendrils curled near him. "You both have other duties to attend to. Finding the witch to aid us in killing more necromancers is in my job description."

"She isn't a pawn." Whynnie hissed, and we stiffened. "Throwen, she is your only priority now. Not because of what she can do for us, but because she needs our help. Her powers hadn't manifested before she was taken. I must teach her about them and how to wield them. It's the only way she might help us defeat Malik. Is that understood?"

"Yes." We spoke in unison.

"It's certainly a new angle," Kallan muttered, and I stood up straight.

"Good." Whynnie rolled her shoulders back. "Echo and Kallan, your missions remain the same. We don't want to attract too much attention. Kallan, you can meet up with Throwen in Graygarde."

Whynnie stood and shuffled to her nearest grimoire. Her quill scratched with the speed of a panther chasing its prey.

Kallan rose slowly and grunted, kissing Whynnie on her head and walked toward his bag near the entrance. Echo tapped their fingers against the table.

"Echo," Whynnie continued, "they will meet you at Fennix's Coven. She will need more protection as the gossip spreads. The Stranatan covens need to come together now more than ever. Once Throwen finds Octavia, Malik will stop at nothing to get her back."

I grabbed my lute, throwing it over my shoulder. Malik would pay for taking her. His torture would last at least twenty-six years, the years he had stolen. Echo didn't respond, their face growing a mixture of orange and red.

Whynnie came back to the table, cupping their round cheeks in her hands. "*Dazzle* them, Peacock." At the nickname, Echo's face softened.

"You will explain *all of this* when we get her back?" Echo placed a hand on their hip.

Whynnie nodded rapidly. "Thank you for always understanding." She squished Echo's round cheeks tightly, pushing their lips out like a fish before letting go. They rolled their eyes dramatically before leaving the table and packing up their things.

I strode to Whynnie, wrapping her in a tight hug. "Tell me what I need to know before I find her."

Whynnie reached for my hands, her eyes coated in a faint silver sheen. "I don't see her often, but when I do, she is flying around the Odraze peaks and the moon is full. But it's very fickle." She huffed, dropping her hands. "We are at the mercy of her choices now."

"I can be there in a little over a week, well before the next full moon. I will stay on those cursed mountains until I find her." Failure wasn't an option, and I said a silent prayer to the Goddess to guide Octavia's decisions.

Sighing, Whynnie grabbed her teacup, warming it with her barely replenished magic. "I've been trying to understand Malik's erratic movements for years, and nothing makes sense. He is as much a phantom as the spirits he defiles. She must have broken through their concealment somehow. If she refuses to go with you, tell her that I'm Goddess-born."

"You really think that will work?" I cocked my brow.

"I hope so." She said, "If you come across Malik or his scouts, use that clever mind of yours to keep her safe. He is pure evil wrapped in silk. Bring her home, Little Miracle."

"I will." I kissed Whynnie's head and joined my siblings outside where they were preparing their horses.

Kallan towered over me and roughly rubbed my head with his knuckles. "See you soon, brother."

Echo was already trotting away, hollering over their shoulder, "Don't do anything I wouldn't do!"

Kallan laughed and rode away.

Birds began to gather on Whynnie's windowsill where she attached letters to their legs.

I threw my bags over Lucky's back, climbing up as she brayed. A wicked smile tugged at the corners of my lips and dark violet wisps swirled around me. I let them join in on the high of my newfound challenge.

I knew that fucker's coven was within flying distance of the Odraze Mountains, and I would not only save Octavia, but I would burn him and everything he held dear to the ground.

Lute firmly strapped to my back, I pressed my heels into her sides. "Time to show off that speed, girl."

Wind whipped my face, the menacing song of war I had been working on clicking into place. I sang low, my vocal cords tickled by the vibrations.

*"Whether flesh or bone, I have touched it all
There is no hiding when death arrives
For I am him and the Abyss calls
I will savor delivering you to your demise"*

Malik might control the dead, but I knew what it was to be one of them.

Chapter 4

OCTAVIA

Droplets splashed against the stone windowsill, and warmth coursed through my limbs.

I latched the lock to the window, muting the celebrations that continued outside; everyone too drunk or too oblivious to notice my momentary escape. "I did it."

My broom whirred, vibrating my hands. I rubbed the knot on my forehead. "*You* owe me an apology."

She hummed louder, and my face softened. "Thank you."

"What a joyous night!" Malik's voice boomed through the walls.

My heart raced. I looked at the broom, then at the door. I needed to hide it, so I hopped down and scurried to the closet to hide any trace of treason.

"Because of yer Looord and Lady, you have nothing to fear!" Malik slurred, the sounds of lovers giggling, sucking, and smacking, sneaking into the ambiance of his speech.

A headache was already forming at my temples, and I shed my wet clothes, pushing them in with my broom. My stomach clenched. She didn't deserve to be locked away. I shifted the tiles back in place, and her comforting hums ceased.

"I'm sorry."

I threw on an old shirt; the fabric tickling the top of my knees. Brutish laughter came from the hall where scouts were stumbling back to their rooms, and I leaned over, holding my stomach as it churned.

"No Theldean ssscum will invade our paradise!" Malik growled, the sound so loud that my feet slipped out from under me. I braced myself just in time to protect my skull from bashing against the tiles.

"Not the humiliating accident I was picturing," I rubbed my tailbone, mumbling as I stood and retrieved a towel.

"I will show you the path to peace, to the true Ether!" Malik droned on.

Grabbing some cotton from my vanity, I plugged my ears. His enthusiasm faded into the back of my mind like an annoying gnat. I usually kept some hidden away in my cleavage after Malik's speeches had escalated into all hours of the night.

I scratched roughly at my neck before lowering to my knees and wiping away the melted snow. Lifting the wet towel to my nose, I tried to relish in the scents outside our boundary, but they were already gone.

You will die the moment you step foot in Theldea.

"But I didn't die, did I?" If Malik was wrong about this, what else was he wrong about?

Decisions and sanity always tangled in a confusing web during the full moon, and I was not immune to its effects, bouncing between guilt and doubt.

What was that shimmering in the distance while I was out on the mountain? Where were the Theldeans?

I couldn't believe how crisp the air had felt in my lungs the moment I crossed through our barrier. Once that fresh air of freedom was gone, there was a crawling sensation as if ants had made their hills on my skin.

Climbing into bed, I layered blankets and pillows over me until I was in a cocoon of darkness. My body trembled, and my tears flowed like rivers. I swore I could feel the curves and grooves of my brain shifting with this new knowledge.

My teeth chattered and my body trembled. "My only purpose is to serve my coven. My only purpose is to serve my coven. My only purpose is to serve my coven."

)))🌀(((

"ARE YOU QUITE well, Lady? You're squirming more than a snail about to be relieved of its shell." Badru, our coven's librarian, wore a vibrant plum robe that dragged slightly behind him as his old legs shuffled toward the desk.

The library was modest and quiet. A handful of witches read at long tables that lined the center of the room. Tall shelves surrounded them and the smell of parchment and leather coated my skin in familiarity.

"Just eager to start my day." I rubbed my sleep-deprived eyes, pushing my pile of books toward him. Two weeks had gone by, and I'd dreamed of my flight every night since. Sometimes I would keep flying right into the bright light in the distance, only to wake up coated in sweat.

"I'll let you get to it." Badru's shaggy white whiskers curled up around his crooked smile as he finished checking the books back in. Everything about him fit together like a completed quilt, from his spectacles to his pink-tinted point of a nose.

"Thank you, I'll re-shelve these." I collected the books I borrowed and spun on my heels, counting the aisles as I went. Every day in our paradise was the same, times and places determined for us by our leader. I had fifteen more minutes of free time in the library before I had to dive into my list of duties for the day, starting with singing and ending with dinner dishes.

The chants of praise for Malik that the bards and I lead made me second-guess everything I knew. They claimed our leader was fearless. But if he was so courageous, why couldn't he take me with him to see Theldea and protect me from its inhabitants?

Pivoting down my favorite aisle, I tried to remember the bite of the frigid wind. I kept my face a mask of cool indifference while my mind raged against the act of betrayal and my heart yearned for more.

Shaking my head, I pushed the thoughts away. Even fantasizing about leaving again was unforgivable. As I walked past the floor-to-ceiling windows, the view of the mountains in the distance heightened my perpetual cynicism.

I stopped and assessed my surroundings. My head only reached the fourth shelf, but I made sure there was no one in sight. After ensuring I was alone, I rested my head against the books by my favorite author, thankful for the steamy fantasies that helped banish my unwanted thoughts over the years.

My throat grew thick and coated with the unwanted taste of nostalgia. I slid my palm down the soft aqua binding. "The Siren and the Sea."

Against my will, my mind rapidly flashed through memories with Calliope. I itched at my ribs, picking at the memories like a scab threatening to reopen. Even my traitorous core heated, recalling our many late nights hidden away in these stacks. I hated the way my body still reacted to those moments, tingling all over at the lie.

"Taking a rest?"

I jumped at Malik's voice.

He sauntered down the aisle toward me. Plucking the cotton from my ears, I then discreetly shoved it back into my cleavage.

"No, Lord. I mean, yes." My mouth went dry, and I coughed. "What I mean is, I haven't been sleeping well."

"Hm." He grunted and reached for the stack of books I still needed to re-shelve. He placed them on the floor, and I cringed, my fingers twitching to put them where they belonged.

"What brings you to the library this morning?" I asked and took a few steps back, pretending to be looking for a book.

"I brought you something from our scouting mission." He reached into his satchel, handing me a heavy golden bracelet. "It reminded me of you."

His smile was soft, but the gold was a constant reminder of the weight of my responsibilities, of being different from everyone, of being trapped.

"Thank you, Lord." I shoved it into my pocket, forever unsure of his true intentions. "Was that all?" My voice was sharper than I wanted it to be, my doubts manifesting in my vocal cords.

"These fantasies are where you find yourself in your traitorous thoughts, is it not?" His jaw ticked, and he towered over me.

I kept my mouth shut and reached for one of the books on the floor.

His large boot kicked my hand away. "You are banned from the library."

"What?" I felt dizzy but straightened my spine, unwilling to show weakness.

"Do you have *cotton* in your ears?" His eyes flicked from my cleavage back to me.

I set my jaw. I had been careless since my return, consumed by daydreams of being back on that mountain. Someone must have witnessed me trying to block him out and reported me. I couldn't trust anyone in this coven.

"No." I grit my teeth. "I don't understand this punishment."

"There are many things you don't comprehend, Octavia. Obedience is one of them." He flicked a piece of lint from his lapel.

"Then help me comprehend how banning me from the library makes sense." The admiration I had toward him was peeling away like dead skin.

"Maybe this will help. You are banned from the gardens as well." He invaded my space and my mouth fell open.

Venom worked its way to the tip of my tongue. "Why would you punish me in such a way? Ripping away the few things that bring me joy?"

"You blame me for your inability to appreciate all the good in your life? No, no." He caressed my cheek, his touch like hot coals. "This punishment is entirely on you. When I was a boy, I was blind to the Goddess's controlling ways, and I refuse to be blind to yours any longer. You attempted to defy me in front of my people. You belittled their safety because you aren't satisfied with what you have here. Maybe you'll learn to appreciate what you do have once it's gone."

I searched his eyes for any hint of mercy but found none. "Malik, please. I'm eternally grateful. Your cause is noble. You save witches like me, witches who had nowhere else to go. Give me any other punishment."

He merely beamed at my praise as he did with every other witch in this coven, his eyes glistening. I used to find comfort in his eyes. But now, they only brought shame.

I latched onto his wrist, desperate. "*Please.*"

He pushed me away. "You're *exactly* like your creator."

I held onto the bookshelf for support, my world spinning around me. "I'm not the Goddess."

"No, you aren't." He wrinkled his nose in disgust. "My decision is final. You will stay in your room until the next ceremony." His tone was harsh.

He signaled the scouts I hadn't noticed at the end of the aisle to retrieve me.

"Malik, please! I wanted to be a scout so I could help the witches throughout Theldea like you. I admire you." My shouts rang out, and I didn't care how unruly I was being.

"Control yourself, Lady!" My head snapped sideways, and the burn of his hand sizzled against my cheek.

"I just wanted to help," I said and rubbed my aching jaw. Scouts huddled around me.

"Help?" Malik fisted my hair in his hand, yanking my chin up. "You don't help, Octavia. You *offend*." He pushed me into the arms of a scout.

Too overwhelmed by the contradicting feelings for my mentor plaguing my mind, everything fizzled into a clouded numbness as I followed the scouts back to my room.

Maybe the cotton had leaked into my brain. I was no longer trapped inside my fleshly prison, but floating just outside of myself.

The punishments would never stop. I wished I could be a savior like him, but a wicked selfishness lived inside of me that no amount of discipline would squelch.

))) ◎ (((

SALIVA SPRAYED ACROSS my face as another scout spit, my trembling chin the only sign of weakness. I stood firm in the center of the labyrinth, hoping the end of the ceremony was close.

"Bitch!" This time, a slap accompanied the spit. The scouts had lined up on Malik's orders, each taking their turn putting me in my place.

"You'll never be one of us." More spit. My face was coated in it, the smells of regurgitation making me gag.

Malik stood a few paces away, chatting with the scouts who had already had their turns. The protector I trusted, passive to the cruelty he inflicted on me.

My eyes and cheeks were hot, and my sluggish heartbeat picked up as the last scout stepped in front of me.

"Calliope?" I whimpered; my hair tangled in my crown. My old lover scrunched her nose at the filth covering my face.

"You're disgusting and pathetic. How dare you think you could leave your coven to fend for themselves." She spat and kicked me in the gut, stealing my breath. I stumbled back.

"Another successful ceremony!" Malik called over the laughing crowd. "You are dismissed."

The crowd scattered toward the conservatory to celebrate. Malik waited for me to gather my strength and straighten. I didn't dare wipe the spit off my face.

"You're looking too thin. Eat more." With one statement he twisted the knife permanently wedged in my bloodless guilt-ridden heart, only to find there was nothing left inside.

He left, following the crowd, and two witches linked arms with him.

"Why did we get picked for traitor duty?" One scout complained as a handful of them led me back to my room.

Two weeks of isolation in my room had gone by and I had gone through the motions of the ceremony only speaking on Malik's precise cues. There was a time when my coven respected me and my power, their Lady of the Grave.

But now, even those I considered friends booed and hissed as I was paraded by. Everything was fuzzy, and I detached myself from the world around me I no longer trusted.

Before long, I was thrown into my room, my knees crashing against the floor. The scouts locked the door behind them.

Crawling on all fours, I made it to the bathroom and turned on the spigot, steam pouring from its mouth as the bath filled. I peeled off my clothes, pulling myself up and over the side of the large clawfoot tub.

Hissing, I welcomed the burning heat. I washed the spit from my face, pretending to accept that the love I had for Malik and my coven would never be reciprocated.

I hadn't bathed since being covered in snow and dirt a month ago, afraid I would lose the earthy scents that were left on my skin and in my hair. I scrubbed as hard as I could with my sponge, trying to wash the filth and treachery away.

"This isn't... *fucking*... working!" I threw the ineffectual sponge and submerged myself in defeat. Bubbles scrambled out of my mouth in currents as I screamed, vocal cords crying out for salvation. I would give them no such thing.

When I finally resurfaced, I took a deep breath, inhaling the sweet-smelling citrus bath salts Malik had brought for me from Stranata. I closed my eyes, imagining fruit juice running down my chin from a freshly picked orange.

"They spit in your face. All of them." Speaking the words aloud narrowed my throat, and I slumped back into the water, covering my limp shoulders.

Burying my unwanted emotions in sweetness and heat had proved to be a waste of time. Scraping layer after layer of skin with the rough sponge and scalding water had made my flesh an angry shade of splotchy red. I released a heavy sigh and pulled my enervated body out of the tub.

The oversized fluffy black towel enveloped my small stature. They were one of the few things Malik had brought me that I enjoyed. My chin quivered, and I patted my ankles and calves dry. Too tired to dry anything else, I wrapped my hair in the towel.

Sleepless nights had hurtled me into delirious reasoning that the glimmer I had seen was another coven, one I could fly to. The corners of my mouth pulled into a deeper frown, which I was certain was just my face now.

I had to come back. For Malik and everyone within this coven who relied on my blood. *I wish I could drain it all.*

Revelry roared outside, the perfect excuse to dampen one's senses and forget the slaughter and hatred they had just taken part in.

I begrudgingly padded over to my vanity and examined my naked appearance in the cracked mirror. My frame was thin; thinner in the span of a month. My body always fluctuated, never truly fitting into a typical mold, but this was different. My collar bones jutted out like the sharp Odraze peaks; some of my usual curves had turned straight. I had stopped going to the kitchen, my appetite for food nothing compared to my hunger for freedom.

"Some fear we are a path to the Abyss, but those Theldean scum are blind. We see past the veil, and I will lead you not to the Abyss but to the true Ether!" I didn't bother putting cotton in my ears as another speech rang through the castle, rattling the paintings on my walls.

"I'm not ok..." I confided in my ugly reflection, my too-heavy arms falling to my sides. Dark circles rimmed my eye sockets, and my skin had lost its warmer tones.

After staring at myself for a brief eternity, I meandered to the window seat. It was a spot that usually brought me comfort, but without my books, it was as hollow as me.

With a shuddering breath, I drew the curtains open for the first time since my flight. Swiping a falling tear, I blinked through soaked lashes. I struggled to comprehend how there could be any fluid left in me from a month of crying, dehydration, and sweat. I sat up straighter, pressing my finger to my upper lip to fight the vicious wave of nausea.

My wet hair fell free of the towel and cool rivulets funneled into a chilling stream down my spine.

The moon was full and dangerous, bringing with her the forbidden fruit of freedom I had dared to taste. There she was, a beacon in the hazy sky I had known all my life. A ripe, pale fruit I wanted to pick from the sky and envelope in my arms.

Would she bring me the comfort and answers I so desperately needed? She was like me, dancing between the shadows of the clouds, never wishing to be fully seen. I scowled up at her and my mark grew hotter.

"This is all your fault!" I hollered at the moon, but in truth, I was speaking to the Goddess. The creator who had abandoned me and thrown me away like garbage. Why did she create me so poorly? Why did she think I wasn't enough?

Perhaps that's why I was left in those woods, I was only a defect. It was easier to blame others than face what I truly was. A monster that considered leaving her people.

I lowered to my knees and opened the windows wide. The shouts of praise gritted ruthlessly against my frayed sanity, and I could see witches dancing and laughing.

Sticky air permeated our coven like a wet rag and clung to my irritated skin. What I wouldn't give to feel the bitter chill upon it again. I had landed face-first in a pile of snow, something I had only ever read about in my books. It had been the most invigorating experience I ever had.

My uncontrollable weeping started again, and I curled into a ball on the plush seat, hugging my knees to my chest. I rocked back and forth. Being alone with my thoughts without normal distractions was driving me mad.

Smile more, Lady. Are you not happy in paradise?

Malik was right. I was ungrateful for his provisions.

Lanterns flickered around the housing, witches finding their homes amongst the coven. The background blurred, leaving only the window's edge in focus.

If I rocked just slightly harder, I would fall from the open windows. It wasn't the first time I'd thought about it since the mountain—hanging, drowning in the tub, a large dose of nightshade. If I jumped, Malik would know I took my life. He'd made it clear that if I did this, my soul would be sent straight to the Abyss. So, I landed on starvation, too cowardly to rid Theldea of its ugliest monster quickly.

I was to be a voice of loyalty, commitment, and reassurance to our coven. But most days I felt as if I was just as in danger here as I would be if I traveled outside our boundaries. How was I supposed to support something I didn't know if I believed in anymore?

Standing naked, I braced my hands on the side frames of the window and curled my toes over the ledge. I stared at the myriads of sharp rocks below; they had never been this much of a temptress. Starvation was taking too long, and I couldn't bear it anymore.

Being the Lady of the Grave was no longer survivable. She had killed Octavia slowly throughout the years, ripping apart every ounce of what was once me.

The demon who lived and prowled across my skull purred in approval at my readiness to give myself fully over to its wishes so that it could deliver me to the Abyss.

The slightest breeze danced across my skin.

My body relaxed for the first time in months, maybe even years. I couldn't stop the contented smile from growing, forcing my face to use muscles long forgotten.

"One tragic, humiliating accident…" I glanced once more at the moon, chuckling. I could barely get my voice to work with the lump of guilt in my throat. "I'm sorry, Malik."

Arms wrapped around myself; I couldn't wait any longer. I stepped with one last laugh off the edge, ready to fall blissfully into oblivion.

A golden barrier collided with my body instantly, pushing me backward and making me stumble like a newborn foal across my window seat.

"What the—?" The air was knocked from my lungs, and I fell onto the floor, forcing out a loud huff. Gulping in breaths, I peered up to my ceiling, begging it to give me answers, any fucking answers.

I sat up on my elbows, peering at the open window, but the golden barrier was gone. "Great, Octavia, you can't even fucking die properly."

A low humming emanated from my closet.

I marched over and tossed aside the tiles without a care. I pulled out my broom to scold it. But as I sat it across my lap, all I could do was admire her recent changes. I had broken off a few twigs during my rough landing and the snow had stained the wood slightly on part of the shaft.

"If that was you, I'm going to chop you up into tiny pieces with an ax and then burn you to ashes." I pulled her into a tight hug, cradling her against my chest and resting my cheek on the smooth wood as if she were the cats I lured in with catnip in the gardens.

"I can't do this anymore," I admitted to her. "Nothing makes sense."

Lowering to the floor so the tiles could cool my spine, I held my broom tightly. My life replayed in my mind, but there were gaps, things I couldn't remember. My memory was empty in places like the porous bone marrow that formed the ceiling.

"I know I came back, but... I can't endure this life anymore."

Malik's rejection and my loneliness had overshadowed my joy and pride for too long. All I could remember were the years I spent making myself small. The mistakes and poor decisions. The hurt I had caused. I was unworthy of being the Lady of the Grave. Of being their source of protection.

The broom hummed again, tickling my soaked cheek as if begging for one last flight. My fingers shook and something adjacent to hope surged through me as I made one more reckless decision.

If I was dying, I would at least die on a mountaintop I loved with fresh air in my lungs. I would jump off that fucking mountain as many times as necessary to be free of this fleshly prison.

I stood and tossed my broom onto the bed. My hands heated, and I blew hot air to dry my hair. It was too cold past the barrier to fly with it wet. I trudged through my closet and pulled out some items I had traded for months ago.

First, I slid on the thickly lined pants. They were a lovely shade that reminded me of freshly picked raspberries. The lace-up sides were adjustable. I cinched them tightly just below my belly button and turned to assess my ass's reflection. Still delirious from trying to kill myself and the increase in adrenaline, I smirked. It accentuated and lifted in all the right places. The perfect pants to die in.

The old plum-colored long-sleeve wasn't very thick, so I threw on another thin layer — a light brown shirt that was open in the front. I wrapped the two sides tightly around my breasts before securing them with one of my thick black belts. It hugged my waist comfortably just above my hips.

I sat on the floor, pulling on my thickest pair of socks and my light brown boots that reached just above my ankles, tucking my pants into my socks. "One more flight."

My coven and Malik would hate me for leaving. But I tried my best to stay here and, just like most things in my life, it ended in bitter disappointment.

Remembering the welcome bite of the cold that the snow had brought me a month ago filled me with recent nostalgia, pushing my doubts into a corner. It was the happiest I had ever been, looking out over that peak into what I assumed was Ozuria based on my research in the library.

Hurrying, I refused to give my heart or mind any time to deter me from my decision. Fear drove me to strap on my thigh holster and sheath my golden dagger. I wanted to die but on my own terms. Murder by Theldean lunatics sounded much less appealing.

With a radical death wish, I grabbed my broom and my cloak and jumped up to the window's ledge once more. Taking flight, I left my crown and the Lady of the Grave behind.

Chapter 5

OCTAVIA

This would be the most helpful thing I had ever done for my coven. I dangled my feet over the steep drop, snow plummeting to the sharp rocks below. My decision to jump was resolute.

The attempt from the window was imperfect, but now I was even more prepared to say goodbye, my failure only spurring me into a deeper spiral rooted in anger and confusion. Something about the idea of falling even further to my definite end soothed me.

I gripped my broom with steady hands and caressed her wild bristles, gold light flowing through them. "I guess this is goodbye."

I smiled softly and stood, taking a deep breath as the first signs of sunlight leaked from the horizon.

"One day I spoke to the raven
She told me to go find the crow"

Loud singing echoed against the rocks, and my heart stuttered. I snatched up my broom, knuckles white, and took to the air, hiding within the sharp peaks. My breaths came fast as I braced myself for a swarm of Theldeans.

A single witch strutted into the open area I had just occupied, strumming a black lute. His white furry hood covered his face, a small misty cloud rising around the opening like a dragon's breath. He sang a song I had never heard; his warm baritone was smooth as silk.

> *"It was quite a one-sided conversation*
> *Was this crow a friend or a foe?"*

Snow fell in heavy chunks, collecting on my hair and lashes, and I blinked it away.

He danced around, his shiny instrument swinging like his dance partner. As he hummed, he sought shelter under an overhang that one of the sharp shards of rock created.

I flew closer, lurking behind a large boulder to get a better view of this strange Theldean who braved the mountains with nothing but a lute and a small bag.

Chuckling, he continued to play, and as he did, lavender tendrils wound around his body. I covered my mouth, suppressing a gasp, and nearly losing my balance. The tendrils looked similar to the billowing red ones that appeared when connected to Malik's Ether. But these were more languid, a merry dance, instead of thrashing violence.

My broom moved of her own accord toward him.

"No, stop." I hissed, but she barreled straight for him. I stifled a scream as I was ripped from a horizontal position to a vertical one. "No, no, no! Don't do this to me again!" I begged in a hushed whisper as I clawed at my broom. Gravity pulled me to the ground and I fell on my ass with a splat. My broom fell on top of me, and I scrambled away from the stranger.

"Well, darling, I have to admit that was a better landing than last time." Slowly clapping, he strode out, chest thrust forward.

I shot a fireball at him, then a stake of ice. They dissipated against his air shield. I scrambled to my feet, my backside sore, but I had to ignore it. I held out my hands, more fire ready in my palms.

"Let's take a breath," he said, his voice gentle as he lowered his air shield. "There's no need for violence."

He moved closer, pulled down his mask, and lowered his hood. His lute hung lazily in his free hand, but he still looked lethal. His skin was pale, and I followed the purple and blue veins winding across his cheekbones like a spider's web.

Gentle *tings* drew my attention to where he clicked his fingers together and my eyes widened. His hands were as black as a fresh pot of ink, clearly affected by some type of magic compared to the rest of his incredibly pale skin. Golden butterfly picks adorned all ten of his slender fingers. They were smooth and looped in a semicircle just above his first knuckle and flowed into a rounded arch just under his fingernails. The picks individually were impressive, but together against his charcoal skin they were a masterpiece.

His cropped hair was dark, and it matched the stubble he scratched.

I called on Malik's Ether and slowly raised my arms; red tendrils thrashed up my body like overgrown roots. The magic scorched my wrists and fingertips, eager to be unleashed.

This witch might have been the most beautiful thing I'd ever seen, but beautiful things were often the most dangerous.

"This is your *one* chance," I said. "Leave now, and I won't have to do this."

"I'm only here to help." He quirked his eyebrows, taking a step closer.

I bared my teeth. "Don't!"

He pulled his shiny black lute in front of him, the intricate embellishments on the body catching the sun as he moved. He strummed a low chord, and the purple tendrils licked at my boots.

"Fine." I widened my stance. "You fucked with the wrong witch, Theldean scum."

"Okay, now you're just trying to be hurtful." He flashed a smile that would have sent any sane witch to her knees. Instead, I scoffed at his charisma.

"Oh, *come on*, I've elicited multiple swoons with this smile." He pointed to his mouth and my eyes widened. This cocky witch refused to heed my warnings.

"Go. Away." My strained voice echoed between the black shards surrounding us, and my hands lowered ever so slightly.

"No. I don't think I will." He took a deep breath and sang.

"How could the raven befriend the crow?
I don't know… I don't know"

"You're going to what? Sing me to death, bard? Attack me with your lute?" I laughed.

He squinted and tapped his boot against the snow, a frown pulling at his smug lips for the first time.

I curled my hands into fists, pulling them tightly into an X across my chest, and leveled my gaze. "I thought you were actually a threat."

He inched closer and I could see now that his eyes matched his magic, a swirling cacophony of differing shades of purple. "I'm not a normal bard, darling."

With a guttural shout, I thrust my hands forward, bombarding him with all the elements at once. He fell flat to the ground, dodging my powerful magic. Everything crashed against the rocks behind him.

The manic laugh coming from my expanding lungs sounded unnatural and cruel and part of me knew it didn't belong to me but the magic pulsing through me. I had never used my magic to protect myself before, and I smiled savagely at the power and control that came with it.

He shot to his feet, still smiling back at me, and sprinted behind a boulder.

"Stay down!" I yelled and ran after him, but froze when I heard a sharp *crack* beneath my boot. All movement ceased as it echoed against the large rocks.

My broom was mangled, the top half sinking and sticking out of the snow, her bristles broken into tiny pieces. A single tear rolled down my cheek.

"No…" I swayed slightly. The sudden loss held my heart in a vise.

"Octavia, are you okay?"

My spine shivered, and it wasn't from the bitter cold. How did he know my name?

The bard's head peered out from behind his hiding place. As soon as I saw those hypnotic eyes *pitying* me, adrenaline replaced shock.

"Aaaaah!" I screamed, and it was so piercing that he covered his ears.

"Stop! You're going to cause an avalanche." he pleaded, but I didn't care.

I was prepared to die now more than ever.

Lifting my aching arms as high as I could, I sent everything I had toward his face. I smothered him in my misplaced anger like honey covering a spoon, hoping to drown him in it. If I was going down, he was going with me.

He dodged my attacks, jumping swiftly from left to right, distancing himself from me. I launched another fireball that whizzed past his head so close it singed the fur on his hood.

"You're dead, bard!" I prowled toward him; a predator ready for her kill.

He circled back, entering the overhang containing his supplies.

Laughing, I cornered him. "Nowhere left to run."

"I could easily solve this through violence, darling, but with the two of us, that will never be the answer," he answered from inside.

I stumbled. If his answer wasn't violence, what was it?

He knew my name, which meant he already knew too much. I pummeled the air shield he had thrown up around himself with rocks, ice, and fire. Sweat dripped down my forehead; I was overheated with the use of so much magic.

He strummed a slow melancholic tune, and calmly sang his melody.

"When darkness falls and you can't find your way, I'll stay, I'll stay
The Goddess will raise the sun soon to banish your fears"

Violet coils ensnared my ankles, crawling up my body. My breaths came quick and shallow as I reached for my dagger. He walked slowly toward me with a gentle smile, his composure petrifying.

His magic swaddled me like a newborn, and my powers fizzled out. A weariness dragged my eyelids closed as my body relaxed. The only thing I could do was listen to his voice.

"I'll catch your tears until the Goddess nears, sleep now, sleep now"

"Please! *Please*! Don't hurt me!" I wailed. "My mentor will give you whatever you want."

His boots crunched in the snow as he grew closer. "You're the one who attacked me, remember? I should beg *you* to stop trying to kill me with that fucking abomination you call magic."

"Abomination?" I whispered, my question fading with my tired voice, and I forced my fluttering eyes open.

The tendrils eased me gently into the snow before dissipating. Strapping his lute to his back, he crouched down. "I need you to tell me that you will not try to kill me again. Nod if you agree."

He was so close and smelled like a freshly lit match, dangerous but alluring and untamed. I nodded, my lethargy fading. He stood and offered me his hand, and I slapped it away. His eyes widened and an exhausted grin spread across his face. I stood up shakily.

"What do you want from me?" I glared, hating how handsome he looked this close. His eyes reflected the magic he controlled. Lavender swirled within his irises, deep purples bursting around his pupils. His jaw was sharp, and his lips were full.

He tightened the white bracers on his forearms. "I'm here to take you home."

He tugged his hood up and walked to retrieve his bag.

I scrambled after him. Black spots danced across my vision. If he took me back Malik would disown me entirely. The punishments would be worse and never-ending. "You can't take me back. My coven is concealed, you'll never find it."

"The Coven of the Grave is not your home, Octavia." His words were so certain it made my mark glow brighter.

I lifted a hand to the back of my clammy neck.

"It's okay, I know you're Goddess-born, I'm not here to hurt you." He placed his lute on the ground.

My head shook violently, and I reached my hand to my upper lip, pressing hard. The witch hadn't hurt me, staying on the defensive the entire fight. But he could just be delivering me to someone worse. I took a few steps back.

"How do you know my name?" I asked through the nausea, looking longingly at the cliff's edge. Jumping would be easier than playing into his delusions.

With a few long strides, he closed the space between us, blocking my view of escape. "My name is Throwen. My mentor, Whynnie, knew you as a child and sent me to find you and take you back to Goldhaven."

Goldhaven? My stomach erupted with the giant moths that were said to live there. He was offering me a chance to see Goldhaven, to take me there. Or perhaps leading me to something much worse.

I rubbed my chest to calm the pounding of my heart. "How did you know where to find me?"

His stance was wide as he entered my space again. I had to look up to watch him. "We saw you in a mirror."

"Ew! *What the fuck?*" I pushed his chest hard, blowing him a few feet away with my air. I blanched and took a step back, attempting to cover my body with my arms. "You saw me in my mirror? W-what did you see?"

Throwen's cheeks bloomed a pale amethyst. "Whynnie is Goddess-born. She can tap into magic no other witch can. The Goddess gifted her with sight, and we saw you flying on your broom."

"No. No, that can't be right." My jaw dropped in disbelief. I pulled my hood tighter. My chest was aflame, shooting its sparks behind my eyes as tears welled. "You're lying. I'm the only Goddess-born in Theldea."

"I wouldn't lie to you." His face was soft, never taking his eyes off mine.

"Why should I trust you?" My body shook, and my knees buckled, my eyes threatening to roll back into my skull.

Throwen's hands wrapped around my shoulders as he pressed warmth into me with his magic. "Hey, stay with me."

"Who else knows about me?" I looked around, searching for threats. Was this one of Malik's elaborate ruses to see what I would do?

They will siphon your powers until there's nothing left.

Malik's warning chilled my already frozen bones, building up layers of crystalized paranoia.

"I'm alone. I have two siblings we would meet along our journey who also know who you are. We want to protect you and get you to Whynnie.

That's it, that's everyone who knows you exist beyond your coven." Throwen's grip was still firm around my biceps as I tried to steady myself.

"*Our* journey?" I squirmed out of his hold and took a step back, his outstretched hands lingering before lowering to his sides.

"That flicker"—he pointed to a dot in the distance—"is Oxvein. That's our first stop."

Licking my chapped lips, I admired the glimmer across the expanse of ice. It was validating to know my conjectures were true.

Then I looked back to where my coven lay behind the concealment. I couldn't see it, but flashes of Malik and our members threatened to pull me back.

"How will you get back without your broom?" Throwen's voice wasn't malicious but concerned.

I swallowed, my throat constricting as I located the remains of my broken broom. She deserved better than my blind rage and fear for her demise.

"Why would I go with you?" I whipped around to face him again, my face growing hot.

"Whynnie sent me to find you and bring you home, so that's what I would like to do." Throwen started walking the way he came. Toward Oxvein.

"What do you mean, it's what you would *like* to do?" My trembling chin lifted. "As if I have a choice."

"When you're with me, darling, you will always have a choice."

My vision tunneled with Throwen in its center. I tilted my head to the side, seeing if a new angle would show me his true intentions.

"Not to mention, I *saw* you in that mirror a month ago. Your desperation to flee. You have the same look in your eyes now. You and I both know you wouldn't have come back if you didn't need to see more." His eyes gleamed, and he crossed his arms.

I broke eye contact, turning and walking solemnly around the markings my destructive magic had left behind. When I reached the remains of my broom, I knelt in the snow beside her.

"I'm sorry I broke you. I love you." I sniffled and pulled one of her twigs from the scattered bristles, tucking it into my cloak. I maneuvered around the rubble to Throwen.

The sun had risen over the mountain peaks and a beam of natural light stretched across the ice.

He reached out a hand. "Theldea is a lovely place if you give it a chance."

I stared at his open palm. How many times had I stared at my own hands, desperate for answers? Now, Throwen's mysterious hands offered hope.

If I stayed here, Malik would eventually retrieve me, which would end in punishment. If I went with Throwen, Malik would find us, and we would both be punished. But, with Throwen, the punishments would be delayed, *and* I could see the lands and witches I'd fantasized about since I was a child. I inhaled an icy breath.

"My mentor will come for me, and he gets violent when he is angry. If he catches us..." I didn't want to think of the horrible punishments he would inflict on Throwen because of my selfishness.

Running a hand through his hair, his posture went rigid. "He won't catch us."

"You don't know him. He is more powerful than any of us, even you. I don't want to put you or your loved ones in danger." I tried to help Throwen see that this plan of his was too risky.

"I know what I'm signing up for, I've faced your mentor's scouts before." Hands clenched at his sides, he gritted his teeth, jaw ticking.

"If what you say is true, Whynnie can teach me about my magic?" I tapped my fingertips against my dagger. Even considering this was foolish but I couldn't go back to my coven with the knowledge of another Goddess-born. I *had* to meet her.

"Yes. And trust me, out of all the siblings you could have been stuck with, I'm the best one. I'm not *just* a bard." Throwen smiled wide.

I grimaced at his confidence, resting my hands on my hips. "Is that so? And how sure are you that you can keep us safe?"

"You've seen what I can do." Throwen clicked his picks together, pushing out his chest.

I chewed on my lip and raised an eyebrow. "Yeah, so? For all I know, every Theldean has your abilities and you're lying and taking me to be raped, tortured, murdered—"

"No one touches you unless they come through me." He stepped close enough that I could see the steam rising from his heated skin, my morbid thoughts evaporating with it.

If this witch was an oil painting, I would stare at it endlessly. He looked lean, and I wanted to peel away his furry layers to see what other marvels he hid.

"Why purple?" I blurted, flustered by his proximity.

"Do you mean my eyes, darling? Well, I suppose I got them from my mother or father, but I like to pretend they never existed, so... who knows?" He winked with a laugh.

"What kind of magic is it? And *stop* calling me darling." I crossed my arms, unimpressed.

"I can't, nicknames are a tradition where I come from," His eyes darkened, his canines making an appearance. "And I doubt you want to insult the culture of the first Theldean you've met."

Scoffing, I rolled my eyes, pretending his correct assumption and charm didn't affect me.

"I'll make you a deal. If you want to come with me, I'll tell you anything you want to know. To the best of my ability... I'm a bard, not a scholar." He offered his hand again. "Deal?"

My stomach dropped. This was it. The precipice of a decision that would alter my life forever. I came here to die and Throwen had offered me life. The demon in me hated him for it, but my heart was always too curious for its own good.

I reached out a shaking hand and when our palms met, a jolt of electricity shot through my limbs. With wide eyes, I looked to see if he had felt it too, but he showed no signs of anything amiss. I dropped my free hand to the dagger on my thigh in case this was all an elaborate trap.

"Excellent." He kept his hand in mine, leading me away from my coven and into the unknown.

Chapter 6

THROWEN

"So far Theldea sucks!"

I peered over my shoulder at where Octavia walked behind me. Her hollow red cheeks sucked in deep breaths of air, her hands on her hips. Her mark glowed, emanating warm light around her hood and illuminating her dark mocha hair. It was even more marvelous than the Odraze Mountains on this cloudy morning.

"I agree, this part sucks, but look." I pointed just below to where Lucky drank from a pool of water, just where I'd left her. "That's my horse. We are almost there."

She groaned and lifted her legs high, trudging after me. She was so short that each step of mine was three steps for her, the piling snow rising to her knees.

I usually found negativity annoying, but with her, it somehow came across as cute. She complained, but she never gave up.

We'd walked for a few torturous hours with only minor cuts and bruises, clearing the slippery shale and now closer to a brief respite. I had a feeling the bruise Octavia had from her fall off the broom was probably worse than her minor climbing injuries.

I waited until she caught up to me, then we slid carefully down the steep icy incline leading to Lucky. "Having fun yet, darling?"

"Tons." She deadpanned. Her skin was an olive tone similar to Whynnie's, but Octavia leaned toward a cooler shade.

I bent my knees, leaning onto the slope to pick up speed. She slid along with me, mimicking my posture flawlessly. She wobbled, but kept her balance. A lightness filled my chest watching her perseverance.

The sun illuminated us with a merciful break in the clouds. Warmth soaked into my dry skin and aching bones. I rubbed my wrists as we walked the last paces to Lucky.

Octavia's hair billowed around her drawn hood, whipping her in the face over and over as she tried to spit it out of her mouth.

Trying to contain my entertained smirk, I untied my necklace, slipping the crystal held within the black leather string into the pouch strapped to my thigh. "Here."

She just stared at it for a long moment. Her chin tilted down, kicking tiny ice particles with her boot. "I... I don't have anything to trade you for it."

What the fuck does that mean?

"No. I'm giving it to you. Here." I held it out to her once more and her dark brows knit together.

This close, I could see bands of lighter cinnamon hair blending into the darker strands. An unfamiliar part of me wanted to comb through those tangles and see what it felt like between my fingers.

I shook my head, clearing it from my trance. "It's for your unruly hair."

Her nose scrunched up, and she folded her arms across her chest. "In my coven, we trade for items. It wouldn't be right for me to take it without giving you something in return."

I grabbed her hand and placed it in her palm. "Well, in my coven, we help our friends without needing something in return."

"Um... Thank you." Her cool fingers grazed mine, and I had the immediate urge to get her warm.

Her eyes bounced from my lips to my eyes. Normally, Theldeans looked into my eyes with a hint of fear. The only way to describe how she inspected me was innocent curiosity, like that of a child experiencing strangers for the first time—with no judgment.

Octavia pulled her hair into a low ponytail at her nape, and it cascaded down to the center of her back. She returned the hood over her head, and small curls, wet from sweat, framed her face.

Turning, I bit my lip and continued forward, eager to get us to Oxvein before nightfall.

"So... you're a bard?" she asked, thick ice creaking under our boots.

I pulled my lute forward, strumming some chords. "I am."

"What's your favorite part of being a bard?"

My strumming faltered. Nobody had ever asked me that before.

"I enjoy being around witches from every walk of life, playing for them, making them laugh and dance." The spirits serpentined between my knuckles, wanting to come and play at the mention of a good time.

"Do you have many friends?" Her questions were coming in quick succession, and I welcomed them.

"Yes, they love me at the taverns." I picked quickly, showing off my skills. "Don't worry, you'll see what I mean when you have the honor of experiencing one of my performances."

She was quiet, touching her pointer finger to her nose. "I don't think that a true friend is someone you have to perform for." Her words were melancholic and pierced through me in the most excruciatingly beautiful way.

I turned and winked at her just as we reached Lucky. "You're quite a clever little witch, aren't you?"

She glared at me. Lucky whinnied, happily prancing at my return.

"Hello." Octavia's voice was soft, and she timidly approached. Lucky snorted in response, shaking her shiny black mane. She was a head below Lucky's withers.

"This is Lucky. Lucky, this is Octavia." A loud neigh echoed around us in the expansive glacial terrain. "Have you ridden before?"

"Yes, but it's been years." She ran her fingers through Lucky's mane and cooed sweet nothings to her.

"Here, give her these." I pulled out some frozen carrots from the black saddle bag resting on the ground. "Feed her and she will love you forever."

Octavia laughed and the melody it created demanded to be accompanied by my music. It was ethereal, and I never wanted it to stop.

"She sounds a lot like me." She snorted and fed the carrots to Lucky.

I strolled a few paces away and started packing fresh snow into our empty canteens. Keeping her protected was my top priority, so I wanted to use as little magic as possible to ensure my reserves were full.

"How many witches are in Oxvein?"

I jumped and my high-pitched scream ripped free. "*Goddess's tits*, Octavia!" My cheeks heated and I clutched my chest. "I knew you were going to be bad for my health."

"I'm so sorry. I didn't mean to creep up on you, I'm just curious."

This woman was good at sneaking around. I couldn't remember the last time anyone had sneaked up on me. I laughed a huge belly laugh and she couldn't help but join in. It was refreshing, the changes she was already bringing into my life.

The sounds of our joy intertwining made me want to dance with her, let the spirits coil around us. But there would be time to enjoy Theldea together later once we grabbed some supplies.

She rubbed the back of her neck. "So, how many? Is Oxvein a large coven?"

I passed her one of my canteens still full of water and she drank from it greedily, water dripping down her chin.

I swallowed hard before answering. "Oxvein is one of the smaller covens. Maybe around twenty thousand witches."

"That's about how many are in my coven too." She took another sip, appearing very interested in the sky.

My ears rang, and I buried my dread deep where she wouldn't see it. We had no idea Malik had so many, figuring a large majority were dead. I tacked up Lucky and prepared her for a harsh ride to distract my hands from the rage deep inside.

"How does their coven operate?" Octavia stared out over the vast sheet of ice we had to travel across to arrive at the entrance of Oxvein.

"The people are deeply connected to one another and their land. They hunt and gather mostly, live off the land and what the Goddess blesses them with from year to year. Some years are hard for them, but they always band together and accept the Goddess's provisions, whatever they may be."

"So, they worship her, the Goddess?" She spoke our creator's name like a curse, as if hatred roiled within her.

"Yes. Most covens in Theldea do, but not all witches still believe in the Goddess or worship her."

Octavia's jaw ticked. She brushed some snow off her cloak and pants. "And how long until we reach Goldhaven?"

"I can make the journey in nine days, but we might need to slow down and, knowing Echo, we will have to once we reach Stranata." I shook my head, thinking of the antics they must be getting up to in Fennix's territory.

"Echo is one of your siblings?"

My chest hummed pleasantly at her focus on details. She might not be the most physically adept, but she was keen and intelligent, and even in her state of shock up on the mountain, she had paid attention.

"Yes. They are... Well, you'll just have to see. Let's get going." Lucky neighed in agreement, ready to stretch her legs. I reached to help Octavia onto Lucky's back.

"What are you doing?" She stepped back and wrapped her arms around herself.

"I'm helping you up." *What is she hiding behind that carefully built wall?*

She peered up at Lucky, and her eyes widened as if realizing there was no way she could reach to climb up herself.

She took a hesitant step toward me. "Fine."

When I lifted her, a sweet citrus scent wafted off her skin and snapped my senses into focus. She weighed close to nothing and was much thinner than when I inspected her in the mirror. Was Malik starving her? I would fucking rip his limbs from his body.

"Thank you."

I hopped up behind her. Our bodies melded together, and an inferno started in my stomach. I fumbled with Lucky's reigns and coughed through the heat she provided between my legs.

She struggled to find her balance, so I tightened my thighs around her so she could get comfortable.

A small gasp escaped her. She squirmed more and I smirked, even if she couldn't see it. The way she felt moving there—

Abyss consume me!

I opened my legs slightly, offering her more room. This woman needed to sit still, or the ride would be unbearable. It had been some time since I was this close to a woman, and it felt like a sip of cool water after a drought.

I signaled Lucky to walk and Octavia wobbled again. I wrapped my arm around her waist firmly, pulling her flush with my body. I called on my magic to wrap around her waist just in case.

She went rigid. "You called my magic an abomination. What did you mean? I pull the spirits directly from Malik's Ether."

I opened and closed my mouth, realization hitting me like one of Kallan's left hooks. She didn't understand her magic. Didn't know she was being manipulated, damaging her own soul by using necromancy.

"Throwen?" Her voice shook, and she turned, the sun lighting up her honey-brown eyes. Her thick, snow-covered lashes fluttered.

I hated this feeling. I didn't even know what this feeling was, I just knew I had to rip the worry out of her.

"More answers after you rest. You'll need your energy." My throat tightened, recalling the many necromancers I had annihilated over the years. My targets had likely been someone she'd known, considered family, maybe loved. I couldn't imagine befriending someone who hurt my family, so why should I expect her to trust me?

She bit her lip and nodded, facing forward. After a few moments, she relaxed into me.

Beads of sweat gathered on my forehead.

"Are you going to tell them who I am?" she asked, yawning.

"It's best if we try not to draw any extra attention. For all anyone knows, you are my friend, and I'm helping you travel back to Goldhaven. The cloak will keep your mark hidden. You're safe with me."

The bottoms of her ribs relaxed under my fingers. Her body was resting heavily on me.

"Why did you pick Goldhaven as your home?"

"We all have to find our place in the world, Octavia." It wasn't an answer, but it was all I had. Emotions were hard for me to put into words, so instead I sang the lullaby I had used to contain her rage softly against her hood.

Chapter 7

OCTAVIA

Otherworldly howls made the hairs on my neck rise. I sat straight up, now fully awake. I swiveled my head, frantically searching for the source of the unnerving sound.

"Relax darling, it's just wolves." Throwen spoke calmly into my ear.

"Are they close?"

"No, their howls can be heard from miles away and they echo in the tundra." I was acutely aware of every part of his body that was touching mine. My head rested into the crook of his neck, my hot breath billowing in clouds around us.

The sun was setting. Its glow painted the arctic sky in skilled strokes of pinks and oranges. I had never seen such vivid colors. Without the haze, the sky was so much more alive.

A flat white landscape lay before us with mountains rising all around. Glaciers floated in sporadic holes throughout the ice. Other holes led to deep caverns with thick walls of ice and snow.

He pulled me even closer, wrapping me tightly in his cloak. Having this much concern focused on my well-being was baffling. *Why would he take on such a burden?*

"We are safe, just listen." He whispered the last part into the shell of my ear through my hood.

The smell of fresh crisp snow flooded my senses. My breaths grated against my sore throat and my chest ached from all this unfamiliar cold air.

It was bitter and painful yet still the most incredible experience of my life. My world was opening up like a flower in the morning sun and it was exquisite.

I closed my eyes, leaning back, and did as he said.

The long keening sounds echoed and another distinct howl sounded from somewhere behind us. This time the pitch rose and fell delicately, like the moon's passage through the night sky.

The sounds continued to bounce back and forth in a captivating exchange, a mastered cadence.

"Wow…" I whispered. It was unnerving but at the same time, a distinct cognizance ran through the animals' melodies.

I took a steadying breath and sat silently, listening to the wind, the wolves, and the gentle cracking of thick ice and snow below Lucky's hooves. Throwen's breaths matched my own as we listened. "I've never heard something so… connected."

"Wolves are very well connected. They howl to determine each other's locations."

"Have you ever seen one up close?" I craned my neck to look up at him, imagining what the stubble under his chin might feel like.

When he wasn't using his unique magic, his eyes were a softer lavender that reminded me of amethyst. The contrast against the white fur of his hood made them appear even more vibrant.

"I've seen an *entire pack*." He emphasized his words, teasing me with the possibility of a great story. I could see why he was so confident. He was an enticing witch, and he knew it.

I couldn't help my stupid crooked smile and turned back to the ice shelves ahead. "Will you tell me about it?"

He pulled me closer again, still sporadically warming me with his palms. "It was years ago. I was on my way to Miren, it's a small coven in Ozuria, not easy to travel to."

"Is anything easy to travel to in Ozuria?" I asked, my tone dry.

He chuckled, his chest shaking against my back. "I slept in a cave along the mountainside and as I lit my fire, a low *growl* sounded from behind me." He animated his words, growling himself.

The way he wove this story had me holding my breath. The same sensation my fantasy novels gave me, but hearing a tale vocalized in this way was an entirely new experience.

"The beast snarled and lowered his huge white muzzle, inching closer." He walked his fingers along my arm. "I readied my magic, but I wanted to see what would happen, so I stayed still and silent, waiting."

"You're insane." I said.

"Soon more wolves surrounded me, their long white fur hypnotic as they circled. The alpha advanced on me and I reached out my hand." He reached his hand in front of my face, holding me steady on Lucky with his strong thighs.

I was flushed, and I didn't know if it was from the intense story or our proximity.

"Then…"

I took a small breath at his soft tone and exaggerated pause.

"He bit my hand clean off!" he yelled and pinched the tip of my nose.

Lucky snorted, and I let out an embarrassingly loud squeak.

Throwen held me tight so that I didn't fall. I turned, making sure he was looking to see my glare.

He was laughing so hard tears welled in his eyes. The sweet sound of his joy was too infectious because instead of my normal bite, I laughed too.

I didn't recognize my genuine laugh anymore. Not forced or calculated.

How long had it been since I laughed like this?

Our laughter subsided, and Throwen gripped his stomach. "Oh, you're going to be so much fun. I've told these stories so many times that my siblings would be groaning. But you remind me why I love them so much."

"You're an ass." I bumped my shoulder into his chest, I was weak and the laughing had taken more out of me than I wanted to admit. "What actually happened, Throwen?"

He chuckled and soothed Lucky with some firm pats.

"Nothing. Wolves rarely attack unless we encroach on their territory. I was tired and lazy that night. I should have known the wolves were there. As soon as they started circling, I created an air shield, backed out of their cave, and apologized."

"Wait... you apologized to a wolf?"

"*No.* I apologized to an entire pack of wolves. Were you listening to my story at all?"

"I was. It's just that it's a pretty boring story compared to the wolves I read about in the library." I shrugged.

"I make my living on stories. People *love* my stories." His tone was playful and infectious.

Just as I thought, a typical bard. I laughed, but it faded at the sight before me. Two enormous ice shelves almost met, leaving a thin tunnel leading straight toward what must be Oxvein.

I sat up straighter and held onto Lucky's reins. My vision tunneled, and I fell forward onto Lucky's neck. My throat swelled, and I clutched tightly at my neck.

"Hey." Throwen tried to pull me up.

"*Fuck.* We need to stop!" I said over a lump in my throat, trying desperately to get my vision to come back into focus as I hyperventilated.

Cursed Abyss! I hadn't lost control of my emotions in front of another witch like this in ages. I had learned to never show fear, but walking into a Theldean coven was too overwhelming.

"Are you ok?" Throwen's voice was full of that infuriating concern again and he signaled Lucky to stop. She snorted, shaking out her mane.

"I'm fine. I just... I need a minute."

He slid off Lucky and helped lower me to the ground. My legs buckled, and I almost fell to the icy floor. I was a burden, weighing Throwen down with my growing madness.

"I've got you." He sought to reassure me, but I didn't care if I fell.

I pushed him away roughly and dove across the ice, sliding into a clumsy fall. I landed hard on my hands and knees and new cuts and scrapes seeped blood through my pants. I heaved bile all over the ice.

A loud snap echoed from below my knees. The crack fissured in fractals all around where I knelt.

"Octavia!" Throwen shouted, his expression petrified. He sprinted for me, purple tendrils beginning to wrap around his fingers. But he was too late. The ice was giving.

It would be better this way. He would be safer without me.

The same peace I experienced jumping out my window overtook me, and I gave up control, allowing the ground to consume me.

I couldn't help the scream that escaped as my body fell through the ice. I didn't bother trying to use an air shield, accepting the fate I had put off for too long.

The demon purred with satisfaction against my skull for only a moment before my hands and knees collided with a cold, powdery surface.

Throwen followed shortly after, but he had dove into the hole head first and his face smashed into a thicker pile of snow. I laughed my painfully bruised ass off.

He sat up and wiped the snow from his face. "What the *fuck*? I don't know why you're laughing. Sometimes the canyons below the ice are much much deeper. You got lucky."

My laugh continued, but it had a cynical edge to it now. The lack of food and sleep was taking its toll, and my mask was slipping.

"Octavia. It's not funny. You could have been hurt or killed."

"That's *exactly* why it's so funny. What's your problem? You barely know me." My biting tone made him flinch slightly. I was just a stranger who would only bring him pain.

"Do you have a death wish or something? Or are you just one of those witches who are attracted to danger?" His nostrils flared, and we panted together.

"I'm just not used to the thrills of adventure, I guess." I rubbed the back of my neck. It was an answer, but I was adept at hiding things beneath my words. He had no idea what he was dealing with.

"I must say, darling, your sense of wonder is intoxicating." His anger left just as quickly as it had come. He replaced it with humor, his tone positive once more.

I wiped my mouth self-consciously. I must have been quite the sight with my anxieties splashed all over my cloak and shirt. He either didn't notice my dishevelment or didn't care.

"Let's go." He offered his hand and helped me up.

"You want to know a secret?" I hopped on my toes a bit, feeling lighter from another near-death experience.

He laughed and bumped into me lightly, making me slip on the ice. "I want to know all your secrets."

We crawled out of the shallow hole and made our way back to Lucky. I patted her mane before Throwen grabbed her reins, pulling her along behind us.

It was our shared genuine curiosity about each other that drove me to tell him something real this time.

"I thought my sense of wonder died a long time ago. I know I can be a little... cynical, and Goddess knows I'm horrible company." I laughed, but his head snapped down, his eyes glowing a deep plum.

As he stared at his boots, I could tell he was trying to think before he spoke, to reign in his emotions. Apparently, he didn't find my self-degradation as funny as I did.

"I have thoroughly enjoyed your company thus far, even when you were trying to kill me or forcing me to dive into a hole after you. You don't have to apologize for who you are. Besides, Kallan will love having another grump to bond with." With his extra height, he rubbed the top of my head playfully with his knuckles.

Throwen was an anomaly. Not just because of his magic, but because of his willingness to befriend me.

We paused at the opening of the ice shelves.

"Are you ready? I'll be right here the whole time." He slipped his hand into mine and I was shocked at how natural it felt.

I left because I wanted to meet the witches in Theldea. To help them. I took a steady breath. "I'm ready."

"Keep your cloak on. If asked, you're assisting me while I help you get back to Goldhaven."

I frowned at my current state, covering up my bloodied knees with my cloak. *What a fucking disaster.* I snorted. "Assisting you with what? Singing and getting witches drunk?"

I scratched roughly at my neck, staring down at my frozen toes. The world around me spun. I had no idea what I was walking into. Despite Throwen's reassurances that these were peaceful witches, I couldn't shake Malik's words.

If they see what you are, they will cage you.

"Hey." Throwen leaned down so that I was forced to meet his eyes.

I couldn't focus, the unknowns drowning me in fear. "Huh?"

"Where did you go?" He studied me closely, but not in the way I was used to. This felt like curiosity, not scrutiny.

"Throwen." I worked to speak over the lump in my throat. "I don't think I can do this, I—"

"Back again, Angel? I didn't think you would be foolish enough to show up here again so soon after your last visit." I whipped my head up and focused on a tall woman with long black braids striding toward us. She was wrapped in a beautifully patterned maroon parka. Her large teal earrings complimented her lovely, tanned skin. She was a vision, and I was very aware of my stinky, sickly appearance.

A large white wolf pranced along her side happily, tongue lolling out the side of its mouth.

Throwen took in my uncertain expression and pulled my cloak tight around my chin before winking.

"Nova, just the witch I wanted to see. How are you?" He bowed low.

Her thick, gray fur headband rose with her eyebrows. She crossed her arms. "What do you need, Throwen? We are still grieving, as I'm sure your mentor has informed you, and I don't need your shit right now."

Throwen held up placating hands. "We are just here to gather supplies for our journey back to Goldhaven."

Nova scoffed. "That's what you said last time, and my best fishermen ended up dead outside the tavern."

My stomach tied itself into knots and I glanced at Throwen, confused.

His jaw ticked. "Perhaps they should have been more discreet about the company they kept." Throwen's voice held an edge.

I pulled my cloak tighter, and the movement caught Nova's eye.

"And what of the company you keep?" She moved around Throwen, stepping into my space. "Who are you?"

I wouldn't let her unyielding gaze break me, so I donned the mask of the Lady of the Grave, speaking as I'd witnessed Malik present himself for years. My hair lifted along my arms, but I remained a picture of confidence and charm. "I'm Octavia, and I'm assisting Throwen."

Her dark brown eyes examined me skeptically and when her lips pursed, the black tattoo reaching from her bottom lip down her chin stretched even straighter. "And what is it you do, Octavia?"

She stroked the top of her wolf's head, eliciting a low growl. Lucky let out a protective whinny and Throwen attempted to step in front of me.

"She's—"

"I'm a healer," I blurted and pushed Throwen out of the way.

Nova was hardened; it was easy to see, but there was something beneath her cool exterior. She smiled and moved closer, completely ignoring Throwen who stared at me with a cute quirky smile.

"You seem to have captured Throwen's attention. That's no easy task." She turned her attention to Throwen. "Tell me, Angel, where did you find such a healer?"

"Come now, Nova, if you want information, you'll have to give me some in return. And I highly doubt you have any intel since the last time I was here. But your rangers are always more than happy to tell me all about what's *really* happening in Oxvein after some ale and singing."

Nova clicked her tongue, and chuckled. "You're a *Goddess-damned* pain in my ass, Throwen. Come, you can stay for one night. I can tell she is nothing but trouble if she's working with you. You'll leave first thing in the morning."

Nova turned, and I stepped to follow. Her wolf barked and jumped up, wrapping its enormous paws around my shoulders. Her jaw unhinged, and a scream got trapped in my throat as the beast licked me from my chin up to my forehead.

I couldn't have stopped the childish giggle that escaped, even if I wanted to. Fear and excitement were colliding rapidly. It was a potent combination, leaving me feeling dizzy and delirious.

"Petwa is affectionate with those she trusts." Nova scrunched her nose and Petwa scampered back. As she massaged Petwa's ears, her eyes softened and reminded me of my relationship with my broom.

She waved, signaling us to follow, calling a flame to her hand as the sun finally set. Thrown pulled Lucky along, locking his free elbow around mine.

Those Theldean scum are incapable of empathy.

"Are you ok?" He leaned in close, whispering so Nova couldn't hear.

Well, Malik, apparently this witch had empathy.

"Why did she call you Angel?" My blood was pumping through my veins so hard and fast I feared I would fall dead. I was losing my shit, falling apart at the seams, and distraction was my greatest ally.

"I told you, nicknames are a thing in Theldea."

Why would depraved witches endear one another with nicknames? None of this made sense. If Malik was wrong about Theldeans, what else was he wrong about?

The weight of my coven returned, pressing on my chest so tightly that each inhale burned. My mind slowly slipped away from my body, unable to handle any more emotions as we walked toward Oxvein.

I craned my neck, using the clear night sky hovering about the thick icy walls to ground myself. Stars littered the sky, brighter than I ever imagined they could be.

Waves of bright greens and turquoise crashed around each other wildly. I let my mind float up there with them in their unpredictable movements. They alternated between bright and vivid to barely perceptible.

"Octavia?" My name on his lips was muffled, barely audible, but it had me lowering my gaze.

"Hmm?" I reached up to rub the kink in my neck.

"You were touching your nose." Throwen's mouth was pulled up into that playful smirk.

"No, I wasn't." I frowned deeply, drawn back to the large ice shelves towering over us on either side. I was a rat being led straight into a trap.

I could hear other coven members just ahead and tucked my panicked shaking hands into my armpits.

"You were." He dramatically pointed to his nose and peered with an open mouth in mimicked awe at the sky. I couldn't endure his humor right now.

"How much longer?" My voice was breathless and rushed and my palms were sweating. I was about to see Oxvein.

This wasn't right.

I turned and looked back to the way we had come and blinked. Malik was rushing toward me, intent on destroying.

You selfish cunt!

I curled in on myself, trying to cast out the panic-fueled vision. I wasn't supposed to be here. Breathing heavily, I rubbed my ribs and poked Throwen's side.

He crouched down, and I pushed up on my toes and whispered in his ear, "Malik will come for me, Throwen. I can't put Nova at risk, or you, or these people. I just can't."

I turned, ready to flee, but he gently grabbed my hand and held it flat against Lucky's side while pouring heat through our entwined fingers. Lucky sighed contentedly.

"Try to match Lucky's breathing," he commanded, and I scoffed but did as I was told. "You're not in your coven anymore, Octavia. You're with me."

His words were like a salve to my blistering thoughts. Breathing with Lucky eased the pain in my chest.

The path entered into a coven like a river to the ocean. Oxvein and its people unfolded before me, and I had to hold my breath. Keeping a hand on Lucky to ground myself, I took in the large open space, unsure what to focus on first. Stone huts littered the coven in small groupings where witches of all shapes and sizes gathered around fires.

Nova chuckled and veered off to speak with a woman who was staring daggers at Throwen.

Giant, hairy orange oxen with large horns lazily waddled around, grazing on small patches of grass growing up through the ice. The majestic creatures had fully captured my attention, and I wanted to touch their long fur to see if it was as soft as it appeared. Some oxen pulled around large carts. I pointed and said, "They're beautiful."

Throwen chuckled and laced his fingers through my free hand, which shook more with excitement than fear. He squeezed gently, and we continued through the coven.

A large river flowed through the coven. The water was a dark and hypnotic gradient of blue. I followed the river to an opening in the ice shelf, then noticed that there were several openings, which I assumed had to be exits. I took a relieved breath.

Something furry sprinted in front of us, and Lucky snorted. I pointed wildly in the direction it fled. "That was a white fox!"

"First fox?" Throwen raised an eyebrow.

My cheeks heated. I found that I thoroughly enjoyed those eyebrows. The witches in my coven rarely showed emotion unless it was in praise of Malik, and it was nice to know how Throwen truly felt just from the expressions on his face.

"I've only ever seen illustrations of them in books. I didn't know they could be white."

Throwen's smile grew wider, and I hoped I wasn't making a complete ass of myself. Why wouldn't Malik include such information in our biology section?

A group of witches wearing thick fur jackets paused what they were doing to gawk at us while we passed by. They had been sharpening spears and harpoons. Throwen didn't take his eyes off them. They either respected or feared him. *Maybe both.*

We kept moving, but I looked back. Their demeanor changed, challenging each other to hit a wooden target with ice stakes they were crafting and manipulating with their air. They were very accurate, and a chill ran down my spine at the thought of trying to outrun them.

"This reminds me a lot of our coven—"

A fetid odor permeated the air, and I covered my nose and mouth firmly with my hands. The group of witches crossing in front of us carried loads of fish on a large wooden sled, which was pulled by wolves. Many of the men and women carried large fish over their shoulders. One child was pulling a fish larger than herself by its tail, practically skipping with her spoils of hard labor.

Nova strode over to us, and I lowered my hands to my sides. "Well, looks like the last hut is already taken. You may stay in the igloo." She spoke in a sarcastic tone, narrowing her eyes at Throwen.

"Come on Nova, put me in there, but Octavia needs food, warmth, shelter. Please, I'll pay." He started digging through one of his pouches when a small gasp escaped my lips. Both of them paused.

There was a vast flat plane, the only area devoid of huts. Instead, crystal arches scattered the ground like stars. Large, fluffy sheep with curling horns meandered around them. The undulating colors from the dancing sky reflected off the crystals and the majesty nearly brought me to my knees. "What is that?"

"You don't know of the Oxvein arches?" Nova narrowed her eyes at me and crossed her arms over her chest.

"Oh, um... yeah, of course I just have never seen them in person. Can we go see them?" I searched Throwen's expression for some kind of direction. His eyes flitted to the arches and back as he coughed.

"I think we should get some rest, we have a lot of travel ahead." The moment he sensed my disappointment, he grimaced. "Can I show her your *marvelously morbid* arches before we go to the *fucking igloo*?"

Nova's smile widened. "Of course, Angel. Then get the fuck out of my coven before I let Petwa hunt you again."

There was an intensity between her and Throwen that I couldn't place. Not rivals, not confidants, but something in between.

She leaned in and kissed Throwen's forehead. I blushed and looked away. *Is this how all Theldeans say goodbye?*

Just as I rose on my toes so she could reach my forehead, she turned and stepped away, shoving her middle finger up as a final goodbye. I liked Nova. I could see myself being friends with a witch like her.

"Octavia." I didn't like his tone and when I found his eyes, it made my blood boil. Pity. *Fucking pity*.

"Don't *ever* look at me like that." My voice was that of the Lady of the Grave, demanding, final. I had the urge to summon Malik's Ether to prove how serious I was, but suppressed my rage.

He flinched at my change in tone. "Octavia, you're my friend and I'm telling you that you will not like what you find down there." He was serious and claimed dominance, blocking my view of the arches.

"I left my coven to see *all* of Theldea. Show me. I want to experience it in its entirety, not just the parts you favor." The back of my neck buzzed, and I realized just how much I meant those words.

Desperation laced my voice; I needed something, *anything*, to hold on to. "Will you promise me, Throwen? To show me everything you can? I *have* to see as much as I can."

A forced laugh spilled from his mouth before he took a deep breath and smiled. "I never make promises, but for you, darling, I'll make an exception."

))) ◉ (((

I FELT COMFORT amongst the graves, the nearness of bones familiar. As we walked between the delicate arches, it reminded me of the labyrinth, a place for self-reflection and shared grief.

"They bury their people here. Each arch is a fallen member of Oxvein," Throwen explained. "They chisel the name of their lost and stories about their lives into the crystal."

"Can I get closer?" I asked, and Throwen nodded, indulging my morbid curiosity.

I studied the crystals and delighted in the images of hunting, celebrating, childbearing, and growing old with a lover. These graves were masterpieces.

"We should get some sleep, the igloo is just over there." He pointed beyond the graveyard to a house of ice alone in the snow.

A glossy rock drew my attention to a small slope behind him. I pushed him aside and strode toward the large black structure that looked out of place amongst the aesthetic arches. "What's that?"

It had been carved into a giant wolf standing atop a large, square platform. This rock was from the Odraze mountains, an abrasive contrast against the snow and ice. It reflected in the clear night.

Throwen said nothing, and a melancholic gust of wind cut across my face. When amongst the huts, we were protected from harsh winds, but out here in the open, the bite of the cold returned.

I rested my hand against the cool surface and began reading the names on the monument. Rose, Kaya, Seda, Pilip.

My blood chilled and my mouth went dry. I backed away, shaking uncontrollably. "Throwen, what is this?"

Visions of Rose cooking in our kitchens flowed into ones of Seda and Pilip gathering berries. It had to be a coincidence. Maybe these names were common in Theldea.

"Octavia, I'm sorry." Darkness crept into the corners of my vision, and Throwen's voice sounded like he was underwater. His hand was on my back, and I flinched away from his comfort.

I moved around the wall, searching for more names. Beric—a well-trained scout. Anka looked forward to doing laundry because she enjoyed separating the colors into neat piles. Griffin—a bard just like Throwen.

My finger grazed a name I hadn't thought of for at least five years. *Jatan.* I had slit his throat for being caught worshiping the Goddess at one of our ceremonies.

Murderer!

"No. No. No. No." I lifted my hands to my ears beseeching the aggressive thoughts pummeling my skull to stop.

Throwen threw up an air shield, inching closer.

"What the fuck is this?" I screamed, focusing on my misplaced guilt and rage.

Tears burned hot, but I refused to let them fall. It was too bright, and I glared up at the night sky. The lights I thought were the most beautiful thing I'd ever seen only minutes ago now turned against me, overstimulating my senses.

"It's a shrine for members of the coven who are... missing." Throwen's comforting voice wrapped around me despite my slowly fading control. Hysteria plagued my body and mind, I couldn't stop it now.

I inspected the freshly carved names.

Missing? Deep droplets of red trickled from each chiseled name. I fell to my knees, gasping for air. "None of this makes sense! These are *my* people!"

I punched the ice on the ground only twice before Thrown pulled me into his lap and pressed my face into his chest. As he embraced me, he pulled my hood down so he could pet my hair, covering the back of my neck with his large hand. He tightened his grip and pulled me close.

"Octavia, I promise to tell you everything you need or want to know."

I peered up at him through tear-stained, windburned cheeks. I could barely make out his glowing irises. My eyes were closing of their own volition. This was it; the moment I went insane. I could practically hear the snap.

Any grip I had left on who I was or what I believed was gone. All the vomit, sweat, blood, and tears I had shed were, in reality, my sanity slowly seeping out of my body forever.

"I've made promises to the Goddess but never to another witch and here you are plucking two from me in a single day as if they're fruit ripe for the picking."

An incoherent laugh pushed out between my sobs, and he stroked my hair. I giggled because I didn't care anymore. "Strawberries are my favorite."

My ears popped as he lowered the air shield. His arms tucked around the crook of my knee, and he wrapped my limp arms around his neck. The world began to fade with my lightheadedness. "Noted, darling."

Chapter 8

OCTAVIA

Smoke billowed out of the hole in the top of the igloo, the fire lighting the space in a warm glow.

My life is a lie.

I shuddered and pulled on the clothes Nova had left for me. The brown pants and top hung heavily on my body, accentuating how petite I was.

Wobbling, I pressed my palm against the icy wall, still not fully recovered from passing out. Throwen had carried me here. I peeked over my shoulder to where he still faced the wall.

The skin on his hands were coated in what looked like dark oil that spilled up his forearms before tapering out at his elbows where it was met with abrupt pale white skin. As he pulled a black shirt up and over his head, lean muscles flexed.

I spun around to face the wall. My body ached, and I unclenched my hands, searching my palms for answers they would never provide.

"Have you finished?" I jumped as Throwen's soft voice ripped me from my thoughts.

"Yes." Finding a spot by the fire, I sat, pulling my knees to my chest in a tight hug.

He brought over some supplies and mimicked me, sitting an arm's length away. He opened a jar of thick yellow paste, applying it to his cracked knuckles. "We should take care of our wounds. We don't want infection to set in."

"What is it?" I grimaced at the thick, stringy texture. He handed me the jar, and I hummed, holding it up to my nose to smell the sickeningly sweet scent.

"It's a honey mixture that Whynnie makes. Helps with the healing process." His eyebrows drew together. "Do you not use something like this in your coven?"

"We rarely treat minor injuries in our coven. Enduring them strengthens us." Was that another lie too?

"You told Nova you were a healer. Is that what you truly wish to be?" He moved closer.

I sighed. How could I think of a future while my past was collapsing? "I don't know what I want anymore."

"This can be your first lesson," he said as I handed the paste back with shaking hands. "Let's start with your knees."

I rolled up my pants, revealing my legs splotched in scrapes and bruises. They were nowhere near as damaged as my mind and soul, and I laughed at them.

Grimacing, Throwen's nostrils flared. He grasped my foot, and I gasped as he gently twisted me so my knee rested on his lap.

"First, you clean the wound with a wet rag." He gently patted the scrapes across my right knee. I grit my teeth and he shifted his other hand under my knee, his picks tickling the sensitive skin.

I bit my lip. "We could do this with your cuts, you know. I heal quicker than you."

"And people say I'm a braggart," he teased with a coy smile, sticking his pinky finger into the mixture.

"Next, you apply it to the wound. It may sting at first." He delicately pressed some of the paste into the wound. I welcomed the sting. Deceit was far more painful than any of my physical injuries.

"Throwen," I said in a hushed tone. He froze, eyes locked on my knee. "I need to know what's going on."

"Then you wrap it snugly, but not too tight." He ignored me, wrapping my knee rapidly.

"Throwen," I whispered. He exhaled and his eyes met mine. They were as dark as the midnight sky. I pulled my leg back, but he held firm, the veins in his neck throbbing.

"You still want to be able to move your knee and if it's too tight, it also limits blood flow." A single tear fell down his cheek, ricocheting through his stubble.

"Throwen." I reached over to touch his shoulder, and he deflated, finally letting my foot go.

"I know." His chin tilted down, and he rubbed his eyes, clearing them of any lingering tears before he faced me. "You said the missing witches on the monument are your people."

"Yes, but it doesn't make sense. The witches who join our coven, they're always poor, suffering, broken… outcasts. If they had people who cared for them, why would they ever leave? And yes, Malik had an extensive hit list but not innocents. He targeted those who were targeting us, to keep us safe."

I searched his eyes for all my unanswered questions. He opened and closed his mouth, and I wondered if the lies he was about to unravel might instead tangle around me so much that I would suffocate.

"Theldeans call members of your coven necromancers." He spoke the words like a curse. "Malik—"

"What does that mean? *Necromancer?*"

"Any magic can be used immorally," he continued. "Magic can cause destruction or harm, but necromancy is scorned by Theldeans, since it causes the worst and most destructive kinds of suffering and damage."

I breathed heavily, waiting for him to give me a substantial answer. Malik didn't cause suffering or damage. He was a savior. My stomach clenched and time seemed to slow.

Throwen looked away. "Necromancers rip the dead from the Abyss and bind those they kill to it."

I shot up, pacing around the fire. "No! No, that's not true. Our coven is a community of witches that the Goddess turned her back on. We are survivors, just like these Oxvein witches. We pull our spirits from Malik's Ether, and we do *not* bind them. They transform into blissful existences."

Throwen remained still on the ground. "Necromancy is unnatural. It's not of the Goddess."

"Fuck the Goddess! She abandons her creations!" I laughed at the absurdity. "She left me in the Furothian Forest to die. She made me *wrong*, Throwen. A mistake with too much darkness. She discarded her failure."

Tears streamed down my face and my chest heaved.

Throwen stood and strode over, taking my clammy hand and guiding me back to our spot by the fire.

"How did you feel when you attacked me on that peak?" he asked softly as if too much noise would spook me.

I stared at where my hand still rested in his. "Scared, angry, hopeless."

"We are friends now, right?" He grabbed my chin between his fingers and turned my face to his.

My eyes bulged as he wiped my tears. I didn't trust friendship, but the way he treated me with patience and gentleness made me feel safe. I nodded in agreement, the lump in my throat too swollen to speak.

"Do you agree friends should be honest, even when it's hard?"

I offered another hesitant nod.

"Darling, the Goddess *never* abandoned you." His eyes glazed over with unshed tears. "Malik abducted you when you were about three years old. Whynnie was supposed to be your mentor. You grew up in a cult full of necromancers."

I blinked slowly, and my ears popped.

Malik abducted me from Whynnie.

Don't cry, little Lady, we just have to get through this tunnel and we will be home.

I shook my head rapidly. Malik never wanted me.

Your purpose is to keep us concealed. Focus!

He only wanted my blood.

Your blood is needed to keep your people safe. How dare you risk leaving our coven so some Theldean trash could waste it all, bleeding you dry.

All the memories of Malik's words came rushing back. The hidden meanings. The lies. The unreciprocated love and respect.

"Octavia?" Throwen shifted, so he was directly in front of me. He ran a hand over my hair and his eyes searched mine.

"Why didn't you tell me?" I asked through a tight throat. "You said you were my friend."

He released my hand, biting his lip. "I *am* your friend, Octavia. Would you have believed me? Would you have come with me if I told you all of this on that mountain?"

My shoulders shook with my sobs. Throwen was right. I would've dismissed him, writing him off as another Theldean lunatic. I wouldn't have come. But there was still part of me that doubted his radical claims about Malik.

He tucked a piece of hair behind my ear. "I'm sorry I didn't tell you right away." He fidgeted but held my gaze, as if his eyes were pleading with me to understand.

The evidence against Malik was strong, but he was a good witch. He cared for our people. Didn't he? "How could I have been so blind?"

"You weren't blind. Malik indoctrinated you." Throwen's thumb rubbed my cheek, and I closed my damp eyes, leaning into the comfort he offered.

I wept. "I don't—" Squirming, I moved out of his grip. "I don't want to think about this right now. My brain feels like it's about to leak from every orifice on my face."

Throwen nodded. "I understand." He retrieved his lute and a plate of cooked fish that Nova left.

I shifted back into a cross-legged position, massaging my temples. He sat a plate beside me, and I took a small bite despite my uneasy stomach. I couldn't remember the last time I had a meal. Sweet seasonings danced across my tongue, and it flaked apart in my mouth.

A gentle melody filled the diminutive space. Throwen's magic coiled gracefully around his arms, licking at his fingers as he strummed.

"How does it work? Your magic?" I took a sip of cool water, letting it soothe my aching throat and chapped lips.

"I'll show you." His smile was wide, and he bumped into my shoulder playfully.

"I looked to the stars"

As he sang, the tendrils crawled up his arms, caressing his protruding veins. I followed their movements up his firm torso and around his neck. When I found his eyes, his cheeks were colored. Even his blush was an adorable shade of amethyst.

"Begging to find them a tether"

The strands reached out, tickling my toes. I giggled at the sensation.

"Stop that."

Throwen chuckled, still strumming the song. "I don't control them. I can communicate my intentions, but I always ensure they have free will to help me or not in whatever way they see fit."

My rapid pulse slowed with his music.

"Most of the time I'm simply a gateway," he continued, "and I let them enjoy their brief trips back to Theldea from being with the Goddess in her Ether."

I will show you the path to the true Ether. To my Ether.

I bit the inside of my cheek, no longer sure what I believed about the Goddess or Malik. "So, they're drawn to music, that's your pathway? If I learned an instrument, could I replicate the magic myself?"

"I don't think it's music specifically. That's just one way I learned to connect with them. I think they enjoy the same things they enjoyed while they were here. Joy, positivity, zest for life."

"From what I can tell, you have those things in abundance." My dry tone was at odds with my crooked smirk. His magic was attracted to all the things I wished I'd had in life.

I looked at Throwen, searching for something, but I had no idea what.

"I guess I do." He ceased playing, never taking his eyes off me. If I stared much longer, I would be lost to those eyes forever.

"Goodnight, Throwen." I crawled over to my bag, laying out a fur to sleep on and allowing myself to crumble to the ground.

My mind raced. A cult? Perhaps our ways were a bit fervent, but there was no way I grew up in a *cult*. I was teetering on a fine line, unsure of who I was or what I believed. I curled up into a ball.

A moment later, Throwen laid more large furs over me, pulling them up under my chin.

The wind whistled through the monuments outside.

"What would be on your archway?"

There was a long pause, but I could feel him moving behind me. "I could tell you hundreds of dramatic tales of my adventures. But it would be the time the Goddess has gifted me with Whynnie, Kallan, and Echo."

"Thank you for the truth." My lip quivered, and I closed my eyes, silent tears rolling down my nose and the side of my face as I thought of the horrors that would be depicted on my arch.

Chapter 9

THROWEN

"It's like I told you, I don't control the spirits. Necromantic magic demands. It's a perversion of the natural cycle and keeps souls from the Ether for eternity. The Goddess laments her lost creations."

Lucky snorted, shaking out her mane as she carried us along the icy plane. We had spent an entire day answering Octavia's many questions.

"So the Goddess's Ether is where witches can reunite with their creator, family, and friends and live free and happy. And the Abyss leads to eternal separation from the Goddess's Ether, but *what* is it?" Octavia reached into the saddlebag, pulling out some nuts and berries and popping a few into her mouth.

Her question reminded me of my newfound sense of purpose. To end the Abyss's hold on Theldea. The Goddess sent me back for this. Octavia was our chance to end necromancy, and I would cut down anyone who dared try to take her from us again.

"That's a problematic question," I replied, admiring the dark orange glow of the afternoon sun high in the sky, doing little to warm the chill in the air.

"I think we have plenty of time for a complicated answer." She gestured to the icy landscape. *Goddess,* that sass did things to me I didn't want to focus on with her pressed so tightly against me.

"Good point." I paused, trying to comb through everything I knew about the Abyss. *Goddess's tits*, I hadn't had a conversation this philosophical in ages.

I rubbed my aching chest where my heart bled for Octavia. I tried to imagine a life where I was fed lies and needed efficient answers. "There are countless legends about the start of it all. The one Whynnie used to tell us about the Goddess's brother is the story I'm most inclined to believe. The Goddess's brother loved her, but she loved us, her creations, more. They were equals at first, but there was a fight of some kind. Some stories say the power struggle caused collateral damage that almost resulted in Theldea being destroyed entirely."

I gave her a moment to process, but she wasted no time. "So, what you're telling me is that witches go around Theldea not knowing what the fuck is going on?"

I laughed because that's exactly what we did.

"It's called *faith*, darling." She snorted derisively and I fought the urge to pull her hair to the side and kiss her glowing mark, to soothe that never-ending wheel spinning in her mind. I enjoyed holding her close, the way I wanted to last night.

We barely knew each other, but I cared what she thought of me. I was a performer with thick skin. Normally, I could care less what others thought of me.

She took a long swig of water. "Why did Nova call you Angel?" There was a slight tightness to her tone.

"Sometimes the spirits..." My muscles stiffened, unsure how to tell her this truth. These hands brought laughter, healing, and joy. But they also delivered justice. Those who crossed me knew how quickly a good time could turn into a death sentence once outside the taverns. The lethal bard. To my enemies, I was death personified and no witch in their right mind wanted to cross death. I swallowed, settling on, "They aid me in my work."

"My coven members call me Lady of the Grave." She offered one of her truths in return.

There was a pause while I waited for her to give me more. Conversations with her were easy, and I found myself enjoying when she spoke about herself. I couldn't help the taunt before it slipped past my lips. "Are you ever going to tell me why they call you that?"

She was quiet for a moment, stroking Lucky's mane. "Not today."

Tapping a finger against her thigh, I thought back to the arches, to how it felt to cradle her against me when the world was too much for her to handle.

"By being here, I'm hurting every witch in my coven, especially Malik…" She curled in on herself, and I pulled her closer.

My gut clenched. She'd suffered enough, and all I wanted to do was distract her. Octavia was an enigma and the need to figure her out tainted my every thought and interaction. "If you could do anything, what would you do?"

Her head lifted, and she sighed heavily. "I've always dreamed of traveling throughout Theldea and healing. Not just physical healing though, healing entire covens, teaching them of the true path to Malik's Ether." She shuddered. "I guess I just like helping people."

Malik's Ether. I ground my teeth. When I saw Malik, I would enjoy tearing that fucker to shreds for manipulating so many.

"I craved freedom all my life," Octavia continued. "And once I reached that peak, I knew that was it for me. I couldn't function, trapped inside my room, that *fucking* castle." Sniffing, she wiped her nose on her sleeve.

"They locked you in your room?" It came out low and defensive. Hot rage sizzled through my veins. My skin tingled and I could barely contain the urge to release my magic.

I reined it in. My vengeance—my anger—had no room here. I wanted to be her safe space, needed to be her safe space. My pulse raced at the realization, the intimacy of it.

"It was my fault. I publicly challenged Malik." She exhaled, white puffs of air floating back to me. "I usually enjoyed when my punishment was isolation, I loved all the extra time to read. But Malik took my books away and without them…"

How the fuck does she think any of this is her fault? The inside of my cheek stung as I bit hard. Isolation as punishment was something she *enjoyed*? It took everything in me not to turn her around and grab her jaw before I vowed vengeance on those who hurt her. She deserved to know just how much of a treasure she truly was.

Instead, I laughed, burying my anger. "You can challenge me anytime, darling. I rather like a good challenge, life would be boring without them."

"Is it weird that I like the danger? I expected savages to murder me as soon as I landed on that peak, but then I found you, and later when I fell in that hole—" She laughed loudly.

I memorized it. My fingers itched to play along with her laughter. The melody had to be captured.

Lucky whinnied and trotted happily along with us, the thinning ice sloshing under her hooves.

"That was the most fun I've had in a long time, I can't recall my risks ever ending in laughter."

I breathed in the crisp air. Perhaps she was my muse, a gift from the Goddess, forcing me to pluck at heartstrings I didn't know existed as my need to connect with her grew. She made me want to spill all my secrets in front of her like an offering.

"I enjoy that kind of danger, too. The thrill of making it out alive." I swallowed hard at the admission.

She looked over her shoulder. The afternoon light lit up her face. Her dark eyebrows were raised, and a wide smile appeared on her face. Making her laugh and smile was quickly becoming my obsessive, personal quest.

"But you have a family in Goldhaven, a home. I'm sure they don't want you jumping headfirst into danger." Tiny flecks of light brown swam in the honey tones of her eyes.

Her natural beauty took my breath away. In the mirror, her makeup was smeared, her hair matted and wild, and I could barely make out her features in all the snow.

Now with clearer skies, she had pulled her dark hair into a low ponytail at the base of her neck to hide her mark without having to wear her hood. It cascaded down her spine, and I wanted to wrap it tightly around my fist, knowing the hues of her wavy hair would pair nicely with my golden picks.

Spilling a small truth had brought me a lightness. Sharing genuine pieces of myself with someone other than my family was an exhilarating new experience, and I couldn't help but continue. "I've always been restless by nature. It's like if I stay in one place too long, I'm afraid I'll grow roots and never be able to leave."

"I can understand that." Hunching, she turned forward, breaking my trance.

I wrapped her in my cloak. The temperatures were warming, but I was selfish and wanted her pressed against me.

"My family is my home, and we know the risks we take protecting Theldea," I said against the shell of her ear. "It doesn't matter where we are, they are my home." My belly warmed as I thought about introducing them to Octavia.

"Will you tell me more about them?" She straightened her spine, feigning confidence, but I could hear the fear and hesitation in her voice.

"Whynnie has a thing for picking up strays. She often speaks of a time when she used to travel throughout Theldea, but by the time she found me, she stopped trusting other witches and refused to leave her hovel."

"So, she trained her strays to do her work for her? That sounds like what Malik does with our scouts." Scanning the land around us, her head swiveled as if the mention of Malik and his scouts had spooked her.

"No." My voice hardened. Whynnie was *nothing* like Malik. "She wasn't some power-hungry witch grooming children to do her bidding. We weren't slaves. We chose our paths because she always asked us how we wanted to use our skills while she raised us."

"What paths did they choose?" Interest laced her tone. My neck muscles relaxed slightly.

"Echo wanted to travel and wield their status to become loved and accepted by all, making Theldea better from the inside out. They succeeded, every coven leader always allowing them in." I cherished Echo, and I smiled. There was no doubt in my mind that Octavia would become quick friends with them.

"Kallan wanted to keep balance in this world and fight for those who couldn't. Luckily, his love of an exercise routine made him a hulk of a man that nobody wanted to mess with. He saved countless witches throughout the years. He is a grump like you." I poked her side, and she released a breathy chuckle.

"If Echo is the brains, and Kallan is the muscle, what does that make you, Throwen?" There was a taunt on the tip of her tongue.

The sound of my name on her smart-ass lips had me reeling. Her question was pointed, cutting right to the heart of my role in this life.

"Um…" I shifted away. *Abyss consume me!* "I wanted to experience all Theldea offered. I'm a big hit at all the taverns. The Goddess gives us all different gifts."

Octavia was quiet for a long moment before speaking. "Sounds like you're the spirit of your family."

Her words heated my blood and my fingers twitched, aching to let the spirits play in the joy her assessment brought me. My body was responding like a youth, my heart pounding hard in my chest as the hairs on my arms stood at attention.

"I guess you could say I'm something like that. Theldea is too beautiful not to experience. It's like the Goddess painted our world, one stroke effortlessly weaving into the next. Just wait until we get to Luftor, I think you're going to love it. The views from Graygarde's balconies are breathtaking."

"As long as I can take a hot bath, it will already be my new favorite place." Her dry humor elicited a chuckle from me, and she echoed my amusement with one of her own, each laugh a small victory.

"You can bathe, and I can shave. It will be *paradise*." That was brilliant. "Damn!"

"What?" She sat up on high alert.

I opened the songbook strapped to my belt and scribbled the words messily. "I have to jot this down, that's definitely the start of a song."

She scoffed. "How many witches are in—" The crack of a footstep echoed from behind a small glacier just ahead.

"Don't. Speak," I whispered into her ear and pulled her hood back up over her head as she grew stiff.

As I dismounted Lucky, three scouts sauntered out from behind the glacier.

Desperation to shield Octavia from these monsters, from her own people, mixed into an intoxicating adrenaline. I helped her down before she could see who they were. "Hood up. Eyes down. Behind me."

She shook slightly but did as I instructed and shifted behind me, keeping her gaze on her feet.

"Well, well, well. If it isn't the Angel of Death." The tallest scout shouted and held a large battle axe made of sharpened bone.

Octavia pressed her palms against my back. "Throwen... what does he mean, Angel of Death?"

The smallest scout held two jagged bone daggers, the handles wrapping around his knuckles. The last scout wore a mask made from the jaws of a wolf, the sharp teeth covering her lips, her bow aimed at me.

Imminent danger permeated the cool air, twisting it into a hot musk. I kept my angled hood low and made a mental note of my daggers and my lute at my back. Compared to the scouts, my clothing was light and my weapons were thin and sharp.

"You usually travel alone... Who's your little *friend*?" The tall one's weasley voice grated against my nerves.

Holding back a growl, I pulled my lute to my chest with a feral grin, my nostrils flaring.

The scout's eyes blew wide and flashed red as tendrils of tormented souls thrashed around their hands and weapons.

They were afraid. *Good.*

"A shame we'll have to kill you both, she looks like she would be a *lively* one," he taunted.

Octavia gasped, and I started picking and humming a low menacing war chant. There was no way I'd let them lay their hands on her. If even their rancid breath made contact with her skin, their deaths would be slow and painful. Purple spirits gathered around my feet, ready to absorb my intent to tear them apart.

Octavia stepped in front of me, and my eyes widened, the hairs on the back of my neck standing at attention. Mistaking her gasp as fear, I now understood that she wasn't scared, she was pissed.

"As your Lady, I demand you to stand down!" She stood confident and firm, but I knew it was in vain. Malik held power over these necromancers, not Octavia. Red danced across her fingers.

I grabbed her hand, whipping her around, and lowered my hood. She found my eyes, and I grabbed her chin gently, breaking through her rage. "I will *not* let you taint your soul any more than that fucker already has, especially not for me. Do you understand?"

A single tear rolled down her cheek and she shook her head rapidly. "I didn't know. I thought it felt wrong sometimes but... I truly didn't know, Throwen, *please* believe me."

"You Theldean piece of *shit*! You fucking abducted our Lady! When I deliver you to Malik, I'll enjoy watching him tear you apart, *bard*!" Their vexing leader stepped in front of the other two who followed close behind. They stomped toward us, only a few yards away now.

"I believe you, darling." I pulled her into a quick hug. "You take the little one for a moment, yeah?"

I pulled away and winked, throwing my lute over my back. I drew two daggers and sprinted toward the massive scout. I couldn't see Octavia, but the smallest one broke away shouting something I couldn't quite hear.

Once I reached the others, I slid along the ground as low as I could, right as the scout's axe landed where I'd been a second before. He was big, but that slowed him down. I maneuvered to my hands and knees and jumped to my feet.

I dodged an arrow and locked eyes with the scout who shot it. A loud grunt sounded from behind, and I ducked as the axe swung above my head.

Octavia's shouts accompanied the explosive sounds of the elements she was hurling at the scout. *Good girl.*

"You useless hunk of meat!" The scout with the arrows didn't hesitate to shoot her partner in the neck. "You move slower than the dead."

I fumbled for my lute, but it was too late. The archer bound his soul to his body quicker than most necromancers I had fought. It turned the unmistakable crimson of a soul forever separated from the Goddess.

"Alex!" the scout attacking Octavia screamed for his lost friend before throwing even more at Octavia's shield. The angry scout's flames wrapped around her air shield, getting closer and closer to her face.

The undead scout was on me as soon as the black blood seeped from their lips. I dodged their right hook, and they struggled to recover. I took advantage of their misstep and landed a quick blow to their nose before head butting them. Landing one more swift punch to their gut, I watched the jolt knock their spirit out of the body.

I ducked and red spirits frenzied like sharks, blocking my vision as they all fought to get into the husk through any opening they could. The scout's body thrashed wildly, and the spirits fought from within him. They fled as the corpse's gurgles emitted dark tar that spewed over its chin.

"Throwen! What was that?" Octavia's panicked shouts cut across the distance between us. I turned for a moment to see horror written into her struggling features. "What's happening?" Her posture shifted, and her air shield was faltering, flickering in and out.

I ran at the new spirit that filled the corpse and they unnaturally dropped to the ground, limbs twisting at impossible angles, bones cracking and popping. I leapt over them, but they gripped my ankle tightly and squeezed, pulling me to the ground.

A sharp pain shot through my ankle, reverberating up my shin as I fell. I hissed and jumped on top of where they still crouched on the ground, pulling out a dagger sheathed to my chest. Dark violet tendrils wrapped around the blade, and I swiftly sunk it deep into the undead's pulsing heart.

As I ripped it from their chest, the spirits burrowed into the gushing wound. A potent sulfuric scent rose from the body, a pungent smell that accompanied a necromancer's death.

My magic sent the livid red spirit to the Abyss, leaving the now useless cadaver on the ground. Red blood and black tar stood out against the icy floor. We couldn't leave any of them alive or they would report back to Malik.

"Octavia! I'm coming, just hold on!" Dodging another arrow, I pulled my dagger free from the strap on my swelling ankle. The archer sprinted toward Octavia, shooting the other scout in the head.

Octavia's ear-shattering scream pierced the air as he crashed to the ground face-first. Flinging the dagger at the archer proved difficult with my hands shaking from hearing Octavia's scream and I missed.

The archer bound the other scout's spirit and turned toward me, preparing to loose another arrow. With a deep breath, I grabbed another dagger and flicked it right into her forehead before she could shoot at me.

She stood there for a moment, lifting a shaking hand to her head, pulling it away to see deep red blood. It trickled down over her eyes and mouth.

I flicked two more daggers into her heart, and she fell to her knees. Only bound spirits were forced to return to the Abyss, and it was a mercy that her spirit would go to the Ether despite all the fucked-up shit she just did.

The only remaining undead scout rose with jerky movements.

Octavia's face was covered in sweat and indecision. She was scrambling to reach under her layers for her dagger. Her air shield fell.

He swiftly tackled Octavia to the ground. She cried out and her head snapped back, hitting the ice below. He dropped his daggers and held her wrists above her head roughly.

He will regret that.

The scout's firm grip coiled tightly around her neck. Red spirits lit up across his knuckles, adding to his strength. She was thrashing, gasping for air, and trying to pull his hands free.

"Octavia!" I pressed the button underneath the head of my lute and it sprung the instrument wide open down the length of the neck. The strings pulled taut and the separated sections of the sleek black body formed the distinctive arch of my bow.

I flicked my wrist, latching it into place, and grabbed the grip that sat between the two halves firmly, my lute doubling as my weapon of choice.

Lavender tendrils of spirits wove together, wrapping around the separated heads of my instrument, creating the bow's string.

Pointing my arrow toward the threat looming over her, I placed three fingers gently below the undulating purple arrow, composed of spirits.

They were more eager than ever to aid me, like their inclination to protect Octavia was just as strong as my own.

Her head was tilted up, neck craning to see me.

I pulled the string back far before letting it fly.

A short *thwang* was followed by a thud. Octavia wiggled and coughed, trying to push the body off of her.

I darted over and lugged the limp body to the side. When she sat up, I couldn't bear the horror that filled her face or the angry red burns around her neck.

The arrow went straight through his heart. Tendrils burrowed into the hole the arrow had made, forcefully expelling the bound spirit from every orifice in the scout's twitching body.

This fucker's death would not be quick and painless. He'd hurt her and wrapped his *filthy* fingers around her perfect neck. This would be the result for anyone who dared touch her.

I sneered as his eye sockets, ears, nose, and mouth leaked a dark, bloody mixture. The red was slowly draining from his eyes, leaving behind their natural pale blue.

"Levi?" Octavia crawled to him and cradled his head in her lap. "It's okay, Levi, it's going to be okay."

My eyes widened, snapping me free of my vengeance. She patted his greasy hair gently as my magic violently purged him of the damned spirit.

He looked into her eyes, only gurgles able to pour out as his last words.

A final red tendril peeled itself out of his body from his bloody, slacked jaw and disappeared into the Abyss.

"I'm sorry. I'm so sorry." Tears flowed down her cheeks, dripping off the chin I held just moments ago. Octavia's sobs shot through me, and I stiffened.

I reached out to rest my hand on her shoulder. "Octavia?"

She pushed me away with her air. "No!"

Her new friend, the charming bard, had morphed into the Angel of Death. She finally knew what I truly was: an assassin, *a monster*.

Octavia cradled and rocked her mutilated friend in her arms, weeping.

Tears filled my eyes as I went to check on Lucky. I couldn't breathe. *She will fear me now, like everyone else.*

Patting Lucky's side, I tried to calm her loud snorts and whinnies. I had never thought of necromancers as being loved or cared for. She was prying my eyes open to things I ignored, and I wanted to force them shut and block her out.

Why did this moment, this decision, feel like the greatest loss of my life?

Losing her friendship and trust dragged me into a panic.

My time with her would be on my archway, because that's what my life was now, before her and after her. With an unsettling clarity, I knew deep in my bones that if I lost her, I would lose myself.

Chapter 10

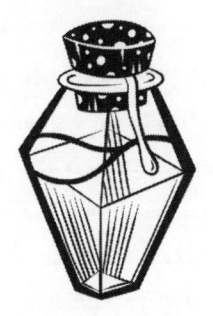

OCTAVIA

The steady drips of water falling from the countless stalactites echoed off the bumpy stone walls. Wind whistled outside, where Lucky rested at the entrance. The cave we were in bore into the ground and tunneled under the mountain. This dark damp place reminded me of the catacombs and all the imprisoned souls I had sent to their cruel, prolonged deaths.

True bliss finds them the moment they enter my Ether, Lady. You are bringing them peace.

Malik's lies stacked like the stones of his castle.

Throwen had peeled me away from the slaughter and now my world was devoid of color as the events of the past two days blurred into a mass of ambiguity.

I retrieved the remaining twig of my broom from my coat and twirled it between my fingers. Its iridescent paint reflected the warm glow of the fire. My life was full of things I had once thought magnificent. They always ended up destroyed.

Nausea turned my stomach thinking about the hyperactive red spirits clamoring to claim the corpse. Malik had kept the worst parts of necromancy from me. I'd never seen the undead act in such a way. They would rather be anywhere but the Abyss. Was everything Malik told me a lie?

I scoffed and tossed the final remains of my creation into the fire and flicked my fingers to fan the flames. The twig disintegrated instantly. My broom was gone and so was my blind admiration of Malik.

Throwen sat across the fire, wrapping his injured ankle. His nostrils flared, and he roughly tightened the bandage. His fitted mossy green tunic accentuated his broad shoulders and thin waist. I could see some dark chest hair poking out from where the ties were coming undone at the tip of his sternum. His sleeves were rolled at the elbows.

As I continued to admire him, my eyes trailed up his arm to his large bicep. I didn't realize how strong and skilled he was until I'd seen him fight. His magic wasn't his only defense.

Throwen hadn't spoken since the ambush, but I didn't mind — I wasn't sure if what was left of my shattered soul could speak or if I even wanted to engage with him. He hadn't been this quiet since our journey began, and I worried his injuries were worse than he let on.

No more history books. Our duty is to our people. If you give any more of your thoughts and energy to Theldea and the vermin who inhabit it, there will be consequences.

Malik's voice in my mind propelled me into motion, and I rocked back and forth on the rock I sat on, hoping the movement would ease the torment of the nightmare that was my life.

Throwen wasn't a vermin. He had been nothing but kind.

It was pathetic how hard I was trying to repair my tattered memory, like the many incompetent stitches I gave myself in the past. I was a murderer. *Levi, Robin, Jatan, Oleander, Ellinor.*

I rubbed my thighs over and over, the friction not helping in the slightest. The insanity was leaking into my limbs, the ducts of my mind in need of some expert repair.

The truth encrusted my hands in innocent blood. This couldn't be the entire story. Malik loved our people. He loved me. His punishments were lessons. He cared enough to teach me and there *had* to be a reason he kept this from me.

"Octavia?" Throwen's voice pulled me back to the present.

When my glazed eyes met his, his cool confidence fractured. He bit his lip, fear and uncertainty circled his pupils.

"What do you want to do now?" His voice was low, and his picks clicked quickly together.

I envisioned briefly what his finger bones and tendons might look like. Would they be purple like his magic?

"How should I know what I want, Throwen? My entire life—" An unwelcome sob caught in my throat, and I knew I was yelling, but I couldn't control the emotions pouring out of me like a weepy child.

I loathed that anytime I became infuriated tears came with it. Blinking them away, my vision blurred, and I heard the echo of Throwen's footsteps as he closed the distance between us.

"Don't you dare." I pushed him back with a gust of air and gripped my dagger. He threw his hands up with no effort to fight back.

His impulse to comfort me was disorienting and my ribs ached with the knowledge that I was so undeserving of his help or kindness. *Persistent bastard.*

"You shouldn't have come for me! Why do you *insist* on saving a monster?"

"Wait…" He froze mid-stride and rubbed his forehead. "You think *you're* a monster? Octavia, did you not see what my magic did to those witches? If *anyone* is the monster here, it's me." His voice stayed steady and assertive.

My breaths quickened and spots filled my vision. His demeanor infuriated me, and jealousy burned hot in my chest at his ability to remain stable in situations that overwhelmed me. Throwen had this way of riling up the beast inside of me, shattering years of perfected composure.

"Oh, fuck off! You have *no idea* what a real monster even is."

"Why do you think you're a monster?" He inched closer, and my lip trembled. My chaotic breathing came in short swift bursts.

Always so sensitive, Lady.

I needed to spoon my eyes out from the amount of pressure building, and I pushed my aching palms into them, hoping to eradicate Malik's words.

"I already told you." I lowered my hands, squinting at him. "I'm an erroneous creation of the Goddess, she doesn't give a fuck about me or you or anyone."

"Well, I *do* give a fuck about you, okay?" He was rigid and his voice was hard.

His dark brows rose, and he took a step back, as if his words took him equally by surprise.

I sighed and rubbed my forehead. The exhaustion of the journey and this tension between us caught up to me and I lowered my voice. "I don't care if I was supposed to be looked after by Whynnie, I still would have turned into *this*. I'm not some witch damaged by growing up in a cult. I was *already* broken."

"You aren't broken." He moved closer, voice serious.

My hackles rose. A fireball formed in my palm. "Don't."

He continued to move confidently forward, determined. I wanted to pummel him, to take this nasty revelation and pain out on him and his incessant need to help me. *It is his fault I'm still alive.*

"We don't have to talk, okay?" He raised his hands again. "Please just let me look at your head."

Dried blood matted my hair, but I couldn't care less. I tilted my head to the side and my neck and shoulder muscles tightened.

Despite my aggressive posture, he approached. He lowered behind me and pressed a cool, clean cloth to the back of my head. I didn't even flinch, the pain coating my broken heart like the tar that oozed from Levi's mouth.

"You have a high pain tolerance," Throwen said.

He had no idea. Perhaps that would scare him off. "I like pain."

Throwen's movements halted only for a moment before he continued pressing the cloth to my head.

"I told you, I'm a real fucking piece of work," I whispered. "You should have just let me die—"

"I will *never* let you die." His words cut sharply through the cool air in the small space between us and he applied the honey mixture to my wound.

And there it is. He would never let me die, and that was a serious problem because all I wanted to do right now was fall asleep and never wake up.

If they find you, they will cage you.

"You asked what I wanted. What if that's what I want?"

Another long silence. I tried to stand and move away, but a firm hand landed on my shoulder.

"Can I check your neck?" he asked through gritted teeth, and I nodded.

Shifting to sit next to me, he peered into the fire with those bewitching lavender orbs. "You aren't the only witch I've met who craves death." His voice was soft. "I've met witches from all walks of life who share that struggle, darling, cult or not. What I'm trying to say is that while I might not know how that feels, that doesn't mean nobody else will. We are never truly alone, no matter the struggle."

Taking in a sharp breath, he tilted my chin up and analyzed the burns lightly with his finger. As he applied the healing mixture, he slowly traced along my neck. His golden picks a cool sensation against the heat of the burn.

"What do you believe in?" I asked, needing something to hold on to as my beliefs lay shattered on the ground, like my poor broom, never to be repaired.

"I believe we aren't supposed to understand it all," he said quietly.

"What do you mean?"

"I don't know, I just—" He laughed, a strangled, ridiculous sound.

He was eloquent with lyrics and stories, but when faced with his own emotions, his quick wit faded right along with his shield of humor. I was always drawn to contradictions though, and his attempts to articulate were more endearing than they had any right to be.

"I don't fully comprehend how the spirits work or always appreciate the Goddess's plans. None of us can figure it all out. But my belief is that is truly okay. I don't want to solve it all, it would be too much."

He licked his lips. "I believe in soaking up the entirety of the Goddess's creation. In protecting my friends and family from bigotry and loving them through their achievements and mistakes. I believe in trying to help Theldea grow and be a safe and enjoyable place for all."

His words were lovely, but I had a frenzied need for understanding in my life. I needed to dissect Malik, my coven, Theldea, the Goddess, our magic, and myself. He was right; it was too much, but I couldn't stop the compulsion.

Failure to suppress such compulsions clung to me like a second skin, both for my people and Malik. I was unsure if I could love them through the mistakes that were now coming to light. The pain of that knowledge was unbearable.

Throwen finished applying the mixture and lowered himself to his knees before me, looking up into my eyes. I could tell he wanted to help, but I didn't even know what I needed.

My throat was so tight I could barely manage words. Averting my gaze, I pulled at an unruly piece of hair. "I don't know if I can keep going if I don't unravel it all."

Throwen's fingers latched onto mine. "I'll help you keep going."

I pulled my hands away and rubbed my chest, hoping to work out the knot that formed there.

"Throwen…" I wanted to tell him everything. An excruciating headache was forming across my forehead and against the base of my skull.

Lips parted, he waited patiently at my feet.

Fresh tears left hot tracks down my cheeks, dripping from my chin like the stalactites above. "I… I don't know who I am anymore, and I don't know how to accept your help."

He wiped away my tears, briefly holding my face in his hands.

Seeing him below me was odd. I was so used to seeing him tower above me. He made himself small to help me, an offering.

"I've experienced dark pockets of time with my family. Whynnie had days, sometimes weeks, where she couldn't function. We did our best, but often the only way to get through it was to get through it."

Another sob escaped me, and he stood, easing me onto my feet for a tight embrace. I crumpled under his comfort despite the part of me wanting to push him away. My tears soaked through his shirt.

"And how did you help her get through it?"

I sunk deeper into his hold. Resting my head on his shoulder. I was grateful for his warmth.

With one more squeeze, he pulled away. "I would play her lullabies to help her fall asleep, Echo would help Whynnie tend to her hygiene, and Kallan would read her ancient stories about the Goddess while he ensured she ate and drank."

My stomach dropped. When I was at my lowest, I was never offered such things. "That sounds nice."

I looked up at the glistening ceiling and blinked through the tears. What would life had been like if someone walked through the darkness with me?

"When Echo was little, they had horrific nightmares. When they woke, they'd always come find me and I would sing them back to sleep."

I smiled and looked at him, trying to picture a tiny Throwen dramatically waking from his comfortable sleep to help his sibling.

A slow smirk pulled at the corner of his lips. He sauntered over to my fur in the secluded corner and placed it near his own. My cheeks heated, and I took a deep breath. Intoxicating herby smells rolled off the loose-fitting black shirt that Throwen had let me borrow.

"Come on, I'll sing you to sleep. You need rest, the journey ahead of us is a long one."

He crawled into his spot and patted my fur.

My jaw almost dropped to the floor. Throwen paid attention to me. Not the way the witches in my coven did—they monitored. Throwen picked up on my shifts in mood and demeanor. He somehow discerned what I needed, even when I didn't know myself. *Is this what true friendship is?*

It would be nice to sleep near him and let his sweet voice lull me to sleep. He was so warm, kind, and gentle, which I both loved and loathed. I wished I could be more like him.

I would stay with him as long as I possibly could, soaking up his friendship like a parched mutt. *Pathetic self-serving wretch!*

"Are you still there?"

Throwen's waving hand appeared in front of my face and I jumped. "What?!"

"*Fuck*! Why is it always my eyes?"

"You startled me." I giggled. I hadn't realized I sprayed him with water when I jumped. And the fact that he could make me laugh even when I was wallowing in doubt and sorrow…

Abyss consume me. He untucked the bottom of his shirt and pulled it up to wipe away the water. A dark brown line of hair traveled down the center of his sculpted abdomen, into his fitted black pants.

Fidgeting, I pushed my thighs together and imagined trailing my finger down the soft path.

He caught me staring and smirked. "Are you going to let me help you sleep, or are you going to fight me the entire time?"

I raised an eyebrow. My impulse was to fight, and he knew it. "I'm tired."

Slouching, I wrapped my hands around my aching head and followed him to the furs. He didn't grab his lute that was far more than it appeared.

"Don't you…" I pointed to his lute, and he merely lowered himself onto his back with one arm resting behind his head. I yearned to be enveloped by his comfort and warmth; I was sick of being cold and lonely.

"I don't need magic to help you sleep."

Sitting next to him, I almost gasped at how beautiful he was this close in the firelight. "Are you always so cocky?"

I started planning out ways to instigate that ego. He ignored my snarky comment and patted his chest. "Lay on me, listen to my heartbeat, and I'll hum. You'll be asleep before I finish the song."

So *fucking* cocky, but I admired his confidence.

I lowered myself, resisting the urge to curl my fingers into his exposed chest hair, and instead rested my palm flat against where his heart beat. Hope and despair clashed like rams' horns inside of me. The back and forth were excruciating, but the vibrations of his chest soothed the pain.

Chapter 11

THROWEN

A drop of water splattered across my forehead and roused me awake. Unwelcome chills sent shivers through my body, the weight of Octavia missing from my chest. I opened my eyes to an empty spot next to me. I maneuvered to my feet, stretching my aching body, and scanned the cave for her.

It was empty. *She's gone.* "No."

I scrambled past Lucky hopeful that was a sign she hadn't fled, and out the cave entrance, slipping on the icy ground.

The sun was rising over the last of the snow-capped peaks, accenting where Octavia stood, completely stoic as the gradients of yellow bled into vibrant teals. A deep frown pulled at her chapped lips. She was swimming in my black shirt, but she didn't shiver. Dark waves of hair twirled over her shoulders and down her back.

"I miss my broom more than I miss my coven." Her voice was rough and devoid of emotion, her arms hanging straight by her sides and her grip tightened around something.

I moved closer slowly, my feet cracking the icy morning dew clinging to what little grass poked through. She didn't flinch or move to stop me, her unblinking expression so far off I questioned if she was even truly here with me.

The object in her hand gleamed menacingly in the morning light. *Her dagger.*

A foreign pain overtook me. My heart pounded violently against my ribs and my ears rang. My steps were no longer hesitant, but long and purposeful. Why was I so scared?

Finding her hands clenched tight, I helped ease them open.

I removed the dagger from her stiff fingers and slipped it into the sheath closest to my heart. "I'll give this back once we start moving again."

She didn't respond, and I examined her for injuries or blood but found none other than the angry crescents she had created on the softest parts of her palms.

Thank the Goddess.

Her stare was still vacant. I'd hoped removing the dagger would ease the fight-or-flight response she seemed to live in constantly.

Pressing her knuckles to my forehead, I lowered my chin and pleaded to the Goddess.

Please help her feel safe. Help her know I want her here with me.

I was shocked when Octavia spoke to me last night after witnessing me brutally murder her friends. The desperation I felt to tether her here with me instead of wherever her mind was taking her made me want to scream, but I remained calm for her.

I pushed heat into the tops of her hands, massaging her fingers gently. She was so cold. "What do you need? How can I help?"

"You can't help, Throwen. I'm a lunatic, more than you know," she said, her voice didn't fluctuate, sounding as flat as the landscape.

"Friends help each other carry the weight of this world when it's too heavy. You don't have to tell me anything, but know that I'm always willing to share the weight with you."

We stood in silence, watching the sun slowly rise higher over the mountains. As I massaged her forearms, her body slowly relaxed.

"I'm scared, and I honestly don't know how to talk about any of it." The laugh that fell from her lips was frenzied and her chest heaved. Her eyes darted wildly. "If I'm crazy what's the point?"

The dread of hearing about her life in the cult vanished. I wanted to be the one she waded through her trauma with, to help her see how even her sorrow and cynicism were incandescent. Even in her darkness, I saw light.

"I see visions all the time." She ripped free from my grip and paced around as her cold mask of indifference slipped away. Her movements were more animated, showing me a glimpse of the woman she was underneath the cocoon she had built around herself.

"They're things only I see, and they're usually *extremely* fucked up, but they seem so *real*. Sometimes I don't even know if what I'm seeing is truly happening." She shook her head and peered at me with those huge fucking eyes that might as well have been golden moons.

I understood the constant fight or flight she lived in. She had to hide to survive. She didn't know any other way to live. "Did you always have them?"

Her pointer finger found her nose and an adorable scowl lined her brow, as if she was in a fistfight with her own memory. "No. They started around my eighteenth Name Day. They get worse when I'm tired or stressed."

As she combed her fingers through her tangled hair, warmth heated my chest when I noticed my leather strap wrapped multiple times around her delicate wrist. She winced when her fingers grazed the wound on the back of her head.

My instinct was to tend to her physical needs, but I was learning that her emotional wounds were just as severe, if not worse. I forced myself to stand still instead of going to her. "That had to be difficult to keep to yourself for so long." I imagined her curled up in her bed as a young adult plagued by fear and loneliness.

"At first, I thought everyone was like me. I thought all the witches in my coven imagined phantom blood oozing from the walls." She laughed half-heartedly and wiggled her fingers in a downward motion like blood dripping down a wall.

Her smile eased some of the tension in my chest. I was well acquainted with using humor to handle hard things and I had to admit, her dark wit was growing on me.

I stepped closer to her. "Does anything help when you're having them?"

She scratched at her ribs. "No." Defeat laced her voice, and I hated how it sounded.

"I have an idea." My stomach quivered at the intimacy of it.

She inched closer, crossing her arms against her chest and raising her dark brows. Those damn tiny curls bounced around her face. They may as well have been wrapped tightly around my pounding heart.

"If you start seeing something, grab onto my hand or arm and squeeze. That will let me know it's happening without anyone else having to know." It would be an unspoken secret that tied us together. I reached out my hand. "Then I can be something in the moment that you know is real."

Her eyes were less vacant, like she was about to agree, but her face contorted into despair as her chin dipped back down to the brown tips of her boots poking out from beneath her pants.

"There's this beast that crawls beneath my skin and in my skull... I wish to be free of it." She clutched her chest. "I'm *selfish* and I'm a *coward* because I would rather die than face Malik's disappointment. I betrayed him. Despite all that I know now, I still love him like I would a father. I should have never left him or my people. If I'm gone, it would spare everyone all this death and trouble for my reckless decisions."

She sniffed. I reached up, and with the pad of my thumb, wiped away her tears. Entwining my fingers with hers, I pulled her back toward the cave. "Those feelings are all valid. But you aren't selfish or a coward for seeking the truth."

We settled next to the small fire and started to eat the last of the sweet berries Nova had sent with us. For a witch who hated me, she sure seemed more than willing to spoil Octavia.

Witnessing the relaxation in her posture, and how sharing her secret brought us closer together was magic. Sharing all of me with her without fear was a dangerous craving.

But she never judged me. Not when she witnessed my appearance or what my magic did. My family were the only witches who knew my story, and I had ended many relationships with women who wanted more truth from me than I could give.

I coughed, drew my shoulders back, and spoke over the lump in my throat. "I died once."

The sentence tingled on my tongue.

"You... died? How?" Her mark emanated bright golden light around her neck, and she leaned closer to me. She was... *eager*.

Such a morbid little witch, but it somehow drew me in more.

"Whynnie found me accidentally one night when she was collecting herbs," I said as Octavia popped another berry into her mouth. "I have no memory of any time before Whynnie. When I awoke there was only her. Even in the beginning, she explained the truth, that my arms and hands were a sign that I had touched death. I died in those woods that night and the Goddess chose to send my spirit back after finding her in the end."

"How old were you?" Empathy pulled her lips into a frown, but her wide eyes and parted lips were welcoming.

The way she looked at me made it feel like she was the friend I had been missing all my life. It felt good telling someone who actively listened.

"Around six or seven, there was no way to tell. But it doesn't really matter. I have no intentions to discover the witches who left me beaten and starved in those woods."

She held her hand over her heart and curled in on herself, as if taking on the pain of my past.

"Whynnie called me her Little Miracle, and I always wished I could repay her for saving me and taking me in as if I were her own. She nourished without coddling and challenged without deriding. We were lucky to have her to look up to." I smiled and tipped back my head, taking a long swig from the canteen before offering it to Octavia.

"Another nickname?" Her eyebrows lifted as she drank.

"Yes, unfortunately, she *still* calls me that, and sometimes my siblings do too."

That almost elicited a full-blown smile. But her posture was still deflated.

"I made it my life's purpose to experience everything this world offered to honor the Goddess's gift. Thanking her every night for my life, usually through song." I flashed her my swoon eliciting grin, and she chewed on her bottom lip, as if fighting a smile.

Goddess forgive me, why does the way she makes me work for her amusement excite me so much?

Octavia popped more berries into her mouth. They were staining her lips a delicious shade of eggplant and I peeled my eyes away, focusing instead on packing up our things.

"To others, my appearance may be alarming, but to me, it's like armor that the Goddess personally bestowed upon me. I knew there was a reason she sent me back and I've searched every inch of Theldea looking for it."

I hauled the bag over my shoulder and her mouth fell open slightly, those tempting lips parting just enough for me to see her purple-stained tongue. "Every inch of Theldea? Have you truly seen all of it?"

Pride made me puff up my chest. "Not *every* inch. But most of it, yes."

A small brown curl spiraled down her cheek, wrapping around the bottom of her chin. "What's your favorite place? I've always wanted to visit Volgsump. Is it true their entire sky lights up because of bugs that can set the lands on fire?" She straightened, sitting taller.

I did not know what books these necromancers were reading, but they had twisted the most beautiful parts of Theldea into something to be feared. "They have fireflies, yes. But they're harmless. Volgsump is a unique place, I know you will love it. We won't be passing through there, but I can take you after we meet with Whynnie."

An adorable, crooked grin spilled across her face like the light peeking through the trees. She followed me, grabbing her pack.

"Whynnie said it's been ages since the powerful magic I wield manifested and we don't fully understand why, what it is, or even how it works. We only know it is from the Goddess and that she sent me back for a reason."

"How do you live like that?" She threw her arms wildly over her head and huffed. Her lively irritation was cute. "Not knowing things is torture for me."

"Well, it's not like we know *nothing*. I know there is a level of intent, and the spirits can choose not to help. For example, they never help when I'm sparring with Echo and Kallan. I think *they* think I'm being childish, but *they* are the ones who act like little children and—"

"What was your intent when you saved me from Levi?" She paused her movement, staring at me through thick lashes.

My mouth went dry, and my palms broke out into a sweat. Taking a steadying breath, I shoved my hands into my pocket to avoid anxiously clicking my picks together. The truth had been easy until this point.

"I wanted them to suffer. Especially Levi after he tackled you. I... I couldn't control my intent." It was too hot, and a fresh wave of nausea rippled through my gut.

She patiently waited for me to continue. Her honey eyes held no judgment, only a ruthless pursuit of the entire truth.

"I've worked very hard to perfect my intent over the years and it's usually not quite that brutal, but seeing someone try to hurt you..." I blinked back tears. There was nothing I could say to make my truth less horrific, so I said the only thing I could, "I'm sorry, darling. I hope with time you can forgive me."

Waiting for her reaction, I braced myself for her anger and disappointment. I was too cowardly to look at her face, so I looked to the ceiling instead.

Small arms wrapped around my back, and I pulled her tight into my chest, holding her in my arms. She squeezed me. "Thank you, Throwen, for saving my life, even if I don't want you to. And for telling me the truth."

I pressed my cheek to the top of her head. I needed to study her mind. Learn how it worked. Push and challenge to figure out what made her so otherworldly aside from her Goddess-born blood.

She pulled away and tended to Lucky, feeding her carrots and kissing the shiny black bridge of her nose. I instantly missed her cool skin against mine.

I unbuckled my songbook, mumbling the words aloud that needed to be put on paper.

"When an enchanting witch
Fell into the snow..."

The next line was undetermined, but it would come to me if I gave it time.

Chapter 12

OCTAVIA

Deep navy clouds shifted unhurriedly across the late afternoon sky, threatening to unleash rain at any moment. The snow was gone, but the air was still pleasantly cool, just enough to pebble my skin. I breathed deeply, filling my lungs with the crispness. Who knew the witch who'd paced around her room wrapped in a blanket most nights would welcome the cold?

The sounds of Throwen sharpening his blades sounded from inside the cave behind me. It was a place he frequented, and he had supplies stored there.

Stretching my arms high above my head, I managed to alleviate some of the sharp pain shooting from my tailbone up my spine.

The Zattia peaks were unusual. Instead of sharp pointed tops, these mountains fractured and pulled apart. Large blocks and chunks jutted out, forming irregular peaks. The stone itself was full of differing gray, white, and charcoal lines, as if the Goddess meticulously stacked them on top of one another.

A vision assaulted my senses. My skull fractured, cracks forming along every curve. But instead of filling in the cracks with gold like my crown, shards erupted through my skin. Large chunks of bone forced to shift, jutting out irregularly just like the new peaks.

Theldea broke you. I will save you.

"It's not real. He's not here," I said my mantra even though I smelled iron and felt the tinny blood dripping down my forehead.

Wincing, I clutched my head, trying to hold together my fracturing skull. Terrains weren't the only thing changing.

I was changing. No... not changing... shifting. My mind was reshaping my beliefs, but my subconscious was punishing me for the treason.

After a few more forceful blinks, the vision subsided, and I lowered my hands.

"Allow me to summarize my astute knowledge of Octavia." Throwen strutted next to me, strumming his lute.

Smirking, I rolled my eyes. Throwen valued happiness and optimism, two things I had lacked my entire life, and I was still getting used to the attention.

He paced back and forth as he played. "Your window was your favorite place to nest."

"Yes, but it was only appealing if I had a good book." It seemed books were something I could confidently talk about. I'd spent half of our day's ride describing our library and telling him about Badru.

Spending the day with him was a breath of fresh air. The pain of riding was worth the open communication, smiles, and when he was lucky, laughs. It was oddly exhilarating to speak without fear of my words reaching Malik.

"Why's that?" Throwen was like a toddler, constantly asking me why so I'd share more and more with him.

"Reading was the only time I felt free, living vicariously through the lives of my favorite heroes," I admitted and switched my focus on him. "You love celebrations and performing. Stranatan covens have the best audiences and Graygarde produces the most coin."

Easing witches' burdens through song seemed like a lovely way to live.

He shifted his lute to his back, stretching his arms and legs. "Yes, but performing in Goldhaven is my favorite."

I squinted, focusing on the patches of lush green grass that adorned the new mountains. Even amongst such extreme rocky conditions, this vegetation thrived.

Could I do the same?

Could I enjoy experiencing Theldea and my blossoming friendship with Throwen while being assaulted with grief, guilt, and confusion at the same time?

"Your favorite thing to do outside of your room was feeding the animals, tending to the gardens, and secretly helping children tend to their wounds," he said with a satisfied smile.

The cloudy sky dripped black, and the sun finally disappeared. He moved to stand beside me, and I sighed. "Our assigned tasks were either rewards for doing well or punishments for even the slightest of failures."

I was the Lady of the Grave. My life's purpose was to help Malik and my people in whatever way I could. Or was I just his dog, trained to perform one very important trick?

"I'm happy you could find some joy amongst the oppression," he said, his voice holding an edge.

I sighed shakily. I was absorbing an abundance of new information while simultaneously deconstructing my entire life. I needed to focus on something else for a moment. "You've been attacked by an assortment of animals, including Petwa."

Throwen's life sounded so remarkable that I kept finding my own life experiences falling short. He must think I'm the most *Goddess-damned* boring witch in all of Theldea.

"Yes, but Petwa loves me despite what Nova thinks. Her nips tend to be playful." He chuckled.

A cool, light breeze lifted my hair, and I pulled it back into a high ponytail with the leather strap Throwen had gifted me. It was the first gift I was ever given that I truly appreciated.

Throwen's gifts were selfless, unlike the manipulative gifts I was used to. Every uncomfortable dress, every humiliating piece of jewelry, and those *fucking* heels and corsets. They all flashed like a play before me, and I swallowed back the bile rising in my throat.

My attempts at focusing on the present were challenging, the demons of my past scratching at my memory like a scab. "What about Luftor and its people?"

Turning, Throwen walked briskly toward the fire, and I followed him, letting the cave swallow us whole.

"They're a scholarly bunch. The covens within Luftor are full of advancement and education. They have wonderful amenities. But overall, the covens are excessively wealthy. Despite all their knowledge, they still have areas of obvious inequality."

"I planned to take you to Graygarde's library. It's the largest in all Theldea." He beamed.

I struggled to keep up with his long strides. "That sounds like a lovely plan."

"It's a strategic plan, darling. If I can't make you swoon, the library will." We reached the fire, and the mischievous smile on Throwen's face made my stomach drop.

"Why are you smiling like that?" I grabbed a pastry from his trove. It was stale but filled with chocolate, so I endured the rock-hard covering.

"Like what?" he asked with a tone that sounded innocent, but he forgot to hide his suspicious, shit-eating grin.

"You look like you're about to run over and pull on my ponytail or something else childish." I crossed my arms and narrowed my gaze.

He had ditched his furs for a comfortable pair of gray pants that he tucked into his brown boots. His songbook was connected to his belt with leather straps. It paired perfectly with his loose-fitting dark yellow shirt.

"Did you have any scout training? Combat? Weapons? Anything like that?" He took off his lute.

"Not technically, no. I've asked Malik countless times to make me a scout, but his answer is always the same. He told me I was too sensitive to be out in the field, too indispensable."

"Why were you so valuable to him that he would imprison you?" The easygoing smile was gone with the mention of Malik, and he effortlessly shifted into the Angel of Death they claimed him to be.

He was an assassin through and through, digging for information like an impatient dog. Unfortunately, this dog was sweet and had the most adorable eyes.

"He didn't *imprison* me. We used my blood to conceal our coven. Without me, all my people would be vulnerable, open to attacks from the very atrocities they fled."

Throwen scowled, poking at the fire. "Theldea is not full of atrocities. It has its problems like any society. But we don't cower and isolate. We work to make things better."

I ignored him, returning to his original question. "I've watched countless battles to the death, and I'd like to think I could recreate some of the techniques I've seen."

"You've watched *countless* battles to the death?" His Adam's apple bobbed as he swallowed hard, rolling his shoulders.

"You haven't?" I said over a full bite of crunchy pastry sustenance, holding back from eating the rest in one bite.

He turned to face me. "No. I only fight when necessary, and I don't kill if I can find another way."

"Oh." That must be nice, but that was never an option for me. "Sometimes members are chosen to fight and earn their place amongst the living or be honored in death by slipping into Malik's Ether."

My chest ached. Those witches died for nothing, and now they would be tormented for all eternity.

"Do you want to talk about it?"

He was too good at following the ebb and flow of my ever-changing moods. *Did I want to talk about it?* I thought Theldea was a depraved world, but I was coming to see that wasn't the case.

"The worst months were when a child's name was drawn. They always died quickly and efficiently at least..." I trailed off, not ready to face the truth of our ceremonies or try to rationalize why Malik had them.

"Their parents allowed them to fight?" Throwen blanched.

Bile threatened the back of my throat, and I spoke through the burning. "Children in my coven don't stay with their parents. As soon as they can walk, they're placed where they would be most useful to the coven."

"I see." He stabbed at the burning twigs with sharp movements, and flames lit up the shadows dancing under his set jaw. "Did he ever make you fight?"

I pressed my lips together. "No. I read the names of the fighters and helped them transform when defeated." I fumbled awkwardly with the last bite of pastry and caught it just before it hit the ground.

Throwen's laughter at my embarrassing movements echoed off the dripping walls. "I would have pegged you as a savory girl, not sweet."

I frowned and stuck my tongue out at him before licking my fingers clean, savoring the last bit of sweetness. He laughed, clutching his stomach.

How were his humor and laughter so fucking infectious? Even

without using his powers, he could naturally transition my moods and the atmosphere around us.

"I want to teach you how to shoot my bow."

My mark tingled, and I grasped the back of my neck but it was too late, he saw the pulsing glow.

His wide grin grew. "*Oh...* you *want* to shoot my bow."

"Seriously? You would let me shoot? I'm afraid I'll mess it up or something. I couldn't..."

He stepped closer, lowering his gaze to my rambling lips. "Beloved things are meant to be used and enjoyed, darling. *We both know you want to.*" He waggled those *Goddess-damned* emotive eyebrows.

Cursed Abyss! I pulled my bottom lip between my teeth, knowing I was terrible at turning away from a challenge.

"Show me," I said confidently.

He picked up his lute and swiftly flicked it into its bow form, never taking his eyes off me. It sent chills up and down my spine.

My crown and broom were mediocre compared to his marvelously crafted instrument of death and when combined with his picks, he was truly mystical.

He set up his half-eaten apple on an uneven rock a few paces from where we stood before striding over to me.

My senses were heightened, and I felt lighter and more awake than I had in months. It was an exhilarating kind of adrenaline that I wasn't used to but could easily become addicted to.

"We'll start with your stance." He handed over his bow, and my traitorous palms sweat, my nerves building to a crescendo. "Show me what you've got."

The moment my fingers contacted the weapon, an invigorating rush of energy pulsed through me, tingling all the way to my fingers and toes.

"Woah." My mark hummed, and I knew it was glowing brightly from the way Throwen was looking at me with reverence. He respected the Goddess, and that respect extended to me even though I felt unworthy as the lavender tendrils tickled my skin.

"See? They already like you." Throwen winked and gestured for me to continue.

Indignation pooled low in my stomach. I had observed the scouts practicing archery daily, watching them through my towering window greedily or sneaking around in the shadows on the practice fields. Every day I had wished I could learn to use their weapons.

I lifted my arms confidently and stood with stiff legs. Throwen was granting me another wish. How many of my fantasies could he fulfill on our journey?

I was grateful for Throwen's constant distractions. Solving puzzles always had settled some of the restlessness inside me, and shooting a bow seemed like one I could solve.

"Not bad. May I?" He stared at my hips, and my ears heated, my frown deepening. *Okay, not as naturally gifted as I hoped.*

I nodded, allowing him to help me. Having someone ask before touching me expanded my chest with a sense of safety. It was as if my trapped heart was swelling, and I feared this man would tear down all the walls I had spent years building. I didn't know who I would be without them.

"We are about ten yards away. You'll want to stand perpendicular to your shooting line." He stepped behind me and placed his hands around my hips, twisting them to the right, stretching the muscles tight. "Good. It will feel a little unnatural at first, but with time, your body will remember what to do. Don't lock your knees, try to bend them and relax your muscles."

Relax with his hands enveloping my hips? Yeah, sure. No problem.

He bent down, pushing the backs of my knees slightly and my kneecaps creaked.

"There you go. Don't forget to relax your neck." His hand moved from my hips up to my neck where he massaged it from the base of my skull down to the tip of my spine.

I shivered. The picks were cool, and they glided across my skin in a way unadorned fingers couldn't. Throwen worked the knotted muscles and all the tension I stored there melted away like butter on a hot pan.

"Feet shoulder width apart." The toe of his boot pushed against the insides of my feet until they were in the ideal position. He placed his warm palm on my lower back, sending a small amount of heat through my shirt. "Do you feel that? Your lower back is arched."

He moved in closer, his body now against my back. Reaching one arm around my waist, he pressed his other hand against my stomach. His pinky finger grazed the top of my waistband where my shirt had lifted, and I had to suppress a gasp.

As he applied firm pressure, the arch in my lower back straightened and my abdominals tightened.

"Archery is like a dance. Your entire body must be in tune," he said.

The only thing my body wanted was for him to slip those fingers lower. Guilt coiled around my throat where the burns from Levi choking me were quickly healing. I had to fight the urge to flee this interaction, fearing I was taking advantage of his willingness to teach me.

"Take a moment to feel your chest, torso, and shoulders. They should all face straight forward."

I adjusted them slightly, reaching out to be aware of each tendon and muscle, and faced the direction he indicated.

"You're a natural, darling." His praise was even sweeter than his songs, and when he removed his hands, my body revolted at the loss.

Wrapping his hands around the sides of my head, he was careful not to touch the healing wound. My eyes were locked on the apple. He leaned in so close that his nose brushed my ear.

Thin smoke coiled around the ends of the bow, forming a string.

"They're eager to share this new experience with you," he whispered, and I hoped he couldn't feel my racing pulse. "Whatever you're feeling might be intensified."

Judging by the wetness gathering between my legs, I'd say that was pretty accurate. "Um... yeah, I definitely feel... something."

He held me in the stance. "I'm going to form the arrow and notch it. Once we get you your own bow, I will teach you this part too."

Once we get my bow? He envisioned a future where he would continue to teach me.

I was at a loss for words. Only a few days together, and he was treating me better than any of my friends in my coven. Even though he thought of a future with me in it, he would eventually grow tired of my hysteria and distance himself, like everyone else.

My mouth fell open as the arrow formed. The spirits were breathtaking this close. They swirled with varying shades of purple contained to the shape of an arrow. Three fletching feathers lined the back in gradients of lavender. The colors fluctuated in graceful movements.

"They're so beautiful. Their movements remind me of the lights dancing across the night skies in Oxvein." I invited them in, letting their comfort wrap around me.

The spirits I was used to wielding felt nothing like this. They usually thrashed and fought and were hard to control. But this felt so calming and natural.

Throwen moved my fingers one by one into position, each of his touches now shooting pure electricity through me. "Relax your fingers and loosen your grip."

My index finger held the string above the arrow and my middle and ring fingers rested below. Taking direction from him was easy, and I worried I liked it a bit too much.

There was no judgment or condescending tone, which only ignited my drive to learn quickly and efficiently.

"Drag your arm across your chest while staying relaxed and use your upper back muscles to pull your shoulder blades together. You want to make one solid line towards your target."

The spirits formed a delicate line for me to follow. "Thank you."

"You're welcome."

My nose scrunched. "I wasn't talking to you. I was talking to them."

His breathy laugh tickled my cheek. My body was melting, my core growing hotter by the second.

He brushed tiny strokes against the corner of my mouth with his thumb. It must be the spirits making me feel so... lustful wasn't quite right, but something lust adjacent. Throwen had said they feed on our experiences, and it had been a *long* time since I felt anywhere near this level of attraction.

"When you pull the string back, use your mouth here as an anchor point." With one more gentle stroke, he shifted, reaching out under my extended elbow to steady my shaking arm. "Don't bend your wrist or break your stance until after you release the arrow. Aim for the center of the apple."

That should be easy enough with the line the spirits were creating.

"You can think of your intent, but I'll guide the arrow with mine. I'll count, release on three."

What is my intent? To hit the apple? My heart was beating hard, wanting to break free from the confines of my ribcage. Throwen was warm and smelled of campfire smoke, and his stubble brushed my cheek as he held me close. Clarity pulsed through me, and I took a slow deep breath, letting myself feel my appreciation for him.

I pushed my intent toward the spirits, and they pulsed and twined around our arms, binding us together.

"One. Two."

Please help me impress him. I exhaled and released the arrow before he could finish counting.

He jumped back with a shout of surprise and the arrow flew straight, but before impact, it separated into eight smaller arrows, circling the apple menacingly before plunging into it all at once. The apple exploded into chunks, juice splattering the dark rock below.

I screamed and jumped up and down. "Not too bad for my first time, huh?"

Throwen's hands were on top of his head, his mouth hanging open.

Abyss consume me! Gloating had *never* felt this good. *Who's the cocky one now?*

"*Sacred Ether*. Did you just...? What the fuck was your intent?" The proud smile beaming across his face was like water after a drought.

I threw my arms up, nearly hitting myself in the face with his bow.

He paced, and it was like watching a fly try to escape through a closed window. "Whynnie attempted to connect with them and never could. So, it isn't because you're Goddess-born."

"What are you talking about?" My body buzzed with adrenaline, but his reaction had a seed of worry blooming in my stomach.

"Octavia, I was the *only* witch in Theldea able to create a direct connection with them."

The spirits danced around us, and my brows knit together, unsure how to process what he was saying. "What about Echo and Kallan? Have they used your bow?"

"*No.* I don't let anyone else touch my bow, especially my siblings." His wide eyes found mine and looked panicked before spewing his next words in a rush, "Teaching Echo or Kallan anything is like trying to teach children, I love them but they're horrible students."

He shook his head and bit his bottom lip. "What I'm trying to say is that *without bias*, what you just did was fucking *impressive*. It took me years to convey my intent to them."

I let his words wash over me. But that meant...

He was in front of me now, holding me tightly by my shoulders with the widest grin I'd ever seen on his face. He was still rambling, but his voice faded into the background and my ears rang.

I should focus on the newfound ability to use his magic, but all I could think about was the fact that I was the only other witch he had allowed to touch his bow. *How could I have earned his trust so quickly?*

I added it to the list of things that made little sense and tried to focus on Throwen instead. "Well, you're not alone anymore. You better not piss me off or I might use that bow against you."

He barked a laugh. "Wow! Look at that, you do smile with your teeth sometimes."

He squished my cheeks between his fingers, and I flicked my finger, pushing air hard into his ribs and forcing out a woosh of his breath. Rubbing at them, he laughed at my souring expression.

"You know, I think you're actually better at frowning."

I expect you to smile and show our people how grateful you are for my salvation and this place of safety. Your disposition for frowning is appalling.

My glower fell to my aching feet. Malik would be so disappointed.

Throwen shifted, the rocky ground crunching beneath his boots. I gasped as he grabbed my chin. His eyes were bright and glossy. "Don't fret, darling. I find your smile and frown equally exquisite. Think you could teach me that trick with the arrows?"

I was transfixed. His fingers holding my face, and genuine smile nearly undid me. The distance between us was too much, and I wanted to push up on my toes so I could see what he tasted like.

Hoping my out-of-control emotions would settle, I thrust the bow back at him. He said the spirits intensified emotions and surely my attraction was being amplified.

"I'm pretty sore." My muscles ached and every so often, a sharp stabbing pain shot through my body. "I think I need to massage my feet again."

"I have a better idea." He sat the bow down and, without another word, laced his fingers with mine. As he pulled us deeper into the cave, I was more than happy to follow

Chapter 13

OCTAVIA

Humidity poured from the opening just ahead and the smell of damp rock permeated the air.

We were deep inside the mountain now, and craggy gray rocks towered around the mostly circular cavern. Small pools of cloudy water littered the floor and slabs of rock lined the edges of each one. Water rushed over a small waterfall, pouring directly into one of the pools. I followed its path up the long straight side of the rocky mountain to where it disappeared close to the top.

The ceiling was glowing bright fluorescent blues. The colors pulsed as if we were in the chest cavity of the mountain, watching its heartbeat. My jaw dropped and I shook my head in disbelief.

"What kind of magic is this?" I twirled in a circle committing the sight to memory.

"Glowworms."

Worms? I had to give the Goddess credit. So far, her creations were extraordinary.

Through a large opening in the cave's top, I could see the clear night sky, blanketed in the twinkling lights of the stars. The faintest scent of almonds lingered in the large space, reminding me of the days I would gather mushrooms for our feasts. My skin pebbled and the hair on the back of my neck raised despite the lazy heat coating my skin. "This is *unbelievable*."

Water lapped the edges of the pools, and I could hear the clicking of bats. They soared in and out through the opening above. It was just like the crows that flew in and out of Ombra Lurra and for the first time since leaving, I felt a tiny prickle of homesickness followed by a rush of guilt.

Throwen strutted toward the largest pool in the cave's center that the rest of the pools flowed into. "Luftor is filled with hot springs. Most witches are afraid to venture so deep in the mountains, though."

"Should I be afraid?"

"That depends. Are you afraid of water?" He tossed a cheeky smile over his shoulder before turning and peeling his shirt up over his head.

Sacred Ether! The pools were no longer the most alluring thing in the cave.

His skin glistened, and the heat caused his veins to stand out more than normal beneath his pale skin. My fingers itched to claw into his lean back muscles that were accentuated by his slender build.

He turned to face me, dark chest hair curling at the top of his pecs and trailing down in a straight line to his abdomen before disappearing into his pants. I wanted to grip that chest hair between my fingers and pull. *Fuck me, he could be an angel.*

"See something you like, darling?" he said with a slight laugh.

"The pools they're... majestic."

An amused hum fell from his lips as he sat and kicked off his boots. "They are."

He stood and started unbuckling his thick black belt. All that remained were his pants. My cheeks were blazing, and I hoped he was too far to see. *Abyss open up and consume me now.* "What are you doing?"

"I don't know about you, but I need to wash this filth off my body." He slowly pulled off his trousers and I couldn't look away. A very short pair of thin black underwear left little to the imagination.

He tossed his pile of clothes on a nearby rock before wading into the pool, where trails of steam drifted up from the water. Throwen's deep primal moan struck me as he slowly submerged his dark hair beneath the bubbles.

White cloudy water curled into spirals, reminding me of our coven's labyrinth as they blocked my sight. Some greenery poked through in some areas, and I ambled over to a patch, kneeling to inhale their aroma. The purplish-red flowers blooming from the tall stalks spread sweetness and opened into four pointed petals.

"I bet if we dried these they would smell even —"

Throwen's cropped hair and pale skin were nowhere to be seen.

"What the fuck?" Standing quickly, I slipped over wet rocks to where he had descended into the water. I crawled on all fours, probing every inch of the pool. Stories of terrifying sea monsters who prowled in the waters of Theldea swarmed my mind.

"Throwen?" I screamed at the cloudy water, obstructing any view I might have of him.

"Shit! Shit! Shit!" I needed him. I couldn't survive in Theldea, or my mind, without him.

Water flew into the air as he breached the surface, soaking me. He was laughing, but I didn't appreciate the joke.

I scowled at him, grinding my teeth together. "You. Asshole!"

"Well, since you're already wet... or do you need me to teach you how to swim too?"

I shot a stream of water directly into his eye. "Fuck off!"

"Ahhh! Okay, I deserved that." He rubbed his assaulted eyes, and I shook my arms and legs like a wet dog. The hot water that had hit me was heavenly, though I would never admit it.

"At least try it. I promised to show you everything, remember?" He pleaded, and his muscular shoulders bobbed in and out of the water, the steam creating droplets along every curve and dip.

He was right. This was why I left my coven, to discover new things and choose for myself what I wanted to do. And right now, I wanted to wash away the coating of grime covering my skin.

The fact that a gorgeous man who had taken an interest in me for some reason was wading in the water was just a bonus.

I winced and shifted from my throbbing knees to sit on my bruised ass. Unlacing my brown boots, I slipped them off and curled my aching toes.

At least Whynnie's honey mixture was healing my throat and head quickly, working in tandem with my Goddess-born blood.

When I looked to Throwen he was watching me intently with an eagerness in his expression that made my stomach clench.

"How many witches have you brought to this place?" I acted like it was an innocent question, but I wanted to know if he had other friends, perhaps a lover. Who was I kidding? He probably had the women in each coven lining up for a chance to fuck him.

"None. I work alone."

"You're kidding me, right? You're a bard."

"And?"

"Bards never shut up. How do you survive without someone incessantly giving you feedback?" A smile pulled at my lips, and I had to bite down to suppress a laugh.

I shimmied out of my pants, thankful that Nova had provided a pair of black underwear too, but I kept my shirt on, my nerves taking hold. Wading in slowly, I let the hot water slide over me like silken sheets.

"Not just a bard, darling. The Goddess gifted me with the heart of a bard and the mind of an assassin." He arched a dark brow. "I hope you aren't one of those witches who put individuals into neat, tiny boxes."

I laughed because he had no idea the tiny box I had to fit inside my entire life, always wanting to burst through its walls. Malik had put us in boxes, arranging them to suit his purposes.

"That's fair," I conceded. "But you have to admit that most bards *do* love attention."

A mischievous smile curled across his lips. "No arguments there."

I wanted to help him stay in this carefree state forever, but as soon as we left this pool, he would once again be burdened by me. Who I was. What I've done.

I squelched my toes into the muddy bottom, and it squished pleasantly between my toes. The steam warmed my face and neck, and I gave in, letting out a small moan.

The water was already doing its job, releasing the tension in my muscles as my aches and pains faded away. I licked my lips, and the taste of salty sweat clung to the tip of my tongue. I was still too nervous to look at Throwen, who I could hear swimming closer.

In a moment of panic, I submerged myself. I was back in my coven, under the scalding water of my bath. Usually, I would be screaming, begging to burst like the rapidly floating bubbles around my head. But with Throwen next to me, I had no desire to scream or focus on the past.

The water tickled the bridge of my nose as I poked my eyes out of the water.

Throwen was floating lazily nearby, laying on his back and dragging his golden picks across the top of the water. I imagined myself to be like a sneaky siren from one of my favorite books, eyeing up her prey before devouring it.

"Do you ever take them off? Your picks." I asked, finding a new well of courage and pushed up on my toes to see him more clearly.

He raised an arm straight above, the light of the glowworms and stars shining through his fingers and reflecting off the golden picks. "No. At this point, they feel like an extension of myself."

"They're beautifully crafted. Where did you get them?"

"Well, that's actually a very funny story. Kallan was in Stranata with Echo. Do you know anything about Stranata?"

I frowned, already aware that my knowledge of Stranata would be greatly construed. "The books I read talked of pirates, sea monsters, great big cats who would eat you whole…"

"It's wrong that someone thought it was acceptable to dictate what you read." He swam toward me, the distance between us shrinking with each word. "*But* some of that is true. Stranata houses the most lawless of covens. Whynnie despises having to deal with them. She says it is like dealing with us when we were children."

I poked holes in the cloudy water, watching the rings spread out around them. "Tell me about the picks."

He hopped up and sat on a rocky ledge a few feet away. His chest hair looked darker when it was wet, and I was tempted to follow that trail down… I blinked slowly and forced myself to focus on his face.

"Kallan and Echo were in Fennix's Coven picking up these picks they had custom-made for my Name Day. That night, in their room at the tavern, Echo wanted to examine the picks again. I mean, look at them." He stretched out his arm toward me, spreading out his long fingers.

My eyes snagged on his protruding veins that went up his forearm like hypnotic, flowing rivers. His biceps were a hill winding naturally into his shoulders.

"They're exquisite." But they wouldn't be on their own. Only he could make them look that beautiful, with the fingers the Goddess had gifted him.

"*Exactly.*" He pointed at me dramatically. "So exquisite that Kallan pick-pocketed *his own sibling* and bet with them right under Echo's nose in a game of poker with Fennix."

"He did not." The way he told stories was always enthralling and I was powerless against participating.

"He did. And he lost." Throwen barked out a laugh, and I joined in.

My natural laugh was still a foreign thing to me, and I cut it short, afraid that I sounded like an insane witch, but Throwen didn't seem to notice.

"In the end, Echo threatened to cut off Fennix's cock in front of his entire crew if he didn't return the picks."

I blanched and felt the blood rush from my face.

"How did they get away with talking to a coven leader like that?" If someone said that to Malik, he would not only kill them, but anyone in the close vicinity.

"Echo deals with Fennix more than any of us. He may kill freely amongst other Stranata covens, but he would never kill Echo. The other coven leaders would demand his head on a spike. Echo does a lot to ease tension between covens." They sounded both intimidating and awe-inspiring.

"Deep down, he knows I could end his life at any time. We let him think he is powerful when, in reality, he holds none."

I marveled at him. I hadn't fully understood the scope of their work with other covens.

"Kallan apologized and bought me my songbook holster. We all laughed about it while we celebrated and ate way too much cake."

My eyes welled with tears. His life, his family, everything about him, sounded like the loveliest of fantasies. Flashes of my Name Day raced across my mind. The wretched outfit, the so-called 'transformations,' challenging Malik. His rejection, all the blood, my sacrifice to conceal our coven for another year. It all seemed so far away and surreal now that I was safe next to Throwen.

I cleared my throat, shaking my head to banish the memories. "It sounds like your family cares deeply for one another."

A merciful cool rain started pouring in on top of us from above, washing away the perfidious tears now falling down my cheeks.

"Let's get back! We should try to get some rest!" he shouted over the pouring rain and dove toward me. We exited the pool, rushing away from the downpour. His joy entwined with mine and we laughed, making our way back toward our clothes.

The sounds were pacifying. I pretended it was possible to leave my demons behind in that pool to drown in their malevolence.

Once we were safely under a rocky ceiling, the rain slowed; the cave echoed in the silence. Water fell to the rocks from our soaked bodies. My heart beat much faster than the steady dripping rhythm, and I was very aware of our proximity and near nakedness.

Stepping back, I slipped on a rock. "Woah!"

Throwen's arms shot out to catch me, but instead, his hand slipped against my wet skin under my shirt. He made contact with one of my most shameful secrets, and fear rushed through me. We stood frozen, gazes locked, as he supported my weight.

Making hesitant but tender circles against my left ribs with his thumb, he pulled me closer.

"Octavia?"

My face heated, and I was certain it was now the deepest shade of red my skin could muster.

"It's nothing. Just a birthmark."

Throwen's sharp jaw ticked, and his nostrils flared. A million questions washed through his pained expression, and the rain and wind picked back up with an urgent fierceness.

His stare pinned me where I stood. "Are we lying to each other now?"

How did he see right through my defenses? It was *infuriating*. I didn't want to lie to him, but I couldn't help it.

Pushing him away gently, I bit my cheek, and I gathered my shirt under my breast with shaking hands. Lightning struck, illuminating the cave enough to reveal the large branded M on my ribs.

"*He fucking branded you?*" he growled. Another bolt flashed, displaying his bared teeth.

I knew that look. His expression was like mine the night before I lost control and punched my mirror.

An unnatural silence fell between us, and I waited for him to explode the way I had. I shrugged it off, trying not to think about the last witch I let past my defenses and how her reaction to my brand was nothing like this. Calliope was thrilled with Malik's choice of punishment, claiming it was the highest of honors and I let myself believe her all these years.

"It's not uncommon in our coven. Malik brands all the scouts with a skull on their ribs, it's a true honor. I don't remember much of it; I was twenty-four and I think I passed out at some point."

Throwen was panting, and he examined my other ribs, no doubt making sure there weren't other hideous disfigurements.

"There are these gaps in my memory when my brain leaves my body," I said, disregarding his concern. "I know that makes me sound ridiculous, but it's true. It's not a big deal. I barely remember it."

"It doesn't sound ridiculous at all, it sounds like survival. And it's a fucking big deal to me," he said as if he was losing control of his rage. "He covets control, Octavia, he wanted to own you."

"No. He loved me."

I will mark you as many times as it takes for you to be civil, you ungrateful child! Don't worry, I will help you learn.

The phantom of Malik's rough backhand against my cheek coiled its way free. I grit my teeth. "When you care about someone, you discipline them. It was my fault for trying to escape through the catacombs. How else would I have learned?"

Throwen looked a dangerous shade of rage, his eyes deepening to a dark plum instead of the easygoing lavender I'd grown used to. Instead of yelling, he surprised me by wrapping his arms around me and squeezing. The pressure soothed the sting of the memory.

"Would *you* brand someone you love?" he asked, his chest rumbling.

His question threw me off balance. Luckily, he was holding me steady. My lip quivered. *Keep it together, Octavia.*

"No, but..." I could not face the truth of his words. I was ugly, marred. Inside and out.

I looked up to the sky through the large opening and a dark cloud moved ominously, snuffing out the light. Thunder shook the very rocks we stood on, and I welcomed the deafening noise vibrating through my bones. It was as if the sky itself had broken a lock inside of me. The rumble of thunder and flashes of lightning spurred me on.

I locked eyes with him, seamlessly transforming from sensitive Octavia into the imperturbable Lady of the Grave. "Consequences result in learning and growing. I care about making you the consummate Lady for our coven. *Rejoice* in this consequence, knowing it will bring you one step closer to serenity." I mimicked Malik's tone and cadence with an eerie perfection.

I had never spoken Malik's words that replayed in my mind endlessly out loud before, and hearing them pour from my lips had me questioning Malik's love. His once sweet and caring words turned sour both in my mouth and mind.

"That's what he said," I continued, "right before pressing the branding iron to my ribs."

Throwen's eyes welled with tears, and his thumb rubbed tenderly at the repulsive brand.

"I always hoped I would earn a skull here next to it." I pointed to my other side where my ribs were bare.

Throwen's other hand squeezed tightly against the unmarred skin. "With all due respect, I'm going to kill that fucker," he said, tone terse. "And it won't be quick, I will make him suffer!"

I took a step back from his embrace, fumbling as I lowered my shirt. "Throwen!"

"He fucking—When people hurt you, I—" His thoughts were disjointed, and he threw his arms up in the air, tears falling down his cheeks and getting lost in the stubble on his face.

Closing the gap between us, I threw my arms around him, reaching up on my toes. Seeing him sad and hurting ripped all reason from me. I latched onto him and squeezed tightly, no longer caring that we were both wet and half-naked. He was shaking; tight fists curled at his sides.

"It's okay, Throwen. I'm okay, I'm with you, remember? I was lucky. Not everyone survived Malik's punishments."

He pulled away, cupping my chin. "I should be the one comforting you through this, not the other way around." His eyes followed the curly hair framing my face, and he tucked a wet strand behind my ear.

"You are. You're helping me fill in the gaps and even though they're painful to face, I *need* you to keep doing it. These unknowns... they scare me, Throwen. Do you know what it's like to not be able to recall information about yourself or your life's history correctly?"

A small laugh escaped his lips. "Actually, I do."

How had I so quickly forgotten that he had no memory from before the Goddess sent him back?

"Would you want someone to fill in those gaps for you? I mean, if they could?"

He rubbed his hand over his head, splashing water droplets down his back. "No. But I understand why you need to, and I'm willing to be there for you along the way."

A large knot formed in my throat, but I spoke through it. "Thank you."

He was offering me so much, and I had so little to offer him in return. Throwen always seemed so content. He didn't need me or my help.

I shivered, the cool night air and rain pebbling my skin. I missed the warmth of the pool.

"Let's get you back to the fire. I have a dry shirt you can borrow." He smiled and kissed my forehead gently. Then he walked past me and retrieved our clothing.

I pressed my hand to my forehead, trying to press the kiss deeper. These feelings I had were not those of friendship, but something deeper — something I'd never felt before. Maybe it was a residual effect of using his bow and connecting with the spirits together.

He disappeared behind a large boulder before returning with a fluffy towel. He certainly did store items all over these caves.

"I'll even let you use my *only* towel. You're welcome." He bowed low, offering it to me like he was my humble servant.

I flicked some nearby pebbles at his shins. "*You're* the one who soaked all my clothes."

We both laughed, and he enveloped me in the towel. I pulled it tightly around myself, letting the warmth it had gathered from the steam soothe me.

I straightened my spine. These moments with Throwen tore me apart but also healed me. "Will you sing me to sleep again?" I was getting too used to his melodies sweeping me away and the cadence of his heart when I laid on his chest.

"I will serenade you anytime, darling." He wrapped one large arm around my neck and shoulder, but he was still tense.

I had to give him something in return for his care and comfort, even if he didn't need it. This was all a dream that couldn't last. I would have to face Malik eventually. But for now, I wanted to enjoy my time with Throwen while I still could.

"Throwen. I'm here too. I mean for you. If you ever want or need to talk."

He stiffened slightly and pulled away. "If anything comes up, you'll be the first to know."

He slipped his hand into mine and I hoped that one day I could be as carefree, helpful, and content as him.

You're going to get him killed.

Oh right, I had almost forgotten about the roaring demons in my head. They crushed my momentary hope like a cockroach beneath their boots. My fate was sealed the moment Malik took me to his coven and even Throwen couldn't save me from the imminent condemnation coming my way.

Chapter 14

And Sew It Begins

THROWEN

Stone buildings lined the winding streets of Graygarde. The coven was built into the side of the mountain, buildings clinging to its rocky surface. Octavia craned her neck, taking in the flora pouring over the balconies like overflowing cups. I couldn't help but smile at her wonder. She led Lucky by her reins and the street widened as we walked out from under a row of arching, ivy-covered colonnades.

The center of the main courtyard was lined with granite tables, merchant's booths personalized with brightly colored tablecloths and awnings. It was mostly empty but for a few mumbling stragglers closing up shop.

Octavia gaped and covered her mouth as the setting sunlight refracted off the mosaic beneath our feet. Shards of glass in every color imaginable fit together to form one artist's interpretation of the Goddess. She had bright yellow hair and silver eyes. A jeweled crown floated above her head and her arms were outstretched, as if welcoming you in for an embrace.

I nudged Octavia with my arm. "Nobody truly knows what she looks like. I always wished I could recall seeing her when I died."

"She's so full of light." Octavia hunched, curling in on herself.

"All I remember are echoes of peace, euphoria, and compassion." All things Octavia brought out in me. Even if she didn't want to admit it, she was connected to the Goddess.

The artwork was nothing compared to Octavia and her unabashed open-mouthed smile, her adorable finger pressed to her nose in contemplation and fascination.

Her attention danced from one empty stand to the next. She licked her lips and inhaled deeply, no doubt being lured in by the lingering aromas of fruits, meats, and sugary treats.

Spirits tickled my fingers, wanting to join in on the energy this new experience was bringing her. The way they reacted to her was fascinating.

I couldn't blame them. I was drawn to her too, like a moth to a flame. I savored her constant presence, and it scared the shit out of me. Boredom usually followed me like my extra unwanted shadow, but Octavia was as far as it came from boring.

She froze in the center of the courtyard. A large fountain depicting foxes chasing each other in a circle burbled. She squinted, eyes searching all the alleys and exits, like she had done in Oxvein, assessing for any threats.

"You're safe," I reassured her and squeezed her shoulders.

Her face morphed from assessing to guilt and fear, but then they slowly faded away as she nodded and straightened her spine.

A carnal part of me wanted to be the one to rip that mask off. Maybe then she could finally take a full breath and know that who she was at her core was worthy. I wanted to see all that she was with the same intensity she wanted to uncover Theldea's hidden secrets.

But *she* was quickly becoming my treasure, my instincts demanding to hide her away like a dragon with a precious hoard. But I wasn't Malik, and I'd never cage her in such a way. Despite the terror seeping into my veins at the thought of Malik coming for her, I would not hide her away.

A young witch carrying a tray caught my eye. It held one puff pastry oozing with chocolate. I latched onto Octavia and pulled her with me toward the boy.

"Throwen, wait!" She stumbled, and Lucky chuffed, but I kept them close.

My new life's purpose was to keep that wild sheen in her eyes, cultivate her wonder, and push until her laughter bubbled through the night air.

"How much for that last pastry?" I called out to the boy, and when we were close enough, his eyes widened.

The sun had set, and lanterns were being lit. Dark wisps of clouds floated over the twinkling stars. They seemed closer here, up in the mountains of Graygarde.

"N-n-n-nothing for ye, sir." His pale blue eyes were wide and the freckles along his cheeks quivered slightly. He averted his gaze and lifted the tray to me.

The children outside of Goldhaven feared me. They told greatly exaggerated stories about 'the Angel of Death'. In reality I was great with children, the ones in Goldhaven loved singing and dancing to my music with the spirits.

I lowered myself to his level, and his body shifted, as if to flee. "How about this? You give me that pastry and I give you double the coin. You keep half and you give half to your...?"

"My mother." The boy's thin eyebrows knit together, and he looked between us.

"Wonderful. Your mother then." I offered up the coin, and he gasped when my death-touched hands grazed his. Those types of reactions used to unravel me, but I had become numb to them long ago. So I smiled, instead.

"Th-thank ye!" He handed me the pastry, the trembling subsiding in his body replaced with the innocent confidence of a young witch. He grinned, his front left tooth missing. "Mom's not gonna believe me when I tell her *ye* were the one to buy our last pastry! I'm gonna give her all the coin, if that's okay?"

"Of course, it's yours to do with as you choose. It's quite noble to help your mother."

His chin shifted back to his tattered shoes. They were falling apart, his big toe sticking out. Graygarde was a wealthy place, but there were still those who suffered from poverty.

"My father disappeared about a year ago." The boy sniffed. "He was traveling to Stranata for some supplies and… he never came back. We will be eternally grateful for yer help. Thank ye." He threw the tray under his arm and hurried home.

"I thought you said we need to save our coin for our survival?" Octavia arched a dark eyebrow, giving me an icy stare, but there was something beneath that stare I couldn't quite place. Was it admiration?

"Don't worry, darling, I'll give the performance of my life tonight. We will have so much coin we can buy Lucky a month's worth of carrots." Lucky whinnied happily as I guided her beside us and back to the middle of the large courtyard. I warmed the pastry in my hands just enough for the chocolate to melt.

"Why didn't I think of that?" Her pouty lips, combined with her crossed arms, were magnetic. I handed it to her and she took a bite, immediately rewarding herself with another. She examined the pastry with pleasure. "Thif tasfes amafing!"

I chuckled, and she devoured it. The growing sound of witches' voices interrupted her excitement as they approached the courtyard. Its wheel-like design had witches pouring in from every spoke, through the ivy arches.

Turning, she attempted to flee, but I grabbed her hand, not wanting us to get separated.

"It's okay, they're just gathering to relax after a long day's work."

A band started tuning their instruments in preparation to play and my fingers twitched, wanting to join in. The music started with a loud jaunty tune and soon witches were dancing all around us.

"No. Throwen!"

I looked at Octavia, hoping to see more joy and wonder on her face. My heart stopped as I took in the unbridled panic, turning her face hot and sweaty. I lowered myself to be eye level with her, searching for an answer to what was happening inside that great expanse of a mind. "What's wrong?"

Her eyes darted wildly around like she couldn't find a focal point. "I can't. See an exit! I-can't-see-an-exit! I. Can't. breathe!" She was hyperventilating, her words coming in rushed bursts.

Clutching her chest, she started scratching at her healing throat with her other hand. She stood on her toes, trying to see over the towering crowd of witches.

Fuck! Why had I not thought about this? She was short, unable to see over the heads in the crowd. My idiotic obsession with showing her everything made me blind to her needs. *I did this to her.*

"Hold on," I said as I guided us to a post and placed her hand on my chest. I tied Lucky with fumbling hands. Banishing my self-doubt, I scooped her into my arms and maneuvered our way through the crowd. We snuck behind some rambunctious guards monitoring a private spiral stone staircase leading to one of the many balconies adorning the main courtyard.

I doubted the owner of this loft was home. He had a penchant for the brothel two streets over. It wasn't wise to trespass, but Octavia made me reckless. My mind wrestled with the thought for only a moment because she was still scratching at her neck and my only priority was calming her down.

When we reached the top, my ankle ached, and I sat her next to me on the stone bench overlooking Graygarde. "Can you see it? There are the exits. All of them. And I can take you through them at a moment's notice."

Her body was still shaking. Could she even hear me? Could she see the mountains in the distance, or the city below?

I pulled her hands from her neck, held them tight, and did the only thing I knew how to do. *Please show me how to help her.* I pleaded to the Goddess, and then I sang.

"One day I spoke to the raven
She told me to go find the crow
It was quite a one-sided conversation
Was this crow a friend or a foe?"

The spirits stroked her hair as I sang and some of them swirled in a bullseye pattern around the top of her sternum, in the center of her chest.

Sacred Ether. Sudden clarity washed over me like a soft morning mist, reverberating throughout my mind. They were showing me what to do, how to help soothe her.

"I searched near and far
My purpose to bring them together
I looked to the stars
Begging to find them a tether"

Her expression was still panicked, and she wheezed, her eyes glazed over with hot unshed tears. I rubbed the spot with my palm, creating gentle circles that followed the pattern of the bullseye.

Her eyes flicked to me, my singing and rubbing mercifully penetrating her anxiety. The spirits were never so direct, but they did seem to care deeply for Octavia. Or was that my intent being pushed into them?

"How could the raven befriend the crow?
I don't know… I don't know"

Wrapping around my knuckles, the spirits showed me to apply more pressure, but I could tell they were irritated with me. It wasn't exactly easy or familiar for me to be attempting so many forms of comfort at once.

I pressed firmly now, with no hesitation. She wasn't frail; she was the strongest woman I'd ever met. To go through what she had, see what she's seen, *feel* things as deeply as she did…

Her breathing slowed, and she gripped both hands tightly around my wrist.

"Octavia, it's your friend, Throwen." I kept my tone playful, as if this wasn't happening at all, and provided consistent eye contact to give her something else to hold on to. "You're here with me. We are in one of the *highest* balconies in Graygarde."

Her breathing was slogging its way toward a normal cadence, and her grip relaxed.

"I would love to show it to you when you're ready."

A small, exhausted smile spread across her lips, and her eyelids fluttered. "That's the song you sang on the mountain when I found you."

Joy pulsed through me, so powerful the spirits licked at both our fingers. *She remembered my song.* "I like to think I found you, but yes, that's the song I was singing."

"I'm sorry." Her words were music to my ears, even though her voice was raw from hyperventilating.

As her round chin trembled, I felt a strong sensation in my chest cavity I thought had hollowed out years ago. My heart rattled, and she shifted her body away. I wanted to continue caring for her, *cursed Abyss*. I would dote on this witch, support her and give her whatever she needed. I swallowed my pride and asked, "Sorry for what?"

She scowled at me. "For being a sensitive burden who can't control her mind or body. *Goddess's tits!* I had such tight control over this back at my coven. Maybe the lack of sleep and travel is just... it's harder to fight it when I'm stressed. Oh!"

She stood and made her way to the railing, her mask in pieces at her feet as she took in the entirety of Graygarde laid out before her.

The whooshing wind sent her dark hair flying. She twirled her fingers around the ivy that was wrapped around the cement railing. She almost had to stand on her toes, and I gave her a moment before I sauntered up beside her, resting my palms flush against the cool stone and ivy.

Silence lingered for a long moment and my mouth went dry. I had to help her out of this pit she'd fallen into because of me. I would never let her go through these struggles alone if I had any say in it. Her pain and sorrow tore me apart and helping her through it filled me with a new purpose. *She is becoming my purpose.*

"You don't have to apologize for things that are out of your control, darling," I said. "Friends don't pick and choose the pieces of each other that they like or even feel comfortable with. They embrace the discomfort, the fear, the anger. I accept and thoroughly enjoy your company, whether or not you are in control. Please don't hide parts of yourself away from me. I would much rather learn how to help and walk those shady paths with you."

Confusion knit her dark brows. Octavia did not know how to accept compliments, but I would teach her.

Her eyes called out to me as the light of the stars and hanging lamps reflected in them. Dark curls framed her face, and her lips were full. She bit on the bottom one and blood rushed through me, my arousal about to become known as I leaned in, inches from her lips.

"Hey! Who's out there?"

We jumped apart and my hand found hers; it was sweaty and trembling. "Think you can run?"

She narrowed her eyes and tapped her foot. "We aren't supposed to be up here, are we?"

Her glare promised retribution for my careless actions. She punched me lightly on the shoulder.

I rubbed the spot and smiled widely. "If we don't get caught, you get the first bath."

The challenge summoned a spark within her eyes.

"Ye *fucking* kids!" A gust of strong wind reached us and a large woman with a thick Luftor accent waddled towards us with a large cast-iron skillet. "Take your tryst somewhere else or next time it won't just be air shooting at yer thick skulls!"

"Run!" Hand in hand, I pulled her with me back down the long spiraling stairs and we laughed like youths enjoying a bit of trespassing and getting thoroughly dizzy.

I missed this feeling.

She made me feel alive again. Like the world had new experiences for me as long as she stayed by my side. I would hold her when she was wrapped in shadows, and she would be my illumination in a world that had turned gray.

"HERE WE ARE." I dismounted and secured Lucky to the post outside the shop. "This is Enoch's place."

We were all hungry and tired, but Octavia needed clothes for tonight. I would not force her to stay in our room in my oversized shirt, though she looked adorable in it.

Octavia snorted and pointed at the sign above the store with a large button next to the name, *And Sew It Begins*. "And what, precisely, am I looking for?"

"Don't worry, Enoch will know exactly what you need. He's the best." I led her through the bright violet door that matched the button on the sign. A loud ding rang out from the bell above the door. Octavia gasped.

The small shop was covered floor to ceiling with smooth stone shelves. Red silk flowed into orange and yellow, a rainbow of finery.

"I'll be with you in a moment!" a raspy voice called out from somewhere in the back.

I locked the door behind us and discreetly flipped the open sign to closed. To Octavia, I said, "Make sure whatever you pick hides your mark well."

She nodded in agreement, checking to make sure her hood was drawn tight.

"Throwen. How delightful to see you." Enoch raised his thick-lensed goggles atop his brown hair. He was a tall, lanky man, and he had to lean down to wrap me in a hug.

He wore a pair of puffy salmon overalls with a brown shirt underneath. Across his chest was a belt of threads and buttons, organized by color with red at his shoulder and purple at his hip. Enoch had become a close confidant over the years.

Octavia shifted behind me as he grabbed me by the shoulders, scrunching his nose in disgust. "What the fuck are you wearing?"

I stared down at my mundane Ozurian fashion. "These are on loan from Nova."

Enoch rolled his eyes. "That witch wouldn't know fashion if it bit her in the ass."

He pushed me aside, stepping up to Octavia, who stood stiff as a board. "This won't do at all. Your gorgeous olive skin is hiding beneath this oversized bag." The backhanded compliments were sprinkled in effortlessly and sincerely.

He pulled out measuring tape from the front pocket of his overalls. "May I?"

"Of course." Octavia held her arms out wide.

Enoch moved around to her back, taking her measurements.

"We don't have time for dress-up today, Enoch. I need to perform tonight." I stepped back and Enoch straightened, taking his final measurements of Octavia's bust.

Enoch pouted. "For a theatrical bard, you are the biggest creative cock-block I've ever met."

"Enoch is the most sought-after fashion designer in Theldea," I clarified for Octavia and bowed low before him.

"Flattery will get you nowhere, Angel." Enoch chastised with a smirk.

"Oh, you love praise just as much as me." I winked, and he spun on his heels, waving a hand for us to follow.

Octavia let out a small sigh of relief and bounced on her toes. She tapped my chest, and I bent down as she whispered, "I've never picked my own clothes before."

The information was bittersweet, and her eyes lit up when he pointed to a row of flashy dresses in every color and style imaginable. Enoch pointed to a row of navy curtains.

"Your size is over here. Take your time. When you find one you want to try on, the alcove is just over there."

"Thank you." She moved hesitantly, brushing her fingers gently along the different fabrics lining the walls.

"And I suppose you want the usual?" Enoch's frown looked like it was painted on as he tapped his foot at me.

"Please and thank you." I offered my award-winning smile and Enoch lifted his eyebrow.

"Just over there." He turned and disappeared to the back.

I stretched my torso, eliciting a series of cracks down my spine, and swiftly grabbed a pile of my usual performance attire. Casually, I pretended to peruse a different section so I could discreetly observe Octavia from behind some shelves.

She was like a squirrel hiding nuts for the winter, twisting and turning without a real pattern. I could tell she was overwhelmed, but this was nothing like her panic attack. The smile on her face was radiant, even in the dim light.

Pausing in the middle of the section, she pressed that *Goddess-damned* finger to her nose and spun slowly in a circle. She scowled at the clothing, no doubt berating it for overwhelming her.

An abrupt laugh left me, and her posture went stiff. She whipped her head around, now aiming that scowl at me.

Flipping around, I pretended to be looking for — oh, great — leather underwear. *Nice,* Enoch.

A chuckle sounded behind me, but I was too embarrassed to turn around, even for one of Octavia's laughs. My cheeks continued to heat, and I ran my fingers over the stubble growing over my head.

Her footsteps tapped about and my legs felt weak. This witch was consuming me, and it felt like I had no control. Giving up, I glanced back over my shoulder. She was grabbing items with determination.

She hustled into an alcove on the far wall and pulled the curtain shut. I listened as she shed her layers and my heart rate picked up, blood flowing to places that would be extremely inconvenient right now.

Her pants dropped to the floor, and it sent my head spinning. Dainty feet kicked her other clothing aside, and I envisioned rubbing away the aches in her arches and tiny toes.

After a lot of shuffling, the curtain swished open, and time stopped around me. I moved out from the row of shelves to face her, taking slow steps that I had no control over. All I knew was that I had to get closer to her.

Nothing could have prepared me for her emergence. My jaw dropped and my cock started throbbing.

A plum piece of fabric was wrapped around her neck multiple times before leaving a short tail trailing down her back. The perfect accent to hide her secrets—*our* secrets. I curled my hands into fists at my sides, wishing I could wrap them around that scarf and pull it tight until she begged for more.

"Well?" She bent nervously, smoothing the lightweight lavender material that cascaded down just below her knees. As she bent, the plunging neckline gave me a perfect view of the inner curves of her breasts.

"It's... um..." I struggled to use my words, and she stood up straight, resting a fist on her hips.

Her annoyance drew my attention to the bodice of the piece. Daring cutouts revealed the delicious skin of her hips and abdomen, wrapping all around her lower back. They were connected through rings of varying sizes, creating a hypnotic pattern I couldn't tear my eyes from. A tempting ellipse of exposed skin I wanted to trace with my finger, lick with my tongue.

"See something you like?" The sly look she gave me as she repeated my words back to me was unbearable.

Divine, salacious, ravishing, ethereal. I wanted to say all those things to her and let her know how beautiful she was, but none of the words were good enough. She deserved for me to worship at her feet and worship the rest of her body, too.

Fantasies of her twirling and dancing to my music in the tavern filled me with anticipation. It was the perfect dress for dancing.

Her playful demeanor switched in the blink of an eye and her face fell, her momentary comfort and confidence evaporating. She hunched, trying to make herself small. "What? Will I not blend in? This is what most of them looked like."

There will be none of that.

I strode toward her, blatantly analyzing the outfit. My eyes dragged up and down her body. Her cheeks flushed a delicious shade of red that I wanted to sip like a sweet wine.

"You are flawless." It still wasn't enough, but it was the best this affixed bard could come up with. She tucked a curl behind her ear, but I knew it would soon spring free again. They never stayed put.

"Nobody is flawless." There was an inkling of challenge in her voice and *Goddess forgive me*, I loved a good challenge.

There were only a few feet between us, and I looked hungrily at her bare shoulders, admiring the sultry straps that mimicked her cold-shoulder style. This witch did not know of the control she held over me.

Hesitating, I took a step back. A tense silence built between us, and I shoved my hands into my pockets.

I never wanted to be tied down. I enjoyed the spontaneity being a wanderer gave me. My family was my everything, but I didn't want them with me daily. But for her... I could see myself making her my home.

These emotions were too strange and new. I wanted to tell her how I felt. That I wanted more. But she was traumatized and trying to figure out who she was, what she wanted, what she believed.

I had moved forward like a moth to a flame and took her hands in mine. It was all a blur; I was so captivated by her I wanted to give her every ounce of attention I had. But she also made me leave my guard down and in my profession that was a death sentence.

Octavia's eyebrows drew together, worry lines appearing on her forehead. "Throwen, are you okay?"

"Fabulous! I'll make a few quick adjustments," Enoch said, and I gasped, taking a step away. Her usual frown fell back into place. Enoch thrust two bags into my arms and unlatched the purple thread from his belt. "To-go bags for you and the lady."

He lowered to his knees and sewed around the hem of the skirt. "So, you assist Throwen in his duties?"

Octavia cleared her throat. "Yes."

"Come back and I'll collaborate with the jeweler to get you a poisoned hairpin. Very convenient if you're assassinating a corrupt official. I recommend starting with Mayson, but don't tell anyone I said that."

I pressed my lips together to avoid smiling, but Octavia's open-mouthed grin and raised eyebrows were electrifying. I shook my head. "Thank you, Enoch. But we were never here."

Enoch froze at my hard tone. I crossed my arms, clicking my picks gently together. It was by far my favorite and most effective intimidation tactic.

He peered over his shoulder with fear in his eyes. "Of course, Throwen."

"Good."

Octavia glared at me, and I shrugged. I wasn't being mean. I was ensuring our safety.

Enoch cut the final thread then stood on knobby knees.

"It was lovely to meet you, Enoch. Your work is inspiring." Octavia shook his hand.

"A pleasure my dear." He pointed a sewing needle held between his fingers at her. "But next time, I *will* have the perfect piece for you."

"Thank you, Enoch. We have to get going." I handed Enoch a pouch of coins, and he shooed us toward the door.

"Yes, get out, I have a lot of work to do." Enoch winked at Octavia and enveloped her in an unexpected hug.

"Let's go, I need to get ready to perform." I moved passed her to the door, and as our hands touched, energy shot through my body like a ball of fire.

My heart barely beat at all unless I was experiencing something new and now this witch had it beating as if it had never truly beat before.

"Won't performing bring more attention to us?" Octavia scurried behind to keep up with my agitated steps. I snuck a look back to catch another glimpse.

"Oof!" I stumbled straight into Lucky, and I fought back a groan, grabbing onto her reins.

Fuck! I couldn't keep my eyes off her.

"It's the only way we are getting enough clothes and food to get us to Goldhaven." My voice was harsh. "I have to perform."

She didn't say another word and a pang of guilt pierced my heart for being so short with her, but my rapidly growing feelings weren't safe for either of us. So I said, "Don't worry, you'll be safe. You're just my friend and I'm helping you get to Goldhaven."

Her expression soured further. "Right."

Padding beside me, she analyzed the architecture and people. In the silence, we navigated the narrow, winding streets to the tavern with ease.

"Which songs are you going to sing?" she asked, cooing to Lucky and patting her mane.

"You'll have to wait and see." I elbowed her gently in the arm and she staggered into Lucky who snorted in response.

"I don't like surprises," she said dryly.

I linked my arm through hers, pulling her just an inch closer, keeping her far enough away that I wouldn't let her body heat incinerate any rational thought I had left. "Maybe it was never the right kind of surprise."

"Maybe..." She fought a smile, but I caught the slight twitch at the corner of her mouth. *There you are, darling.* I vowed to coax that smile out of her tonight, to help her be here with me and nowhere else.

Chapter 15

OCTAVIA

Ale and smoke filled my nostrils as I looked at the tavern thriving below us. Music lifted up through the air to our room on the fourth level of the building, and I leaned over the railing outside our room to get a better look at the bright, orange glow below.

"Shall we?" Throwen's voice pulled me back to our door, the only empty room the tavern had left. It was small, and clearly meant for one witch. I swallowed, wiping my sweaty palms on my new dress, and turned toward Throwen as he locked the door. We had both bathed and I kept forgetting that he no longer looked disheveled like he had the entire trip.

His maroon-fitted shirt hugged his muscular arms and torso. He had a cape clasped to his lapels that draped around him. On any other witch it would appear over the top, but he pulled it off. A tight pair of black pants hung on his hips with a dark brown belt keeping the shirt tucked in. Two gold earrings hung in his left ear that were reminiscent of the metal used in his picks. He'd shaved, leaving behind a dark mustache that ended right on the corners of his lips, accentuating his flirtatious smile.

"We shall." An odd combination of hesitation and giddiness flooded my body; it wanted to flee and break into a dance simultaneously.

"Are you ready for some fun, darling?" Throwen bowed low, his pale skin poking through his closely cropped hair. He offered his arm.

"Yes." I took it, welcoming his warmth and unable to take my eyes off him. An ache pulsed through all the places I wanted him to touch me.

Sacred Ether. He exuded charm, and I was extremely horny or, even worse, feeling things I had no right to feel. More than just lust, a deeper connection that I was afraid to look at.

I focused on my feet as we walked down the several flights of stairs, making sure I didn't embarrass myself before the night even started. Once we reached the bottom, I looked up and my jaw dropped at the sight of the tavern.

The bottom of the steps were situated beside the bar where patrons shouted out their orders. It was more spacious than I had expected, with sporadic tables surrounding a pit of musicians. Fire flickered from glass orbs placed atop fancy stone sconces. Boisterous witches sang, gambled, and chatted.

At the tables closest to us, sat a group of witches wearing fitted white pants with a matching white top, sleeves flaring before buttoning tightly around their wrists. Thick navy sashes draped over their shoulders littered with differing amounts of gold pins that had to be a sign of rank. They appeared pompous like the scouts back home, except in a dapper way.

"Throwen. A word." A witch called out, untying her apron, and tossing it to one of the other witches working behind the bar. A ropey blush dress clung to her generous hips. Her lipstick matched the dress, and it created a fabulous focal point against her dark skin.

"That's Harlin, the owner." Throwen patted my hand and unwound our arms. "You can go to that alcove there." He pointed to the opposite corner of the tavern. The thought of a long walk through a crowd of Theldeans made my skin crawl. Throwen gripped my scarf, and I gasped. He tightened it slightly around my neck and pulled me away from my fears. "Keep this on. For now."

I bit my lip and nodded. Taking a deep breath, I put one foot in front of the other. I focused on the group of witches I passed. Compared to the fancy witches, they were more involved in the music and dancing, not caring what they looked like in front of others. I supposed without the burden of high status, they had a freedom not allotted to those constantly saving face.

I settled into one of the alcoves, sliding across the plush seat. There was a dark curtain I could hide behind if I wished. I imagined Throwen drawing it closed and pressing me flat against the mirrored wall surrounding the alcove.

When I looked back across the tavern, his conversation with Harlin looked more like an argument. Harlin's arms were crossed, her hip popped to the side, a sour frown on her lips. A young witch hurried to clean up a spill near them and Throwen shook Harlin's hand.

She returned to the bar, hopped on top, and magnified her voice. "The charming bard, Throwen, has graced us with his presence tonight! Tell yer friends!"

The witches hooted, raising their glasses. A few rushed out the door, calling out to their friends. I laughed, understanding how his confidence could grow from such praise.

Throwen leaned against the bar, speaking to a barmaid. She smiled brightly up at him, and my stomach sank. I envied the witch's ability to give her smiles away so freely. Throwen deserved the smiles he invoked.

A moment later, she handed him a mug of ale, and he turned, strutting toward me. "First song." He placed the mug in front of me. "Wish me luck."

He kissed the top of my head, and butterflies erupted in my stomach as he rushed to the recessed circle in the middle of the room.

The other musicians nodded with huge smiles as Throwen spoke. He quickly tuned his lute, and they began a jaunty piece, my foot already tapping to the beat.

Couples took to the floor, dancing wild and free. I followed their steps, and their subtle glances at each other's lips. How many nights had I dreamt of something like this?

Sighing deeply, I forced myself to face the mirrors lining the alcove. To my surprise, I didn't balk at my reflection and I was thankful that Enoch included makeup in my bag. My kohl-lined eyes were enlivened and my plum-painted lips weren't arched into their usual frown, but a straight line.

Slap!

I flinched at the ghost of Malik's slap across my ten-year-old cheek. He found me laughing and painting on fake lipstick made from berries with my friend Rachel in the greenhouse when we should have been tending to the vegetables. She was chosen the next week to fight for her life at our ceremony. Her death was delivered in less than a minute.

You will wear the makeup I provide for you when it's provided. You aren't some Theldean whore.

The mirror cracked and red smoke slithered from the fresh openings in the wall, burrowing in through my mouth and eyes. I forced them both shut.

Nope. Not now. Not in front of all these witches. *Goddess's tits! Keep your shit together!*

I opened my eyes and took a deep swig of fruity ale, letting it wash away the vision in one burning gulp.

The fast-paced instruments crescendoed and came to an abrupt halt. Witches cheered, clinking their mugs together. I clapped, but I much preferred hearing Throwen's voice with the music.

The song he used to calm me mere hours ago, The Raven and The Crow started and I relaxed my shoulders. It was a lovely tale of unlikely friends finding each other after eons of searching. I could relate to that raven. I had only known Throwen for a short time and I felt like my soul had been searching for a friend like him my whole life.

He was so alluring, I couldn't look away, his cape gliding along with his movements. Throwen gently sashayed around the other musicians and used his magic, allowing the spirits to delicately dance around as he played. More witches poured through the door. Compared to our nights alone, the spirits were hushed here, moving just enough to keep the viewer's attention.

His shifts from baritone to tenor worked their way around my body like a long gentle caress, and I shook my head, realizing I had been staring. I diverted my attention back to the tavern as if it would make penance for my less-than-sacred thoughts.

I looked longingly at the couples dancing, wishing I had the courage to join them. Harlin's long, black braids swayed back and forth with her languid movements as she filled another tray and worked her way around the room with a sultry smile. She batted her eyelashes at every customer.

Stomping over to where I sat, she glared at me, and tossed a bowl of stew on the table with some rolls and butter. "From Throwen."

I took another deep swig of ale to ease the discomfort of being around so many rowdy Theldeans. I coughed; the ale was overly sweet, but it did its job.

Feeling a slight buzz, I dug into the stew. Maybe food would comfort me while Throwen was busy. The hot potatoes and carrots mixed with the soft seasoned beef, and the moan that ripped free was carnal. *Sacred Ether*, I missed hot food.

As I chewed, the tender meat fell apart in my mouth. Tones of garlic, onion, and wine mixed into an intoxicating combination. My eyelids felt slightly heavier, and I was more satiated than before.

A small black cat trotted over happily, lapping up the previous patron's spilled ale near my feet. I rubbed her ears, and she nuzzled into my caress, purring loudly. "I bet you're a great little hunter, aren't you?"

Animals were always easier to connect with than witches, and it would be fine by me if she were my only companion tonight. I dreaded the inevitable interaction I would likely have with one or more of these other Theldeans.

The song faded, and everyone clapped as the musicians bowed. Thrown spoke with the witch playing the harp and she twirled her blonde hair around a finger. She nodded profusely.

My jaw tightened and Thrown started walking toward me.

Three witches stumbled in front of Thrown who elegantly maneuvered around them. He was in his element here, just as much as when he was battling for our lives. A jack of all trades so comfortable in his skin that he could blend everywhere, stand out anywhere. It was *his* choice, and he was in total control.

"I see you're making friends." He gestured to the cat, who had jumped up onto my lap for a nap.

"Cats are better than witches." I scratched the cat's ears and lost my breath as my gaze collided with Thrown's.

He smiled wickedly. "Vixen."

I choked on my sip of ale. I squinted up at him towering over me and used the back of my hand to dab my mouth where some ale had dribbled out, hoping not to smear my lipstick. "Excuse me?"

He laughed and pointed at my lap. "Her name is Vixen. Harlin keeps her around to catch the rats."

"I knew it. You're fierce, aren't you?" I rubbed the soft bridge of her pink nose. She purred and snored despite the noise of the crowded room.

When I looked back up, Thrown had moved closer, the scent of burned matches wrapping me in their comforting arms. He mercifully moved to the other side of the alcove, drawing the curtains slightly to block out the sound. "So, what do you think?"

"I think you have quite a lot of admirers for being a big, scary assassin." I giggled and took another sip.

Thrown cracked his knuckles. "I have a no-violence indoors policy with all the taverns." He tilted his head to the side. "I meant the music. What do you think of the music?"

"You *mean* what do I think of you? Are you always so annoyingly charming?" I took a large bite of the roll that I had smothered in butter and raised my eyebrows in challenge. The ale was doing its job, and social interactions were becoming much less painful.

He leaned forward, placing his arms on the table. "Do you always think in contradictions?"

"Yes." Smirking, I took another bite of stew.

"You're drunk." He laughed, and I joined in.

My cheeks heated and warmth spread through my limbs. "Only a little."

"I'm thrilled you're having fun, but we do still have to be alert, just in case." He took away my empty mug and raised his hand, a small flame on the tip of his finger. A server rushed over and took the empty mug. "Water please, thank you."

I didn't argue. My stomach had been starved and now I was stuffing it with way too much. I was a little lightheaded, too. I squinted at the blonde harpist, who was craning her neck to get a peek through the small opening in our alcove.

"She wants to fuck you." I played an invisible harp for Throwen.

"No. She doesn't. She just thinks she does." His serious tone took me by surprise.

"How can you tell the difference?" I licked my spoon clean and swished it around with my questions. "Is there a difference?"

"Time to go." He exited the alcove quickly.

I called out after him, "Do you always use spontaneity to avoid expressing difficult feelings?"

He laughed a full belly laugh at my taunt and strummed his lute. "Yes!"

Throwing his arms wide, he announced his next song. "This next one's for whoever you call darling!"

He strode up to some crates that were stacked around the rest of the band. Witches hooted and hollered. This was clearly a crowd-pleaser. My pulse quickened. *Is this song for me?*

The music came quick and fast, and Throwen whipped around, leaning his shoulder low before walking around the recessed space in a slow circle.

> *"My lover wanted painted*
> *I was happy to pay the fee*
> *With her tits I was well acquainted*
> *T'would be a sin not to let others see!"*

His gruff voice hollered the last line, and the crowd cheered wildly. *Right then… this song is not meant for me.*

Bobbing his head from one patron to the next, he sang, being sure to lure them all into what was sure to be a lewd tavern song. Rubbing the back of my hand across my mouth, I suppressed the smile forming. I *loved* a good smutty story sprinkled with humor.

> *"He met her up in the attic*
> *The lighting was better, of course*
> *Their private session was very… climactic*
> *Their voices becoming quite hoarse"*

Hopping up to where witches were eating and gambling, he smashed the invisible barrier between dancers and squatters.

The tables were filled with young, well-dressed witches. Throwen swayed in a circular motion, drawing out their laughs and reluctant participation. Some witches swooned at his nearness, and I didn't blame them.

"I may not have been the smartest
My sweet darling loved me so
Until she met... the artist"

Playful booing sounded throughout the tavern, before he finished the chorus.

"To my heart she dealt the death blow"

Holding his heart in feigned pain, his mouth opened wide to cry out his song. He stepped up onto a bench and then right onto the table, closer to me than before. The rest of the tavern joined in, singing along.

"The painting took longer than predicted
Darling's beauty required days to convey
My access to the attic was restricted
For the surprise I was bid keep away"

His heated stare pierced through me right as a witch delivered a bowl of fresh red chocolate-covered strawberries to my table.

"From the bard." She clicked her tongue before she trotted off.

I returned my attention to Throwen's extravagant performance. With a wink, he jumped high, landing on the ground in a crouch and slowly rising with the music as it crescendoed.

"With the endless waiting of days
My curiosity finally took hold
I ascended to the attic in a craze
Upon entering my heart had turned cold"

The band played as one, and Throwen raced back to them as the chorus repeated. He twirled in a circle, his cape billowing out around him, and the instruments stopped, his phony sorrowful voice the only sound. The crowd grew quiet, listening.

"Red handprints littered her body
The painter's hands red, too
His masterpiece unfinished and shoddy..."

He ran, placing his foot up onto a crate and leaning into a sexy deep lunge, strumming his lute so hard I feared the strings would break. My heart slammed its fists against my chest. Lifting his chin to the ceiling, he sang out.

"Now his eyes are black and blue!"

With a final strum, all music stopped, and the tavern erupted into applause and laughter. Everyone was standing, including me.

The cheers continued, and I admired Throwen, panting to catch his breath. He was a phenomenal performer, and his hat was filled with coins of happy patrons.

This was it. The freedom I'd been craving. Life didn't always need to be sunshine and rainbows, but without moments of light, the dark would consume me. That's what had run dry in my coven. There were no more brief respites of light moments left.

Throwen held up a finger, showing he wanted to play one more song. I gave him an awkward thumbs up, lowering back into my alcove.

Another song started, one of the other bards singing about a brothel and some incident with getting kicked in the head by a horse. I let it fade into the background and I indulged in the strawberries.

Rich chocolate mixed with the sweet fruit and a memory pricked me suddenly like a bee sting. *He remembered the strawberries.*

I paused with the green leaves of strawberry number two pinched between my fingers. I didn't have to see him to feel his boiling gaze.

With a deep breath and a last burst of confidence from my rapidly fading buzz, I lifted my chin to where he played. He was sitting behind a singing tambourine player, making sure not to bring any unwanted attention to himself, silently observing me.

Legs spread open, lute across his lap; he blocked my view of his cock. But I was almost certain I knew what was happening underneath its infuriating cover.

I hesitated, holding the berry so it grazed my lips. Something palpable filled his cavernous eyes, a challenge, a demand. His muscles tensed and he strummed some deep chords.

Without breaking eye contact, I wrapped my lips slowly around the strawberry, not caring if it messed up my dark lipstick. His strumming didn't falter, but it did grow louder.

Heat pulled at my core like sweet forbidden honey, and I crossed my legs, pressing, needing friction. Throwen's lips parted, and his tongue darted across his bottom lip.

"Is this seat taken?" I was startled and a large witch with tattoos peeking from his finely tailored collar helped himself to a seat across from me. Quickly covering my mouth, I finished the bite of strawberry.

"Um, my friend is sitting there." Wrapping my fingers around the scarf at my neck, I made sure it was tied tightly. It felt like a noose under his sleazy gaze.

"Haven't seen ye here before."

The music continued, and a group of witches moved to obstruct my view of Throwen. It felt as if a strawberry had gotten lodged in my throat but it was only fear.

"I'm traveling." I filled my tone with disdain, hoping he would catch onto my complete lack of interest without causing a scene.

"Where would a pretty girl like ye be traveling to?" *Pretty girl? Who the fuck did this witch think he was?*

This time I couldn't control my anger, and I didn't want to. "That's none of your—"

His white-sleeved arm reached across the table. With his other tanned hand, he yanked the curtains closed.

"Yer a fighter, I *like* that," he said as he grabbed onto my wrists.

I conjured flames in my palms. This was the depravity Malik wanted to protect us from. This Theldean scum would regret ever laying his eyes on me. Satisfying sizzles accompanied his screams. I drew my dagger from my thigh, raising it to stab right through his entitled scummy hand.

He bared his teeth, and his nostrils flared. "Fucking tease!"

The music stopped abruptly, and gasps echoed outside the alcove. Purple tendrils slipped through the curtain, winding up the witch's arm like the ivy covering the architecture of this place. It coiled around his thick neck, covering the tattoos, and his chest heaved.

The curtain flung open, Throwen's eyes a shade so deep, it almost looked black. He grabbed the witch's blistering wrist, slamming it to the table where the spirits held it in place.

"I should take your hand for that." Throwen gripped harder.

"So much for not shitting where ye eat, bard!" The witch spit at Throwen.

Breathing deeply, a pure calm overtook him and his lips slowly curved up before he pulled a knife from his belt and chopped the witch's finger off.

The witch screamed and tried to pull his hand up to cradle the bleeding mess, but the spirits held it tightly in place despite his thrashing. Some sick part of me enjoyed watching the blood pour over the table, spreading across the smooth stone.

"What the fuck?!" The witch's face went pale.

Throwen growled in response, lifting his blade to take the whole hand. The spirits wrapped tighter around the witch's throat.

The sound of Elenor's neck snapping from the pressure of Malik's whip flooded my senses. I shot out of my seat. "Throwen, wait!"

We were going too far. Malik's hatred for Theldeans was laced into my mind, but I refused to let it win. Throwen leaned over the table, ready to annihilate this witch for disrespecting me, but he wouldn't become a monster on my behalf. That wasn't him, and he wasn't thinking clearly. If we drew too much attention, Malik would hear about it and be able to track us.

I spoke softly and pressed my palm gently to Throwen's chest, "I'm safe. Let him go. It was a mistake. *Right?*" I looked at the pig across from me. He needed to know I was the one who spared his life and this would be my final mercy.

"Yes!" the witch said, his neck turning purple.

Sheathing my dagger slowly, I leaned back in my seat. The witch continued to bleed all over the table. *Goddess* Throwen took it all the way down to the knuckle, a precise cut.

"Hey!" Harlin pushed her way through the crowd that the commotion had drawn. They were disgustingly eager to see the Angel of Death show his face.

He reluctantly let the witch go and the spirits vanished all at once.

"We're going to bed. Let's go." He guided me to the center of the room, where he collected the coins that had accumulated in his leather hat. The crowd dispersed, and we ascended the stairs when Harlin grabbed Throwen's forearm.

Heat gushed over my body, and I conjured a small ball of fire in my palm. *Is this what Throwen felt?*

"I told ye she was trouble. Don't ruin yer reputation for *her*. She isn't worth it."

Her words might as well have been a slap across my face. But she was right. I brought Throwen much more trouble than I was worth. *Worthless.* It used to be a painful thought, but now I simply wore it like a hermit's shell.

Throwen took a steadying breath. "Harlin, I would throw away my reputation and *much more* for her. Slander her again and I swear to the Goddess I will never play in your place of business again. And in a few years, when word spreads, I will write a song about the poor bankrupt *barmaid* who made the grave mistake of insulting my lady."

His lady? Never before had the word brought warmth to my chest.

"Yer burning bridges, Throwen," Harlin spat. "Don't come crying to me when ye get burned by the flames. I want ye both out by sunrise!"

Throwen stomped up the steps, and I rushed to keep up with his long strides. The words he used to defend me circled my skull like rapidly growing brambles. If I got too close to them, the thorns would rip into my skin, leaving inevitable pain and sorrow.

Dread sat like lead in the pit of my stomach. I had no idea how to deal with a truly unhinged Throwen. He was usually so carefree and bright.

When this specific shade of darkness fell over him, I wasn't sure how to help. Did he need me to listen? To be a distraction?

I could think of a fun way to be distracting. The desires his possessiveness brought out in me were unmatched. No witch had ever defended me before, and it made my toes curl.

Somehow, the idea of staying in a room with a door together was much more intimate than sleeping in a cave. My mind raced as we walked over the threshold.

Chapter 16

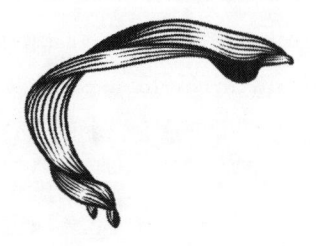

OCTAVIA

Thrown placed his hat and lute by his pack and ran shaking fingers through his freshly cropped hair. He roughly kicked his boots off and paced back and forth between the small window on the far wall and the bathroom door on the right.

I stood flush against the closed door, waiting for him to unleash his thoughts and feelings. But they never came.

"Are you okay?"

"Yes. I just need..." He ran his hand down his face. "*Fuck*, I don't know what I need."

I was grateful for when he would distract me; the least I could do was provide one for him, so I asked, "Why aren't they as perky when you perform?"

He dropped his fists to his sides, lifting his chin to look at me. "What?"

"The spirits, they didn't act like they did in the caves." I shrugged, pleased that the distressed wrinkles that had formed between his brows relaxed. They were begging me to rub the frustration away with the pad of my thumb.

"I think they might find offense to *perky* as a quality." He chuckled.

"Okay..." I bit my lip. "More hushed or muted?"

"I ask them to keep a low profile when we perform. It builds anticipation, and people want to keep watching without being afraid they'll be targeted."

"Is that what Harlin meant? About me ruining your reputation?" I fidgeted with the hem of my dress, wishing I could shed it for one of the comfortable shirts that smelled like him.

"You haven't ruined anything. I took one finger, not his life." He swallowed hard. "My instincts got the better of me."

"I honestly didn't mind. I wanted to get out of there, anyway. You may be a social butterfly, but I'm more the hibernate-in-my-room-until-I'm-forced-out type."

He took a step closer, placing a hand on the door above me. I swallowed at the look in his eye—shades of different purple fighting for dominance. My instinct was to step back, but I had nowhere to go, my back still against the door.

"When you're with me, there's no hiding," he said, his tone low and strained.

Not hiding from him was both exhilarating and terrifying. I ducked out under his arm, plopping onto the bed. My legs dangled from the side, too short to reach the floor.

"If everyone knows what you're capable of, why do they still come to see you play? They loved you, Throwen."

He sighed, defeat lacing his posture. "Not killing in taverns is a pain in the ass. Sometimes I wait days for my target to come out or I have to track them when they bolt mid-performance."

He grabbed his lute, strumming softly. "I have been gifted with the burden of being skilled at both healing and hurting with my magic. When they come to the taverns, they know I offer healing. To them, I'm *Throwen: the funny, charming bard.*" He twirled for emphasis.

"I help them work through grief, forget their troubles, just something to hear other than their own thoughts." His eyes met mine. That was what he'd done for me our entire journey. He was helping me heal.

That *Goddess-damned* smolder fell over his face, "They're at ease in this environment with me. I never mix assignments with performing and everyone knows it. Taverns are a safe place. Well... not *safe*. There's no better place to get intel than from a bunch of inebriated witches."

"And if these same witches you heal and help encounter the Angel of Death?" I tilted my head, my scarf tickling my arm.

"Then they know their fate." His veins protruded as he strummed, and softly sang along with a high-pitched tune.

"Have you ever been
Two sides of the same coin?
Imagine if you can
That they joined"

The dam I worked so hard to build around my heart punctured with the lyrics. A wound buried so deep I would never let it see the light of day. We both led two lives.

He was the bard when he wanted to be, and the Angel of Death when he had no other choice. In this, we were the same, except I no longer had a grasp on who Octavia was. I had been forced to be The Lady of the Grave for so long, Octavia had gotten lost in the transition.

If anyone addresses you as Octavia, they will be punished.

I stared vacantly at a sky-blue rug on the stone floor beside the bed. It reminded me of the one from my room that I vomited all over. That's how all my memories of my coven played out now. Things I thought normal and beautiful were tarnished by Malik's cruelties coming to light.

"What say ye to a trade?" Thrown drew my attention back with a convincing Luftor accent.

His posture shifted into something more laid-back, and he smiled. He let go of his anger and turmoil like it was dust in the wind. I once again wished I possessed his honed emotional regulation. The way I held onto the hot coals of my emotions with tight fists always ended in inevitable festering burns.

I kicked my feet lightly against the side of the bed. "What kind of a trade?"

"A song for a dance."

"Excuse me?"

"You serenade me, and I'll dance with you," he said. "I took away your chance downstairs and I would hate to rob you of that because I couldn't control my temper."

I put my palms flat on the bed and leaned back, cool and confident. "How do you know if I even want to dance?"

"When you watched those other witches let go down there, you had hunger in your eyes. You want to be wild and free, darling. *I see you.*"

Fuck. Me. I exhaled slowly. It both infuriated and delighted me that he could see me, even if I didn't know myself.

"I-I can't sing." I couldn't even remember the last time I sang. We did a lot of chanting in the coven, but it was thoughtless.

He picked his lute; the notes coming at a rapid pace, his fingers gliding around the neck, bending the strings to his will.

"I'm quite the skilled dancer." As he played, I bit my lip, his hips swaying like a hypnotic pendulum. "It would be the best part of your night, hidden away like you prefer. Just one little song."

An ache formed between my thighs; he was too fucking enticing. With a sigh that could only mean reluctant compromise, I kicked off my flats and situated myself against the headboard, fluffy pillows the color of thistles behind my back. They felt heavenly as they swallowed me up and I folded my legs, holding onto my ankles.

"Do you know 'The Siren and the Sea?'" I pointed beside me.

He joined me on the bed, sitting at the foot of it and mimicking my posture. With a widening smile, he tested out different chords. In no time at all, he found the right ones.

"Is this a good key?" The golden picks plucked the chorus in an alto's range, and I nodded. His expression was aglow with expectations I knew my awful singing would never fulfill.

But he was right, I wanted that dance with him. My mouth dried out, remembering his heated stare when I enjoyed the gift of his strawberries. I coughed and timidly began, wanting to get this over with.

"The sea she has her secrets
The siren does as well
The captain he was heedless
Falling deeper to her spell"

Taking another deep breath, I focused on a thread that hung from the hem of my dress. I wrapped it around my finger languidly to the beat of the song.

"He sailed to the darkest oceans
Hoping he would find
The one to drink his potion
His love was truly blind"

Throwen continued playing, matching my cadence and flow perfectly. I looked everywhere but at his face, my voice low and shaky. Joining him in his music, his passion, connected us somehow pulling us closer together than we were before.

> "Be careful what you wish for
> Not all that glitters is gold
> The one you most adore
> Is the one who holds control"

I sang with unshed emotions I had bottled up long ago. I wanted to share them with Throwen, even if I couldn't exactly identify what it was I was truly feeling.

> "The siren he did locate
> He thought he'd finally be whole
> His delusions made him her mate
> She already had his soul"

My stupid throat fought not to close up, but I pressed on, determined to *earn* that dance with him. I ripped the loose strand completely free from the dress, reaching out to let it fall to the rug below.

> "He reached out to touch her
> She reached for him as well
> Her last sound a sweet purr
> He'd meet her where she dwells"

A heavy weight was upon my chest, a sinking feeling pulling me lower. Tears threatened to fall, but I bit them back. I vowed I would shed no more tears for her.

I took a steadying deep breath and lifted my chin, signaling Throwen to finish the final chorus.

"Be careful what you wish for
Not all that glitters is gold
The one you most adore
Is the one who holds control"

Throwen strummed the final chord, and then tossed his lute to the cushioned bench at the foot of the bed. "*That.* Was hauntingly beautiful."

He removed his cape and unbuttoned the top buttons of his shirt, rolling out his neck as if the fancy clothes bothered him more than he let on.

"We don't have to dance," I said, trying to ignore my bleeding heart. "We should change and figure out sleeping arrangements."

He ignored my excuses and bowed low, offering his hand for our dance. "Octavia, I have been waiting to dance with you all night. I'm just ashamed I acted like an asshole. I want to see what that little dress you picked can do."

A lifeless giggle escaped me, and I sniffed back the tears I refused to let fall.

His fingers called to me in a 'come here' motion. As my hand landed in his, I was struck with the comfort and familiarity that had formed between us. He was warm and safe. It gave me the courage I needed to follow through with this deal.

"Have you ever danced before?" His eyes were saucers of empathetic lavender, heart-wrenching. I laughed, and his concern melted away.

"Yes, I danced. It wasn't *all* bad, Throwen," I said. "Most of the witches I know are kind, caring, and hard-working. They just lost their way at some point when they lived in Theldea. They had nowhere to go, or at least that's what I had been told. I always thought I was helping people, but I might as well have been their jailor…"

We moved to the small open area, our feet padding softly on the ground. Everything was too much. The cool stone beneath my feet, the feel of Throwen's hand in mind, the emotions wanting to be released. And most of all, I didn't know how to reconcile my feelings about my coven. I loved them but how could they have stood by and said nothing to me of the truth. They were scared, but did it justify their complacency?

Throwen's fingers left my hand to glide up to my neck. He started unwinding the scarf as if peeling off a venomous snake. "This can't be comfortable, and I want to see you. I don't like it when parts of you are hidden away."

The scarf loosened, and Throwen threw it towards our packs. As it floated delicately over our supplies, I could swear I heard the clank of the invisible collar of oppression I wore crashing to the floor at the same time.

Cool air licked at my bare skin, my mark glowing and warm at the back of my neck. Throwen wrapped his large hand around to rest his palm against the mark and my skin pebbled all over. His thumb stroked the side of my neck, the cool metal soothing against my overheated skin.

Throwen maneuvered us into a basic dancing position. His left hand held my right, and I placed my other hand on the top of his shoulder, his arm snaking around my mid-back, pulling me close enough that our chests were almost touching. Fighting the urge to dig my nails into his hard bicep, I swallowed tightly. He led, and I easily followed.

"Sometimes," I said, "if Malik was in a particularly prickly mood after a ceremony, he would demand that I dance with *every* member who requested it. And because every witch jumped at the chance to impress him, I would dance all night, sometimes until the sun was up and my feet were bleeding through my heels."

I smiled at the memory because to me it wasn't a tainted story. The pain was worth it to see the cheerful faces of our people, to hear their laughs amidst the uncertainty they constantly lived in.

He stopped dancing and released me, taking a step back. "We *never* have to do anything you aren't comfortable with."

"No! Sorry, I didn't mean to turn this into some morbid cult story," I said, breathless. My body needed him closer, to feel more of his touch. "I love dancing. I would do it a lot when I was alone in my room and sometimes late in the library when I would sneak out after curfew."

Throwen's mustache curled up. "I'm glad you had moments of joy amidst the suffering."

I looked at my bare feet against the dark gray floor. Throwen was offering me something important. My demons would always cling to me, but he wanted to help me tame them.

I wanted this.

Reaching for his wrist, I wrapped my fingers tightly around it. His tendons strained around his pounding pulse. He was my tether to joy and freedom. "I want to dance with you."

Without another word, he steered us back into position. He started leading us slowly, getting used to how our bodies worked together.

"Your voice is bewitching. I might start asking you to sing me to sleep at night." His intense expression burned me from the inside out, our noses inches apart.

"Is that so?" I smirked. It wasn't my usual outright denial of his compliments, and his mustache pulled up at the corners with his smile. He guided me expertly to his right, his arm on my back moving up slightly. We moved in a circle with me on the outside.

"Indeed. You're no *Throwen the most magnificent hunky hilarious bard,* but..."

I blasted his face with some light air before playfully stomping his black sock beneath my bare foot.

"Oof!" He laughed and quickly recovered, twirling me into a spin away from him. Just like what I imagined when watching the witches of Goldhaven dance at our ceremonies.

He wound me back in. This time we were closer together, my body now pressed tightly against him.

"I deserved that."

"You deserve most of the things I choose to do to you," I said, my voice lowering an octave and sounding much more sensual than I meant it to. My core heated. Embers that had been waiting fanned by his close presence.

"'The Siren and the Sea' is a very old song. It originated in Stranata. How did you come to learn it?"

"My friend taught it to me." The words came out rushed as he swung us from right to left.

"Were they from there?" We shuffled back and forth, and my hips loosened, swaying naturally to his slow tempo.

"She was. But she didn't talk about it much. Remember how I said I would sneak out after curfew?"

He nodded, listening intently.

"We would meet in the library. I stole a key from Malik's office when I was cleaning."

Moving us right two more steps, he lifted his arm so I could twirl underneath. My dress fanned out, drawing Throwen's attention to my thighs. The candles in the room flickered brightly as I danced with my suave bard.

"Sounds like you and your friend were quite the little troublemakers."

I chuckled. "We were. I would read a chapter of 'The Siren and the Sea' every night and she would sing the song to me at the end." My heart ached, begging me to stop the story now, but I continued, "She would always insist on sending me back to my room when I inevitably started falling asleep amongst the shelves."

"You loved her."

I stumbled over my feet, but Throwen caught me and effortlessly lifted me back into position. We continued to move like a wave against the shore; his proximity and empathy a balm to the lacerations crackling across my heart.

"How did you know?"

"You got this silly little grin when you thought about the time you spent in the library."

"Maybe I just *really* love libraries."

"Oh, I have no doubt, and I *will* be taking you to the library tomorrow, but first I want to hear more about this girl who stole your heart."

Releasing a deep sigh, I knew I was ready to talk about this and felt comfortable with him. The movement of the dance soaked up the usual jitters associated with my anxiety. "Fine. But after this story, I'm putting on a shirt and going to bed."

He laughed, pulling me back into his chest. Some of his chest hair was poking out, and I discreetly inched my fingertips around the hem of his shirt to get the slightest touch.

"Her name was Calliope," I said as he swayed us gently, and I let myself get lost in his lavender gaze, as if the spirits themselves were comforting me through this memory. "We did everything together. Cooked, cleaned, meditated, whatever our tasks were for the day, we always worked together. She was a hard worker, as most of our members are."

I tilted my chin down. "But her drive and ambition were so strong it scared me sometimes. Her approval was signed to start scout training three months into our relationship, and she insisted we had to keep our love a secret."

Throwen's grip tightened, and he pulled me closer. I rested against his chest, and he placed his chin on top of my head.

"So, I did. She became the scout I always wished I could be, and I continued to be their Lady, nothing more than a tool for Malik to maintain control." My throat tightened. "We met in secret, fucked in secret. I think she got off on it, the secrecy of it all."

Throwen had listened to me more than any witch in my life, and I wanted to let go of this. I *needed* to let go of this.

"It all went to shit when I was twenty-four." A single tear fell down my cheek, and I knew the rest were soon to follow. The dancing was slow and comforting.

"One night, she told me she wanted to help me pass the boundary. She was a scout and knew the way and could get us out of the coven. We agreed we would spend five minutes outside in the fresh air and then come right back to my room."

Throwen's shirt grew damp from the emotions leaking out of me, and I let the tears fall freely.

"I met her at the entrance of the catacombs, showering her with kisses and dancing along a path I never traveled. I rarely was allowed in the catacombs…"

The weight of retelling my shameful story crushed my body and my knees buckled.

"I've got you." Throwen lowered us to the floor and laid my head in his lap. He ran his fingers through my hair, easing out all the tangles. "Whenever you're ready to talk, I'm ready to listen. *You're* in control now, Octavia. If that means we go to bed now and you never speak of this again, then that's fine, too."

Taking a shaky breath, I continued, "We made it to the barrier and the opaque red glow of the concealment flickered. I could see snow, but not much else. Then scouts poured in from the other side of the barrier. They circled us and Malik strode through them."

You entitled fucking cunt! Is paradise not enough for you? You're a greedy whore, just like the Goddess who disowned you! Get her out of my sight! I'll deliver your punishment when we get back to the castle!

An ugly sob wracked its way out of my throat. Throwen gently massaged the tension growing between my eyebrows. I wept and clutched onto the leg of his pants.

"Calliope never loved me. It was all Malik from the very beginning. He planted her in my workstations. Told her to test me. See if love was enough to make me break his most sacred rule."

A cynical laugh burst out of me. "At least she got that promotion she wanted though, right? It was part of her reward, heating the brand that Malik used that same night. She laughed and watched, cooing to me that it was an honor I didn't deserve."

My body shook uncontrollably, and I could smell my burning flesh, feel the boils growing over my skin.

Throwen swept me into his lap and cradled me, resting his chin atop my head. He rubbed my back with firm gentle circles, the way he had on my chest during my panic attack.

"Thank you." I clung to his shirt, no longer caring what a mess I was. Everything about him was comforting, and I let myself get lost in the rapid thumping of his heart.

"If she was here, she'd tell me that I'm too sensitive. She told me that a lot." I sniffled. "I loved her, Throwen. Truly loved her. That's been my whole existence. Feeling things so deeply, but it only ever goes one way. I give and they take."

"What she couldn't comprehend, darling," he said, "is that being sensitive to the emotions of those around you, and even the ones riling within yourself, is not a weakness. To some, you might seem sensitive, but do you know what I see?"

I pulled away, my soaked face inches from his. "What?"

"Passion." A sad kind of laugh pushed out through his lips that made me want to put him in my lap and rub his head instead.

"Octavia, I think a part of you loves everyone you meet, even the most awful of people. I'm not saying you're a bad judge of character, but what I mean is that your level of empathy is unmatched. That's why you aren't the monster your brain tries to make you think you are. You genuinely care and want to help witches. She was an idiot for not taking the time to see you, the real you that you wanted to share with her."

A small laugh tumbled from me. It was like the abscess covering my heart had burst. The exhaustion came next. This always happened when I had my episodes. I would feel a sudden rush of emotion immediately followed by a crash. Fatigue took hold and I slumped into his chest. "How do you do that?"

"Do what?" His throat rumbled against my head.

"You can always make me laugh."

"Hasn't anyone ever told you, darling? Laughter is the most potent healer of them all."

I stood up, ready to change and sleep. I reached down to help him, and he lingered, his eyes rimmed with dark circles.

Cursed Abyss. Had he even eaten since we settled in? Has anyone ever stopped to take care of him and see his needs? Earlier I would have wished he kissed me, wished he would touch me. The only thing I cared about now was taking care of him.

"You eat that." I pointed to a tray of food that was left in our room. "I'm going to change."

"Yes, Ma'am." He saluted and made his way toward the bed to sit and eat.

"Ew. Never call me that again."

"Oh right, I forgot you prefer, darling."

I groaned in response, too tired to deal with his smart ass. Grabbing the black shirt he had let me borrow for the past few nights, I headed toward the bathroom.

"Wait, you can have my new one." Striding over, he offered me a similar white shirt that I bet would look delicious on him.

"Here." I untied his leather strap, instincts driving me to trade him for it. He grabbed my wrist, and a gasp escaped me at his firm grip. I swallowed; there was no way I was going to let him know I liked that.

"Don't you dare start that shit. I already told you when I give you something, you owe me *nothing*. Just let me help take care of you."

"Fine," I said and trudged toward the bathroom with both of his gifts clutched tightly in my hands.

"Oh, one last thing," He chimed.

I huffed in irritation. I wanted to fucking sleep, get comfy, and most of all, I wanted *him* to rest.

"What, Throwen?" I put my hand on my hip and his tongue darted across his bottom lip.

"That dress is mesmerizing, thanks for the song and dance."

Looking down, I ran my palms over my dress and hoped he didn't notice my flushed face. I closed the bathroom door and leaned my back against it. All his stories of making witches swoon were true. And I was now one of them, a huge grin pulling at the corners of my lips.

Chapter 17

THROWEN

Octavia clung to me like I was Nova's wolf, her fingers laced in my chest hair. Our bodies found each other during the night, meeting underneath the comfort of a soft blanket.

Exhaustion made me careless last night and I fell asleep in only my underwear while she was showering. Now, my cock throbbed, begging me to caress the soft skin of her right leg haphazardly thrown over my thigh. Instead, I kept my arms wrapped around her waist, holding her close. She was warm through the shirt I had basically forced her to take.

Waking up with her in my arms was the best gift the Goddess had bestowed upon me. As her breaths made her chest rise and fall, I praised our creator for allowing her some rest.

I had never seen her muscles so relaxed, her face so tranquil. I took a deep breath of the sweet citrus scents from her bath that rolled off her soft brown hair, tickling my neck and chin. It took everything I had not to run my fingers through it.

The connection between us was symbiotic. She was my moon, pulling me in with her gravity, washing the tides of perceptivity over me. I was her sun, keeping her warm by staying consistent through her phases. It felt like we both needed each other.

I knew a lot of witches, and the lovers I did take never lasted long. I never let anyone in like this except my family. But this felt different. Octavia gave me little choice by drawing my rawest emotions and truths out of me, ones I didn't even know I had, simply by being herself. I wanted her to be mine. That's the thought that pounded through my skull last night when I drew my blade in the tavern. When I saw his filthy hands touching her, red consumed my vision. It overpowered me and there was no choice but to act. *Mine, mine, mine!*

Cringing, I reassured myself she wasn't mine. She wasn't some object to be won. I wasn't fucking Malik. Ownership wasn't what I craved. I wanted her to choose me, like my untamable heart was already doing with her.

My pulse raced and for a moment, getting Octavia back to Whynnie wasn't the most important thing. I would show Octavia everything. I would be there to help her as she healed. I would mold her natural curiosity into fascination.

Before this was all over, she would love Theldea just as much as I did. We would wipe away every terrible memory, one new experience at a time until the present was able to overcome her past.

Humming happily, Octavia interrupted my thoughts as she clung to me tighter, her pelvis pressing into my thigh.

Goddess forgive me! I should have woken her or moved, but I liked how it felt too much. With a few more agonizing wiggles, she stiffened, her grip loosening on my chest but not pulling away.

Terror filled me at the thought of speaking and ruining this perfect moment with her in my arms, in my bed. I hesitated before whispering into her hair, "Should we get up?"

"I don't know... Should we?" she whispered.

It was still dark outside our window, the sun not yet up but looming. We laid there for a silent moment, skin hot against each other, our breathing in tune but labored. Our need for each other was so fucking palpable, I swore a cloud of heat and desire molded around us.

"Tell me what you want, Octavia." My voice was rough from a night of performing.

She inhaled sharply, and if she moved even the slightest inch, she would feel how hard she made me. But I needed her to be thinking clearly if this was going to happen. I was certain this was where last night was heading before she sifted through my charm, finding an exhausted man underneath.

"I don't know what I want." Her words had a bite, but she stayed glued to my side.

Vocalizing her needs and wants wasn't natural for her, but I would show her the way. I wouldn't decide for her the way Malik did. Sliding her away was torture, but I needed her to look me in the eye.

"Darling, I know the way you fight for what you want. I knew it from the first time I saw you in that mirror. You're allowed to chase what you want and hold on to it once you find it. And if you don't know what you want, I'll help you figure that out too. But this *can't* be you using me as a distraction or to cope with everything around you." I cupped her cheek in my hand. "You've been through so much, and I *refuse* to take advantage of you."

Humming, she leaned into my touch, her skin a dazzling contrast against my death-touched fingers. Resisting my feelings felt like it was no longer an option. The fear that she would be the witch to unravel my lifestyle was gone. With her, I had purpose, and she would never take away my freedoms. Her autonomy had been ripped from her for her entire life, but I would help her get it back and enjoy killing that fucker who took it in the first place.

Those honest, honeycomb irises fell on me, wrapping their way around my soul. "I'm not sure of anything right now. Other than that, with *you*, I'm safe to be myself. I'm still figuring out who I am, but I know you can help me find that without manipulating me into a version of myself that suits you."

A wicked smile pulled at the corners of my lips. Her answer was my undoing. I tried to stop myself from falling, but it was too late.

I pinched her chin between my fingers, her pupils dilating at the firmness of my grip. "I have to hear you say it. Tell me what you want."

Her tongue darted out across her bottom lip, and she trembled slightly, her hips twitching back toward me with anticipation. "I want you, Throwen."

Kissing her forehead gently, I traced my fingers along her side. I grazed the side of her breast, all the way to the middle of her thigh where I teased under the hem of her shirt. Leaning down, I purred into her ear, "Good girl."

She gasped as I latched onto her hips, pulling her on top and holding her above me. I angled my thigh to rest her weight on, holding her firmly in place, the perfect position for her sweet pussy to soak me in her juices.

Allowing her core to graze my thigh, I provided her with a minimal amount of friction. Then I lowered my leg flat on the bed, removing all contact as I held her in place, hovering above me.

"What are you doing?" Fighting with my firm grip, she clenched her teeth and tried to press herself back against my thigh. It was adorable, and I had to stifle the laughter building in my chest.

"We don't do *anything* you don't want or feel comfortable with. If you want me to stop, you say strawberry."

She froze as she took in just how serious I was. Her hands were braced beside my shoulders. Glowing brighter than usual, her mark lit up around her chestnut hair like a halo, and I could see her beautifully silhouetted tits through her shirt.

She caught me admiring her and, with a sultry smile, peered down at me through thick lashes. "Strawberry, huh?"

Everyone thought I was an angel, but it was her all along. Except the hungry way she looked at me wasn't at all innocent or angelic.

"Yes, *strawberry*. Because I can't fucking control myself when you wrap those smart lips around them."

"Okay, strawberry it is."

With her comfort and safety established, I plunged my fingers into the hair at her nape, pulling her down into a punishing kiss. She moaned into my mouth as I held our bodies together. Feeling her weight against me was utter bliss, as if my body had been searching for hers since the beginning of time. I slowly slanted my thigh for her, kissing along her neck before she returned to bracing herself. With a bite of her lip, she pressed her core against me.

"*Fuckkk.*" I hissed as she wiggled into place and I grabbed onto her ass, pulling her forward along me.

"Are you always this wet for me, darling? You're dripping through those tight lace panties." I ran my finger under them, teasing the sensitive skin around her inner thigh and back to her ass, where I pulled the delicate material almost to its breaking point.

"Don't rip those! They're the only extra pair Enoch gave me." She panted, laughing as she set her own rhythm.

"Fine." I let the band go, drawing out a loud *snap* and a satisfying yelp.

"Hey!" She rubbed a finger up and down the red mark now curving around her sweet ass. A feral grin filled her face.

"Mmm." The grateful hum that left her lips nearly had me coming. Leaning down to nip at my neck, she ground against me slowly at first but quickly picked up speed, finding a new rhythm closer to the edge she was seeking.

Good. I wanted her to need me. I wanted *all* of her. My new purpose in life would be worshiping every fucking inch of her skin until she learned to appreciate it herself.

I moved my hands back to her hips and gripped them roughly, feeling her skin squish between my fingers. My picks would leave bruises, but from the smile plastered across her face as she dripped onto my thigh, I could tell my muse liked pain with her pleasure.

I pressed her down harder, and she gasped. "Yes. That. Keep doing that."

She was panting, chasing an orgasm but it was too soon. I wanted to bring her right to the edge and pull her back until she screamed my name. I relaxed my thigh and lowered it slightly. A snarl of frustration ripped free from her chest and *fuck*, I was so turned on by this untamed side of her.

Stradling me, she punched my chest before crossing her arms. "I will not say please, so don't even try that shit." She quoted me, attempting to mock me but failing to capture my bravado.

I loved it when she got feisty. My cock pulsated at the thought of her lips wrapped around it. Seizing the hem of her shirt, I lifted it higher to expose her abdomen. "Oh, I'll make you say please."

Sliding my hand under her shirt, I reached up to the swell of her breast as her skin pebbled under my fingers. Running the pad of my thumb over her peaked nipple, the chill of my pick's cold metal caused her to shiver. I cupped her breast and massaged it as her head tilted back. "I'm going to play you *so well…*"

I slowly glided my fingertips back down to her hips, gripping them firmly. As I smiled up at her, she gasped. "You're going to make beautiful music for me."

Desperate to hear more shouts of her pleasure, I arched my thigh back up, slamming her down onto me. She cried out as I pulled her forward, then thrust her down and back. "You're my muse now."

"*Sacred Ether!*" Elbows bucking, she struggled to hold herself up.

I pulled her back and forth harder and faster each time. "That's it, sing for me."

Grunting, she peeled my hands away, discarding them to the sheets.

She used my chest as leverage, digging in her nails as she rode me exactly the way she wanted.

I moved one hand on her thigh and shoved the other into my underwear to stroke my thundering cock.

"Oh Goddess, Throwen, I'm close. I need more," she begged.

Fuck! I was close too and *Abyss consume me*, if I couldn't last long enough to make her orgasm at least two more times.

I released my hand from my underwear, and grabbed onto her throat, testing with a gentle squeeze. Her golden glow that illuminated us intensified.

"Is that what you need? Is that what you want?" I tightened, and she nodded in blissful approval. "You know the rules."

She whimpered as I loosened my grip, continuing to grind against my thigh. Her arousal soaked through the thin lace, spreading over me. I couldn't wait to dip my finger into her sweet heat once I helped her finish.

"Yes. This is what I want. Don't stop."

I gripped her throat firmly with a low growl. "You're going to sing for me now, darling. I'll even count you in."

She was panting and grunting as rhythmic moans accompanied her composition.

I continued to guide her through her pleasure. "On three."

"Okay. *Fuck*." She kept up her tempo, ready to release her song.

"One." Her head dipped, and I lifted her chin back to my face. I needed to see her come, and she needed to know there was no hiding from me.

"Two." Sweat dripped down her jaw as my body felt the effects of the heat, too. I flexed my thigh as hard as I could as a gasping sob fell free from her throat.

"Three." Crying out, she crashed against me, coming hard. I pet her damp hair, her body twitching as she panted against my chest, riding out the final waves of her orgasm. I kissed the top of her head and stroked her arm as she settled in next to me.

I ran my fingers along my thigh, and brought them to my lips, lapping up her sweet juices that I refused to let go to waste.

She gaped at me, not used to seeing this side of me either. It was fun showing these repressed pieces to each other.

"What? You soaked my thigh, and I wanted a taste."

A burst of laughter erupted from her as she hid behind her hands. I curled my fingers into her panties and pulled down, ready to eliminate these infuriating layers between us. I pulled her in close, kissing her passionately. She opened for me and our tongues met as the kiss deepened.

I mumbled against her lips, "You sang so well. Are you ready to sing again?"

Reaching down, her finger tickled softly along the hem of my underwear. A finger slipped in slightly, teasing me in the same way I did her. "Maybe it's your turn to sing."

She sucked on my bottom lip, and I climbed on top of her, fully prepared to ravish her —

Knock! Knock!

I wrapped my arms around her protectively as my attention shot to the large door and then to the window.

"The sun is up!" Octavia squirmed out of my grip and jumped out of the bed, racing to the bathroom, her ass bouncing hypnotically beneath that damned shirt I never got the chance to rip off.

Knock! Knock!

"I'm coming, Harlin! We were just getting our stuff and leaving!" I wiggled into my tight pants from last night, covered in mead and sweat, and now Octavia's satisfaction. I looked frantically for my shirt but gave up when it was nowhere to be seen.

I stomped over to the door and flung it open. "We were just leavin—"

Kallan stood like a bear in the doorframe. His brows knit with confusion that morphed into a huge grin plastered across his face. "I heard some asshole bard started a fight over a gorgeous stranger." He eyed my still engorged state. "Would you know anything about that brother?"

He laughed his deep, burly laugh. "Looks like you *definitely* know something about it."

I curled my fingers into a fist. The fingers I had just been licking and hoping to sink into Octavia's deliciously dripping pussy. "You're a dick."

"Yeah, and it looks like *yours* didn't get any attention." Only my siblings could get away with this shit. They knew me too well, and if he knew what happened with Harlin, he knew I was already in too deep.

"Whynnie is going to *kill* you once she finds out you hooked up with her missing ward. Please let me know when you're going to tell her so I can watch." He wiped at the tears that had fallen from his laughter, holding his sculpted abs like laughing could even phase them.

The bathroom door squeaked open as Octavia peered out. She looked at me with a creased brow, confused by all the laughter.

"Can you *please* distract Harlin long enough for me to shower?" My head was reeling as I came down from the rush.

He pulled on his beard thoughtfully. "Of course," he said. "Hey, are you okay?"

"I'm fine. I just didn't get a chance to shower after my performance."

"Sure thing, brother." He clasped my shoulder firmly. "I can't wait to meet the witch that made you break one of your silly little rules." Shaking his head, he strode down the hallway as I locked the door.

"Who was that?" She ran her hands along her hair, trying to tame it.

"Kallan."

Her mouth parted and her eyes bounced to the door and back to me. "Your brother?"

"Yes. He's always been quite the cock block." I ran my fingers over my mustache that I wished was currently between her legs. "I need to shower quickly. Do you mind waiting?"

"Of course." She sat on the bed, blushing.

"Thank you." I rushed to the bathroom, slamming the door shut behind me. My body shook.

This witch had my heart in her hands. Malik would come eventually, and she would be forced to make a choice. I wasn't sure she would choose me.

Chapter 18

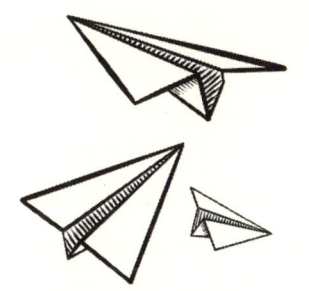

OCTAVIA

Old stone arches surrounded the back entrance of the tavern covered in red ivy. Graygarde was elegant in a way I never expected. Columns and statues were scattered around the square space. The marble structure across from me gleamed in the morning light.

Throwen spoke with the stable hand, paying him for looking after Lucky for the night. He wore a sleeveless cedar brown shirt that ended at his chin where it could be rolled up into a mask. It hugged him so tightly I could see each and every toned muscle. His songbook was at his waist, his lute at his back.

I bit the inside of my cheek to quell the inferno he started within me this morning. If Kallan hadn't interrupted us, I was positive Throwen's ego wasn't the only part of him I would've stroked. My body ached to finish what we started while my mind tried to tarnish what happened with doubt and fear.

The stable hand looked from Throwen to me with wide eyes, and Throwen was in his intimidation stance. He turned and winked as the man retrieved Lucky.

Lowering my gaze, I focused on my hands, where I stretched the deep maroon fabric of my gloves between my fingers. My dress had a narrow cut around my shoulders and accentuated my curves, flaring around my hips. The dress was cute, but it was also functional. It had a collar that wrapped around my neck, but it was so light it felt like there was nothing there. There was an attached mask that could be worn up or down if I needed to cover my face.

Lucky whinnied, and I ran up, welcoming her with open arms.

Throwen chuckled. "Kallan's just out front, he had to take care of a few things with Harlin." He took a step back and looked me up and down. "You look fierce."

My cheeks heated, and I squeezed his bicep. "Thanks, so do you."

Did he have any idea the war he had started within me?

He had blocked my path to death more than once. The thought that this carefree bard could effortlessly give me reasons to live, reasons to *want* to stay made my heart flutter in my chest. I knew that he felt something too. It riled the demon inside my mind and it roared its disapproval.

He banished all my thoughts with a single kiss. I moaned, and he lingered, licking my bottom lip with his tongue. This morning, I had absolutely drowned in ecstasy and even with the world-shattering release, I *needed* more of him. Groaning, he peeled himself away and led us around the side of the tavern.

I ran my fingers along the smooth marble railing that led into the street where Kallan stood with his horse.

He shuffled a deck of cards in his hands. His height and physique made him look like the perfect subject for a sculptor. Dark brown skin was scarred from fighting and his black hair was pulled into locs atop his head.

"Kallan." Throwen punched his brother playfully. Kallan didn't move an inch, probably because he was built like a wall. He was the size of the Theldeans that fueled my nightmares as a child.

Instead, he pulled a metal case from his pocket and slid the cards inside, tapping the lid three times after closing it.

Throwen laced his fingers with mine, pulling me closer. "Kallan, this is Octavia."

Kallan's brow lowered, as if assessing me. Throwen pointed his head toward me and his eyes widened, as if begging his brother not to embarrass him.

I shuffled my feet, kicking at pebbles on the side of the wide street.

Throwen sighed. "Right, well... this is going *exactly* as expected. Octavia, this is Kallan. You'll have to excuse his lack of words, he has the social skills of a potato."

I plastered on my best Lady of the Grave smile. "It's nice to meet you. I've heard great things."

Kallan's dark eyes shifted to his brother and back to me, his lips staying in a flat line.

Throwen laughed. "See. Potato."

Kallan turned to his horse, searching the saddle bag for something. I looked to Throwen for answers, but he merely shrugged.

Kallan thrust a pair of umber-colored boots into my arms. "These are for you." His voice was deep.

"Thank you?"

Throwen bit back a smile. "I told you, she has boots, Kallan,"

"And I told you Lydia's boots are *far* better quality," Kallan said. "It's worth the extra coin if the traction on her boots saves her life."

"You just like flirting with Lydia, don't pretend this is some altruistic endeavor." Throwen laughed and Kallan grunted.

I kicked off my boots and tugged on the new pair. They rested just above my calf and had thick support around both ankles. They were a perfect fit, and I fought hard against the urge to offer something in return. "They're lovely." I beamed at him. "Thank you, again."

He nodded. "All right, let's go."

"Oh, so when he gives you a gift there's no fight." Throwen mumbled and I scrunched my nose at him.

Kallan led his horse toward the street. He was brown and much taller than Lucky, which made sense if he had to carry someone as large as Kallan.

I reached up to scratch the horse's chin, and he nuzzled into my touch. "What's his name?"

"John," Kallan said.

"It's nice to meet you too, John." I gave him another scratch.

"Shall we head to the library?" Throwen asked.

My stomach lurched as I pulled my hood up tighter. "Are you sure we have time? We should probably get going."

I looked down the street and my mind conjured images of scouts peering around buildings. I reached out, squeezing Throwen's hand. It helped ground me, but my mind still sifted through the worst outcomes. Malik could kill his way through all these innocent witches going about their day, and Throwen and Kallan's necks would crack beneath his whip.

Throwen jerked me from my fear by running a finger along my jaw. His expression wasn't judgmental, just open and searching. "Do you *want* to go to the library?"

My shoulders relaxed slightly, but my neck was stiff. "Y-yes. I *love* books. I'm just... We made a big scene at the tavern and if Malik hears..."

"We will protect you." Throwen brushed a thumb over my cheek, and I tilted my head at Kallan curiously. *Would he protect me?*

Kallan's jaw ticked. "Honestly, I wish the fucker *would* show up so I could tear his head from his body myself."

I stopped in the middle of the street, witches grumbling and pushing their way around us.

Throwen rested a hand on my back. "Octavia..."

Kallan turned, towering over me. "I *will* kill him and any who fight with him. Necromancers don't know the meaning of mercy, especially Malik."

My blood boiled. He didn't know my people. Most of us never left the coven. "Why?" I spat.

Kallan frowned, eyebrows pulling together. "Why what?"

"Tell me... Why do *my* people deserve to die?"

"She's very perceptive, brother. If you don't tell her now, she will pull the truth from you later," Throwen said, sounding as if he were both proud and sorrowful.

Kallan looked at me like a gentle father about to teach his child a very important, but painful lesson. "Fine."

My stomach clenched. I didn't want to know where his drive to kill us came from, didn't want another reason to be a traitorous bitch.

"Let's walk and talk." Kallan grabbed onto John's reins and led him toward the library. "I was born in Volgsump. Drybourne was my coven."

My mind weeded through any knowledge I had retained about Volgsump. A laugh fell free and I covered my mouth.

Throwen and Kallan paused and surveyed me, their heads tilting to the side.

"It's just, I always thought the covens in Volgsump were cults. The irony was too much." I giggled again, unsure if this was funny or the only way I could cope with being the one actually raised in a cult.

"What? Where did you get that information?" Kallan looked insulted and I scratched awkwardly at the back of my head.

"Octavia was limited in her education. Malik restricted what books came in and out," Throwen explained.

The guilt that had settled low in my stomach caught aflame, turning into a pit of bitterness. I bit my tongue and kept quiet.

Kallan's face softened. "Don't worry, O, I know *plenty* about Volgsump and we have quite the journey ahead of us. What do you want to know?"

His use of a new nickname caused a lightness to overflow from my heart throughout my entire being. It wasn't like Throwen's name for me that sent bursts of electricity sparking between my veins. Kallan's name for me felt like a powerful hug of acceptance.

"You mean other than why you want to decapitate my mentor?" I smirked and lifted a brow at him. He chuckled low, the sound emanating from somewhere deep inside his broad chest.

Witches bustled in and out of shops. Some carried their supplies in a hurry, while others took their time chatting with other witches.

"We will get to that. What did your histories say about Volgsump?" Kallan asked, his voice softer now, but his muscles were still rigid.

"Volgsump is a swamp with swamp witches," I said, struggling to sift through all I could remember. "They worship the Goddess fanatically and dance naked by the light of the moon. They speak with snakes, lizards, and all kinds of reptiles. And..." I hesitated, not wanting to continue.

"And?" Kallan and Throwen spoke in unison. My eyes widened at how they seemed to be so at odds with each other, yet in sync. It was a strange dynamic and absolutely fascinating.

I squeezed my eyes shut. "They sacrifice babies and... eat them."

After a brief pause, Throwen and Kallan erupted with laughter. My expression soured as I opened my eyes and ripped myself away from Throwen.

"No, darling. We aren't laughing at you. It's just that Volgsump witches *cherish* their children above all else."

My nostrils were flaring, my body tensed, and I crossed my arms over my chest. *Another lie.* Not just a lie, but the outright opposite of how things apparently were. I loved Malik but couldn't come up with a justifiable reason he would rewrite Theldean history other than for his own control over us.

My skin was growing hotter by the second, my cheeks flushed with irritation. "We can discuss my fucked-up education later. Tell me why the people of my coven deserve to die."

We walked into a large opening, much like the courtyard from last night. A new mural decorated the floor, this one of a hand holding a quill. It was mostly empty but for a few witches, painting the beauty around them and reading books. Kallan led us toward a massive stone building with a glass dome on top of it.

"When I was ten, my family was taking a trip to Stranata. We sold eggs and poultry mostly, and Stranata had a festival where we could make good coin." Kallan stroked John's muzzle as he spoke softly so only Thrown and I could hear. "My mother and sisters *loved* going each year. I didn't like traveling much, but seeing their faces light up the entire week before as we packed and planned made the disruption to routine worth it."

Cobblestones clicked with Lucky and John's hooves. Thrown reached over, lacing his fingers through mine. It felt like it had always been this way between us. He was a comfort I never knew, but one I nestled into. He was growing more in tune with my needs with each passing hour.

Kallan's bright smile slowly fell right along with my stomach. "Our caravan was ambushed about halfway to Stranata."

Biting my lip, I fought back the burning already starting in my eyes.

Kallan's eyes glistened. "Five scouts and Malik. I remember it all so clearly that if I had any skill with a brush, I could easily recreate it. Sometimes I can still smell the sulfur that followed their attack."

I flinched, knowing all too well what a vivid hallucination felt like.

"The scouts raped and killed my mom first, making my sisters and I watch." Kallan cleared his throat. "Malik cracked her neck with his whip before binding her spirit to her corpse."

A tear fell down Kallan's cheek and mine were soon to follow, despite my efforts to remain in control. "I knew then all hope of reuniting with her in the Ether was gone."

Kallan sat on a stone bench that surrounded a large fountain, and I sat next to him, my ears popping. A high-pitched tone vibrated my skull. *This can't be real.* Kallan's warm arm rested beside me. I wanted to hear him, to *really* listen, but I felt myself slipping away into a nagging numbness.

His large shoulders sagged. If I knew him better, I would try to comfort him, but I wasn't sure how.

He covered his face with his hands and rubbed roughly. "As soon as the scout's daggers pierced Sage and Daliah's hearts I swore my vengeance on all necromancers. I knew because they destroyed my sisters' hearts, I had a chance at seeing them again. So, I fought and ran."

My heart pounded wildly in my chest, fearing I ruined this new friendship before it even started. "Kallan, I apologize… I didn't mean to pressure you to tell your story."

"If anyone needs to hear this story, it's you." He turned his dark scowl toward me, its depths offering a warning. "Your coven is poison. I've tortured many scouts, and I know the extent of Malik's brainwashing."

"Hey, Kallan. Easy, that's her family." Thrown stepped in, trying to shield me from Kallan's harsh reality.

I looked down at my shaking leg. *What am I supposed to say?* Malik had done horrible things, but his intentions were still noble, right? Maybe he just got lost along the way, like the rest of our coven.

"I know what you're thinking." Kallan rested a hand on my back. "He can't be saved, O. Necromancy corrupts the soul. Whoever he used to be, or you thought he was, died years ago."

A vendor with a cart wheeled by and the witch dragging it morphed into a red-eyed corpse. I recalled Malik and the scouts coming back with bound spirits.

Tragic losses because of radical Theldean maggots. These poor innocent children, forced to join my Ether before their time.

The claps of my coven faded along with the vision of contorted tiny limbs.

"I'm sorry for what my people did to you and your family. I'm sorry for a lot of things that Malik did." I wiped away my useless tears. Crying wouldn't save or heal anyone.

Malik had killed so many, but killing him in return couldn't be the answer. If Kallan killed him, he would be corrupting his soul as well and would be no better than Malik.

Kallan rose to his feet, offering me his hand, and I took it.

"Luckily, this Little Miracle" — Kallan rubbed Throwen's head roughly, and I smiled at the gesture— "found me wandering around the forest near Whynnie's hovel a few months later."

Kallan shook his head with a small chuckle. "He made me laugh and smile for the first time since seeing my family butchered, but I refused to go with him. So, he brought Whynnie along the next time and, well, you'll see, but you can't exactly say no to her."

Throwen shot a stream of water at Kallan from the fountain. They both laughed and started shooting water at each other and blocking with barriers from the dirt in the potted plants nearby.

Throwen was an expert at pulling others from their sorrow, and I envied their relationship. I wanted to be that for someone. There were so many types of love I never knew were possible. My friendships were always shrouded in fear and uncertainty.

"Are you two taking me to this unbelievable library or what?" I wanted to keep moving. My beliefs were scattered like the mosaic beneath our feet, and I couldn't figure out how to rearrange them to make a clear image.

They wiped their faces with their shirts and, *Goddess forgive me*, I would gladly eat off both their abs.

Throwen flashed a devilish smile, his canines poking slightly into his bottom lip. "I'm going to have to teach you some patience, darling."

Tingles erupted in the base of my spine, and I smirked back; his lavender eyes swirled with a darker shade of purple. "Good luck, bard."

He took my hand, and we strode toward the large domed building as he stroked my pulsing wrist gently with his thumb.

))) ◐ 🌀 ◑ (((

"WELCOME TO THE Graygarde public library!" An enthusiastic young witch greeted us as soon as we entered through the large doors. He kept his tone low enough as to not disturb other witches, but I could hear many hushed whispers creating a soothing ambiance like distant rain.

He wore a finely tailored outfit, and the white collar of his shirt flared out drastically, accentuating his thin neck and pointed chin. He looked to be eighteen or nineteen, his features showing his newfound adulthood.

"My name is Finian." His unruly golden hair fell over his silver-rimmed round glasses and into his bright smile. Flicking his finger, he blew the hair up and away from his face. "Is there anything I can help ye with today?"

"Hello, Finian," Throwen said, shaking his hand. "If you could give us a quick tour, that would be appreciated."

Kallan did the same with a patient smile, quiet and relaxed. Lastly, Finian bowed low before me.

"I'm Octavia, it's an honor to meet you."

Soon, all Theldeans will bow before me! We will show them the path to the true Ether or die trying!

I wanted to bash my head against the pretty marble columns lining the long hallway just to get Malik's voice out of my fucking head. Trying to focus on the thrill of a new experience in a new place was proving difficult because I could only think of what Malik might do to Finian if he obtained the power he wanted.

"What would ye like to know, Octavia?" Finian twirled to face us, walking backward. His expression was distinct, he was under the library's spell. I too was susceptible to their specific type of allure.

Throwen and Kallan both looked at me. *Right*. I was the only idiot confined to a library of lies for my entire upbringing.

"Um..." I struggled to form a response. "Do you work here?"

Finian laughed, the light glinting off his crescent moon brooch pinned to his periwinkle cape.

A vision of Badru materialized behind the boy. He reminded me so much of my friend and my heart hummed with pride for my coven's eccentric librarian, who did what he could with what he had.

"No, I have to complete my education to be on staff, but I hope to be head librarian one day." The splattering of freckles across his light cheeks lifted slightly with his eager smile. "I volunteer here and it helps me earn credits for my intentional community course."

Credits must have been a reward system of some kind. Our coven would never waste a healthy young witch in the library. They were always assigned to manual labor, even the children.

I covered my mouth and gasped as the long hallway opened up into the largest building I had ever stepped foot in. Immense domed ceilings were adorned with gorgeous elaborate frescos that appeared to be a historic timeline of scholars and inventors. It drew the eye upward, which must have been the intended goal of the building's architect with all the clean vertical architecture.

This place was beyond magical, it was bewitching. Large spiral staircases climbed up to a second level. Countless tomes filled towering shelves. The tall, majestic columns continued throughout the room, creating many hidden nooks and crannies.

Tears threatened to break free.

All these books, all these stories I would've never discovered if I hadn't made that broom or jumped out of that window. There was an entire world I knew nothing about. Just as I thought the emotions would overwhelm me, Throwen grasped my shaking hand, squeezing gently.

"Ah, first timer! My favorite kind of patron." Finian practically clicked his heels together with joy.

"Finian." I grinned. "Show me the best spot in this library. Where do *you* go to read?"

His eyes twinkled with wisdom far beyond his years. He recognized a book lover when he saw one, and I knew he would show me the best place in this paradise that seemed to stretch on and up endlessly.

You are ungrateful for this paradise I provide. Always wanting more. What makes you think you are so deserving of more, Lady?

Malik couldn't fathom my idea of paradise if it bit him in the ass. I could only feel anger toward him since hearing Kallan's story and being surrounded by all the books he never let me read.

"Well, that depends entirely upon yer preferred genre."

"Fantasy." Also known as my escape from reality.

"Any subgenre?"

"Uhh…" I was not about to ask this adolescent to take me to some toe-curling romance.

Throwen wrapped his arm around my waist, tickling my side. "She reads smut."

I placed my hand on top of his, pushing more heat than necessary into the back of his hand. He yelped, pulling it away. Shaking out his hand, he wore a matching boyish smirk with Finian, who was stifling a laugh.

He thought he had poked the bear, but I wouldn't let him have that satisfaction. I took a step into his space, poking his hard chest. "I'm *proud* of the books I enjoy reading. It takes a true artist to whisk you away from reality while simultaneously aiding you with self-pleasure. Wouldn't you agree, Kallan? It's *so* much easier to just get things done yourself."

"It's a lot less drama," Kallan deadpanned, and I snorted, covering my mouth.

Throwen rolled his eyes, "Seriously, brother?"

Finian stepped in clumsily to help but also to take control of the loud patrons he oversaw. "Witches should read what they want. Yer going to love our romantic fantasy section, Octavia. Miss Penelope is in charge of it, and she is always bringing in more books from new authors throughout Theldea."

Always bringing in more books? I attempted to open my mouth and articulate but the concept was beyond me, so I just opened and closed my mouth like a confused fish.

"This way, we are going to take that staircase there." He pointed to the steps in the far-right corner near a bright colorful space contained within a honeycombed tinted glass dome. As we walked towards it, I tried to commit this moment to memory.

Breathing in the unmistakable smell only a library could provide, my muscles relaxed. The paper, ink, and bindings slowly broke down to create one of my favorite smells. Their decay brought every witch in this place a twisted kind of pleasure. We moved quickly, trying to keep up with an over-excited Finian.

"Our collection is the most extensive in all of Theldea." Pride lit up Finian's face and he confidently strode backward, a guide eager to entertain visitors. Long tables lined the different sections that seemed to stretch on endlessly, some disappearing into rows of shelves. They were filled with witches of all ages and backgrounds.

A paper airplane hit Finian in the head. He adjusted his glasses and opened it up, read it, and blushed as he turned to a table of young witches giggling and finding great enjoyment in his embarrassment.

Many paper airplanes floated about the library, witches using their magic to pass messages to each other.

It was a beautiful sight watching these witches freely speak with one another. They were unafraid to send public messages that would've had someone killed in my coven. Malik had sentenced many to transform after finding letters they wrote or confiscating diaries.

Finian coughed, trying to banish his awkwardness. "Apologies. They should know not to bother me while I'm guiding guests. What sections are ye interested in?" He addressed Kallan and Throwen who both grunted.

"Today is about Octavia, just the filthiest fantasy you have. Thanks." I chose not to respond and Throwen frowned. He thrived on my reactions and giving him none frustrated him, and *Goddess forgive me*, I really enjoyed instigating him.

We meandered past the colorful dome, and it was packed with children running around dancing, singing, and spinning. Short bookshelves lined the perimeter of the contained room with stools throughout for little witches to climb. The glass must have been thick, because their shouts of joy and excitement were encapsulated within.

"You allow children to… play in here?" I pointed to the frenzy.

"Yes! That's the children's section. They're having a story time currently, but as ye can see, it usually ends in dancing and bubbles instead of reading." Finian laughed, nostalgia scrunching up his button nose. "Ye know, the children's section is where I first decided I wanted to be head librarian. The program is fantastic, and my father would bring me every day after school."

School. I had read about schools. They were something Theldeans used to manipulate and brainwash their children into being tiny soldiers of chaos and destruction.

Finian threw his arms wide. "What better way to learn and apply all of this knowledge than through play?"

Playing is for witches who have become idle. If you have become idle, Lady, I can find many more ways for you to contribute to your coven.

But my contribution was never enough. Keeping us all concealed and safe wasn't enough.

Finian continued, going on about founders and milestones for the library as we ascended the spiral stairs.

"Playing is superior to reading in my opinion," Throwen murmured, pulling me close and tickling my back. I elbowed him in the side. If he thought he even stood a chance at winning my attention over books, he was sorely mistaken.

"Well... I wouldn't go that far..." Finian's face was sour as well.

"Ignore him Finian, he is just grumpy because he knows if he skimmed through the poets before his time, they might put him to shame." Throwen scoffed, but I knew what I said rang true.

"He couldn't sit and read an entire book, much less a paragraph." Kallan winked at me over the top of his brother's head. "He has to be moving. It takes a miracle for something or someone to capture his attention for longer than a day."

"You wound me, brother!" Throwen knelt as if shot through the heart with an arrow, grasping his chest. Finian winced at his volume.

"See?" Kallan shook his head, ignoring Throwen's dramatics, and we stepped off the landing of the next level.

Finian walked us down an aisle until we landed at a section of the library with rows upon rows of vibrant, beautifully bound books. Fantasy writers had a thing for pretty books. It was one of the many reasons they were my favorite.

Finian pointed down the row we stopped at. "At the end of this row, there is a large window that looks out to the Zattia Mountains. There are two egg-shaped white chairs. Trust me, they're the best in this place. Miss Penelope sits in them any chance she gets."

I wanted to meet this Miss Penelope Finian seemed enthralled with.

"Rows fifty-five through sixty-two are romantic fantasy. If ye are looking for something more specific, there should be a volunteer shelving books somewhere in this section should ye need any assistance." Finian beamed.

"Thank you, Finian." I curtseyed, and he blushed, an adorable shade of pink blooming across his cheeks and the tips of his ears.

"Finian, can you take me to the shop?" Thrown retrieved some coins from his pocket. "I want to pick a few books for Octavia to bring on our journey."

"Wait, what?" I quickly covered my mouth at my exclamation that came out more like a squeak.

They all gawked at me with concern.

Coughing, I wanted to figure out how to articulate my question without seeming like a complete idiot. "What I mean is... you can buy books to keep as your own *forever*?" I was talking with my hands, disbelief mixing with elation at the notion.

Finian looked to Thrown as if questioning my sanity. *Great job blending in Octavia.*

"There is a store set up in the library where witches can buy slightly damaged or out-of-date books for a reduced cost." Finian grabbed a stack of books off the cart that was next to him. "It's called weeding. We weed through our books frequently."

Thrown continued, "They use the profits for needs that come up."

It was a brilliant idea. This library was a living thing, growing and thriving. I wanted to find its heart and follow along its many winding veins, consuming the worlds begging to be discovered.

"I hope yer visit lived up to yer expectations, Octavia."

"Finian, this place is special. You make it special, and all the witches who work here. I hope that next time I visit, you'll be on your way to that head librarian position." I gave him a warm smile of appreciation, and his face lit up with delight.

"Okay, Finian, don't go falling in love now. We have to leave in a few hours," Throwen joked, and the young witch shook his head, entranced by my words.

He swallowed hard before turning his attention to Throwen. "Right this way."

Finian strode away and panic seized me. I analyzed the many hiding places within this place. Realization hit me that since leaving my coven, Throwen hadn't left my side. A sinking feeling pitted itself low in my stomach. I quickly grabbed onto Throwen's arm. "Is it safe?"

Please don't leave. I begged him with my eyes.

Taking my hands in his, he gently kissed my fingertips that were poking out through my gloves. "Do you trust me, darling?"

I nodded without hesitation; I trusted him more than I trusted any witch, including myself.

"Kallan is my brother, and now he is yours, too. *Right?*" He looked to Kallan who grunted a half-assed confirmation. "I'm only going downstairs; Kallan will keep you safe until I get back."

I glared, displeased at his obvious attempt to push me out of my comfort zone.

Chuckling, he leaned in close and whispered against my hood, "If you're a good girl, I'll buy you more books and you can read me the steamiest parts later."

Molten heat dropped to my core. I had no idea there was this devious side of my sweet bard. I kept forgetting that he was more than that. He was a honed, lethal assassin with hidden hungers.

Finian coughed, ripping us from our inappropriate public exchange. "The store is by the entryway."

He fidgeted with his collar, and a wave of embarrassment washed over me. Throwen had this way of making me feel like we were the only two people in a crowded building. He gave my hand a final squeeze before following Finian to the stairs.

"I guess it's just us." I cleared my throat.

"I think the infamous chairs are this way." Kallan trudged down row fifty-six.

I felt on edge, seeing red orbs peering at me through gaps in stacks of books. *It's not real. It's not real.*

Clasping my hands behind my back, I followed by his side, my head lining up with his bicep.

I wanted to see Theldea, and Throwen couldn't always be with me. Was he trying to help by leaving me with Kallan to show me I could be safe without him?

Assuring myself this unbearable feeling of separation would pass, I traced my fingers along the spines, letting the familiarity calm my fraying nerves. I wanted to make Throwen proud of my brief independence.

I looked up at Kallan. "Do you read?"

He offered me a conspiratorial grin. "Will you tell Throwen?"

I pressed my lips together, pretending to lock them up and throw away the key.

"I'm only telling you because you're the only one who might appreciate them." He rubbed his arm. "I enjoy high fantasy."

"I've read a few." I shrugged. "Sometimes they go over my head, if I'm being honest."

Two white chairs sat at the end of the row, directly across from a huge waterfall. Water stretched up to the sky and plunged to the rocky depths below. We floated in the center of the falls within the safety of the library.

Passing right by the chairs, I pressed my hand against the glass. I could feel the vibrations and the sheer power behind the gushing water made the hair on the back of my neck stand up. "Wow. This is unreal."

"If this isn't the best chair my ass has ever sat on, I'm reporting Finian to the head librarian for lying," Kallan said, so dry that I thought it could've fallen from my own lips.

I laughed and tsked, joining him to observe the notorious chairs.

"I think we've harassed that poor boy enough."

Smiling sheepishly, he gestured for me to pick a chair. Giddiness overwhelmed me and I chewed on my bottom lip, bouncing on my toes. Choosing the seat on the left, I plopped into it.

A scream erupted from me, and the world tilted. The chair rocked back before returning forward. I gripped the sides as if they were my last lifeline.

Kallan burst out laughing.

"Oh, fuck off, he didn't mention they rocked." My irritation faded, and I let myself settle into the chair. I curled my legs up, holding my knees, and rocked gently back and forth. "*Goddess's tits*, this is the warmest, coziest chair I've ever sat in."

Kallan sat with a huff. "I'm too big."

I turned to where he was attempting to fit into the oval opening. His arms were hunched inward, his back too.

He shifted to the floor, pulling out his deck of cards to shuffle. His metal case had a large K engraved on it.

"What's your nickname?" I asked. I wanted to get to know Throwen's family, and it felt like a nickname was a natural starting point, reminding me of my beginning with Throwen.

My heart raced at the memory of the first time Throwen called me darling. He could've easily ended that fight through violence, but even when I attacked him and he knew nothing about me, my safety was his priority.

Resting his elbows on his knees, he continued to shuffle. "What nickname?"

"The one Whynnie gave you. Throwen said she gave one to you all."

Kallan rubbed his temples, and I fought back a smirk. I reached for one of the books displayed on the table beside my chair. "That bad, huh?"

"Teddy Bear." He grimaced.

I hid my smile behind my book.

"Whynnie says it's because I might look like a scary bear on the outside, but underneath the muscle, I'm all fluff."

It seemed a perfect fit for him. Whynnie must be very adept at nicknames, and I couldn't help but wonder what she might call me. Kallan reminded me a lot of myself. I put the book in my lap. "I like it. It suits you."

He had his own unpleasant flavor of childhood trauma, but he relied on Whynnie and his siblings to help him through it. I was glad that they'd found each other.

Rainbows cascaded where the sun shone through the mist. I rocked, the motion soothing me. "Why high fantasy?"

Kallan shuffled again, pulling his cards into a tight bridge. "I love everything about them. The languages, the maps, the strategies and epic battles. There's an order to it. A push and pull of opposites colliding."

It made sense, Kallan appeared to be a creature of habit.

"I can appreciate that. I think it's cool that you like to read. Maybe you could show me your favorites sometime."

Kallan laughed and grabbed the pillow from the chair he couldn't fit in, sprawling out on the rug and throwing an arm over his eyes for a nap. "The Almondgrove Chronicles. Start with those."

Taking a deep breath, I stared up at the ceiling painted with bright pink fluffy clouds. I curled the book tightly to my chest. "Can I just stay here? Pretend everything outside doesn't exist?"

"You could try, O, but I have a feeling Throwen isn't going anywhere without you."

I was slowly realizing I didn't want to go anywhere without him, either. This game we played was dangerous. Eventually I would have to face Malik and my coven.

I never knew I needed a family. Just like that first broom ride, I'd had a taste and didn't want to let it go.

Chapter 19

OCTAVIA

Crossing the enormous stone bridge leading out of Graygarde was like passing between two different worlds. The stone path shifted into soil, and it didn't take long for the forest of Stranata to engulf us. These were the forests I dreamt of in my coven.

The trees were tall, and some were speckled with a pale purple bloom that looked hairy in its center. Vines overlapped above our heads, creating a mesh for the hot beams of sunlight to filter through. Rocks and downed trees lined the path we were on, and birds twittered in a seemingly endless song.

Throwen slipped his hand into one of my pockets, gripping my thigh tightly through the thin fabric. "Remember the time Whynnie caught Echo throwing a huge party near the hovel using all of her teacups for her friends' ale?"

Kallan's chuckle was low, barely perceptible.

"What is Whynnie like?" It was something I pondered on and off. I was apprehensive about meeting her. *Another Goddess-born witch.*

"She is the hardest worker in Theldea. Whynnie knows how to examine a concern and use logic and intellect to solve problems." Kallan sat taller on his horse, John, proud of his mentor. "Covens throughout Theldea have grown and thrived with her help."

Lucky squished bright flowers under her hooves. They lined the path, shooting up from the ground along a stalk, sticking out in alternating sharp spikes.

"She is like a fox. Suspicious of new people and introverted." Throwen rested his chin on my shoulder. "But loyal to those she trusts and even more devoted to the Goddess."

My grip tightened on Lucky's soft mane.

The Goddess.

Theldean's thanked her for the good in their lives and beseeched her in the bad. Now that I knew she hadn't *technically* abandoned me, I didn't even know where to begin with my thoughts and feelings concerning her. I called out to her in the past and after years of no answers, I gave up, accepting her disdain for me.

"Whynnie sounds very practical." I failed to picture what she might look like, only able to conjure an older version of myself.

"She is, but I think she's lonely, too," Throwen said. "Most of her correspondence with witches are through letters or us. Working behind the scenes suits her and we do the rest. Our mission has always been the same, to help Theldea grow and thrive."

I kept seeing scouts mirraged in the growing humidity as the sun mercifully began to set. My right leg bounced, and I double-checked the dagger still strapped to my thigh. Another new constant comfort.

Throwen rubbed up and down my thigh, trying to soothe the shaking. I closed my eyes, focusing on what they said about their mentor. Though from the way they spoke of her, they might as well have called her mother.

"She chose a life of predictability and consistency instead of experiencing the very covens she was trying to help?" I spat it out, the disdain reaching my vocal cords.

"It's not like that," Kallan spoke now, defensiveness lacing his tone.

"He's right. Whynnie is warm and thoughtful behind that tough exterior. Remind you of anyone?" Throwen poked me in the ribs, and I had to fight the urge to bite him in retaliation.

"When she found you... you're all she cared about. She told Throwen to drop everything, that you were his top priority." Kallan offered me an optimistic smile.

"Your family sounds selfless." I pressed a hand to the hollow feeling in my stomach.

Family. I no longer knew where I fit, if that word could even be attributed to me. My coven was my responsibility, and Malik was my mentor. I loved them but did any of them care for me the way these witches did? The answer I already knew filtered numbness into the void I wanted to fill with pain.

Kallan took a long swig from his water, and it dripped into his immaculately trimmed black beard. "Tell us more about your family."

I tensed, unsure of what to say that wouldn't make me seem like a witch to be pitied. "They address me as Lady."

I shifted with discomfort and Throwen pulled me in tighter, whispering into my ear, "There is no pressure with Kallan. His questions are genuine, not an attempt to find your weaknesses, but an attempt to get to know the witch who is so important to me."

Relaxing slightly, I reached to find the right words. "It's short for Lady of the Grave." Hearing it now, I cringed.

"What were your duties as Lady? It sounds like you were important," Kallan asked, and I snorted with amusement.

"No. Not important. Necessary." There was a hard edge to my voice, and they sat patiently, waiting for me to continue.

"I was something to fear. When Malik was away on scouting missions, I instantly made our coven think of him. Most of them were nice, out of trepidation or hope to get closer to Malik through me. But not all of them.

The librarian, Badru, was the witch I interacted with the most. I think maybe to him I was important."

"So you were necessary to instill fear?" Kallan looked at me curiously, like he knew I was holding back. Lacing my fingers with Throwen's, I gripped tightly for his guidance. He knew the truth, that my blood was used to conceal my coven to keep them safe.

Reading my cues, he pressed warmth into my palm, letting me know my secret was safe. I bit the inside of my cheek, slipping on my familiar mask of neutrality. "I guess so."

"Hmm." Kallan patted John's side.

"It's not easy to have a clear perspective anymore." I injected my vagueness with as much truth as I could manage. "I'm still their Lady and I care about them. All of them."

His hatred for Malik ran deep, but so did my love for him. Malik's actions were despicable, and I wanted so badly to turn it all into contempt, but I couldn't.

Kallan shifted his attention to Throwen. I could tell he was about to lighten the mood by instigating his brother. Getting a rise out of Throwen seemed too easy for Kallan and I had to admit I enjoyed it.

"Tell me about your lovers," Kallan said. "A woman who loves romance like yourself *definitely* had some interesting relationships."

Throwen's grip tightened on me, and he rubbed his thumb against my wrist, my pulse picking up as his heart pounded against my back.

I laughed low in response. "The few lovers I had loved me in their own way. They knew I was around, knew I was reliable. But I was mostly unnoticed, expected to be doing what I was told. It's like the way you love a fancy piece of furniture. Everyone was terrified to sit on me, let alone fuck me."

The boys burst out laughing, startling John and Lucky into

disgruntled snorts. I laughed too, happy that my self-degradation was finally being appreciated.

Arching my back, the disks of my spine cracked into alignment. "How much longer until we make camp?"

Throwen massaged the kinks out of my lower back, and I fought a moan.

Kallan spoke methodically. "One more hour and we will make camp well off the path. Then we will eat and sleep. We will head to Fennix's Coven at sunrise."

Pressing my lips into a thin line, I suppressed a smile, knowing Throwen would hate the idea of such a precise schedule.

"Kallan likes *lists* and *plans*," Throwen drawled, and I flicked a rush of air into his face.

"Hey! What was that for?" Scowling, I turned so that he could see my earnest expression. "Kallan is wonderful. Plans and lists are what's going to get us through the rest of this journey. *You* like taking unnecessary detours." I turned to face forward.

"And you made me promise to show you everything Theldea had to offer. That requires *many* detours." Throwen's grip on me was punishing.

As he pressed himself into my back, his hard length rubbed against me, and my aching spine became a puddle. He maneuvered his hand covertly under my dress, inching closer and closer to my core. It was so hot I felt like I might combust. "What? No sarcastic remarks?"

"I'm just waiting for you to quit hiding behind your positivity and face the fact that you love your brother because he likes routine, not despite it." I flicked a tiny ball of flame behind me.

"I knew I liked you." Kallan laughed, trotting ahead of us and speaking over his shoulder to Throwen. "It took me almost five years to like you."

Throwen flicked him off with a grin before winding his fingers into the hair at the base of my neck, massaging out the tension. "If you were a fancy piece of furniture, I would sit on you."

Biting my lip, I allowed myself to sink into his hold. His cock was hard as the stone we left in Graygarde and I wanted more than anything to sneak my hand behind my back and stroke him. But I would be way too mortified if Kallan caught us.

"Hmm... if you were a piece of furniture, you would be a stool." I taunted, and he gasped in horror.

"A stool?! That's the best I get?"

I laughed, knowing how offended he truly was. "It's because you're always lifting people up."

We burst into laughter, Lucky whinnying along with us.

He nipped at my earlobe. "And if I was this stool you speak of, would you sit on me?"

The heat spreading from my abdomen to my core had my sanity slipping away. I drifted my hand back, grabbing his cock through his pants.

Sacred Ether. He felt good in my hand, like his thick cock was made just for me.

"Fuck." He hissed, and I let go, worried I had gone too far. He bit my neck playfully, eliciting a shocked gasp of pleasure. "I'm going to *kill* Kallan for interrupting us again."

"What?" I looked up. Kallan was off his horse and strayed from the path.

Dots burst across my vision. Panic laced my every thought. "What is he doing?"

With four long strides, Kallan was covered by foliage and out of sight.

Throwen slid off Lucky. "Stay here."

He flicked his lute swiftly into a bow and disappeared into the forest, running toward his brother. I heard a grunt of frustration, followed by aggressive hushed whispers.

I patted Lucky's long black mane, quietly slipping off and sneaking her and John a carrot. "Shhh. The boys are fighting."

I took a deep breath and tiptoed over the wild roots toward their muffled argument. Pulling a large leaf aside, I saw them crouching low behind some thick logs. I could hear the rowdy laughter of other witches in the distance now. Kallan snarled, looking through a spyglass.

Inching closer, I pushed the limits of my dress's fabric. Still, it made no sound, and I paused where I could hear them. *Please don't be necromancers.*

"Kallan, we can't risk drawing any more attention to ourselves. We'll report it to the guard, and they will take care of it. We aren't in Fennix's territory yet."

Kallan's muscles tensed. "Oh, you mean like *you* risked everything at the tavern?"

He poked a finger firmly into Throwen's chest and I summoned a flame in my palm defensively.

"That was different." Throwen grit his teeth and stared unflinchingly into his brother's vengeful expression.

Kallan laughed, a dark cynical thing that reminded me too much of myself. "You're absolutely right. *That* was you being a lovesick idiot who can only think with his dick when around that witch. *This!*" He gestured to whatever awaited us in the distance. "This matters. You and I both know Mayson will give them only a slap on the wrist."

I inched forward. "Who are they?"

They both startled and glared at me from where they were crouching. Kallan's neck vein throbbed. "Traffickers."

"No necromancers?" I scratched my neck.

Throwen crawled to me and took my trembling chin between his fingers. "No necromancers."

Throwen's brief reassurance gave Kallan his opening, and he strode confidently into the danger.

Pinching the bridge of his nose, Throwen groaned. "*Cursed Abyss*! Do you have any idea what this is going to be like when Echo joins us? Chaos. This group is going to be complete and utter chaos. *This* is why I work alone." He pulled his collar up into a mask. "Keep a firm hold on your dagger. If they fight, you protect yourself until I can help."

Nodding, fear mixed with an erratic excitement, sending my heart into an intoxicating cadence. I doubted a few regular witches could stand a chance against Kallan and Throwen.

An odd sense of empowerment rushed through me at Throwen's inclusion of me. He thought I was strong enough to handle this. I crouched behind him, following in his exact footsteps. Pulling up my mask and hood, I unsheathed my dagger.

My dream was to be a scout and while I never loved the idea of hurting people, I would have made an excellent addition as a healer.

A healer? They endure the same training as the scouts, and you know where I stand on that. Stop searching for loopholes, Octavia.

As I recalled Malik's words and having to publicly apologize at the following ceremony, my heart sank. My delusion of strength faded, and the panic and fear crept in the closer we got to Kallan and the other witches.

"Ross!" Kallan bellowed. "Last time we met, you were fleeing as I freed the women and children you planned on trading."

Standing together in a huddle, the fumbling witches threw up air shields. There were carts with cages and some crates set up around their camp. If Kallan's accusations were true, I didn't blame him for seeking vengeance.

"That was all a misunderstanding. I'm done with that life. A reformed man," Ross said, his tone confident.

The other witches were trembling, and mostly preoccupied with Throwen. I knew a power-hungry leader when I saw one. If we took Ross down, the others would possibly surrender and wouldn't have to be hurt.

Kallan cracked his knuckles and neck, preparing for a fight.

Throwen stepped forward, striding right up to the air shield, his nose touching it. "Hello," he purred at the witch who couldn't take his paranoid gaze off him. "If you let down your air shield, I'll only break your nose. If not, well…"

Purple tendrils wrapped around his limbs, stringing themselves around his bow to make it lethal. "This might hurt a lot more than it has to."

"Toni, don't you fucking dare!" Ross attempted to reel in his control over the witch, but it was too late. He let his part of the shield down, creating a hole for Throwen and Kallan to race through.

"Wait!" I yelled. It didn't have to be like this. If they subdued Ross—

A fireball whizzed past my head and I dropped to the ground, using my hood to cover myself from the dirt flying around. Staying flat, I threw up an air shield, searching for Throwen.

He punched Toni in the nose, who fell to the ground in a fetal position, blood gushing down his face.

The witch with bright blue hair spotted me and created a tunnel of air, running through it straight toward me.

Standing quickly, I conjured fireballs to rest in my palms. I held up my hands placatingly. "Stop! I don't want to hurt you!"

"Working with the dog and the Angel is a death sentence!" she screamed, launching herself at me.

I held up my hands, and a dark violet arrow popped through her shoulder like a parasite. I screamed, unsure if this was reality or just another hallucination brought on by adrenaline and fear.

As she went down, I knew it was real. But instead of sorrow or guilt, morbid fascination consumed me. The spirits didn't tear her apart from the inside, but sunk back into Throwen. Her soul wasn't tainted. The Abyss had no hold on it. The girl was small and quickly passed out, succumbing to the pain.

I watched Kallan catch Ross's kick, pulling him in close before head-butting him. Ross cried out in pain and was easily pushed back by Kallan's sheer size. Kallan laughed, as if excited to catch this rat who had escaped him in the past.

Throwen was on the ground with another witch, thighs wrapped tightly around his neck. His target slowly went limp and Throwen released his hold. Without hesitation, he leaped from the ground to his feet, fearful eyes searching for me as the chaos subsided.

I waved at him with a sheepish smile, and his posture relaxed.

Kallan's fist collided with Ross's jaw. The crunch of bone I was all too acquainted with hurt my ears. Ross thudded into the soft soil with a splat, knocked out.

Throwen flicked his bow back into a lute, playing a few chords as the spirits gathered up the fallen witches, holding them against a large tree. The boys wasted no time binding the witches together tightly with thick vines. It was like our assembly lines in the kitchen, smooth and practiced. They panted as we walked back to the horses.

Throwen wiped his sleeve across his brow, soaking up the sweat. "I hope it was worth it."

"If even one woman or child is spared, then it was more than worth it." Kallan clapped his hands, shaking off the extra dirt.

"So, you just leave them there?" I asked, paying attention to my feet as my boots squished into the muddy ground.

"It's in the Goddess's hands now." Kallan burst through the last large leaves and John trotted with excitement.

"What he means is it's much more torturous if nature kills them than if he does." Throwen helped me back up on Lucky. When we were pressed together once more, the feel of him in my hand came rushing back.

"Let's go, this fucked up our schedule." It seemed as though Kallan thought his concept of morality was black and white, unknowingly blind to the gray of his own soul.

Chapter 20

THROWEN

Calls of the wild filtered through the lush flora surrounding our campsite. The sounds of nature had always inspired me, given me rhythms and melodies to capture in my songs. It was a relief to take a break after a full day of travel.

Edward gave a small salute like a tiny deckhand. "Sorry I'm late sir. Echo's map was confusing. No necromancers detected."

I tousled his dark brown hair. "And Fennix?"

"He has been at the tavern the past five nights. Echo burned off the tip of his beard last night during one of their debates. It was hilarious! The Captain jumped up and down like a freshly caught salmon!" The boy's laughter was contagious, and I pictured the idiot jumping about and Echo laughing their ass off.

"Thank you, Edward. Great work, as always. Are you up for one more job?" As I peered down at him, his bright green eyes twinkled with mischief.

"Aye, sir!"

"Find Echo and ask them to book us two rooms." Placing the bag of coins in Edwards's hands made me realize how much he had grown in the past year. He was getting taller, almost ten now. Soon, I would have to find another little spy.

"Aye, thank you, sir!"

I stroked my mustache, shaking my head. "Edward, it's Throwen, not sir."

"Right." His abysmal attention span shifted to where Octavia sat next to Kallan by the fire. They were laughing and eating stew. When I turned back to him, a huge grin with a few missing teeth, filled half of his small round face.

"She's... beautiful." He shifted on his toes, trying to get a better look.

"No, Edward. Many witches are beautiful. That one"—I pointed to her through the large leaves hanging around our campsite—"she's divine. For a long time, I thought she was the Goddess herself. Do you know what I mean?"

The boy scrunched up his nose, staring hard at Octavia. "Nope."

He turned and strode back toward Fennix's Coven without another word.

Chuckling, I thought of the children of Goldhaven that I often played for. They never held back and I adored how unpredictable children's responses could be.

Pushing some leaves and vines aside, I strode up to camp.

Octavia's playful smile beamed from across the fire. "I still think you're an ass for using a child to do your spying for you. You're a terrible influence."

"Children go unnoticed. Nobody suspects they're listening. Most even think them incapable. But some of the best spies I've worked with have been children. We don't give them nearly enough credit."

I finished stirring the stew and ladled some out for myself. My mouth watered at the savory smell. Finding a seat across from Octavia, I kept my head down. I knew I was pulling away from her, but the more I thought about how this would end, the harder it was to foresee a positive outcome.

An ache formed in the back of my throat at the thought of Malik prevailing and taking her away from us. *Take her and run.*

I clenched my fork tightly, devouring each potato like it was my enemy and I was crushing his manipulation between my teeth.

"Are you okay?" Her soft voice penetrated my negative thoughts.

"Fine, darling. Just hungry." I squirmed and took another bite of stew. She had enough problems without me airing my doubts and fears.

"You look stressed, brother." Kallan stood and dug into his pocket. Pulling out a joint, he handed it to me.

Taking it, I flicked a flame to life at the tip of my finger, lighting the tip. "You are a lifesaver."

He shrugged. "I figured you were out." Kallan always brought me joints and I loved him for it.

As I sucked in, the burn and heat coated my throat before moving down into my chest. I held it for a few seconds before blowing it back out.

Soon the relief took hold, bringing me back down so I could feel happy and comfortable with my thoughts. I inhaled again, holding the smoke in for a moment before blowing it out in a thick cloud.

Rustling leaves bathed us in a pleasant ambiance.

Feeling my eyelids relax, I found Octavia again. Her hair was blowing in the gentle breeze and her curls were more prominent in the humidity. With her head tilted to the side, she eyed me with something akin to suspicion and curiosity. She was like a cat, my little witch, and I wanted to pet her. *Why did I sit all the way over here?*

"Have you ever smoked cannabis?" I licked my lips slowly and took a drink of water.

"No. Malik said it would only lead to stupidity and laziness. But when I snuck around the training yard, I would see him smoking with the scouts." She scrunched up her nose. "The smell is unmistakable."

I stood up, feeling much lighter and in control of my fear and uncertainty. They were mercifully dormant for now. "Would you like to try? No pressure, Kallan doesn't partake."

Kallan huffed while he shuffled his cards.

Sitting beside her, I crossed my legs the way we usually sat together. Her legs looked like a little pretzel all curled up in themselves.

"Does it hurt?" Her question would seem innocent to any other witch, but I smiled wickedly, knowing she enjoyed small amounts of pain with her pleasure.

"It will burn in your throat and chest. Since it's your first time, you're going to cough a lot. But don't be embarrassed, it's a rite of passage."

She gave me her rapt attention, a little too eagerly as she squirmed closer to me. *Such a good girl, helping me keep my promise to show her everything.*

I spoke low so that only Octavia could hear me, "Promise me this is your own decision and not me pressuring you."

She scooted even closer, and my cock twitched eagerly in response. When her sweet citrus scent mixed with the smoke, it was intoxicating. Leaning in closer, she held her body against me. "If I want you to stop, I know the word, Throwen."

My name on her lips confirmed that my deprived cock was starving for attention. *Sacred Ether*, she was perfect.

"The important thing to remember is to ensure you're taking a deep breath." I took her hand, pressing her palm flush against her stomach. "Fill your belly and blow all the air out slowly and gently if you can."

Determination straightened her spine, and she reached for the joint.

"Allow me, darling. Don't hold it for more than a few seconds, or this is going to be rough."

As I held it for her, she wrapped her lips around the joint, sucking in deep. Her pupils dilated and her cheeks puffed up before she coughed. She glared at me through watering eyes.

"You sucked it into your mouth and throat instead of your belly."

With a final cough, she panted and took a drink of water. Clenching her fists, she pressed her lips tightly together and tried again. This time I let her hold it herself and she breathed in deeply, her belly expanding to allow the smoke in. She blew out a large puff and coughed uncontrollably as I held her close, rubbing her back.

"*Sacred Ether*! Who would do this for fun? That was..." Her eyes unfocused for a minute and a very slow smile pulled at the corners of her lips. "Oh... *oh*."

I laughed as the high hit her. "That's why."

Her smile grew, and she held her hands to her lips.

Malik kept this herb from most of his coven. The Goddess gave us the treasures of the soil to help us through this life until we could join her in the Ether. It would have greatly eased Octavia's many struggles and lightened the weight her mind put on her.

"What should we do?" She looked between Kallan and me eagerly, giggles pouring from her. Kallan just shook his head, but a content smile accompanied it.

I'd never seen her this carefree, and I wanted to test the limits. "If you could do anything right now, what would you do?"

As she eyed me hungrily, the message in those golden pools she called eyes was clear. *She would do me.*

I shifted in my seat, my body simmering with need. She bit her lip before her eyes bounced to where Lucky and John slept next to our bags.

"I want to try on my new clothes." She shot up and rushed over, unwrapping her neatly packaged clothes like a child on their Name Day. "No peeking!"

She rushed into the dense forest and an instinct to chase her had me arching my back to fight the ache in my hands that wanted to explore her body. "Not too far! I don't want you getting eaten by a huge cat!"

"You're soooooo funny, Throwen. Ha. Ha," she dryly called out through the darkness, but excited cackling followed.

Goddess forgive me, I wished she would have just stripped right here in front of me.

Kallan plopped down next to me, pulling me away from my fantasies. "I've never seen you so smitten before, Little Miracle."

I wiped the dopey grin off my face and took in one more deep breath of smoke. When I let it out, it was in a frustrated sigh. "Yeah, I guess."

Pulling my lute over, I opened my songbook. I strummed, trying to figure out the notes for the chorus of her song.

"You guess? Really?" He scowled at me, and I knew exactly where this was going.

"If you have something to say, brother, just say it." It came out more defensive than intended.

"I've never seen you look at a witch the way you look at her. You look at her like if you lost her again, you would burn everything down to find her."

I bit the inside of my cheek. "That's because it's exactly what I would do."

My playing ceased, and I found the courage to meet Kallan's eyes. They widened and his jaw dropped. He rested a hand on my shoulder. "Do you love her?"

"I... am a pirate!" Octavia strutted over to the fire and spun in a circle with her hands on her hips.

"Well, you'll certainly blend in." Kallan's voice sounded far away as I took in the Goddess-born artistry before me.

I was fully awake, heart pounding with adrenaline, my sole focus on her. My jaw had dropped and the worries of what exactly I felt for her faded away. If I hadn't already been sitting, she would have brought me to my knees and I would have kissed her feet, thanking her for allowing me to be in her presence.

She wore a white blouse that crossed over her breasts, twisting up around her neck, covering her mark but leaving her arms and back bare. It was tucked into a black leather corset belt that hugged her waist, accentuating her hips.

Plunging her hands into her hip scarf, she swayed back and forth to make the golden coins along the hem jingle. "And look. Pockets!"

I was hypnotized, following her movements as I scanned past the scarf to the black split-thigh skirt trailing down her front and back. Her legs were wrapped in fishnets that were just begging to be ripped off.

Another flash of gold glinted as she twirled, her dagger still at her thigh.

When she moved just right, I could see where her thigh met her hip and the delicate curve of her ass. *Thank you, Goddess, for your bountiful creation.*

"And what do you need pockets for?" Typical. I wanted to proclaim my reverence for her, treat her body as a temple, making sure to give it my undivided attention, but a taunt came out instead.

"For these!" She whipped out two oddly shaped black throwing stars. "Kallan got them for me."

"Of course he did." I smiled, knowing I would be the one who would get to teach her how to use them. "Let me see."

She hopped over to where we sat by the fire, her tits bouncing right along. The next time we were alone, I was going to sink my teeth into them. Shaking my head, I attempted to clear away the lust so I could properly enjoy her innocent excitement with her.

"I know I don't know how to use them, but they are so badass. Will you teach me?" Her glazed squint found me, and her dark almond hair appeared warmer in tone in this new environment. The unruly waves were gathered in a high ponytail, held up with my leather strap.

"Hmm…" I twisted one of the curls near her temple around my finger, drawing her in. "I'll teach you, but there's a condition."

"What's the condition?"

These little games made me feel more excited than I had in years. It was as if she shot lightning throughout my body, always originating in my heart. My fingers ached, wanting to rip the outfit off to see the perfection beneath. This was nothing like the anxious itch to play my lute. This was all-consuming. A needy and insistent pull.

Raising my eyebrows, I said, "A dance."

Eyes ablaze, she jumped up, opening her arms wide to welcome me.

"With Kallan," I specified.

Her bottom lip pushed out in an adorable pout, her arms dropping to her sides. Then a devilish grin spread across her face, and she found her target. She rushed toward Kallan.

"No, O! No. I don't dance." I knew his denial didn't stand a chance against Octavia's determination. He laughed, and she pulled on his arm, not moving him an inch.

"Either you teach me yourself or you dance." She stomped her foot like a child, and Kallan crossed his arms.

"I don't dance."

"Okay…" Octavia plopped down beside him, feigning defeat. The only noises were the crackling fire, frogs, and rustling leaves.

Octavia pounced, trying to wrap her arms around him, but they were nowhere close to touching.

"O… what are you doing?" Kallan sighed, Octavia slowly chipping away at his resolve.

"I'm going to keep hugging you until you agree to dance with me." She squeezed him like a cobra.

Kallan's expression soured further, finding me across the fire. He had no idea what to do, and I shrugged, not wanting to interfere in this hilarious battle, if you could even call it that. My brother managed to stand, but Octavia held on tight, grunting and standing with him.

Kallan shook his head. "You can't do this forever."

"Try me," Octavia challenged. He walked away, and she became dead weight, hanging on tightly as he hauled her around.

"Fine. One dance." He rubbed his shoulders and Octavia loosened her grip.

I stood, and she shrieked, sending nearby bats fluttering.

With a flare I had crafted perfectly from years of playing in taverns, I effortlessly swung my lute in front of me and stepped into a deep lunge.

Octavia's cheeks turned pink, and I strummed a jaunty sea shanty.

Kallan awkwardly held her tiny hands in his and swayed back and forth. After a moment of finding their footing, they box-stepped around the fire.

Kallan's white teeth beamed through his smile as his entire face lit up. Octavia giggled and swayed her hips in exaggerated movements to make the coins jingle. It was a moment of innocence and Kallan was no doubt picturing his sisters that he used to dance with.

Octavia was experiencing a childhood lost and the love and support only a devoted sibling could provide. She twirled under Kallan's extended arm and between the humidity and her hips swaying to my rhythm, I was about to burst into flame.

"See. You're good at it, you big bear." Octavia poked his chest, and he laughed, spinning with her in a circle.

The spirits danced around too, sticking close to Octavia's ankles. Chuckling, I admired her bare feet. She was free, if only for a moment. I wanted to watch her dance every night for the rest of my existence.

Continuing to play, I let the spirits know if we didn't settle down soon, I wouldn't be able to keep from acting on my desires. I brought the song to its end and they both fell to the ground. Octavia was panting from staying on her toes to reach Kallan.

"Thank you." He bumped her in the shoulder. "I haven't danced in years."

"You're welcome." Her eyes flicked to mine. "Now teach me."

"Not tonight, darling. We need to sleep."

"What kind of dancing do they do in Stranata?" she asked. "There were witches in our coven from here that could move like serpents. Do you think I could learn that?"

She shifted her hips up and down and the spirits erupted from me, wrapping around Octavia like ribbons. *So much for settling down.*

"Hello there." She stroked them lovingly.

I felt a fissuring tear within me, something filling all the cracks with her emotions. *Hope.* She was experiencing hope, and the spirits couldn't control themselves around her strong positive energy.

I shivered with the onslaught of both our emotions. It didn't seem to affect her the way it was me, and I felt unhinged. I would play her like my lute, pushing and bending her strings to the point of breaking beneath our passion until she was screaming my name.

"Okay, I think I've tired you out enough for sleep." Kallan sensed how overwhelmed I was and mercifully picked Octavia up. He easily threw her over his shoulder, and she shrieked with joy, kicking her feet back and forth. Placing her gently onto her bedroll, he thrust a book into her hands.

"One chapter before bed. And don't even try to read more. Echo tries to pull that crap all the time too. If you stay up all night reading, I am not dealing with your grumpy ass tomorrow." Kallan walked to the other side of the fire.

She pouted, removing the skirt of coins and crawling under a lightweight blanket. It wouldn't keep us too warm, but it did help protect us from bugs.

I would have to thank Kallan later for treating her like she was part of our family. He had no idea how badly she needed compassion and acceptance, and he gave it to her in abundance.

She hummed happily and opened her book, fidgeting, trying to find a comfortable position.

The combined humidity and horniness forced me to pull my shirt up over my head. It was too fucking hot. I frowned when she didn't even look up, already engrossed in her fantasy world.

As I crawled into my spot beside her, I could feel the heat rolling off her skin and I wanted nothing more than to demand that she sleep in my bedroll with me.

But Kallan was right, we needed rest. I pulled out my songbook, determined to figure out the last lines of her song.

"Psst..."

"*Goddess's tits*, O, that wasn't even a minute." Kallan grunted, grabbing his bedroll and sulking over to a spot near a large tree in the distance.

"What, troublemaker?" I turned to look at her. "I'm not letting you ride my thigh again with him right over there, I would never hear the end of it."

"I have a feeling if I climbed back on top of you right now you would sing a different tune, bard." She challenged me.

She was right. Octavia tasted like strawberries and sin, and I wanted to be nourished by her sweet pussy.

"What was it you wanted, darling?" I deserved a special place in the Ether for surviving this much sexual frustration.

She propped up on her elbows, her open book resting on the ground between us.

"What are you writing?" Her snooping eyes drifted to my open page full of lyrics I had written about her. That's all I was capable of writing these days. She completely consumed my thoughts. *My sexy little muse.*

I poked her nose. "That's for me to know and you to find out."

"But if I'm going to find out later, why can't I just know now?"

I closed my book, and she peered up at me through fluttering lashes. The whites of her eyes were glazed pink and a soft natural smile lit up her face. I could sing with how good it felt to see her so at ease, so happy and content.

"Darling, I don't share my songs with any witch until they're complete. Even a witch that has the greatest ass I've ever had the pleasure of digging my fingers into."

She burst into laughter, rolling onto her side, her head on her book and her hands grasping her belly.

"If you two can't fucking settle down, I'm separating you!" Kallan called out over the sounds of the crackling embers and Octavia's laughter. I wanted to throttle him for interrupting her rare moments of undiluted joy.

Sitting up, I pulled her to me by her armpits. She was like a ragdoll letting me drag her so that her head was resting in my lap. She hummed and snuggled in; her lids heavy from the residual effects of the cannabis.

I untied the leather strap holding her hair up and gently wrapped it back around her wrist, tightening it and sealing it with a gentle kiss.

"Thank you." Her sleepy voice was music to my ears.

Tonight, I witnessed her put herself first, make her own choices, and follow her passions. Pride swelled within my chest, watching her grow.

Without guilt, she enjoyed her new clothes. She read the books she loved. Octavia thought she lost herself long ago, but she was in there. She was just too traumatized and afraid to fully emerge.

Malik feigned being her savior for years. She didn't need another savior; she needed a friend willing to protect her if she became too overwhelmed to handle this world herself.

I would spend the rest of my life teaching her how to love herself and nurture her body and passions. Would encourage her curiosity. Would carry her through the darkness. And I would decimate every witch who threatened to hurt or manipulate her.

Her breathing shifted into a slow cadence, the cannabis helping her sleep to be more restful. Usually, she was restless and twitching, but tonight she was in a deep motionless sleep.

I peered down at her relaxed facial features as drool spilled from her mouth onto my leg. Slipping under, I adjusted so her head was resting on my chest.

We snuggled together in our haphazard nest of blankets. I rubbed tiny circles on her back, and I couldn't help the song from slipping free.

"Darling, you only know what it's like to survive
You think there's only darkness, but I see your light"

Chapter 21

OCTAVIA

We led Lucky and John on foot, but they seemed on edge, the wild sounds of the forest keeping them alert to any threats. Their hooves and legs were coated in the rich-smelling soil.

All the muscles that had been momentarily loosened last night seemed even tighter today. Each step I took sunk into the wet ground, squishing the mud beneath. Wiggling my toes in my boots, I recalled how marvelous the soil felt between them as I danced around the fire with Kallan.

The cannabis had calmed my mind, coercing it into a brief peacefulness. Never had I felt so free of guilt. I was grateful for Throwen's marvelous idea. It was a clever way to pull both Kallan and I from our shells. I navigated my emotions as we walked in comfortable silence.

Tilting my head, I appreciated Throwen's profile. His jaw was smooth and freshly shaven, his mustache curled up into a content grin. A loose-fitting sandy brown shirt that could be cinched shut at his waist was hanging wide open, revealing his toned chest. The dark hair contrasted beautifully with his pale skin.

My eyes wandered lower to his long baggy pants that were tight around his ankles, creating a unique laid-back look with his songbook still strapped to his side. After seeing so many new magnificent things, he was by far my favorite.

Last night my fears had faded into almost nothing and I wanted to let myself feel. But today my demon was roaring at last night's momentary sedation. *He could never love a monster like you.*

Fidgeting, I toyed with the coins adorning my hip scarf.

A low growl sounded far off in the forest. Could it be the panthers Thrown had mentioned tearing apart their prey? My stomach turned, and I regretted stuffing my face with fruit this morning.

"Try this." Thrown offered me a dark green leaf curled into a glistening cup.

I took it with a sheepish smile, tilting it up to let the fresh water cool my throat. Some of it dripped down my chin and a bead of sweat tickled along my spine. The heat here was oppressive. "Mmm."

According to Kallan, it rained over half of the year here and I was thankful he suggested I wear my boots until we made it to Fennix's Coven.

The overly sweet smell of rotting fruit on the ground morphed into a potent sulfuric odor. I froze, reaching out for Thrown but he was already pulling me close.

"What's going on?" he asked.

"I... I smell sulfur," I whispered to ensure Kallan didn't overhear something I might be hallucinating.

"I don't smell it. Kallan isn't saying anything, so he doesn't smell it either," Thrown reassured.

"It feels real." It was all I could think of to say.

"It is real for you." He pulled me close to his side, rubbing his hand along my arm firmly from shoulder to fingertips. "I know that doesn't erase the fear, but I'm here."

Cursed Abyss! How was he this fucking perfect? He anticipated my needs the way a dog sensed an oncoming storm, seeing right through me as if staring through freshly cleaned glass. I knew he wasn't perfect, but he was pretty *Goddess-damned* close.

"Thank you. You're very good at helping people." My heart rate picked up.

"Is that so?" Arching a dark eyebrow, he licked his lips. "Is there anything else you might need help with? I'm always open to suggestions." He slipped a finger through my fishnets, pulling and letting it snap against my thigh.

"Hmm…" I slowly ran a hand down my thigh and imagined all the depraved things I wanted him to do to me. "Well, I was thinking you could start between my—"

A tiny bright blue blob hopped out from the dense undergrowth onto the worn path. "Woah! What is that?"

I sprinted ahead, and crouched low, my knees getting covered in mud so I could inspect this bright enigma. "*Oh, my Goddess*, it's so cute! It's a little baby frog!"

A gust of wind pushed me over and I lost my balance as I reached for it. My reflexes saved me from falling into the mud. The little frog hopped back into the jungle.

"What the fuck, Throwen?"

He strode over, hand extended to help me up, while he laughed and winked devilishly. "They're poisonous, darling. Look but don't touch."

I flicked my finger, sending muddy water toward his face, but he threw his arm up in time to block it.

Throwen smirked. "Better come up with some new moves."

I wanted to slap that smirk right off his stupid, distracting face.

"Come on you two, we have a schedule to keep." Kallan urged us forward from behind. He took the flank hours ago when Throwen kept getting distracted, showing me every little detail I might have missed. This place, this life I was now living, was danger wrapped in an alluring package. *But I like danger.*

"We have a schedule to keep," Throwen mocked Kallan with a convincing deep voice and puffed up his chest. "Live a little, brother!"

He used a rag to wipe me clean of mud. My pulse skittered under his touch, his warmth. It was torture being so close but unable to act. "Thank you."

The bright sun and sky glinted through a lush canopy of leaves, making the path below our feet look like undulating green waves.

"How is so much of this place untouched?" I admired the ropy vines covering the trees that mirrored the winding roots below.

"Most Stranatans survive on their resources," Throwen said as he scratched Lucky's chin. "They respect nature more than they respect each other."

Streams meandered alongside us, and I pictured witches foraging and fishing along their banks. Mystical sounds of exotic birds and other animals continuously provided a musical ambiance while they worked.

"How many animals live here?" A vision of a large black cat leaping onto the path and tearing our throats out assaulted me, ripping me from my pleasant picture of daily life in Stranata.

"I don't think anyone bothered to count." Kallan strode up beside us, trying to keep John moving despite the creature stopping every few feet to enjoy some fallen fruit.

I straightened, hearing voices in the distance. It was another panic attack waiting to happen. Taking a deep breath, I held onto the fact that Stranata's population was smaller than Graygarde's.

"Is there anything else I need to know before we get there?" I reached for the back of my neck, ensuring my mark was hidden. They already explained the basics but out of all the regions, the Stranatans seemed to most align with the Theldeans I grew up learning about. Despite knowing most of that was lies, I was still afraid. *Fucking coward.*

Throwen grabbed the hand now scratching at my throat and placed it on Lucky's side. I stroked her coat and Throwen squeezed my other hand. "The goal is to get in and find Echo."

"And not be seen by Fennix," Kallan added.

I turned to Kallan. "What is he like?"

"Fennix is a pompous ass who secured his position with brute force. Most of the witches in his coven and the rest of Stranata were criminals, outlaws, and pirates." Kallan shook his head. "I don't envy Echo's responsibilities."

I didn't want to be seen by Fennix either, but I couldn't comprehend how someone so dishonorable could remain head of a coven. Malik consumed my thoughts, and my next questions came out defensively. "Have you given Fennix a chance? To do better?"

"He's had many opportunities to be a fair leader. But his father beat his beliefs into him, and he feels a responsibility to stick to them. Echo thinks he can change." Throwen said.

Maybe that's what happened to Malik, and he grew up in a similar unhealthy situation.

"If everyone hates him so much, why do they follow him?"

The boys groaned in unison. Throwen smoothed his mustache with his thumb and pointer finger, failing to hide a smile. "Because as much as I hate to admit it, he is the best at what he does."

"And what is that?"

"What pirates do best, of course. Find treasure." He put on a gruff tone, knowing this was *exactly* the kind of thing I would find interesting.

I bit my lip, recalling the sexy captains in my books, fucking on a huge pile of lavish stolen textiles, jewels, and coins. "What kind of treasure?"

"Tomes bring in the most coin, but artifacts are valuable too." Throwen shortened his strides so I could keep up. "Fennix works closely with the

Graygarde curator. He has brought in most of the items they show off in their museums."

We had a museum in our coven, but there were no tomes. All the junk in that dank hallway revolved solely around Malik. Gagging internally, I imagined the entire display of robes he wore during some of his particularly intense orgies.

"He also sells artifacts to the richest bastards in Graygarde for an obscene cost. All that money just so some witches can hang the treasures in their enormous houses and swing their cocks around. That money could go toward making life better for everyone in their coven." Kallan's assessment seemed valid.

"What kind of artifacts?" I asked.

More voices and shouts were filtering through the dense trees, but I still couldn't see any sign of the coven.

"Stuff from old covens," Throwen replied. "Covens grow and die just like anything. The most valuable stuff goes decades back when almost every witch in Theldea worshiped the Goddess."

"Whynnie has tons of that junk." Kallan rolled his eyes. "I'm pretty sure that mirror she spotted you in was given to her by her mentor who got it from his mentor who—"

My vision tunneled, and it was hot, *so fucking hot*. Sweat gathered around my hairline and under my breasts. A dull hum vibrated my skull, and I slipped away from my body.

I always thought I was alone. A fluke. A mistake. I'd never even considered there were others like me and the reality of that was sinking in the closer we got to Whynnie.

I was vaguely aware that someone was touching me and Throwen's muffled voice penetrated my fraying nerves. "Octavia?"

"We're here." The humming in my head ceased as Kallan spoke. My vacant eyes refocused, staring down at shaking hands.

Throwen pulled me aside. "Give us a minute."

"We don't have a minute, we are already behind sched—"

"I swear to the Goddess, brother, if you say the word schedule one more time, I will tell Whynnie you're the one who broke her favorite teacup last year," Throwen ground out.

Kallan huffed and mumbled as he went further ahead.

Throwen cupped my face, pulling me back to him. "What do you need from me right now? How can I help?"

Words evaded me and my throat gradually tightened. Refusing to cry, I forced my eyes wide open, hoping my defiance would dry them out. They pleaded with him to decide for me. I didn't know what I needed. I was enveloped in the strong scent of cannabis. Nuzzling into his warm chest, my body relaxed in his arms. His comfort lifted the fog that covered my mind. "I don't want to think about the Goddess or my connection to her. I'm just... I'm not ready."

"That's okay. She will be there when you're ready." Pulling away, he kept his grip firmly on my shoulders and gently kissed my forehead. "Lucky for you we are in Fennix's Coven, there will be plenty of distractions here."

His gaze shifted to my painted lips.

"Echo doesn't like to be kept waiting and I would much rather deal with them than you. Let's go!" Kallan hollered.

We laughed and caught up. A canopy of trees still surrounded us, but the only difference was that the path was no longer dirt. Instead, a row of boards stretched off into the unknown. Lively sounds of a coven were near, but I still didn't see it. Maybe they had a concealment spell of their own?

"I thought you said we were here?"

Throwen smiled, pulling me a few steps away from the path. As he parted some large leaves, I gasped at the sight before me. Below us sat

Fennix's entire coven, nestled right in the middle of thick vegetation next to where the water flowed out to the sea. Magic did not conceal them, but the nature that surrounded them did.

We returned to the path, and soon the wooden boards shifted into steps descending into the coven. They creaked and moaned as we led our horses down with us.

I clung to the railing made of thick twisting ropes, trying my best not to imagine them as deadly slithering snakes.

It didn't take long to reach the entrance. Time seemed to speed up, as if trying to keep pace with my racing heartbeat. I scanned the glorious scene before me.

Huts standing high on stilts were built along the shoreline, the water lapping lazily against the thick, wet wood. Tied to some posts were hand-built canoes, filled with witches fishing. They hooted and hollered unabashedly, not concerned with the other witches around them. The trees at our backs creaked in the slight breeze and I closed my eyes, inhaling the scent of exotic spices.

Throwen came up behind me, massaging my shoulders. "What do you think?"

"This place smells like *life*. The entire cycle of it. The moisture gives to the soil, which gives to the vegetation and plants until they decay. *Even in death, there is life.*" I said it with reverence, hopeful that it was true.

"It smells like fish and shit." Kallan urged us forward up a hill. He seemed so blind to the beauty around him. Did he purposefully ignore it or had he simply become accustomed to it?

The water was composed of magnificent teals that undulated in a fluid motion, and I imagined a royal blue siren tail flicking up out of its waves. A soft smile curled the corners of my lips. It had been a long time since my mind conjured something fun and pleasant.

"Are there really sirens out there?" I asked as we crested the top of the hill that turned into a street.

"Shh!" Kallan whirled on me and Throwen sealed my mouth with his hand.

Without thinking, I bit hard into his flesh, my fight-or-flight response pulsing through my jaw. He hissed, and I released.

Heat rushed up my neck and into my cheeks, not from embarrassment but from the hungry smirk he gave me. He appeared ravenous, a devilish expression filling his face. *Sacred Ether.* I imagined biting into his thick biceps, his neck, anything that would get me closer to him, into his bloodstream.

"You can't talk about that shit here. Pirates are extremely superstitious." Kallan cut in, redirecting my attention.

"They must have left that out of my history books," I replied sarcastically.

We were deeper into the coven now, the water at our backs. The huts were no longer on stilts but stacked upon one another, creating a row of housing and businesses. Witches lined the streets, but this differed greatly from the markets in Graygarde. There were no bright colors, and their stalls had no roof, using the natural cover of the canopy. These witches were loud, hollering their goods and prices at passersby, while others bartered.

When we passed, witches grew quiet. Some of them tried to avoid eye contact with Throwen and Kallan. Others gawked at me. *Too much attention. We are drawing too much attention.*

The muscles Throwen had just massaged turned back to stone. My heart rushed up to block my airway. I could feel the golden corset crushing my lungs as we paraded to the tree for the ceremony. *Murderer! Levi, Robin, Jatan, Oleander, Ellinor, and so many more.*

"Why are they looking at us like that?"

Throwen leaned down and whispered in my ear, "Stranatans are weary of every witch around them. We're almost there, darling. I'm going to buy you whatever has the most chocolate in it."

"Promise?" I asked with a shaky voice and rested my head against his shoulder.

He gave my hand another squeeze. "Promise."

Fennix's Ruby was painted onto a wooden sign that hung above a large hut's door. Music and laughter poured through the windows where glass had broken. I took a deep breath, ready to execute this perfectly and impress them all.

Kallan led the horses to a stable hand. The witch opened his mouth to ask a question, but upon seeing Kallan's stature and Throwen's serious face, he closed it and rushed off.

As we stepped over the threshold of the tavern, the first thing to overtake me was the noise. Everyone packed in like sardines. It also smelled like sardines, and I covered my mouth and nose.

This place brought my imaginations of pirate ships and crews to life. Witches shouted and sang while playing cards and darts. Barmaids cackled at the lewd jokes being told around the bar, filling their patron's mugs to overflowing.

Everything was made of a deep dark wood with accents of crimson fabric hanging about. Some tapestries of monstrous sea creatures crushing ships sent shivers down my spine.

Throwen discreetly led us to a table in a darkened alcove, using the band playing as cover. I scooched into the worn red booth, Kallan and Throwen my bookends, the only things keeping me from falling.

I took a deep breath, trying to take it in. But the sheer volume of this place grated on my nerves. I instinctively dug between my cleavage, frowning at the annoying muscle memory. When I lifted my chin to look at Throwen for help, his eyes were already glued on the fingers I had shoved down my top. My already boiling skin grew hotter.

Needing a break from the tension, I yelled over the music and cacophony of voices, "Do you have any cotton?"

Broken from the trance of my tits, he leaned in closer. "What?"

"Cotton! Do you have any cotton?"

His look was quizzical but held no judgment and the music mercifully died down. It was still loud, but bearable.

"And why did you think you would find cotton between your tits?" My bard's charming smile only deepened my frown.

Kallan leaned in, resting his arms on the table. "What? Why do you want cotton? Did I miss something?"

Crossing my arms over my chest, I leaned back into the booth. My shoulders hunched, doing their damndest to make me so small I would disappear entirely. "I used to keep cotton on me at all times. I had to be careful where I kept it so that I wouldn't be reported."

"Report you for what?" Throwen's voice was firm, and his anger rippled off of him. The closer he got to me, the more his hatred for Malik grew.

You're betraying him. You're betraying them all.

"Oh, just a minor thing, it would only earn me a public confession." A public confession where I was pummeled with stones and berated by the witches I thought were my friends.

Throwen grabbed onto my thigh under the table, giving it a reassuring squeeze. He wouldn't push the topic if I didn't want to talk about it. But part of me was desperate to share the weight of this with someone else.

I looked over at Kallan. His demeanor was so peaceful that I questioned how he could ever be violent. A Teddy Bear. It was perfect.

"Um." I coughed, unsure how to vocalize something I've only ever talked about to myself. And she was a real bitch sometimes. I preferred that. I didn't know how I would feel about telling someone who might actually care. "Malik liked to make speeches. He used his magic to carry them throughout the entire coven so every member would hear them."

The sound of clashing metal drew my attention. Two men brawled on a raised platform while others cheered them on. I couldn't see much, only a bright red feather sticking straight up in the air above a crowd of heads.

"They were that loud?" Kallan asked.

"Well... no, not exactly. It's just..." I sounded like a child, unable to morph their thoughts into complete sentences.

Throwen squeezed my thigh harder, shooting a burst of adrenaline through me like liquid courage.

"He made them all the time. It wasn't always like that, but by the time I was six, he was making them all hours of the night, always at random times. The cotton helped me drown it out." Bile rose in my throat, and I pushed at Throwen. "Let me out."

Squirming out of the way, he kept my hand in his. As he tightened his grip, I scowled and felt the urge to bite his hand again and force him to let me go. "Octavia, it's okay."

"No." It would have been a sob if I wasn't gritting my teeth so hard. I turned to look at Throwen, the bard who saved me. "I shouldn't speak of him in such a way."

My lip quivered and Throwen pulled me into a tight embrace, kissing the top of my head.

"Well, if it isn't the Angel of Death!" A man wearing a large tricorn hat with a huge red feather sticking out dragged his chair loudly across the creaking wooden floorboards. It was more of a throne, towering over the others with plush red cushions.

"Oh, fuck." Kallan rose standing in front of me. The rest of the patrons fell silent, parting as the witch stalked toward us.

"You can't possibly be foolish enough to do this with all of us here." Throwen gestured to Kallan, sounding more bored than annoyed.

If he was scared, he didn't show it, but he stood defensively in front of me, his brother forming the rest of the wall.

I peeked through an opening between their arms. The witch wore an extravagantly long crimson coat with a dark blue sash tied around his waist. The white shirt he wore was unbuttoned, and his tanned chest stood out. He drew the cutlass strapped to his side. An image of some sea creature was tattooed across his exposed chest, tentacles wrapping up and around his neck.

As he neared, I made out a lifetime of scars and hardships hidden under that beautiful ink. Was this witch always so hardened? My mind naturally landed on Malik.

Kallan stepped closer to the snarling witch. "I'm not in the mood, Fennix. Where's Echo?"

My eyes widened. This was Fennix. Everyone was staring at us. I scanned the room, looking for faces I might recognize.

One by one, their irises turned crimson and their mouths opened in silent screams, red smoke pouring from their mouths onto the dirty floor. Fear tainted my veins. Would this be the time my panic-driven madness decided to consume me? I curled my fingers into a claw, ready to call upon the Abyss if necessary because we were trapped in the corner surrounded by lawless pirates.

"Why did the music stop?" A breathtaking witch stepped out of the back where the rooms to rent must have been. They were tall and curvy and tattoos littered their arms, a living breathing piece of art. Their flowing pink dress draped across their shoulders and fell to their knees.

"Teddy Bear! Little Miracle! You made it!" They raced over to where we stood, tight platinum blonde curls clung to their tanned round cheeks. The same height as Throwen, they leaned forward, kissing him on the forehead. Kallan leaned down for his forehead kiss.

"If everyone is done *reuniting*." Fennix gripped his sword firmly, shifting into a fighting stance.

"Julian, not tonight." The witch dismissed him with a wave. Their voice was soft in a way that made you lean in to listen more closely. Fennix was drawn in too, reaching out to touch them, but gazing at Kallan and Throwen, thought better of it.

His brows furrowed as if hurt. "I asked you not to call me that."

"You had no problem with me screaming it last night. This is my family, we all know your name."

The crowd started chattering again, pretending not to notice their leader's humiliation. Kallan snorted, Throwen gagged, and I remained silent.

"This is *my* coven."

"No. This is *their* coven." The witch gestured to the patrons gathered around, playing cards and getting so drunk they flopped over wooden barrels throughout the tavern. They seemed happy in an ill-natured sort of way. "You can't own a group of people, *Fennix*. That's not how this works."

"Echo, I swear to the Goddess, if you don't start respecting me in front of my people—"

Echo stepped into his space, their noses touching, eliciting a sharp gasp to fall from his parted lips.

Of course, this was Echo. A strong delegate, ensuring the importance of the coven's members.

"Then *do something* to earn my respect." They remained pressed against Fennix.

Fennix's jaw ticked, and he scratched his unkempt beard. His hazel gaze softened, and he took a step back. Opening his mouth, he spoke, barely above a whisper, "Okay. Fine. I hear you Echo, okay? *I'm listening.*"

Echo reached out and tugged his singed beard playfully. "Thank you."

"You're welcome to stay," he said through gritted teeth. "*But* I've heard the bard no longer honors his little 'no violence while performing' rule."

Throwen stiffened.

"Do we need to put a leash on him?" Fennix's sneer revealed some shiny gold and silver teeth.

I curled my hand into a fist at my side, trying to control the urge to throttle him for calling Throwen out.

"Don't worry Fennix, I'm not performing tonight." Throwen reached for me, rubbing soothing circles around my palm.

Fennix cut between us and scanned me from head to toe. I wanted to shiver, but I held my chin high, playing the part. "And who is this?"

"I'm Octavia. It's nice to meet you. I've heard you're the best treasure hunter in all Theldea." I held my hand out to shake, and he stood taller.

An endearing crooked smile revealed a dimple on his right cheek. There was no ill intent in the gentle shake of his hand. I was quickly learning that I wasn't the only witch in Theldea who hid behind a mask.

Nova hid, too. Maybe all the leaders did the same. A silent thank you rolled through his aged eyes, pulling at his crow's feet. Throwen stepped back between us.

"That is the *only* time you ever get to touch her."

Everyone fell silent.

Echo looked at Kallan, who shrugged. Then they squinted at Throwen. Their mouth fell open, their attention fully pulled away from a scowling Fennix.

"Family meeting." They pushed their way through, but Fennix grabbed their arm.

Through a tight and pleading tone, he asked, "Wait, can't we finish our discussion first?"

Echo wrapped their arms around his neck, grabbing his hat and placing it on their head. "We will finish it tomorrow, Tiger Fish."

The Captain's grip tightened on Echo's wide hips, eliciting an irritated sigh. "But—"

"You need some fun tonight, too?" Echo questioned, and he nodded, joy pulling at the corners of his lips.

Echo kissed the tip of his bulbous red nose, the veins bursting from years of consuming alcohol. "Say please."

Groaning, he leaned into them. "Please."

"Good boy. Okay, enjoy your fun!" Echo pushed Fennix roughly into a very inebriated witch, breaking his bottle of dark ale.

The witch wobbled and looked perplexed, staring at the floor, as if wondering how his bottle had got there. Squinting at his assailant, the oblivious man cocked his arm and punched Fennix right in the jaw. He fell into another witch, who shot another in the eye with a stream of ale. The band started up and a full-on brawl started.

Witches were flung onto tables and food flew around the room. A fireball zipped past my head and I shrieked, ducking to the floor before it could singe my hair. A barmaid walked calmly over to the now burning curtains, palms up as she shot water at them, dousing the flames. She was unperturbed, as if this happened every night. A mother to these wild witches, tolerating their tantrums and shenanigans.

Kallan and Throwen were crouching next to me, giddy expressions on their faces. Echo was nowhere to be seen.

"Time to go?" Throwen laughed.

I tilted my head to the side, pursing my lips. I was covered in sticky liquids. My new favorite outfit was filthy, my hair almost burned off, and I made a terrible first impression on both of his siblings. "Yes."

There was so much going on, so many witches who might have noticed who I was. I felt like I was trapped in a room with no air, slowly suffocating. Reaching back, I made sure the fabric was fully covering my mark.

Kallan joined in the laughter, popping up to hit a witch with a vase of bright pink flowers.

Standing with Throwen, I had difficulty getting my sense of direction back. We just needed to make it to the back of the tavern. I was pushed to the side as two witches screamed, pulling each other's hair and yelling insults. Huffing, my frustration won out. "Is it always like this?"

"This is fun!" Kallan laughed, and he launched potted plants at some particularly bloodthirsty pirates fighting in the corner.

I scowled at the boys as witches drew their swords, the sounds of clashing metal putting my nerves on edge.

"Come on! Our rooms are this way!" Echo hollered from behind the bar where they crouched, a huge mischievous grin on their face.

We rushed toward them and one witch standing on the edge of a table took a long swig before leaping over us onto another witch's back.

Throwen grabbed my hand, and we ran, an exhilarating habit we formed on our journey thus far. It was utter chaos, but I had to admit there was an element of fun to it.

A glass bottle flew toward Throwen's head, but he ducked out of the way, and it shattered against the wall.

When we reached the bar, Echo stood proudly wearing Fennix's hat. They bowed low as we all laughed, racing down a long hallway until I was tugged into a large room. Echo flung the door shut with a loud thud and the three of them fell to the ground, holding their bellies as they laughed.

A lump formed in my throat. This was what a family was supposed to look like. My heart knew it, but the beast within me roared. Swallowing all the longing in my heart, I rationalized to appease it. Malik did his best. Just because my family didn't look like this didn't mean it wasn't real.

Chapter 22

OCTAVIA

The room we found ourselves in was another assault on my senses. A maelstrom of organized clutter. Every inch of the wood-paneled walls were covered in knickknacks and treasures. Shelves were piled high with gold, silver, and shiny jewels. Varying sizes of bottles were flipped on their side and held miniature ships.

Long swords hung vertically on the far wall surrounded by throwing knives, machetes, and axes. Ancient maps decorated another wall. I pivoted to see the door outlined in hats that hung from hooks.

There were piles of clothes, books, and large wooden crates filled with bottles of ale. Throwen sauntered over to one, grabbing a bottle.

We settled in at the small round table in the center of the room, atop a crimson rug. Kallan and Throwen appeared unphased by its intricacies.

"This room is... unforgettable." I searched for a way to describe it as I sat on the hard wooden chair.

"This is Julian's room. Most of the coven heads always put me in the best rooms. But I never minded people kissing my ass." Echo winked at me, "I don't believe we've been properly introduced. My brothers have no manners as I'm sure you already know."

Echo pulled off the blonde wig, revealing dazzling teal hair, and my mouth opened. It was cut into a short bob just below their round chin.

Echo was pure light and warmth pulling me close.

They reached out their hand, and my eyes were drawn to a Peacock inked in black that took up their forearm. "I'm Echo."

"Octavia." I took their offered hand and shook it weakly. I swallowed — my confidence nonexistent.

"You look like her, ya' know?" Echo said.

My heart stopped, unsure what exactly they meant. I blinked, searching for a response.

Echo snatched an orange, peeling it while keeping eye contact with me. "Whynnie. You look like her."

"She does?" Kallan and Throwen asked in unison.

Throwen looked green, like the thought of me looking like his mentor made him sick. I scanned the room, trying to find anything to pretend to be fixating on. Heat crawled up my neck, pooling in my cheeks.

"It's not a physical resemblance. It's a spiritual one," Echo said, drawing a circle in the air around me. "Your aura is mostly purple, with a sliver of white around the outside."

"My what?"

"Oh, please don't get them started." Throwen stretched his arms high, his chest exposed. The lean muscles of his abdomen tightened with the extension. I pushed my legs together, hoping the friction would satiate my growing desire.

Kallan slipped his cards from his pocket, a look of clear disbelief on his face. "That's not a real thing."

"It is real." They ignored their brothers. "An aura is this cluster of energy around all of us. Think of it like a star, the brightest part is condensed right in the middle, and it changes and shifts as it fans out, illuminating the soul. Auras usually adapt based on mood and while yours seems to be all over the place" — their eyes bounced quickly between me and Throwen — "the purple and white never fade."

"What does the purple mean?" I thought of Throwen's beautiful abilities, the spirits wrapping around him happy to share in his joy. They clung to him for happiness, just like me.

But I was a leech deprived of fun, honesty, and care. I'd savagely feed on Throwen until Malik inevitably ripped me off, severing me from my new life source because of my horrible choices.

"Here we go..." Throwen pulled out his lute and began playing a beautiful song. I had a feeling he could play me music for the rest of my existence, and I would never get used to the comfort it brought me.

"Whynnie saw me in a mirror, and you can't believe in auras or things you can't comprehend or see?" I challenged Throwen.

"Oh, I like you!" Echo undulated their fingers, creating a rhythmic gallop with their glittery fingernails on the table.

"I didn't say that I just meant—"

"Hush! The grownups are talking." Echo swatted at Throwen like a fly and a huge smile curled at my lips. I had never been so quickly accepted into a group like this before. *Don't trust them. They will never accept all of you. You're still a necromancer.*

My demon's voice was loud, but I hoped the sound in the room would drown it out.

"The purple is for intuition and empathy," Echo explained.

"Be careful Echo." Throwen reached over, gripping my thigh tightly beneath the table. This was no longer a comforting touch, but a needy one. Cool picks slipped under my fishnets, tickling my overheated skin. "Her empathy infects whoever it touches. Making them pour their secrets."

I shooed Throwen's hand away so that I could focus, but his grip only tightened, forcing me to fight back a gasp. "And the white?"

"Whynnie has the white ring, too. That one is a little trickier. It can mean purity, but not always. Wisdom or spiritual connectedness to the Goddess herself is the more common explanation."

"Oh." It was as if Echo punched me in the gut. The more I tried not to think about my connection to the Goddess, the more frequently it was thrown in my face.

If only Malik were here now to witness my doubt.

I knew the Goddess as a controlling creator for most of my life. But so far, her creation seemed magnificent. The skies of Oxvein, the view from the window of the Graygarde library, the jungles of Stranata. It wasn't evil, there was no way it could be.

"I didn't mean to make you uncomfortable," Echo said, and I quickly flashed a smile to hide my discomfort.

"No, I believe you." I was quick to say. "I just didn't grow up in a spiritual environment, well, at least not what you all consider spiritual."

Kallan grunted along with Throwen. "O, please don't tell them you believe in auras, it only feeds their delusions."

Delusions.

Funny little things, delusions. They take root in the mind, twisting your reality. From the outside, it's easy to see them, but I had been trapped in a world of Malik's delusions all my life. Now that I lived on the outside, it was all too obvious.

I thought back to the first time I sensed something was off, but my memory was foggy, as if I was a child reaching for the highest shelf, never able to grasp what I needed.

My brand of delusions were much more dangerous. Not ones of power and control, but of hope and freedom. Throwen, Kallan, Echo... they could be my home. I wanted them to be my new home.

This is your home, Lady. Can't you see all the beauty here? The fruits of hard work and obedience are glorious if you only take the time to look. This paradise is for us. What more could any witch hope for?

Malik's voice was gentler in my youth. Back then, I had always hoped for more. But that hope dripped out of me slowly throughout the years, leaving me with nothing but disdain and scars.

"Enough about auras." Throwen stroked my thigh. "Let's get back to Fennix."

"Yeah, what about Fennix?" Kallan rolled his shoulders; loud cracks and pops sounded as he straightened his spine. I shivered, hearing the sounds sharper than they were—the snap of Malik's whip.

"Ugh! No more Fennix talk tonight." Echo shook their head. "Whynnie said Octavia is our priority, so what's the plan from here? Were you detected?"

We all looked at each other, none of us willing to start.

"Oh Goddess, I should have grabbed another bottle." Echo scooched their chair back, flinging their feet up on the table and crossing their ankles together. "Well, someone has to tell me or else this plan will be total shit."

"*Fuck.* I made a *little* scene at Harlin's." Throwen didn't make eye contact with his sibling as he said it.

"A *little* scene? Every witch in Graygarde was talking about how you lashed out *at a guard* for some unknown gorgeous witch," Kallan said with a scoff.

I fought the urge to cover my face and hide, releasing the energy through my shuffling feet under the table instead.

Echo rubbed their eyebrows. "*Goddess's tits*! Of all the times to break your silly rules—"

"They aren't *silly*. They're there for all our safety." Throwen glared at his siblings. Echo cocked a brow, looking between Throwen and me. Throwen shrugged smugly. "Besides, Kallan tied up Ross and his gang. Left them behind in the jungle. Doubt they're going to make it."

Echo leaned forward and tapped their fingernail on the table, breathing in deeply through their nose and out through their mouth.

It was eerily silent before Echo spoke through their teeth with forced restraint, "Kallan. You know I was building a case against him. He could have led us to other traffickers. Mayson was being compliant."

Kallan lowered his chin, and his muscles tightened.

"Hey," Throwen said, breaking the tense silence, "it's not as bad as the time you tried to break into Whynnie's archives."

Echo gasped, standing and slamming their palms on the table before pointing an accusatory finger at Throwen. "We agreed. *No spying* in the house! You dick!"

"Whynnie offered me new strings for my lute if I gave you up. *I was twelve.*" Throwen slouched in his chair as if that was an excuse for his betrayal.

"You tried to break in too, Throwen." Kallan lifted his eyebrows cheekily, his anger shifting.

"Hey! We said we would take that to our graves!" Throwen was up now too.

Echo huffed and crossed their arms.

Is this what a family is like? The comfort of revealing even the worst of your decisions and still knowing you'll be loved after the dust settles?

"Hey, you're the one who opened fire." Kallan laughed, holding his hands up in surrender.

"Kallan knits." Throwen crossed his arms over his chest in victory, but Kallan didn't respond.

Echo's eyes were as wide as mine and we both zeroed in on Kallan.

"Oh, come on, say it," Throwen taunted his brother who was gritting his teeth.

"Oh, *please* Teddy Bear, I *really* want to hear this one." Echo sat back down, their posture now open and relaxed.

Throwen the bard, distracting everyone from their frustrations with enticing stories. It was one of my favorite things about him.

"Fine." Kallan shuffled his cards quicker now. "Prove it."

Echo looked eagerly to Throwen, resting their chin in their hands. He grabbed his lute and started playing a tune that reminded me of the snow falling lightly on my lashes in Oxvein.

"It was two years ago. The air was pleasantly chilled, and leaves prepared to shift into their autumn gowns. I was strolling through Blatock." He threw his fingers over the strings, silencing his instrument, ducking down next to my left ear, speaking loud enough so only I could hear, "It's a coven in Luftor, I'll take you there sometime."

Effortlessly, he fell back into his strumming, raising his voice. "I was nearly at the Rock Bottom Tavern. I had a set that night, but something caused me to pause as I passed the orphanage."

Kallan threw his forehead down onto the table, grunting.

"Why, it was my grumpy bear of a brother, handing over a pile of tiny, knitted scarves to Mirra. How nice, I thought. He gathered some scarves to donate. So, I moved closer, ready to give him a firm pat on the back."

Kallan lifted his head. "You were in the shadows, you sneaky little shit. Just get it over with."

Throwen's head tilted to the side, and he pushed his bottom lip out dramatizing his admiration. "Kallan offered Mirra the scarves, who then gave him a bright shiny new pair of knitting needles. His eyes were aglow as he grasped the needles to his huge, meaty chest. In his spare time, which we all know is almost non-existent, Kallan knits little scarves for tiny orphans."

Throwen finished his story with a final strum. Silence filled the room, but it was a comfortable silence I wasn't familiar with.

"Oh, Kallan." Echo punched their brother on the shoulder. "You big softie!"

"Yeah, yeah... Can we please get back to the plan? We need to make a schedule."

"See? Barely any time in his schedule and he still has time for knitting." Throwen said. They all laughed, and I stared in wonder at their bond with one another.

"You better knit me a scarf." Echo demanded through their laughter. "No, wait! I want one of every color."

The siblings held their bellies. Once they settled down, wiping away tears, their postures shifted into that of mission planning.

"I say first light, we go straight to Whynnie." Echo said, a scowl on their face. "We can avoid Squalsend and stick close to the Midloathian Mountains. It sounds like we have drawn enough attention to ourselves already."

"I'll send birds to my confidants and see if anyone has had increased necromancer activity." Throwen leaned forward, resting his elbows on the table. I wished I could take his hand and place it back on my thigh where it belonged.

"O, consider me your new personal bodyguard." Kallan smiled gently, and I trusted his determination to protect me. The whole reason for all of this chaos was to get me to Whynnie and having extra protection could ensure they met their goal.

"I'll deal with Fennix in the morning." A brief twitch of sadness pulled at Echo's lips.

I coughed, drawing everyone's attention. "Can I help?"

Echo and Kallan looked confused, but Throwen understood, an approving smile lighting up his face.

Selfish. Part of me wanted to help, but the uglier part needed them to accept me. *Fucking leech.*

"Are you sure?" Kallan's hands were squeezed tightly into fists. Maybe he didn't think I would stand up to Malik, and maybe he was right.

I had no idea what I would do or say when I had to face him again. I had been avoiding it, hiding away in the pleasure of adventure, but we were almost to Goldhaven and Malik *would* find me. Hopefully it was long enough for me to figure all this shit out.

I sat up taller, mimicking Echo's confidence like I'd done so many times with Malik. "Positive."

"Will you help us put an end to this violence?" Their voice was steady as they spoke, shifting into the seasoned diplomat. "I don't care how you do it, but we can't allow necromancy to continue. It negatively affects every single coven. It also destroys the witches who use it."

I felt too vulnerable. I wanted a rock to crawl under, a granite barrier between me and my radiating shame.

I wasn't sure how necromancy magic truly worked. Malik had explained that for the magic, you had to give the tree your blood in exchange. But was that *Goddess-damned* tree the source of his magic?

My leg started bouncing under the table, the coins on my hip scarf jingling. It gave away my anxiety like a bell around a cat's neck. I stopped it, biting into my cheek hard.

"I promise I will do my best to put a stop to the harmful magic," I said, enunciating each word. "I've seen now what it does to the souls of my people, and I don't want anyone else to get hurt." I didn't have to say it. We all knew I was talking about Malik too. They might have seen him as a lost cause, but I didn't.

"In your work, you take all of Theldea into consideration, yes?"

They nodded in unison, hanging on to my every word. It made me feel powerful and in control of the room. I could see how easily Malik could become addicted to this feeling.

I crossed my hands in my lap. "That includes The Coven of the Grave now, too."

Malik would have to answer for his crimes, and until then, I would have to step in. Maybe that was why he appointed me Lady, in case something happened to him.

They were all smiling at each other, and I hunched over with a deep frown, bracing myself for their mocking laughter, already hearing Malik's in my head.

"I would be honored to serve your coven," Kallan said, and I snapped my head up. He stood and bowed low, banishing Malik's voice from my head.

Tears pricked at the back of my eyes. I knew what that meant for him, to accept my people, including the scouts he loathed. They would answer for what they did, but it would be a just sentence. Nothing like Malik's punishments.

Echo stood next and bowed low with Kallan. "I would be honored to serve your coven."

They looked up with a wink, and a half sob, half laugh fell from my lips.

Then Throwen stood, lowering to one knee. I wasn't sure I could endure this much acceptance at once. Gratitude oozed from my pores, enveloping me in its warmth and light. He pressed a gentle, warm kiss on top of my trembling hand. "I would be honored to serve *you* and your coven."

A single tear fell down my cheek, not missing the way he phrased his devotion. Even in this moment, he put me first.

"Thank you." It was all I could manage, and I wiped away the rebellious tear.

"Have you ever seen fireworks?" Throwen's voice was strained, like he was fighting back his emotions.

"Fireworks?" I asked.

"Throwen, that's a bad idea." Kallan tried to interject, but Throwen ignored him.

His eyes never left mine, as if it were only us in the room. "They look like colorful explosions in the sky, but it's just a bit of science. We should stop at Squalsend. She deserves to see the fireworks before she has to face this."

"I don't know, Throwen, we should get her to Whynnie." Echo bit their bottom lip, looking torn.

He turned to his siblings, his eyes pleading. "*Please*. Just one more stop."

I would eventually be dragged back to my coven and possibly get everyone else killed in the process. Their pitying gazes fell on me, but I didn't have the energy to care. I would take any extra time with Throwen that I could, no matter how stupid and reckless it was.

"I'll work it into the schedule." Kallan rubbed at his temples with a sigh, "But I'm going to bed, you all should too. We still have a journey ahead of us."

As I stood, it felt like the ground beneath my feet was forever changed, sturdier somehow. All because of these new relationships. How could I feel more connected to these witches I just met than my family? The answer was all too clear, and I refused to admit I grew up without a family.

Kallan was already out the door and heading toward his room without another word. Large arms wrapped around me, the scent of vanilla unfamiliar but pleasant. Echo pulled me against their chest. "Thanks for taking care of our Little Miracle."

They were squeezing me tightly, but I managed to get out, "No problem."

Throwen laughed, and Echo sat me back down. I had never felt so accepted, and as Throwen laced his fingers through mine, leading us to our room, I couldn't help but embrace my newfound hope.

Chapter 23

OCTAVIA

Freezing water rushed through my hair and down my aching body, but the ache between my legs was stronger. I was about to crawl out of my skin if something didn't give.

Once Echo had shown us to our room, I'd told Throwen I needed a shower and fled to the bathroom before he could get a word in. It was childish, but after so much flirting and taunting, I was afraid we were building up to something that would only disappoint him and break me.

One must be careful with love, Lady. The result is always a relinquishment of power. Fucking is one thing, but love is a pit you don't want to fall into.

Malik was appalled at the love I held in my heart for others. I loved far too easily, and it often ended in punishments for being too sensitive, too erratic, too impulsive. I'd learned to only give others part of my love, shoving all the extra down. But I found I wanted to share the entirety of myself with my bard.

You're too much sometimes Octavia. Get a hold of yourself.

Too much. Not enough. They were the same thing and after the excitement wore off, that's exactly what I would be to Throwen.

I slowly turned off the faucet; the chill in my bones wouldn't freeze the hot coals of emotion sizzling within. Wrapping a soft towel around myself, I patted my limbs dry, and the humidity rushed back in, clinging to my skin.

Pressure pushed in on me from all sides. I was a clove of garlic being pressed to the point of bursting. Music trickled under the door from our room, and I smiled.

I fondled the fabric of my new clothes. *My clothes.* These were a last-minute grab before we left Graygarde, a set of dark golden-rod pajamas that reminded me of pirate treasure. I knew they would enhance my mark's appearance, but this time I didn't care because it was something I chose for myself.

"You can do this Octavia." Taking in a deep breath, I slid the silky shorts up my legs. They were littered with bruises and old scars. Tiny flutters bounced around my stomach, and I pulled the top over my head. The straps were thin, and it landed just below my belly button. "This is a terrible idea."

I stared at my feet beseeching them to move, to go to him, but they wouldn't. "*Please* move."

Tears threatened to spill. My demons awoke, paralyzing me. *There's nothing left of you to love.*

"Darling, if you don't come out of there soon, I'm going to go mad and carry you out myself." Throwen's voice beckoned to me from beneath the door.

I reached for the handle, swinging the door open and hoping the momentum would let my feet know to pay attention and *fucking move.*

"I have a lot of hair…" I cringed at the idiotic excuse, ducking my chin.

Throwen ceased playing as I entered the room.

I squeezed the towel around the ends of my hair a few more times before tossing it into the bin. The room was quiet, the erratic beat of my heart surging blood through my ears. *Act normal.*

The hairs on the back of my neck rose to attention, and I raised my eyes to where he sat on the floor. The entire room was charged as if he was my new center of gravity.

He leaned against the bottom of the wooden bed frame, but not in his usual nonchalant way. He was as stiff as his lute, resting against the frame beside him. Flexed fingers gripped his bare ankles, his legs crossed in front of him.

In the light I could see his scars more clearly. His body was littered with them, mementos of working as an assassin. I wanted to hear the story behind each one. His broad shoulders were on full display, and his excellent bone structure was wrapped in beautifully sculpted muscle. It was the kind of muscle one could only hone from constant training.

A long pale torso flowed elegantly into his narrow waist, and I fought the urge to lick my lips. He wore only a pair of loose-fitting charcoal shorts that ended on his upper thigh.

His grip was so tight that the veins in his forearms protruded. I pictured licking along each one. I would trail my tongue along them slowly until they all inevitably led me right to his heart.

With a burst of boldness, I met his gaze.

He was magnificent. Tiny rivulets of water fell over his delicious shoulders as he ran a hand over his cropped hair.

"You showered?"

He examined me like I was a snack he fully intended to savor. "Yeah, Kallan wouldn't let me in, but Echo didn't mind. *You* took a long time."

My skittish laugh grated on my nerves, and I answered, "I've always loved baths and showers."

He cocked his head to the side with a smirk. "I snuck into the kitchen and grabbed you this." He offered me a tiny sliver of chocolate cake topped with slices of fresh oranges, keeping his promise to get me chocolate.

"Thank you." I walked over and sat beside him, just within his reach. I shoved a bite of cake into my mouth and moaned. *Sacred Ether*, this was the best chocolate I'd ever tasted.

Throwen chuckled. "They harvest the cocoa beans here. Stranata has the best chocolate in all Theldea."

I hummed in approval, my curlicues tickling my hot face.

"How are you feeling?" His eyes were locked on mine.

The question took me by surprise, and I shoved in another bite, already halfway through the slice.

"Um." A strangled laugh escaped, and I covered my mouth full of food. I was expecting a joke, a story, something to make me smile and distract me from the building tension.

"Honestly?" I asked.

"Always honesty."

I rubbed my forehead as if it would alleviate the permanent stress that had built up over the years.

"I keep trying to think back. Figure out how I didn't see Malik's manipulation. But when I try to remember, everything is hazy." As hazy as the skies I grew up in. Perhaps the skies themselves siphoned my memories, replacing them with a myriad of indistinct images. "There are tiny patches of clarity, but not many."

I took the final bite of the small cake and let it sit in my mouth for a minute, the bitter chocolate mixing perfectly with the tang of the orange. I sat the plate and fork aside, and clutched my ankles, mimicking his posture.

"What's one of the earliest things you remember?" His fingers twitched, as if eager to reach out for me. But we both knew once we touched each other, we wouldn't be able to stop.

I laughed, thinking back as far as my dilapidated brain could manage. "When I was about eight, I asked Malik if I could train to be his head scout. I didn't want to be the Lady of the Grave. But the idea of traveling throughout Theldea along his side thrilled me." A sharp pain radiated from my brand, the mark I had so hoped would signify my acceptance as a scout. "He laughed in my face."

His laughter reverberated through my mind. That's all I would ever be to Malik. A joke.

I admired Throwen's restraint as he grit his teeth and listened intently. He allowed me to work through this without threatening to dismember my mentor.

"I spent two months spying on coven members. When I asked him again, I brought an entire notebook filled with things he could punish them for. I didn't know that young that the consequences of trying to prove myself would bring so much pain and death."

"Octavia I—"

I stared at the floor, not seeing it because I was drifting somewhere in between now and my past. My control slipped and my chest rose and fell, my breaths becoming more labored. "He made me dole out the punishments to every witch I named in that *cursed* notebook. It was the first time I killed another living soul. Eight years old and I was already a monster, a murderer. I was a fucking *child*."

Unsure what to do with the emotions, I threw them into my voice, raising it the more I let the truths spill. "I think he was wrong."

My jaw ticked, preparing to unleash things I didn't dare utter aloud until I barreled into Throwen's bubble of safety. If I didn't let this out now, I knew the explosion would destroy more than just me. "I think if he had never taken me, I would have been the woman I was tonight. The woman I've been when I'm with you and your family."

I didn't realize that tears were falling until Throwen reached out his arms. Cupping my cheeks, he brushed my tears and the invisible barrier between us away. His picks clung tightly to the tips of his fingers, their cooling sensation now a comfort I sought after.

"I could have been a scout *and* a healer. You make your own rules. I mean, who would think a bard could also be an assassin?"

We both laughed, and he pushed some warmth into my cheeks. I dreaded his answer and felt foolish, but I had to ask, "Do you think I could have done it?"

My internal thoughts were bursting out quickly, and I felt myself peeling off the mask I had worn for so long. I thought it would be painful, but it wasn't. I wanted him to see me.

"I don't think you should waste your time on what-ifs. I like who you are now, even with all the cynicism and self-loathing." He moved one hand to the back of my neck, grasping it while moving his other to grip my chin between his fingers.

The way he embraced my negativity pulled me in even closer, giving me hope I was safe to find myself again with his help and support. I clutched onto his wrist that held my chin and reached my other hand up to rub my thumb across the short stubble growing back on his cheek. He leaned into my touch, soaking it up like an offering. And maybe it was.

Throwen wasn't just the Angel of Death others painted him to be. He was my angel, sent back to our plane by the Goddess. My gaze fell to his lips, full and curled up into a smile.

"I think you would make the best healer this world has ever seen. You don't belong in a cage. You never did."

I threw my arms out wide, breaking our embrace, and lowered my head as two hot tears slipped down onto my thighs. I whispered, scared to utter the words out loud, "I'm *so angry*, Throwen."

He gripped my shoulders. "Then *be* angry. You can let yourself feel when you're with me, you don't have to hold back anymore. If you need to scream, or cry, or punch the shit out of a pillow, whatever it is—"

"I'm afraid if I let the anger out, I'll lose control and the bitterness will consume me like a fire." This was my true fear. That if I let myself hate, I would turn into Malik, wiping out any who threatened me. "What if it frees this demon living inside me? What if once I start letting myself feel it, I won't be able to stop?"

He rubbed my arms up and down, his touch bringing a sense of clarity to my confusion. "I'll be right here when you're ready and I will help you carry that weight."

I was enamored with the way he didn't push me. He let me unravel at my own pace and I wasn't ready to unpack the anger.

"When I'm ready, I will let you know." I stared into his eyes. Was it all a dream? Had I really jumped out that window and fallen and this was my comatose fantasy? The tears had dried up and I could take a deep breath again.

Throwen lowered his hands to rest gently on my hips. "*Sacred Ether*, Octavia... Do you even comprehend how enchanting you are?"

"No." I blinked, and his eyebrows rose slightly. Beauty was always something just out of reach, the ugliness of my soul seeping out through the cracks like the gold in my crown.

I wasn't young anymore and had long ago stopped believing I could be seen as anything but an annoying nuisance.

He gripped my hips tighter and pulled me closer. I braced both my hands against his firm chest and gasped.

"Can I show you just how beautiful I think you are?"

In a breathy voice I didn't fully recognize, I said, "Yes."

He leaned in close, our noses touching and lips barely grazing. "Say please."

"Never." I closed the space between us, nibbling his lip and sucking it between my teeth.

He moaned and his tongue glided across mine as his restraint snapped. Breaking the kiss, he wrapped an arm around my back, lowering me to the floor.

His lute fell with a clang, the strings protesting his carelessness. As he knelt over me, my legs wrapped around his hips, and I lifted my arms around the back of his neck.

Sacred Ether this is really happening.

The tip of his tongue found mine before pulling back. He lifted me off the floor and held me up easily. I dug my fingers into the muscles in his back, kissing him again as I pressed my body tightly against his.

"*Fuck.*" Throwen palmed my ass, squeezing hard and burying his face in the wet hair falling over my shoulder. He pushed my hair aside and started kissing along my shoulder as he carried me to the bed. "You know, I've been obsessed with this ass of yours ever since I watched you flying in that mirror. *Goddess*, it feels so much better than I imagined."

A breathy laugh escaped me as he tossed me playfully onto the bed. But when he crawled on top of me, pressing his hot skin against mine, all the humor was sucked from the room. I didn't know skin could feel this fucking good.

He pressed his body flush to mine, and I felt his cock straining against his thin shorts. *Sacred Ether*, he was hard as stone.

Soon I would be fully bared to him. *There is no going back.*

I wasn't sure I even knew how to do this anymore or if my body could handle the things I wanted him to do to me.

My body tensed and he pushed up, hovering over me. I couldn't even remember the last time I found release myself. Other than Calliope, the witches I fucked were just that, a quick release.

"Octavia? What's wrong?" Throwen asked.

This is different. This was going to change me on a structural level. I could feel my mind deconstructing with each tender kiss and kind word.

"Throwen, it's been a while…"

"Octavia, look at me," he said, voice rough.

I didn't realize that my eyes had been closed, scared to face what this was. As I peeled them open, I gasped at his expression. He was looking at me the way I always imagined the heroes in my books looked at their lovers. Like he treasured me above all else.

"Is this what you want?"

My mark thrummed, illuminating his face. His devastating expression, his perfectly trimmed mustache, his cropped hair. *I want to keep him*. It was another stupid fantasy; all we had was now.

"Yes, Throwen." I grabbed onto his hand, guiding it to cup my breast. "I want you."

He clenched the tender area, then moved to cup my cheek. "Don't worry. I fully intend to take my time. And…" He winked and pressed his lips to mine, lingering for only a moment before pulling away. "You know what to say if you want me to stop."

He moved down to the end of the bed, and I whimpered at the loss of his weight on me. Sitting on his knees, he then pulled my left foot to rest on his chest. He slowly massaged, working out the knotted muscles. I sighed, relaxing my sweltering body into the cool linen sheets.

I squeezed my legs together, my pussy demanding friction. He chuckled, pulling them apart before working on the other foot. Was he seriously denying me after all that teasing? Any other time, he would want to give me exactly what I wanted.

I lifted onto my elbows to tell him to fuck me already, but he glided his finger along the bottom of my foot, tickling the sensitive skin there. I squealed and my legs spasmed in an effort to kick him away, but Throwen held my foot steady.

"You have deep, elegant arches." Before I could try to kick him again, he pressed his lips to my ankle, slowly working his way up my calf to my knee. I relaxed back into the sheets, and he trailed kisses higher and higher.

"Your thighs are strong, I've fantasized about what they would feel like squeezing against my head as I lick your sweet pussy. The brief taste I had wasn't nearly enough." He bit into my thigh and my hips bucked as he soothed it with a languid lick and kiss.

My breaths quickened. This felt good, too fucking good. I gasped as he slid his nose along my core through my shorts before looking up at me. He was my angel, and I was his altar.

I wanted him inside of me, *needed* him inside of me. "Throwen," I panted, "I need more."

He chuckled and moved so we were face to face. He kissed along my jaw and nibbled on my earlobe as I writhed beneath him. "More already?"

My eyes bounced down to admire the outline of his cock, and I wrapped the tips of my fingers around the waistband of his shorts. The tip of his cock sprung free. Wasting no time, I greedily grasped what I could reach, running my thumb over the pre-cum beading there.

He grabbed onto my wrists to stop me. "I'm not done." His voice was firm, and *Goddess forgive me*, I loved it.

"But to properly finish showing you just how flawless you are"—he curled his fingers around my waistband, teasing the soft flesh with his fingertips—"these need to come off."

"Yes," I panted and lifted my hips. He pressed a hot kiss to my clit through the thin shorts. "Stop teasing me!"

"Never." Laughing, he ripped the shorts down my body and then pulled my shirt over my head, tossing them to the floor.

Purple swirled around his blown pupils so deep that the color reminded me of fresh grapes. Dread caused me to look away, unable to watch him discover all the scars, both self-inflicted and not.

"Look at me, Octavia." It wasn't a suggestion, and something within me ignited.

I wanted to burrow into him, beneath his content exterior, to where this possessiveness lived. I wanted to see him feral. Wanted to draw it out of him, live on his praise, and let him ravish me.

I swiveled my head to face him again, and he moved to straddle me. "Your body is a *good* body. It's a fucking perfect body, but I know you will fight me on that."

He leaned down whispering into my ear as I arched my back trying to feel him pressed against me, "You agreed you wanted me to show you what I thought of your body, and I get *very* offended when someone chooses not to watch my show."

He bit my earlobe before trailing kisses along my neck and moving down to focus on my thighs again. Rubbing his thumbs along my inner thigh, he pressed firmly and grazed the wetness leaking out. "*Fuck, Octavia. You're making it hard to take my time.*"

I laughed, and he traced a finger along my stretch marks. When he noticed me watching, he smiled approvingly, canines poking into his bottom lip. "In Volgsump, they call these victory stripes." He followed one up the side of my thigh, kissing where it ended on my hip bone. "They believe they're earned by the most courageous of us."

"Sounds like a delusional way to deal with aging but—"

Before I knew what was happening, I was flipped onto my stomach. A sharp slap on my ass made me yelp.

"What was that for?" My question was silenced by a gentle kiss at the base of my spine. I shuddered as he licked up the entire length of it before pausing at my mark. "*Oh, Goddess.*"

He flipped me back over and pressed me down, kissing just below my belly button. I fisted the sheets as he annihilated my need for any explanations.

"And this. This right here is trouble." He traced his finger slowly along my waistline. "Always poking out from those tight little clothes you wear. You drive me mad."

I laughed dryly. "Welcome to the crazy club."

His chuckle tickled my stomach, and I pouted. I'd hoped for a spanking for that remark.

"Mmm…" I hummed as my lids drifted shut, and he worked his way around my stomach. Once he found my ribs, he kissed each one. I tensed when he grazed the brand, but as his cock pressed against me there was no doubting that he was attracted to me.

I ran my hand over his head, his buzzed hair softer than I expected. My hips bucked, and he rose again, straddling me. His cock was still poking out of his shorts, and I licked my lips, wishing I could taste him.

"Honestly." He reached out, squeezing my breasts hard between his fingers. "I've been putting these off because how am I supposed to describe how—"

I squirmed under him, as he ran his thumb over my peaked nipple gently.

He took me into his mouth and my head tilted back, bursts of pleasure sweeping through me. His tongue traced circles around the peak, flicking and sucking as his other hand moved mercifully between my thighs. "Oh!"

He slid two fingers slowly through the wetness, pressing down once he reached my clit. His picks were cool, and the ridges intensified the pleasure in a way I wasn't expecting.

"Throwen—" I gasped, clutching the blanket. "Your picks."

He rubbed slow, firm circles around my clit and my hips rolled up and down against the friction. "Trust me, you'll be glad I kept them on."

I gasped as he slid a finger in deep, his knuckle pressing against me. The smooth ridges of his pick glided against my tight walls adding to the pleasure. He pulled it out slowly before pushing it back in. I couldn't keep track of the noises he was plucking from me as if I were his instrument.

"Fuck," he ground out, "you're so tight."

I tried to buck my hips, but his other hand held me down. He slid in another finger. *Sacred Ether*, I would not last much longer.

"Throwen, I—"

"Not yet." He curled his fingers, hitting that spot that stole the breath from my lungs, and I nearly fell off that edge into bliss. The pressure and friction combined into an intense ache. My pussy throbbed, needing release.

I was on the precipice about to jump off the cliff except this time I wouldn't fall into oblivion but into ecstasy.

The sound I unleashed when I came was filthy, and he pumped relaxed fingers in and out until my walls loosened, drawing the orgasm out. My body tingled, happy to finally be set free. I panted, trying to come back from the stars Throwen just sent me out into. He didn't just push me over the edge, he fucking launched me to the moon.

"Good girl. Now you're ready for me." His lips were on mine again, and I could tell his restraint was failing when I found his hungry eyes. His tongue slid along the roof of my mouth.

"I want you to take a deep breath for me." He pushed my hair out of my face. "Now."

As I filled my lungs with air, he slid into me with one long thrust. I couldn't think, only feel. My mind was peaceful, but my body was ablaze. "Fuck! Throwen!"

"My name sounds so good pouring from your pretty, little lips." He started slowly, rolling his hips as he thrust in and out. Grabbing onto my jaw, he kissed me, pressing me hard into the bed. We moaned together and his pace quickened.

I was dripping around him as his cock filled me, but I could tell he was restraining himself. Biting into his lip hard, I forced him to pull away with a hiss. "I've heard bards fuck hard, or was that just another exaggerated truth?"

Sparks of lavender flashed in his irises like lightning.

With a low growl, his eyes darkened. Then, he finally let go.

I bit into my lip as my body bounced up and down. He was thrusting hard, and my head almost hit the headboard. There was pleasure and pain, and I fucking loved it. He was going faster, harder, and I knew soon we would both jump together.

"*Sacred Ether*!" I shouted again and came even harder.

"Oh, fuck!" With a loud grunt, he finished, his hot cum filling me. He panted, leaned down, and pressed his forehead against mine. As he pulled out, my body relaxed, leaving behind a wet heat.

"I'll be right back." He walked to the bathroom, followed by the swishing of the faucet being turned on. I craned my neck to look around, trying to find something to clean up with.

He hurried back and wiped between my inner thighs with a warm cloth.

"Oh." I kept my arms at my sides. My sexual interactions always ended the same way. Finish and get out. I had always taken care of cleaning myself.

"Why do you look so confused?" He tossed the cloth into the bin, grabbing a second clean one.

This man gently cleaning between my shaking legs with a warm cloth was not the same one who just fucked me. That hunger in his eyes was gone, leaving behind my content friend.

"I've just never been with anyone so… dominant before."

He shrugged. "You bring it out of me."

When he went back to the bathroom to wash up, I peeled the sheets back, sinking into the plush pillows. As the bliss and ecstasy faded, my smile wavered.

These infatuations with the idea of love are a distraction. Your heart is tender Lady, I suggest you thicken it.

I curled into a ball, cradling my head in my arms. Throwen slid under the sheets and pulled me tightly against him. I grasped for what I wanted to say or ask, but all I could hear were Malik's warnings in my mind.

"What's wrong? Did I hurt you?"

I flipped over to face him, cradling his face in my hands. "Goddess, Throwen, no. It was. I mean. Well, you were there."

He laughed, brushing my hair out of my face. "Then what's troubling you?"

I searched for the words, not wanting to sound clingy, so I pushed my thoughts of something *more* away. "It's your family." I reached out to run my fingers through his chest hair. "They're so fucking *nice*. I don't know what to do with their acceptance."

Throwen rested his forehead against mine, stroking my cheek, gently coaxing out my hidden truths as my demon roared.

Too close. You're getting too Goddess-damned close.

"I'm—" I rolled over, unable to face him. "I'm scared they're going to get hurt. I-I'm scared to lose you…"

He kneaded the knots in my back and shoulders. "I won't let that happen."

I wanted to believe him, wanted to hope that this could be my new life. But delusions would get us nowhere. I didn't answer, exhaustion pushing me towards sleep.

He pressed a soft kiss on my head and whispered, "I hope you know how beautiful I think you are. I'm scared to lose you, too."

Chapter 24

OCTAVIA

The jungle was thinning out after spending an entire day traveling. It was twilight, and the skies were smeared in dark blues and greens, the final strokes of color before the moon rose. Echo and I had been chatting all day, and I enjoyed learning about their life. Their hobbies, work, and passions.

I ran my fingers through Lucky's soft mane. I spent a good portion of the ride this morning running my fingers through her tangles as Echo told me stories about their childhood.

There was never pressure for me to share, but occasionally, I got the nerve to join in on the conversation. They were easy to talk to, and I found myself happy to be sharing about my life with someone other than Throwen.

I rode Lucky alone and Throwen walked ahead with Kallan. The distance between us was a mercy because I wasn't sure I could handle being pressed against my bard without needing him inside of me again. Just the thought of last night made me wet.

The boys' laughter carried back to us and they pushed each other around. "Are they always like this?"

"Yeah. I like it though." Echo looked at their brothers from where they rode next to me on John with nothing but pride and admiration. "But don't tell them that."

"I would never." I pulled my fingers across my lips, sealing their secret inside.

Echo smiled, the dimples in their cheeks prominent. That nagging need for clarity clawed at my mind. I needed to learn the way their mind worked, the reason they kept going each day.

So many questions, Lady. Over what? A favorite flower? Those things don't matter.

Echo's favorite flower was a red rose. The way their face lit up showing me their tattoo of one on their shoulder meant something. It meant joy in who they were and what they liked.

I asked my question freely. "Why do you call Fennix Tiger Fish? I know nicknames are a thing in your family."

Echo's lips curled up into a smile that reached their twinkling caramel eyes like they enjoyed my annoying prying. "Tigerfish swim to and fro *but* always with an objective. They're clever creatures." They laughed. "I used to hand feed them down by the docks when I was little and we visited Stranata."

Imagining a tiny Echo scurrying about the docks brought warmth to my chest.

"But…" they continued, "Tigerfish can be territorial and stress other fish out *so much* that they can't live around them. Most witches don't take the time or have the patience to truly see him, but sometimes it's his own fault, ya' know?"

Their face fell and I could tell they wished this part wasn't true of Fennix. I knew exactly how that felt. To be unseen. That is until Throwen saw me.

They twisted a large silver ring around their thumb, a red ruby catching the light, reminding me of Fennix's huge, feathered hat. "He genuinely is quite the treasure hunter."

"It hurts you not to be with him?"

Echo sucked in their bottom lip, worrying it between their teeth before releasing it. "Yes, and no. He wants to be exclusive, and I don't. It's a mess."

They ran their fingers through the strands of their hair like a fish cutting through teal waves before continuing, "Usually, when I'm working, I enjoy my days off. I like pleasure and fun. When I'm working with coven leaders, it's as if I'm a character in my story. I use my skills, and I can easily adjust to the cultures from coven to coven. But with Julian, it isn't just business. I can be myself. But he also isn't the only person who makes me feel that way."

There was a long pause, and I steered Lucky closer to them, reaching out to offer my hand for comfort.

They smiled, grabbing on like we were lifelong friends. "*Every* witch deserves to be valued and accepted. Even Fennix. I know he seems like a brute, but he's special."

Echo's hand in mine was an entirely new comfort. I'd never had siblings, but this was how I always imagined it would feel. Being there, noticing their hurt, helping them through it. I craved a relationship like this almost as much as I craved my freedom. I released my grip, curling my fingers into Lucky's mane. I ran my fingers through it, hoping it would ground me.

"What about necromancers?" It was a stupid question, but I needed to know how they felt. If I could ever be worthy of their friendship.

"Yes, Octavia," Echo said. "Even necromancers."

I made eye contact with them, and my shoulders loosened a bit. For once in my life, I was feeling cautiously optimistic. If Echo could accept us, others could too.

Echo winked and trotted ahead, catching up with the boys. I stayed behind. The extra socialization was taking a toll on me and, as if sensing my exhaustion, Throwen slowed, falling beside me and patting Lucky.

He frowned. "I think Lucky likes you more than me."

"Maybe she just needs more pampering. She's magnificent and

deserves all the affection. Isn't that right?" I lowered my body, wrapping my arms around her neck. She pranced and whinnied happily in response.

"You're going to spoil her, and then she will be even more rebellious and stubborn." He wrinkled his nose at me, his mustache shifting diagonally.

I shrugged. "She listened to me all day with no problems."

Quick footsteps sounded on either side of the path. I straightened and looked at Throwen for reassurance that it was just in my head.

He pulled his lute off his back, flicking it into his bow. "I hear it too."

Kallan unsheathed his weapon, a gorgeous blend between a cutlass and a machete. A twig of sage and a dahlia were engraved on the hilt. His violence carried out for the sisters he lost, and others like them.

Echo pulled two curved teal blades from their back. They glistened and the ruby eyes of the Peacocks carved into the wooden hilts caught the fading sunlight.

The footsteps stopped just as a high-pitched laugh came from the path ahead.

"No," I whispered, and Throwen helped me off Lucky, my legs unsteady.

"What?" Throwen asked as he gripped my hips.

I pushed him off me and sprinted toward the voice. The decision to sacrifice myself to save my friends was resolute. This couldn't end in more bloodshed. I didn't know if I could bear it.

"Octavia!" He raced after me, but I was on a mission, driven entirely by my fear of losing him.

Echo and Kallan were too slow to react, and I zigzagged out of their way, bursting into an opening in the forest lined by trees.

On the far side of the clearing was a steep hill which they stood upon, giving them an immediate advantage. Dozens of scouts were on either side of her, and the two that I assumed ran alongside us made their way back to their commanding officer.

"Hello, sweetheart," Calliope purred, exactly the way she used to, but now, instead of sorrow, it brought me nothing but rage.

"*Don't* call me that!" I was pissed that it was her. *Of course, it was her.*

"*Oh*! I see you've found your claws," she hissed and paced atop the hill.

Lucky burst through the leaves and Throwen leapt from her side, positioning himself directly in front of me. Lucky was at my back and Throwen aimed his bow at Calliope. Kallan and Echo flanked him on either side.

"If you leave now, no one has to get hurt." Throwen's voice was full of the promise of bloodshed.

Calliope cackled and the other scouts joined in. I was back in my coven, my people laughing and sneering as I endured public ridicule and humiliation. I bristled at my new friends' presence. Now they would see how little my title meant. How pathetic I was. How I held no power at all and couldn't save us. I scanned the scouts. There were only a few I didn't recognize.

Calliope tsked. "This is your fault, bard. You shouldn't have made such a scene in Graygarde."

Throwen's arms vibrated, and his back muscles tensed further. I knew he was already blaming himself, especially if they had been tracking us all that time.

I was nothing but a deadly distraction for him. This wasn't his fault. None of this was their fault.

"Calliope, you know this is wrong. Please."

I scanned the necromancers and spotted Indigo, a girl I worked with often. She was only fourteen. The red in her inexperienced eyes flashed in and out erratically. She couldn't control this type of magic. It was too untamed, too feral for her underdeveloped body to hold. She glared at us with more malice than a girl her age should be capable of. It didn't fit on her face, and it made her sharp features even sharper. That's because it wasn't her hatred.

It was Malik's engraved into her.

Bile rose in my throat at the oversized rib cage wrapped around her delicate body as if armor would help her.

Kallan growled behind me, Echo the only thing holding him back.

"Lady, I don't have time for your dramatics." Calliope's red curls bounced in the breeze, catching on the white skull covering half of her face, sharp canines menacingly covering her sneer. "What will it be, my sweet siren? Will you come willingly, or do I have to kill your new *friends* first?"

Throwen's biceps tightened as he drew back his string further, purple bursts of light aching to be unleashed. Closing one eye, he raised his bow, aiming straight for Calliope.

"Is this who you're fucking these days? The bard?" Calliope scoffed. "Or is it the dog? Perhaps the other abomination?"

I cataloged my weapons. The dagger on my right thigh, the butterfly daggers in the pouch across my chest. My fingers twitched, wanting to slice through those lying lips to silence her disrespect toward my friends.

Then she winked at me. Fucking *winked* at me.

This is it. I had to choose between my old family and my new one. My soul cowered, unsure whose side I was on. If I fought these scouts, I'd be a traitor. There'd be no turning back and possibly no way to save my people.

Malik would find me, lock me away forever, and kill Throwen. My demon roared, wanting me to sacrifice myself, but I had no time for *its* dramatics, either.

I stepped in front of Throwen and his siblings. "I *won't* be imprisoned again, and you won't touch them."

Holding my chin high, I called on the only thing I knew could get us out of this in one piece. Blood pounded against my eardrums, and red tendrils wrapped around my wrists. Parts of me I had just discovered were being ripped away as I tried to connect with tormented souls.

All Throwen's sweet whispers and affirmations were cut off. The Abyss was like a deranged child with a fly, pulling my wings off, then my legs, watching me writhe and squirm for its power. Had it always hurt this much or was there simply nothing to lose before?

"I need help," I pleaded with the very souls I condemned.

My arms were pinned against my sides, a furious Throwen at my back. "What are you doing?" He rested his chin on my shoulder, never taking his eyes off the necromancers. "*Don't you fucking dare.* Your soul is under *my* protection now, and you know what necromancy does to it."

He pointed over my shoulder at Calliope, and there was no argument. It was a fact we could all see in her frenzied scowl and the way her head twitched to the side when she blinked.

As he released me, I looked at Kallan and Echo. Their chests rose and fell rapidly, but they stood firm. Fear gripped its tight fist around my throat and tears threatened to fall. They were waiting for *my* approval to attack. Their professions last night, to include my people, were being carried out.

"We can't win." I stretched my fingers wide and released the trapped souls, sending them back to the Abyss. We were all speaking in rushed, muddled words.

Kallan's gaze was locked on Calliope. "I will not let them take you, O. I'm your bodyguard, remember? They'll have to get through me."

My body was recognizing something my mind was only starting to grasp. This was war and in war, witches died. I'd seen hundreds of my people slaughtered before me, but this was different. Witches I cared for were about to die in front of me yet again, no matter who came out victorious. I blinked back the tears.

I took one last look at the scouts lining the top of the hill. I knew most of them by name, their passions, and dreams. My love for my people and my friends collided and rendered me immobile and speechless. *Who do you love more?*

"We stick together. Kallan, right or left?" Throwen was checking his daggers.

"Right."

"We go in from the right and work our way to the top of the hill to take out Calliope. Octavia stays in the middle and holds up an air shield around herself. We are her second bubble of safety." Throwen's plan was rushed but calculated and we didn't have time to argue.

"Times up!" Calliope chimed, raising her arms above her head, along with the others. Bright orbs circled her, ripping through the atmosphere with an eerie red as they waited for vessels to inhabit.

Scouts ran down the hill toward us from both sides. We were surrounded by fallen leaves, tangled roots, and mud.

"Octavia!" Throwen moved, thrusting his hand into the air to grab the weapon flying straight for me. I ducked, and he winced, the bone dagger nicking his knuckles as he deflected it.

A horrific piercing shriek followed a soft wet thud. Then an earthshaking collision vibrated from behind me.

I choked out, "Lucky? *Oh, Goddess!*" I crashed to my knees, gagging and retching up bile. Turning to witness what I already knew I would see felt like tearing out a little piece of my soul.

"No! Don't look!" Throwen's hands were around my face, diverting my gaze, and he wiped my mouth clean. Hot tears stained my cheeks, and I gasped for breath that my lungs refused to share.

"Octavia, we have to move. Air shield. Focus on the air shield." Throwen said, his voice steady. He pulled me up as the sounds of my daily visions came to life.

I was dizzy, but I nodded, throwing up the shield.

Urgency laced his tone "Run."

The word I used to laugh along with as he pulled me to our next adventure was now tainted with too much danger.

Echo sprinted ahead of Kallan gushing a strong stream of water while still palming their weapons. They were clearing a path for Kallan, and he hurled fireballs at the front line of scouts. Echo and Kallan were just as skilled as Throwen, nimbly maneuvering around the twisted, uneven ground.

But the scouts had the power of the Abyss amplifying their magic.

Fire and large balls of rocky soil fell flat against my shield, and I raced to keep up. Feeling utterly useless, I swallowed my pride. I wasn't a trained fighter like them, but if protection was all I could manage, then so be it.

Kallan rushed a scout, their weapons clashing as they collided. He easily overpowered the scout and thrust his sword in and across his abdomen. No sound came from the scout's opened mouth, but his intestines slowly slipped to the ground with a wet splat followed by the rest of his body. I gagged as we moved quickly past him.

"Patrick," I muttered. He was in his thirties. Loved joining in on the chants, treating them more like a song.

Echo danced around the next scout while Throwen loosed arrow after arrow toward the rest, hoping to penetrate an air shield.

Another scout laughed a nasally taunt as she bound Patrick's soul to his body. His intestines sloshed along, and he jerkily straightened back to his full height.

"Aim for their hearts!" Throwen called over the chaos.

Echo was lurching at the scout that raised Patrick, and Kallan made his way back to me.

As another corpse ran toward us, Kallan aimed a fireball for the pulsing red bump in his chest. He missed and the undead scout dropped low to the ground like a spider. Black tar fell from his lips, sticking to his beard.

"Stay still fucker!" Kallan manipulated the ground around the scout's feet and threw another fireball while he was held in place. It hit its mark and the scout's husk dropped, the red orb of his soul seeping out and diving into the tar pit around his unusable corpse.

The stench of sulfur became more potent with every passing second.

Echo whistled from the front; their blades covered in blood. "Keep moving!"

Drip. Drip. Drip. Snap!

Even in battle, my mind conjured sounds of Malik's whip, the period of the sentence. The end of life.

We kept moving, and Kallan took his place back in front. They circled me like a moving, breathing shield, being sure to keep me protected.

I stepped over Echo's victim; her neck severed all the way through, her eyes a pale blue.

"Emilia." I hoped that somehow speaking her name out loud would help her know she wasn't forgotten. She was a skilled dancer from Volgsump. Always a hit at celebrations but lost her daughter during a ceremony and the life never truly came back to her dances.

My arms shook as I held up my shield, forcing their names into the place where I kept them all, deep inside my demon's cage. They would be sure to repeat the names, fuel for the incessant thoughts that everyone would be better off if I was dead.

I looked frantically for Throwen to help me know what was real in the tangle of confusion brewing and bubbling over in my mind. He was still shooting, his body showing no signs of his magic being drained, but I knew time was precious. My companions' magic wouldn't last forever, and we were severely outnumbered.

Kallan and Echo continued to create a path of horror up the hill, as spirits fought for possession of the bodies that weren't hit in the heart.

My mind smeared the expressions of the fallen like an emotional painter, not willing to form familiar faces.

Throwen had moved to my back, shooting the undead Calliope was raising in their hearts. They fled to the Abyss, where they would fight against the other souls for a farce of freedom within a corpse.

After taking down the last one, Throwen yelled ahead to her, "Hey, bitch!"

Calliope whipped her head toward Throwen, snarling as black trickled from her eye sockets. She was using too much power, and her body struggled under its demands.

"I'm going to enjoy killing you for hurting her, you piece of shit!" He smiled, losing three arrows in a row so quickly that I barely caught the movement.

One flew toward her heart, one toward her head, and another toward her knee. *Thank the Goddess, it is almost over.*

At the last second, Calliope grabbed the closest thing to her, ducking behind it for cover.

Throwen balked, falling to his knees beside me.

Indigo fell hard to the ground, one of Throwen's arrows sticking out of her forehead, and another plunged through her abdomen. The tendrils formed a sort of cocoon around her small body.

Calliope growled, trying to bind Indigo's soul, but the spirits wouldn't allow it. Throwen's intent to kill Calliope must have overpowered the spirits' autonomy, but they did their best to protect her now.

Indigo's hair was black as night, and her body was covered in bone armor that did nothing to protect her in the end.

The spirits did their job, freeing the tainted soul from her tiny body. It was so tender in comparison to Levi, a small red orb rising from her open mouth gently as it disappeared into the Abyss.

Throwen roared and shook as Calliope cackled. She was reveling in his pain.

"No." I lowered the shield and ran to him, enveloping him in a hug.

The terrors boomed around us. Wailing shrieks of pain and low unnatural gurgles of the undead.

I released Throwen and covered my ears, hoping the pressure would be merciful and crush my skull entirely, leaving my useless brain matter scattered amongst the dead where it belonged.

Stop this, Octavia! He needs you! I threw up a shield and lifted Throwen's chin, my heart breaking at the sight of his lip quivering. I kissed away his tears as everything fell silent in my mind.

Malik was wrong. Throwen was the only thing that mattered. And he was in pain.

He flinched from my hold, instead turning to exchange a savage look with Calliope.

"Time to move!" Kallan pulled his sword from another scout's side, sprinting up the hill to where Calliope stood in the middle of a group of the remaining scouts.

Spirits clamored everywhere, Throwen's purple mixing with the erratic reds. It was dizzying and I could barely find my footing.

Throwen's knuckles were bleeding and so was his forehead. He had a burn along his right thigh and rocks wedged into his shins. Never had my desire to heal been so strong. *I need to heal him.*

Echo flung their blades, flicking off as much gore as they could. "We will work with The Coven of the Grave." They panted, but their posture stayed statuesque, matter-of-factly asserting their power over Calliope.

Calliope ripped off her mask, striding toward us but not past her scouts. "We don't *want* to work with you. Malik doesn't need Theldea. He tolerates you. But I can assure you his patience is running thin." Tiny black spittle shot from her mouth as she spoke.

I walked toward her. "Calliope. Stop. I *know* you're in there somewhere."

I reached out but was stopped by Throwen. He pulled me back against his firm chest. I swore I saw a flash of green under the deep red of her oozing eyes.

I didn't love her, far from it. But I wanted to prove we could help my people. She could be an example. If I could help her, then I could help Malik and we could change how things were. I could be the healer I dreamed of being and mend the rift between our covens.

Calliope tilted her chin, laughing into the humid skies. "Always so *sensitive*, Lady. This is me!"

She tightened her grip on her dagger and signaled for the rest of the scouts to attack. She threw her dagger at me and Kallan leaped in front, throwing up a shield just in time. A burst of scouts rushed Throwen, one taking him to the ground while the others aimed to hit him with fire.

"Throwen!" I wanted to go to him, but there were too many undead rising between us.

The scouts were tired, their magic unruly and depleting, but the undead fought without pain or free will.

Echo was cut off from us next, three scouts driving them back down the hill. We were outnumbered and despite Throwen's abilities, we were losing.

"Kallan!" I yelled over the sounds of battle, fear for my friends honing my decision-making process. He held the shield steady around us, but it was weak too. "If we take her out, the others will follow."

Throwen was surrounded by dark purple tendrils, and they moved around him like ribbons while the red smoke of the Abyss thrashed against them. This wasn't just a physical battle; it was a spiritual one. The Ether collided with the Abyss, creating a dizzying kaleidoscope of violence. They were juxtaposed, forever destined to be in opposition to each other.

"Stay behind me." Kallan kept up his shield, running straight at Calliope. One of the scouts rushed us and Kallan dropped his shield to raise his sword. It cracked against the scout's staff, small shards of bone flying out and scraping across my cheek.

Kallan grappled with the large scout, their size and stature similar. Roaring in fierce protection of me, he pushed the scout off.

"Oof!" I was tackled to the ground, the air pushing out of my lungs painfully. I had no time to think and kicked the scout off. She was small and tired. "Stop! I am still your Lady and I demand you stop!"

The witch raised her hands in surrender, taking multiple steps away from me. *Finally*, the position Malik had given me was making a difference.

"Hands on your head. Don't move," I instructed, and the witch complied.

I looked ahead to Kallan, who was running his sword through another scout. His lip was broken open and his eyes were swollen. Several wounds were bleeding along his arms.

We were only a few feet from Calliope now. My heart pounded, knowing my friend's magic was almost depleted. But Calliope made the mistake of sending all her scouts at Throwen and Echo.

Kallan and I can beat her. A small kernel of hope popped inside my chest. I smiled savagely at her, but she just smiled back.

Grimacing, something warm and sticky ran down the back of my knee. When I looked to see what it was, a bone dagger stuck out of the back of my thigh.

The scout who falsely surrendered laughed at my idiotic, misplaced trust.

Adrenaline pumped through me so ferociously that I didn't even feel the dagger go in. I tried to hobble toward Kallan, but moving was excruciating. Now that I knew it was there, breathing was becoming hard as my leg was painted crimson. I panicked and screamed as I ripped the dagger free, limping toward Kallan and Calliope.

Purple tendrils wrapped around my thigh and pressed hard against the wound, trying to stop the bleeding. I winced and fell hard to my knees, looking back to see Throwen.

He was hitting the witch who injured me in the face with his bow over and over. Something stronger than hate was driving him. The witch's face would soon be nothing but a pulpy mess.

Calliope hollered over the devastation, "You think your empathy makes you special, but it doesn't! It makes you weak! You've *always* been weak!"

She was right. I was weak. But I would fight until the bitter end.

"Kallan!" More scouts forced Throwen and Echo further back. They fought admirably, but the remaining necromancers were skilled, raising the dead quicker than Throwen could spread out his intent.

When Kallan's fearful expression met mine, I knew what I had to do.

"Kill her." Even though they were my words, they came out in Malik's demanding tone.

Kallan sneered, ready to execute his revenge. "I'll be right back. Keep your shield up."

I threw it up and Kallan rushed at Calliope. She fell low to the ground, a deadly warrior ready to pounce and infect him with her venom. She chuckled and landed a kick to his back before he could turn around.

Calliope's red eyes pulsed. "Ah, the loyal mutt. I've been wanting to bring your undead husk back to Malik."

Kallan roared, raising his sword and bringing it down hard. She moved, but the blade sliced her shoulder, and she cried out. Kallan didn't play into her taunts, determined to land a death blow. They fought hard, Calliope dodging as Kallan came at her again and again.

Something crashed into my shield and it broke. "Fuck!"

An undead scout crawled on top of me, its mouth oozing tar onto my face. I screamed against the pain shooting throughout my entire body with my thigh as the epicenter.

The wound scraped against the ground, and I cried out. The undead's slimy fingers wrapped around my throat as I reached for my dagger.

"Octavia!" Kallan's voice wailed over the sounds of clashing weapons.

The scout grabbed my wrist, and the familiar crack of bone didn't register. I knew that sound so well, but when I looked at where my wrist dangled, bent unnaturally backward, I thought I was in one of my nightmares. Then reality came rushing back like water bursting through a dam. The guttural cry that breached its way through my chest, up my throat, and out into the air seemed endless.

Throwen was screaming too, trying to fight his way past the undead littering the hill. His arrow shot into the scout's body, then another, and another. It gurgled and oozed and screeched on top of me.

My head drooped to see flashes of Kallan running toward me. I smiled a soft smile; the pain making me feel light-headed. He halted only an arm's length away as I reached out my unmangled hand.

"No!" Echo was screaming. "Kallan!"

My blurred vision tried to make sense of the image, and when it clicked into place, I dry heaved.

Calliope shrieked with laughter from Kallan's back. Her hand fell from the dagger she had plunged into the side of his neck. Blood pooled in his mouth and flowed over his lips. Gurgles and splutters shot his blood out into the air. His pupils were blown wide and, for the first time, I witnessed fear in the warrior's eyes.

This is your fault.

I pulled myself up with a cry, doing my best to ignore the overwhelming pain that now came with movement. "Kallan! Hold on!"

I limped to him, blood still pouring down my leg just as he fell hard to his knees. When I got a hold of him, I fell too, failing to hold him up.

Echo was screaming, slicing through one of the scouts as they watched their brother dying in my arms.

The rest of the scouts were surrounding Throwen, while Calliope laughed next to me. I was grateful he couldn't see what was happening, and I considered taking the blade from Kallan's neck and plunging it into my own wretched heart.

I was ripped up by my hair and I shrieked as the roots of my scalp tore. An undead growling scout held me by my hair as I wrapped my good hand around his wrist and my limbs thrashed.

Kallan's skin was dull, and he stared up at me from the ground. I sobbed, remembering how accepted and happy I felt dancing with him, the smell of mint and pine wafting off his clean shirt.

His spirit was passing, and for a moment I thought about the smile he had when we danced and when he thought of his sisters. He could be with them now.

The orb shifted hues, and I begged, "No! Please! *Goddess forgive me!* Please don't do this!" The scout held me tightly as I flailed. "Take me instead! Please!"

Calliope straddled Kallan, binding his soul to his corpse, forever separated from the Goddess and his family.

I will deliver you to the true Ether.

He was gone.

Fuck Theldea and the scum who inhabit it!

Kallan was gone.

Are you not happy in paradise?

She would kill Echo and Throwen too.

Control yourself, Lady, or I will take control for you.

"Fuck off!" I growled at Malik's voice in my mind, pulling my dagger free and shoving it into the corpse's heart behind me. He fell into a pile of sludge with me. My ears were ringing, the sounds of Throwen and Echo's battle cries muffled beneath the sharpness.

I held Calliope's stare, writing death into every sliver of my irises. My mark hummed and my demons roared to plunge my dagger into my heart and end it now.

Calliope hesitated, then raised a shaking hand, pulling an invisible string that lifted Kallan's body from the ground.

Throwen rushed to my side, panting and barely keeping it together. "Fuck. Octavia. I don't know if I have it in me." His voice trembled and his teary gaze lingered on Kallan's pulsing, red heart.

My wounds felt like they were about to pull me into unconsciousness, but my will to protect Throwen was just as strong as his was to protect me. Even if we survived, we now had gaping wounds in our souls that would never fully heal.

Kallan's body twitched and contorted as red smoke fell from where his serious stare should have been.

"Kallan, please." Throwen cried as he pulled me backward.

Calliope coughed on tar as she laughed, not even realizing the magic was taking her mind, body, and soul. Then she thrust her arm out and Kallan pounced.

Throwen pushed me out of the way, blocking a blow from Kallan's sword. "Brother, please!"

"Throwen!" I shouted. Everything burned as he was forced away from me again.

Then I heard it. A new voice in my mind. Not Malik's or my own demons, but Throwen's. A soft baritone whispering against the electricity shooting through my brain. *Let yourself feel.*

Pressing my eyes shut tight, I took a deep breath in and out. I felt guilt, shame, betrayal. But the thing I felt most was rage. Pure, unadulterated rage.

Calliope made the man I adore fall to his knees. She killed my new brother before I could even call him that. She was already dead to me.

This was what a volcano felt like before it erupted; what the wind felt like before releasing its power into a hurricane.

I let my need to keep Throwen safe fill every muscle, bone, and tendon in my body. For once, my mind was clear and so was my intent.

I watched as Echo joined Throwen, their weapons clashing against Kallan's skin with roars of anguish and misery. Tears streamed through the blood and tar that covered their face like war paint.

Come to me.

I called for Throwen's spirits, and they left him, shooting out and wrapping around me in a cocoon like they had Indigo moments ago.

Some scouts fled in all directions, willing to risk the deadly jungle over my wrath.

Throwen yelled over the madness, "Promise you won't leave me here without you!" He was forced to rely on his training without his magic, and Kallan ripped him up by the shoulders and threw him at Echo.

It was good he couldn't see my answer. Because promising not to die by my own hands or others was an impossibility. I could never promise him that.

Pulling out one of my butterfly-throwing daggers, I glared at Calliope and sneered. My mark was buzzing now, shining so brightly that it lit up the near darkness.

Calliope looked terrified, but it was only a taste. I wanted her to beg at my feet.

"You fucked with the wrong *Goddess-born* witch." My body protested as I half sprinted, half limped toward her, the spirits doing their best to wrap around my injured wrist like a splint and staunch the flow of blood from my thigh.

But pain had no power over the hatred I had hidden deep inside of me for years. I flicked a dagger at the remaining unbound necromancers who jumped in front of Calliope. The dagger split into more, circling their necks like collars, just like the apple from the cave. I thought of Malik's gold choker and the suffocation it made me feel.

Make them feel it.

The spirits reacted instantly to my intent, spinning in fast circles as they sawed slowly through the necromancers' necks.

I hoped they felt it. The betrayal, the lies, the regret. Once their heads fell to the ground, I threw a sideways glance at Calliope, who was stumbling backward, trying to retreat.

I thought of Throwen, Kallan, and Echo as I limped closer. My wrist was useless by my side, but it didn't matter when I had control of Throwen's magic.

Calliope stood a few feet away, and I tossed the final dagger straight up into the air. It fractured into countless royal purple butterflies floating around the undead she still commanded. It reminded me of the glowworms that night with Throwen. The first night I experienced this kind of power.

Save her for last.

They all moved at once, tearing into the corpses, violently driving out the magic of the Abyss, just like they had to Levi.

Thick black tar fell all around us, and the red spirits flitted about before dying out with no husk to inhabit. The red glow of the sky was gone, replaced by a cloudy, starless night. Or maybe it was the darkness leaking out of me and into Theldea.

I stalked slowly toward a cowering Calliope, hiding behind her pathetic fading air shield. Once I finished this, I would fade too, hopefully right into the ground with the rest of the murderers.

My demon purred at the notion. Death was always so tempting; it would be so easy to end it now and let Throwen take care of Calliope.

No. I would avenge Kallan and ensure Echo and Throwen's safety. I would keep Throwen's consciousness clean of this blood. He had already spilled too much for me. What happened to me after wielding his magic held no consequence.

"Please, Lady! Have mercy." Calliope begged, and I looked over the small expanse.

It had seemed so large during the fighting, but now seemed small. In the distance, Lucky's body lay in a pool of blood on a bed of leaves. Then I looked at Indigo, knowing her soul was trapped forever in the Abyss.

Mercy is what Malik lacked. If I did this, was I just like him? But then I looked at Echo weeping over the corpse of their brother, their blade buried deep into his heart.

Throwen was panting, crawling on all fours toward me. He needed the spirits back, and fast.

"I'm not without mercy Calliope." I kneeled and cradled her chin in my good hand. She had soiled herself and was trembling.

"Thank you, my sweet siren. *Oh, thank you.*" She bowed before me; I was her true Lady of the Grave. The control was mine.

"But my mercy for you has run out." I used my injured hand and winced against the pain as I ripped her up by her strawberry blonde hair, wrapping it tightly in my knuckles.

I screamed as I plunged my dagger into her throat, hitting the exact spot she'd plunged hers into Kallan. Blackened blood splattered across my face and a feral part of me licked it off my lips, needing to taste her demise.

Wheezing and gurgling, her eyes bulged as I opened her mouth wider, letting the spirits tickle around her lips. Tears rolled down her cheeks, dust in the wind.

"They're going to scrape your insides clean of the Abyss now."

I never knew the lengths I would go for the people I loved, *truly, deeply* loved. But I lived in extremes, and this would be no different.

"Make her feel it. Make her feel *all* of it." I thought of all the witches Malik's cult had hurt. I thought of Nova and Finian. Muffled screams and purple blurs made my head spin.

I let go of Throwen's magic as soon as it was over and crashed to the ground.

Sharp rocks dug their way into my cheek, tearing at my already broken flesh. I couldn't feel it anymore, the pain.

Calliope's lifeless face morphed into my own. That's who I would have become if Malik had accepted my pleas and made me a scout.

Throwen knows you're a monster now.

And there he was, brushing my hair aside. I couldn't see him through swollen eyes, but the calluses on his fingers let me know.

My forehead was wet and sticky, hot liquid leaking somewhere from my skull. Or maybe it was my melted brain leaking out of my ears.

Echo's voice was somewhere far away. Or was it close? "Get her out of here, Throwen! Get her to a healer!"

Bright flashes of light popped all around me. My leg was soaked with blood and my thigh buzzed uncomfortably, almost feeling like a very painful tickle.

I giggled. "I see them. The fireworks. They're beautiful."

"Fuck! Stay with me," he said, his voice cracking. "*Please!* Octavia?"

I wanted to ask him to sing me to sleep, but I wasn't sure how to make the words form.

"I have to carry you, brace yourself. This is going to hurt." His arms were under me and as he lifted me with a cry of his own, the pain came bursting through like lightning striking my body.

I tried to scream too, but I couldn't.

"Goddess, please don't take her from me. Not yet. *Please. Please. Please.*" His sobbing supplications faded as I slipped back into the dark to dance with my new demons.

Chapter 25

THROWEN

An unbearable silence overwhelmed me the moment we entered the swamps of Volgsump. Going from the horrid sounds of battle to this was torture. I was trapped with only the sounds of the water sloshing and my thoughts.

I carried Octavia through the swamp's murky waters for miles, pushing reeds aside until we reached the remains of the abandoned coven. The hut we were in was a corpse of its former self, broken wooden boards with gaping holes throughout. It wasn't ideal, but it would do for now, until I could get us to Drybourne. *If we make it to Drybourne.*

I pulled dozens of leeches off my body and hers when we arrived, throwing them one by one into the fire for daring to taste her blood. I winced as I moved, my entire lower half chafed from my wet clothes.

Octavia's wounds needed treatment before infection set in. By the grace of the Goddess, there was some gravel left in a broken cupboard. After I ran the water through the gravel, I boiled it to make sure it was clean.

Plunging my hand in with a clean cloth, I welcomed the burn across my knuckles. I remembered Lucky's final shrieks, an audible ghost to forever remind me of my failure.

Exhaustion and shock caused my hands to shake as I made my way back over to her with the small amount of supplies I could scrounge.

She lay motionless on a broken-down cot. Her mark barely emanated any light and her pulse was weak. There were so many injuries, I didn't know where to start. Early morning light slipped through the slats of wood, creating harsh lines across everything.

Kallan!

Shouts echoed inside my skull as my memories came to life. I covered my ears as sounds of the previous night plagued me. My brother had been dead for hours, but it felt like only moments ago. My traitorous eyes drooped, and I slapped myself across the face.

"No. Fucking fix this, Throwen." I grit my teeth, forcing myself to look at her, *really* look at her. I landed on her wrist. It was resting on her chest and as I reached for it, I flinched as I heard it snap, relived watching the fucker do it. My sobs fell flat, fading into the damp mossy walls.

Was this how she felt all the time? Her mind reminding her of things she wished she could forget.

I took a deep breath and focused on only her wrist, gently poking around the swelling. Octavia healed quicker than a regular witch, but I worried that in her state her body might not heal like it should.

"This wasn't... I was supposed to..." I cried as I reset the bone and placed it between two pieces of wood from a broken chair.

Bile rose in my throat, but I had no appetite, so there was nothing to purge. I kept seeing Kallan's face, his fucking endearingly serious face with just a hint of a smile. Gripping onto my chest, my heart beat hard enough to crack another rib. I ripped the fabric from my sleeve angrily and, with fumbling fingers, began wrapping her wrist.

Throwen! You have to take him out!

It was Echo's voice in my mind now. They had always been stronger than me. When it came down to it, I couldn't slay my brother. Even if he wasn't my brother anymore. But Echo set him free and because of my weakness, that would haunt them forever. It should have been me.

"If I would have known heading toward Squalsend would lead to this…" I was selfish, holding onto any time I might have with her like it was my only lifeline. My aim was to fulfill my promise to show her everything I could, to spend every day with her until the Goddess called me back.

"*Sacred Ether*, what have I done?"

I shuddered as I moved onto her scalp. The bastard had grabbed her hair close to the roots, *thank the Goddess*. There was only a small chunk of skin peeled off behind her ear, just about the size of a coin.

Sighing, I pulled what was left of Whynnie's honey mixture out of my thigh pouch. The jar had broken during battle, and only a small amount remained. I dipped my pinky finger into it, the thick sticky yellow contrasting against my skin.

Lightly, I pressed my finger into her wound. I had a head injury too, but I refused to use any of the mixture on myself. It was my fault we were in this mess.

Swaying slightly, I recalled Kallan throwing me hard against a rock, felt the jolt that shot down my spine as my head smacked against it without the spirits to lessen the blow. He had charged toward us like the enemy. It was nothing like our training sessions. His jaw was unhinged and oozing tar as red smoke filled his pulsating eyes. The sounds that came from him were unnatural, not his usual gruffness, but something more feral.

Am I to be cursed to remember him that way?

I let him hit me, let him claw my face. When he pushed me to the ground with his hands wrapped around my neck, all I could think of was Octavia. Not my dead brother with a gaping hole in his neck, not Echo covered in blood and fighting at my side, not even Whynnie waiting for us in the safety of her hovel.

When Echo tackled him off of me, I fled, crawling my way toward

Octavia. I didn't watch them plunge their weapon into his heart, but I heard it. It wasn't only Kallan's heart being destroyed; it was Echo's, too. I'd been a coward.

My eyes threatened to close, the lack of sleep and blood loss catching up with me. I quickly moved onto the gash cutting across her forehead, repeating the ways Whynnie had taught me to treat injuries.

If you insist on working alone, learn how to do this yourself. Her scolding was always out of love and concern, and I was more grateful for her shared wisdom than ever.

Octavia was powerful, more powerful than I could have imagined. It had been so cold without my magic, like a crab without its shell. It was a vulnerability I never thought I would experience. But as I had proudly watched her walk with purpose to avenge my brother, I'd hoped she would get to keep my magic. She deserved the armor after years of fighting without any.

Octavia used my magic to tear apart scouts, choosing us over her coven. With a final dab to her forehead, I reached for the mixture but knocked it off the cot.

"Fuck!" I ran a hand over my hair, trying to figure out what to do. I couldn't stand this pain in my chest. The constant burning in my eyes. I scratched roughly at my itchy chin. I hadn't slept, couldn't eat. She was the only one who mattered.

Crouching, I picked it up and winced as the burn on my thigh rubbed against the fabric of my shorts. My shin had rocks and dirt wedged into the skin.

Later, I would clean it later.

With a loud groan, I sat back up, finding there were a few drops left, suspended on the tip of the broken glass. I placed it down safely, the piece of glass cradling the precious mixture.

I ran my fingers clumsily through the ends of her tangled hair. "I was supposed to keep you safe, to never let your precious blood spill again."

Something tickled at the back of my neck, the spirits trying to connect with me.

"Fuck off! How could you let this happen? My intent isn't perfect. I'm not a God."

They vanished.

Being furious with the Goddess was a new experience for me. I'd always known she'd worked in mysterious ways, ways no witch could interpret. But this was too much for even me to handle. I felt well and truly abandoned for the first time since I was a child and the wild, free witch who had taught me the meaning of empathy might leave me, too.

I missed those honeycombed orbs looking up at me. I missed her awkward social interactions and her crooked smile. Missed her cynicism and bluntness. "Please, just bring her back to me. *Please.*"

The spirits returned, wrapping me in a tight embrace. I pressed the warm cloth against her scraped cheeks as I bit my lip and looked away.

The Goddess sent me back to find her, but I had failed them both. I had felt guilty before, but what I felt now was a whole other beast. My insides were being thrown into a meat grinder.

Her perfect face was marred. The gorgeous body she let me worship only two nights ago was broken. "I should have stopped it. I should have been able to stop it." My voice cracked as I itched my skin, dried blood flaking off and onto the floorboards. I couldn't concentrate. The battle was over, but the war raged on in my mind.

A crow cawed in the distance, and I tensed. Malik couldn't have found us. I'd covered all our tracks, trudging through dark swampy waters to get her to momentary safety. *Thank the Goddess* we avoided any animals. Still, my heart raced, preparing for another battle.

But there was a part of me that was petrified. Never again would my brother bail me out, fighting by my side. A world without Kallan was one I would never feel safe in. I needed him and he was gone.

Curling my hand into a fist, I squeezed bloody water out of the cloth, letting it drip onto the already soiled floor.

With shaking hands, I dipped the cloth back into the clean water before pressing it on her scraped knees.

Those fuckers killed my brother. They didn't just kill him; they stole his *Goddess-damned* soul. Next time I wouldn't hesitate. I would kill any fucker who got within an arm's length of my witch. I would tear them apart for no other reason than getting close to the one who owned my heart. Their sob stories would mean nothing compared to how I felt about her.

"Fucking Malik!" I spat his name like a curse and stood up, pacing in the dilapidated hut. This was all his fault. *All of it.* He used his own version of Octavia's story to gain sympathy from his followers and to build contempt for the Goddess.

If he only knew the power of Octavia's empathy. It wasn't some tool she used to manipulate, but a gift she bestowed willingly upon others.

Make her feel it. Make her feel all of it.

I heard her intent in my mind the entire time she siphoned my power and let herself go. It was as if we were one and I experienced everything she did, everything she thought and felt in those tense moments.

It was so consuming that I'd thought I would explode with its intensity. My muse felt everything *so fucking deeply* and I didn't blame her for wanting to push that into her intent, to make someone else feel everything for a change.

Calliope's death was brutal, and I wished I could have been the one to carry it out. Octavia would never forgive herself for the anger she had every right to feel. *If she woke up at all.*

"Fuck." I wobbled back over to Octavia, trying to banish the memories popping through my mind from the lack of sleep and trauma. I'd experienced death my entire life. I'd died myself. Had killed. Tortured. Those things I could compartmentalize, but this...

Teddy Bear? Echo appeared in my mind, stroking Kallan's forehead, unable to pull their blade from his chest.

I wheezed, accepting that this was the new normal. That my mind was forever tainted with my brother's death. Despite all my wounds, this is the one that would never heal, would change the trajectory of all our lives.

After reassessing Octavia's wounds, I decided to use the last of Whynnie's mixture on her thigh. I rubbed at my eyes, wishing I had a joint to get through this next part.

Gingerly, I rolled her just enough to get to the back of her leg. I blew off my emotions like blowing out a candle. Luckily, the wound wasn't deep; it looked like only the tip of the dagger embedded itself. *Praise the Goddess*, the weapon was thrown and not slashed across her thigh, no major blood vessels were hit. I didn't see anything to make me think there would be permanent damage.

It would hurt like the Abyss and take much longer to heal than she was probably used to. I kept the emotional part of my brain turned off as I cleaned it, waving it off as if it wasn't destroying me. Seeing her like this was making me light-headed. My pain was pooling in my heart, breaking down the walls I was trying to erect. So instead, I pretended.

"Please wake up. Then I can be mad at you for nearly getting yourself killed. Then you'll force me to admit that you saved my ass, and you can rub it in my idiotic face." I wiped my cheeks on the sleeve of my shirt in an attempt to dry the never-ending tears.

If she hadn't killed those extra scouts, we would've all died and been banished to the Abyss forever. Her righteous anger and violence didn't scare me. I was honored to be allowed in her presence while she unleashed herself, her power. She was fucking Goddess-born, and it was about time Malik got that message through his thick fucking skull.

"I was supposed to save her. I was supposed to save Kallan. I was supposed to keep Theldea and my family safe." My throat burned and my voice cracked. "Why did you send me back, give me these abilities, if I can't do what I'm supposed to?"

The Goddess was silent.

I stared at my lute haphazardly thrown into a corner with what little supplies I could grab on our rush toward Volgsump. Kallan's pack was the only one I could grab in the chaos, and I had peeled it from under John's lifeless corpse.

I took a deep breath, walking over and opening the pack. After unbuttoning the straps, I dumped it all at once as if ripping off a bandage, and memories fell into place.

My eyes jumped from one object to another, unsure where to look first. His worn metal card case, wrapping papers for the extra joints he rolled and carried just for me, Echo's favorite candies, his knitting needles, and a tiny half-knitted red and blue striped scarf.

My chest was so tight I was sure my ribs would start bursting through my skin. I forced myself to focus, knowing I wouldn't be able to stay awake much longer. Fighting through tunneling vision, I grabbed a pair of Kallan's pants and wobbled my way back to Octavia.

I ripped off strips of the fabric as sobs racked my body. It felt like I was shredding pieces of my brother away. Each tear sounded like the cracking of his bones as he moved around unnaturally, his neck snapping back and forth between Echo and me like a rabid animal.

After cleaning her entire thigh vigorously, I applied the last of the mixture and wrapped her wound. Normally, her cool olive skin would look glorious against the dark red fabric, but her skin was pale. So pale.

My breathing was becoming more labored, and I knew I didn't have long before I passed out.

I hobbled back over to the strewn items and found Kallan's clean bedroll. Of course, he had time to clean it at Fennix's Coven. He was meticulous, and I adored him for it now more than ever.

Trying not to get any dirt or blood on it, I flicked it open. The strong scent of mint hit me so hard I swore I was falling. I panted and my arms dropped to my sides.

"Almost done." I leaned over to pick up a goldenrod shirt that reminded me of the pajamas Octavia wore when we were last alone together. I thought of her body, all the things I had promised myself I would do to bring her as much pleasure as I could. Thought of her laugh and her jabs, always trying and succeeding to get a rise out of me.

With the last of my energy, I made my way over to her and examined her one more time. I made a mental note of every scrape, bruise, and major injury. I fantasized about taking my time with Malik, replicating each and every one so he could feel her pain as his own. Sympathy was something his mind wasn't capable of, so maybe his body would get the message instead.

I carefully pulled the shirt over her head, down her shoulders, and her legs.

When I stood back, I swayed and laughed half-heartedly, realizing it reached past her knees. "You're absolutely swimming in his shirt, he would have loved to see this and tease you for it. He truly was a big Teddy Bear. I miss him so much already, Octavia. Please come help me through this. I don't know how to feel things like you do. *How do you fucking handle it?*"

Her face remained in a neutral state of unconsciousness, the first morning rays trying their best to light up her vacant face. I knew if she was awake, she would know exactly what to do, how to comfort me through something so awful.

Picking her up, I supported her neck and avoided touching the major injuries. Her hair tickled my arms, and she smelled like blood and honey. My tears continued to fall over my cheeks and dripped down the tip of my nose onto her stomach.

"I wrote you a song, you know? I think you're going to like it." I laid her on the bedroll, covering her with the final clean black shirt left on the floor from Kallan's bag. He was still here in that shirt somehow, fulfilling his role as her bodyguard, even if to only give her a semblance of comfort.

I crashed to the floor beside her, the damp floorboards seeping into my already soaked clothes. As I stared up through a large hole in the roof, a blue heron flew by languidly. I hummed her song as the weight of it all mercifully pulled me under.

Chapter 26

THROWEN

"Why am I clean and you're not?" Octavia's stern muffled voice penetrated my haze.

I struggled to remember where I was. It was twilight, and the fading sun caught the lighter tones in her wavy hair. Water dripped in a slow, steady cadence from somewhere outside. "What?"

She laid on her back next to me, her head tilted in my direction, a furious golden glow burned into me.

"You're alive." Tears flowed again, and I shot up, wanting to grab her face and kiss her. But her cheeks still had scrapes on them, and I didn't want to add to her pain.

"Yeah, so are you, so please explain why you're treating yourself like you died." She was angry. Blatantly assessing every filthy inch of me.

"I... I wanted to make sure you were okay first and then I guess I passed out..."

Frustration pulled at her dark brows, but then her face softened, and she held my gaze.

"Octavia, it was my fault. I'm the one who said we should go see those fucking fireworks..."

She reached for my hand through a wince, and I curled my fingers around hers. Her movements were too slow, and she rested my hands on her cheeks. "Your picks."

Their absence conjured tears to flow out and over her waterline.

I gripped her tighter. "I lost them... in the fight."

She looked at me and I did my best to hide how much their loss affected me. But she sensed emotions like the sea senses the changing of the tides. I could tell that this loss was the final straw for her.

"He-he was right. The tread on my boots helped keep me safe. He kept me safe. He had to know that, right? In the end? That he didn't fail. That I appreciated and loved him?" Her chin trembled, and I moved closer to her, reaching out to rub slow, firm circles on her chest like the spirits had taught me.

"Why does this hurt so bad, Throwen?" Sobs wracked her body. "I've watched countless people I cared for die. Sometimes I watched the life drain from them as I slit their throats. I thought it was the most painful thing I would have to endure, but this... it's never felt this consuming, this final."

"It's done. There's no point in dwelling on it." My voice came out more lifeless and sterner than expected, and her look of confusion morphed into her familiar frown of irritability. I fought back a smile because last night I'd thought I might never see that endearing frown again.

"Don't you dare fucking try to pull that shit with me, Throwen. You have feelings too."

Fuck. I was not ready for her to draw these emotions out of me yet. She was just like the spirits ready to purge me of the brunt of these horrors. I grunted and pushed up into a sitting position. Leaning over her, I pulled a smattering of peanuts out of my broken pouch. "Eat these, but slowly."

"No." She tried to copy me and sit up, but I placed my hand firmly on her stomach.

"Excuse me?"

"I said no! You don't get to claim to be in charge of protecting my soul when you don't even take care of yours."

"Seriously? Octavia, you were fucked up. I watched you get beaten nearly to death. I carried you miles through a swamp, spent hours getting this fucking water clean, tended to all your wounds, and you're what? Mad at me for taking care of you?"

"Yes!" She pouted, hot angry tears still streaming down her face.

"You're *impossible*!" I moved away, speaking through clenched teeth. Cringing, I assessed myself. I was coated in a thick layer of blood, sweat, dirt, and who knew what else.

"You're an idiot. If you don't take care of yourself, how are you supposed to take care of me?"

"Gah! Fine!" I stood up and stomped over to the bowl of water. Stripping off my clothes, I grabbed the cloth angrily, rubbing at the caked-on blood. I didn't even know where my injuries were anymore, but I knew where every single one of Octavia's were.

She waited silently on her back, arms crossed over her chest, refusing to look at me. *Fuck*.

"You're right," I mumbled, realizing some of my deeper cuts were already starting to get increasingly red.

"Did you say something, bard? You're not usually so quiet and demure."

I bit my cheek, trying to keep in my negative emotions, but she had pushed me too far. "You were right! Okay? You were right."

As I continued to scrub, I ignored the physical pain. We let silence fall between us for what seemed like hours, but was only a few minutes.

Walking back over, I grabbed the black shirt she was using as a blanket and sat next to her. I spoke calmly and pulled it over my head. "See? Taking care of myself even though I would much rather sit here naked and cold than take away even an ounce of comfort for you." I scratched at the back of my neck, hoping she would accept my act of placation.

Sighing, she squeezed her eyes shut. "I'm sorry, Throwen. I'm so fucking sorry."

She was crying harder now, her breaths coming in quick bursts. I combed my fingers gently through her hair, happy to see her scalp was already healing quickly. *Thank the Goddess.*

"You have nothing to apologize for, Octavia. You protected us."

It was as if a switch had flipped and her crying ceased. Her stare was unfocused, and her face was an eerie mask of neutrality.

"Darling." I leaned close so she could hear my soft voice right next to her ear. "You're safe. I'm here. You don't have to hide from me."

She shuddered. I pressed heat into her palm, trying to ground her and pull her back from wherever she went when her emotions were threatening to overflow.

"I've never had to talk about my feelings much." I rubbed circles against her uninjured wrist. "I was always the content one, the well-adjusted one. And I truly was. My intense feelings are nothing like yours. They come and I'm able to let them go. But since I found you on that mountain, I'm feeling things more deeply. Things I didn't take the time to think about or appreciate. Things I've never even felt before."

She spoke softly, "I don't know why this is different. Maybe because in my coven, we weren't allowed to talk about the dead. Once they became part of Malik's Ether they were a collective, no longer individuals, but magic for us to use as we pleased."

"I have an idea." I smiled, and she rolled her head over to look at me.

We were both a mess, but we still fit together perfectly, like the spirits wrapping tightly around my bow. We were made for each other and even when we weren't touching, I felt her wrapped around me.

As she smiled back, I nearly lost my breath at the sight. I wasn't sure I would ever see her look at me like that again.

"Let's talk about the shitty stuff. Not exactly a promise, but an agreement to at least try," I offered.

"Hmm... all the shit?" She raised her eyebrows playfully.

"All the shit." I leaned over, kissing her gently on the lips and pulling away.

"I think that's a good idea. If we bottle this up, we will explode like I did with Calliope." Her chin trembled.

"Hey." I pulled her focus back to me. "If you didn't, I would have."

She sniffed. "I know. That's why I did it. I was her monster, not you."

"You're not a monster." I leaned over her, making sure she saw my sincerity.

"I am. I was one before you found me. I've killed so many people."

"I've killed too." I rubbed the furrowed spot between her brows.

"It's different."

No response came because she was right, it was different. I killed only when I had to while she was ordered to kill regularly, with no real reason.

She sighed heavily. "Intent. It all comes down to intent." She stared at the hole in the ceiling where warm light filtered through crisscrossing mossy branches.

"What do you mean?" It amazed me how insightful her thoughts were, so quick to dig through all the layers to find the deepest meaning possible.

"On my Name Day, Malik forced my bleeding hand against the tree." She lifted her splinted wrist, clicking her tongue. "Octavia. Intent." She spoke in that eerie voice she used to mimic Malik.

"What did you do? What was the intent?" I was trying to follow her line of thinking, but as always, her thoughts were above the simple bard.

She bit her lip and scowled. "I looked at the witches surrounding me, the witches who relied on me, and poured thoughts of safety and protection into it. I thought they relied on Malik too, but it was only me keeping us concealed. Malik doesn't even truly know why my blood could do that. I remember how he would look at the gold light that pulsed through me and into the tree. He looked at it with longing."

"Lies make cowards brave." It was something Whynnie had said to me sometimes when I questioned the way the world worked.

She hummed.

I wanted to applaud her for even having the bearings to reconstruct what she thought she knew about her mentor.

"I didn't know that the wall I erected for my people was actually keeping them imprisoned. It always drained me in the worst way, like someone was sipping my life up through a straw. I should have known." She used her good hand to smack herself in the forehead, wincing when she made contact with the gash there.

"*Goddess's tits*, Octavia." I pulled her hand away and examined the cut. It was healing, but slower than her scalp.

"Can you help me sit up?" She looked stiff and uncomfortable.

"Of course, darling." I got up onto my knees and slid an arm behind her back. I offered her my other forearm, and she gripped onto it with her good hand. As I helped her up slowly, she winced.

"Take your time," I urged her, "your body has sustained a lot, even for a Goddess-born."

She panted, and I let her catch her breath, assessing her every movement. Her face was still swollen, and I fought back tears.

When she was upright and somewhat comfortable, she ate one of the peanuts, handing me one with a stare that reminded me of the way Whynnie had looked when she chased us around with her broom. I ate it, my stomach clenching in protest.

"My intent with the scouts and Calliope…" She shook her head. "It was vile, I didn't give the spirits a choice."

"I heard it."

Recoiling, she averted her eyes.

"Octavia, look at me." I tried to move into her line of vision, but she squeezed her wet eyes shut and turned away.

She moved to wring her hands but couldn't with the splint. Without the comfort of her anxious tics, she was increasingly restless.

"Look at me, my muse. *Please.*"

With a trembling chin, she gifted me a full view of those healing honey irises. It was my turn to help her heal.

"You aren't evil. Passions can be all-consuming. Trust me, I know. But you need to know I have never and will never see you as a monster. I heard your intent clearly, as if it were my own."

A sob escaped her, and I moved around to sit behind her so she could rest between my legs and against my chest.

"Throwen, my intent always creates more pain and death. Even when I don't know what I'm doing, I'm still the villain."

My grip on her tightened, and the spirits coiled up my legs and around her torso. They were trying to keep us calm, to let us know we weren't perfect, but they were still here.

"You are not the villain in this story, Octavia. Things aren't always good or evil. Sometimes it's a little of both, sometimes it's neither. I told you that we don't control the spirits, but sometimes our intent can get… out of hand."

She traced my veins where my death-touched forearms met with pale skin. "What do you mean?"

"I tried controlling them on that battlefield. I thought my intent was better than theirs and look what happened." I sniffed, seeing the raven-haired girl flash before my vision. "My arrows pierced through that girl because instead of allowing the spirits to aid me the way they were meant to, I ripped their choice from them. My intent to kill Calliope was short-sighted and I shouldn't have demanded from the spirits."

"That wasn't your fault, Calliope—"

"I took away their autonomy, their freedom. *Goddess*, I'm so stupid. I'm no better than Malik."

"Never say that. You are nothing like him." She squeezed onto my arm reassuringly. Lavender wisps continued to spiral around us sporadically.

"I think it's safe to say that we were both willing to demand control because of our fear."

She lifted her good hand in front of her face. Spirits coiled around her fingers, tickling at the tips. "You're right." She spoke to them softly. "I shouldn't have taken your freedom. I know how that feels, and I wouldn't wish it upon anyone."

Purple tendrils rushed around her face, lifting her curls and making them dance around.

I chuckled. "They like honesty."

"Oh, yeah?" She strummed her fingers along my arm and reached to touch the tip of her nose with her broken wrist, grunting when she couldn't.

"Okay, all the shit." She took a deep breath, tapping into the parts of herself she worked so hard to keep hidden.

"I feel like I'll never be enough. My decisions and actions will always lead to more death. I wasn't good enough to see that my actions were imprisoning my people. I wasn't good enough to save Kallan. I've never once been good enough for Malik. I truly believe it would be better for the entirety of Theldea if I just wasn't here. How many lives could have been spared?"

I sat with her words and rocked her gently.

"It makes sense that you feel that way, but that doesn't make it true. I feel like I'm not good enough either. Not good enough for you."

Her neck craned beneath me. "Throwen, this world *needs* you. They need you to ease their pain, to make them laugh and see what's out there that's worth living for."

"And I need you." The profession came out so naturally, and she shook her head in disbelief.

"No, you don't."

As if I hadn't already shown her how I felt. I helped her turn around to face me. We sat like we had that night in Stranata before she bared herself to me. I held her hands in mine and spoke softly, "I need your empathy. Sometimes I can't recognize what others need beyond playing them a silly little song to distract them. You see right into a witch's heart. You see a need and you fill it. I need your ability to focus because *fuck*, I get so easily distracted. I need you to keep encouraging me and my stupid ego."

"Throwen, I—"

"I need your eyes looking at me, seeing beyond the bard and the assassin. Your hand in mine, squeezing every so often to let me know I'm needed and can help. I need your cynicism, your morbidity, your curiosity, and tenacity. *Goddess forgive me*, my life wouldn't be worth living without your smiles and your symphonic laugh."

She stayed silent; the twinkle of the evening's first fireflies reflected in her wide eyes.

"I thought my actions were enough, but I realize now that you need to hear it. Octavia, I am head over heels, writing a fucking ballad, in love with you."

She sat there, as if her brain was trying to catch up and comprehend what I just said. It was as if there was a wall it had to dig under first.

"Octavia, once you materialized wild and free in that mirror, that was it for me." I traced my finger along her jaw. "Then when I met you... you were in my every thought, my every desire. My obsession grew with every insightful thought, every swish of your hips, every smart-ass comment."

"Throwen..." Shaking her head, she let out wavering breaths.

"You asked me in Oxvein what would be on my archway. I knew then that you would be on it. I know with every fiber of my being that I was supposed to find you and help you feel wild and free always, to never let your smile falter."

She attempted a smile. "Throwen, I am not good enough for you. I deserve the Abyss, not this. Not your love."

"Tell that demon purring in your ear to shut the fuck up and listen to me."

She took a few shaking breaths, and her cheeks bloomed red.

I pulled her closer, keeping her thigh still. "I will always choose you, over and over, no matter how many problems you cause me or how many bridges I have to burn. I choose you. You are my purpose. You taught me how to love and I know I suck at sharing my feelings, but I love you. I am in love with you. *All of you*. And I *intend* to keep you."

"Throwen I—"

"Are ya' two out here?" Simulie's voice called from outside the hut.

Annoyance at the interruption almost had me ignoring her to hear what Octavia had to say, but we needed medical attention. I shot up and sprinted for the door.

"Throwen, wait!" Octavia called after me, but I was already outside.

"Simulie! Over here!"

The Drybourne coven leader flicked her head toward the hut and clicked her tongue, using a long paddle to switch the direction of her small boat. "Well, come on then. I've got a coven ta' run. Echo has me out here savin' your ass."

Her long locks were pulled up into a brown scarf. Beads and jewelry covered her as if she were a room full of beautiful trinkets.

"Throwen?" I was jolted away from our rescue to see Octavia limping toward the door.

"Octavia, let me help you."

"I'm fine," she spat and found her footing. Wobbling, she made her way to the door. I didn't want her to feel coddled. She would need to heal as quickly as possible because, before long, Malik would find us.

"I'll grab Kallan's—our stuff."

"*Sacred Ether*. You are ethereal." Simulie had pulled her boat up alongside the hut and fell to her knees before Octavia. "Echo told me in their letter ya' were Goddess-born but I didn't believe them. You are radiatin' divine energy, babi."

Octavia checked to make sure her hair was blocking most of the light from her mark. It had been shining brightly ever since my proclamation of love.

I wanted to know her response, if she felt the same way. But I knew we would have time to discuss it in private soon, after her wounds got proper care.

"Oh, babi, don't hide who ya' are. How painful it is ta' dampen our luminescence. You are safe with me and my people. The creator and her children have our devotion and protection." Simulie rose, taking Octavia's good hand in hers and squeezing. "*Always*."

Octavia's shoulders relaxed and a small smile tugged at the corners of her mouth before I went back inside to grab Kallan's things. Simulie helped Octavia into the boat, cooing to her the way a mother would.

"Don't worry, we will get ya' all fixed up once we get ta' Drybourne. Oh, the girls are goin' ta' start actin' up like a croc findin' a chicken."

My body shook as I threw Kallan's things back into his pack. Within three days, I professed my love both physically and verbally and lost my brother forever. One an ending that would haunt me and the other a possibly life-changing new beginning. The two mixed in a sickening combination of bitter and sweet.

I wiped away the tear that fell down my cheek and rolled my shoulders back, bones cracking. Right now, I would be her strength, her anchor. I would help her heal and in turn, I believed she would help me.

Throwing my lute over my shoulder, I winced. The strings were broken and there was a scratch across her body, but I was thankful she was still intact.

As I walked onto the wooden planks out to the boat, I smiled. Octavia's eyes analyzed the swamp with curiosity. I would continue to nurture that in her, to encourage her unique fascinations.

"Let's go." When I hopped into the boat, it wobbled slightly.

I had hoped to wipe away Octavia's bad memories, replacing them with new ones. But I knew now that wasn't realistic. I lived in the past now too, where my brother died. Could we ever be fully present with a tarnished past?

Simulie ripped me from my thoughts, thrusting a paddle into my chest. "I'm not as young as I used ta' be, Angel. Think ya' can paddle?"

"Anything for you, Simulie." I flashed her my charming grin and paddled us through the twisty waters, praying to the Goddess that I could somehow paddle us through our grief too.

Chapter 27

OCTAVIA

Years of mourning my freedom were nothing compared to how I felt about losing Kallan. Simulie explained that a full day had passed since his murder. It was a foreign emptiness. I lost the past with Whynnie and now I lost any future with Kallan.

I looked at the man who had professed his love for me moments ago. The colliding emotions were making me feel sick as Throwen paddled us toward Drybourne. I couldn't help myself from watching his biceps flex with each stroke.

"Echo sent a bird," Simulie said. "They are safely on their way ta' Goldhaven but they wanted me ta' tell ya' some got away."

Throwen's head snapped up to meet Simulie's dark eyes. They reminded me of Kallan's, and another wave of heartache threatened to pull me under.

"What are we going to do?" I asked.

His brow furrowed, and he paddled harder, as if getting further away from Malik would help. By now, he might already be coming for me.

Simulie coughed, attempting to break the tension. "Ya' shouldn't be out in that mess of history, those huts are haunted ya' know."

"What?" I shot a glare at Throwen.

He shook his head. "You'll have to excuse Simulie, the witches of Volgsump enjoy teasing through their dramatics."

"Sounds like someone else I know," I muttered under my breath, and Simulie laughed.

"Don't fret, babi, you'll catch on quick." She winked at me just as two yellow eyes peered out from the murky waters behind her shoulder.

"M-monster!" I pointed a shaky finger at the eyes that must have belonged to one of the beasts of the Volgsump swamps. From what I had read, they were deadly and could chomp your body in two with their enormous jaws.

Simulie looked over, shaming the beast. "Go away, Ozzy! Stop scarin' her."

I almost scoffed at the hypocrisy. She had just been trying to scare me. The large lizard swam alongside the boat and as it emerged, I had the urge to reach out and touch it.

His nostrils surfaced first, squirting out water. Massive jaws flexed into a smile as he showed off his large teeth. He looked silly swimming along the boat with short legs and webbed toes.

"Is he your pet?"

"Pft. He likes ta' think he is. All the crocs near our gates are spoiled rotten by the guards. Ozzy here assumes I have a chicken neck anytime I leave the coven."

"That's because you do have one." Throwen raised his eyebrows in challenge.

"Keep those pretty eyes ta' yourself." Scrunching up her nose, Simulie revealed a pouch hidden in the many layers of her flowing skirts.

Throwen shrugged and smiled coyly. Always such a showoff. My lip lifted at the corner, and I could feel that crooked grin only he could elicit spreading across my face.

We sat in silence for a moment as Ozzy languidly serpentined beside the boat after devouring the chicken neck Simulie tossed to him. When he jumped out of the water, I could properly admire his thick scaly skin, massive tail, and power.

Simulie pressed a hand to her chest. "Echo told me what happened ta' Kallan."

"Simulie, don't." Throwen's harsh tone was followed by Ozzy's hiss, and he swam away.

Throwen's pain was entirely my fault. *How can he love me?*

"Hush!" Simulie's voice rose an octave. "You think ya' are the expert on death because ya' experienced it? Death affects us all. When someone we love dies, a piece of us does too."

Throwen looked to his feet like a scolded child, and I wanted to race across the boat and hold him.

"I know, I know. I apologize." His voice cracked, and I knew then that Ozzy wouldn't be the one to drag me below the swampy depths; instead, my anguish would pull me under.

The sun was setting, and a curling fog made an appearance around the boat. The trunks of the trees were black, reminding me of home.

This coven is our home, and I am the provider. Follow our laws and you will prosper beyond your wildest dreams.

Malik's recurring speeches buzzed through my mind like an annoying fly that wouldn't fucking leave through the open window. I didn't want him in my head anymore, but I had no control over it.

"Kallan was a rare treasure. He supported and led countless children ta' me. Savin' those in trouble was his greatest goal and I think we can all agree he achieved that." The feathers hanging in Simulie's hair shifted, and she looked to the sky, the paint on her face cracking in certain spots where her skin was wrinkled with age. They were happy lines, and I could see contentment in the way she spoke so freely and comfortably about Kallan.

"He brought the children he saved to you?" I never even thought to ask him about it, and I regretted not showing more of an interest in his work. Now, it was too late.

"Of course he did. Our little collection of polliwogs reside throughout Volgsump."

Croaking frogs became louder, and the sun set fully. Mossy vines crisscrossed amongst the branches overhead. I felt the same pleasant sensation I had when I heard the wolves calling to each other in Oxvein. I latched onto the root of the feeling.

Wolves are very well connected.

Throwen's explanation struck me like lightning. *Connection.* When surrounded by nature, I felt connected to it all somehow, like tiny strings were holding everything and everyone together. My mark grew hotter and glowed brighter with the epiphany.

It was a connection to the creator, a connection between me and the Goddess. That part of her that loved her creations was in me, too. Instinctually, I pressed my hand to the back of my neck.

"Our coven respects the Goddess and, by extension, those born of her. Though it would be nice ta' know your name." Her teasing grin shook me from my existential thoughts.

"My name is Octavia. It's very nice to meet you." I started to shake her hand, but I couldn't with a splint on. Awkwardly, I offered my other hand.

Simulie's expression lit up, and she took it, lifting it reverently up to her forehead.

"Oh, um…"

She continued to mumble some kind of thanks under her breath.

I looked to Throwen for help, but he was already holding in a laugh. I tried to raise my middle finger in the splint at him. Frustration boiled in my stomach, and I did the only thing I could think of, sticking my tongue out at him.

He burst into laughter, music to my ears, but I wasn't about to let him know that.

"That's not necessary, just born of the Goddess, not *actually* her." I laughed uncomfortably and pulled back. I couldn't let her keep deifying a monster.

A vision of purple spirits burrowing into Calliope flashed in front of me. I blinked fast, trying to erase the horrid image. Throwen had seen me use his power to do unforgivable things. And yet, he claimed to love me.

Confusion swirled my thoughts around like the paddles swishing through the water. "I feel like I might be sick."

I scooted over to the side of the boat and threw up the two peanuts and bile in my stomach. The boat slowed to a stop and Throwen moved toward me.

"Sit down." Simulie pushed him down with her air. "Ya' want to get cleaned up? Ya' row. I am the second-best healer in Theldea, I think I can handle a little motion sickness."

He huffed and grumbled as he continued rowing, tapping an irritated rhythm with his foot.

Simulie sat beside me, pulling my hair away from my face and gently rubbing my back. Then it hit me: she was a mother. A mother to all those children Kallan brought her.

"Thank you." I pressed my fingers to my upper lip.

"Here, babi, chew on this." She pulled out a knife, and I put my hands up in front of me defensively, holding a flame in my palm.

Ignoring the reaction completely, she took a strange-looking root and sliced off a thin piece.

Pinching it between two fingers, I popped it into my mouth and began chewing. It had a spicy kick to it and my stomach muscles relaxed as she offered me another slice. "What is it?"

"It's ginger root. When the one you're chewin' on loses its flavor, chew on the next one." A root that helped ease nausea. This was exactly the type of healing I dreamed about learning. There were only two books in the library with remedies and most of them made the conditions worse.

"You're a healer?"

She raised her eyebrows as her bone earrings jingled. "Whynnie taught me."

It was odd seeing a witch not of my coven wear bones. It wasn't at all like the necromancers. Her earrings weren't meant to invoke fear.

Finishing the first piece, I spit it out over the edge and popped in the second. My stomach was soothed, and I enjoyed the spicy taste.

"Does it have other healing properties?"

"Mhm, and I'm sure once ya' get ta' Whynnie she will teach ya' them all."

I scratched at my cheek, unsure how I felt about that. Malik was my mentor, and that didn't exactly turn out well. I didn't know if I was ready to have another one.

Throwen paddled and watched the bats flutter through the foggy night sky. His eyes shifted to the reflection of the moon on the water. I didn't like it when he was quiet; I wanted to know exactly what he was thinking.

That gorgeous angel of a man loves me.

Simulie pinched my shoulder. "You're goin' ta' start droolin' soon."

I smiled and looked sheepishly at my feet.

"Ta' be chosen by Throwen is no small thing." She was whispering, and I was confident Throwen wouldn't hear her over the frogs and bugs.

"He shouldn't have chosen me." I wanted to wring my hands but settled for biting the inside of my cheek instead. Even with so much pain in my body, my mind demanded an immediate distraction.

"Perhaps ya' shouldn't be askin' what he should have chosen and decide what you choose. Ta' take away his choice would be takin' away free will and that is not the way of the Goddess."

I wanted to react with anger, to shut her out. The way she saw right through me had me on edge. "It's not that simple."

"Hmm." Grabbing my good hand, she rubbed her thumbs against my palm, kneading out the tension like she was baking bread. "What do ya' think love is, Octavia?"

"It's... well it's..." I stammered, trying to think of my definition of love. I shook my head in disbelief. Love was always a fantasy, something I read about in my books. An exaggerated emotion that only fools felt.

I coughed, banishing the tears. "Love wasn't defined for me. I assumed it meant keeping people safe and happy. My community was built on stable ideas of belonging and acceptance. But it was all lies and manipulation. That's all I know."

"And how do ya' define it now?" Simulie had pulled me close, an arm around my back. She felt like biting into a hot pie, warm, comforting, and mostly harmless.

I blew out my cheeks and released the air, letting out some of my confusion. "I don't know."

I sniffed, and she turned me to face the swamp while she braided my hair so Throwen wouldn't see my tears.

"Love isn't somethin' ta' be earned. It is somethin' ya' have ta' wake up and choose every day."

I knew this already. The days in my coven were tedious and long, but each day I stayed knowing I was keeping the witches I loved safe.

"Most of the children who came ta' me never knew love either. Do ya' know what I've noticed about my polliwogs?"

Shrugging, I hid my deep yearning to learn her secrets under nonchalance.

"They are the best givers of love I've ever seen. They see a need and they fill it. They see someone hurtin' and they go ta' them. They know how ta' help because they have been through it themselves. But when others try ta' love them in return, they don't yet know how ta' receive it. It's like ya' said, it's all they knew."

"I'm *trying* to keep him from making a horrible decision. I'm not rejecting him—"

"Are you not? By telling him what ya' think is best for him despite his reasons, all while refusin' ta' make your own decision?"

I pinched my lips together, getting increasingly sick of this conversation. She tied off the braid with some beaded bands and grief for the leather strap Throwen gave me leaked into my fading resolve. It was silly to be sad about losing something so small, but it wasn't small to me. It was the first of many gifts he gave me.

I faced Simulie, and she extended a smooth pastel pink stone that was slightly smaller than my palm. "For your worrisome hands." She winked, and I rubbed the stone with my thumb. "It will help with those heavy walls ya' keep around your heart."

"Thank you."

Singing poured from a large gate in the distance. Yellow lights danced about the tops of the wooden stakes of the gate, making it appear to be on fire. A beautiful trick of the moon and the water.

I shifted in my seat to get a better look. "What's that?"

"We like ta' gather at night. We dance, sing, and tell stories." Simulie's chest rose and fell, love for her coven expanding her ribs.

I thought of the witches in our coven who came from Volgsump, they were the ones who most enjoyed working in groups and gathering at the post-ceremony parties.

"That sounds like the *perfect* distraction." I smiled, knowing Throwen was bound to get roped into a song.

Simulie tutted. "Distractions always come ta' an end. Decide what ya' want, babi, ya' know better than most that life is short." She stood, whistling to someone atop the gate.

My heart beat hard against my chest.

"*Oh, my Goddess*! Angel is here!" A witch guarding the gates screamed out over the loud noises of revelry and cheering erupted.

Throwen paused the boat while the gates opened. "I'm not in the mood, Simulie."

"Ha! Tell them that."

As we entered through the gate, floating docks were lined with joyous witches. They all began hollering out song requests and Simulie laughed.

"I lost my picks. I can't play tonight."

Simulie said nothing, just stared at him.

"*Fuck*. Fine. One song. But we need to get cleaned up first." His worried eyes fell to my thigh.

"Perfect. I'll take Octavia ta' Babette, she will want ta' treat her wounds and Flora will throw a fit if she doesn't get the honor of pickin' out her outfit." Simulie rolled her eyes.

Throwen stepped toward me. "Actually, I need to talk to Octavia about something import—"

Pulling me away, Simulie helped me up the steps to the dock. I wobbled, hissing at the pain in my thigh.

Throwen looked as though he was going to protest, but then he looked at my wrist and my forehead. "Her wounds need to be treated thoroughly and re-wrapped properly."

Simulie scoffed. "If ya' want ta' come tell Babette how ta' do her job, be my guest."

I was scared to leave him but more scared to be alone with him, with so many words left unsaid. I was sorting through too much. With murder, grief, and danger clouding my thoughts, I couldn't even stop to think about love.

He pouted and mumbled as he turned and walked to a group of musicians who were wildly welcoming him with open arms. They had no idea his heart was breaking for his brother and crying out for me. He also needed a healer, someone who could tend to his wounds, both internal and external.

"There's one thing I'm certain of," I spoke frankly, and Simulie wrapped her elbow around mine.

Witches marveled at my glowing mark as we passed. I wasn't hiding because it didn't matter now. Malik would find me either way and it was freeing to feel the breeze on the back of my neck.

"What's that, babi?"

"I want to be a healer. I always envisioned traveling from coven to coven, meeting not just physical needs, but deeper ones. I thought I wanted to tell them about Malik and his Ether. I don't know what I could even offer now."

"When ya' accomplish that dream, travelin' and healin', I want ya' ta' come back and let me know what ya' found ta' offer." Her hope was so at odds with my icy heart, leaving us in a lukewarm, tolerable state.

We stopped at a small home and Simulie took my hands in hers. "Babette and Flora are inside. They will help ya' get cleaned up."

"Thank you."

She patted the top of my head and journeyed away, hollering instructions at someone in front of her.

With a deep breath, I slipped through the entrance into yet another unknown.

Chapter 28

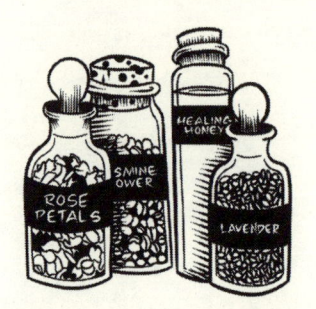

OCTAVIA

Fuchsia fabric parted to expose several layers of beaded curtains. As they clicked together, I flinched knowing whoever was inside undoubtedly knew I was coming.

"Welcome!" A youthful witch with long white hair and cat-like eyes rushed to meet me at the door, a smattering of freckles across her rosy cheeks.

Fireflies flew in and out from the open window, their constant presence a luminous pulse as if they were keeping time with Drybourne's heartbeat. This coven was humming in a way the others weren't, and it reminded me of the gnarled pulsing black tree within my coven.

"I would say sorry for the mess, but we like to live this way."

'This way' was chaos. The walls were lined with bottles, vials, and bowls full of earthy-toned substances. It wasn't like the organized clutter in Fennix's Coven.

"Stop drooling and get over here, Babette," the friendly witch chided.

Another witch hopped down from a hanging swing, speeding toward me. She was pale, with fiery red locs full of gorgeously colored beads cascading just past her hips. She wore an outfit similar to Simulie's, but instead of natural colors, her many layered skirts were a rainbow of fabrics. She blew bottles away from her feet using her air.

As she scurried, a bottle bumped into a perch where a white owl hooted and flew to another across the room. Its enormous eyes were blacker than the darkest night, and I swore I could see stars twinkling within their depths.

The white-haired witch rubbed her eyebrows. "Don't mind Agnes, she always gets fluffed up around strangers."

Sure enough, Agnes had fluffed her feathers out to twice her size.

"I'm Flora," the white-haired witch said. She gestured toward the red-haired witch that stood in front of me, never taking her eyes off my face. "This is Babette."

Babette began moving her hands around quickly.

"Babette's deaf, but she can read lips and sign. I interpret for her most of the time, but a few others have learned her language, too." Flora kept her eyes on her friend as she spoke to me.

We had two deaf witches in our coven at the same time once. But when Malik learned they had their own way of communicating, they were tried for conspiring against the Lord of the Grave and sentenced to the catacombs.

Babette slapped Flora on the shoulder, signing so quickly I wasn't sure how Flora was keeping up.

"Ugh. She wants me to ask what it feels like to have pieces of a deity inside of you." Flora's eyes widened. "*Goddess, Babette*, let her at least get in the bath first."

I couldn't help but smile at Babette. She looked like she was trying to keep from breaking out into a happy little dance. Her large, round glasses fogged up as we hobbled to the bath in the far corner.

"Simulie will want us to be speedy about it." Flora's sour face rivaled my own.

Simulie sounded a lot like Kallan, trying to be efficient about everything and stick to schedules. *Goddess, I miss him.*

The memories of Kallan's unnatural sounds after being bound rattled me, but I kept my face neutral. I didn't want to show any more ignorance or fear. I couldn't even imagine how Thrown and Echo must be feeling.

Biting my lip, I tried to hold back tears. "Yes, quick would be best. Thank you."

"I hope you like your baths hot. You aren't shy, are you?" Flora tilted her head. "I would say we would leave you to it, but Babette has been dying to meet you."

"I'm not shy, but I'm pretty beat up." I toyed with my splint, choosing to embrace the vulnerability.

Babette swiftly spun around, leaving me with Flora as she dashed along on her tiptoes, pulling jars fastened to thick strings hanging from the wooden beams in the ceiling.

"Don't worry, Babette lives for that shit. The grosser the better." Flora scrunched her nose. "She insists on popping my zits all the time."

I smiled, looking at the odd pair.

"Oh no, it's not like that. Totally platonic. No witch alive could meet that one's high standards."

My laugh was cut short as Flora finished gently removing my splint, frowning at the swollen mess. I fought back tears while she peeled Kallan's shirt off my back. I held on tightly, unable to give away another piece of him.

"I need this back." I didn't mean it to come out so demanding, and Flora patted my forearm gently in response. These witches knew how to manage trauma. It was evident in Simulie and now in Flora and Babette. Kallan had brought countless traumatized women and children here, and now I was counted amongst them.

Flora spoke with patience, "I'm just going to wash some of the blood and puss out if that's ok with you?"

I scrunched up my nose. I didn't even notice that my wounds had seeped through the yellow fabric. Nodding slowly, I let go with trembling hands.

I blinked and was back on the hill, Kallan just out of reach. Silent tears fell down my cheeks, and I held in the sobs.

Babette ran up, filling the space Flora left, and I was happy they didn't leave me alone. She wiped my tears and smelled of fresh lavender, like comfort and healing. Silently, she supported me up the steps to the wooden tub that looked like a giant barrel. Steam rose off its surface.

Babette helped me carefully sink into the water. I hissed and moaned the entire way until I submerged my head completely. It was too quiet under the water, the only sound my racing thoughts.

You're the villain now.

I burst through the water's surface, panting for breath and splashing Babette with water.

"*Oh, my Goddess*! I'm so sorry." The tips of my ears grew hot.

Babette merely laughed and wiped her glasses clean with her long skirt. She sprinkled a mixture into the water that must have been vanilla from a potent orchid. It smelled sweet in a cozy way. She sat next to the tub, sponge in hand.

"How do I say thank you?" I asked as she handed it to me.

She beamed, as if thrilled by my interest in learning. Pressing a flat hand to her lips, she moved it forward and down toward me. I mimicked her and she clapped dramatically for me.

I laughed, and she pulled a book from somewhere beneath her layered skirt and began reading, staying close in case I needed help but not being intrusive.

I took my time soaking in the heat and gently scrubbing my body. A lump formed in my throat for chastising Throwen for taking care of me. I had no idea the extent of my injuries.

What was I supposed to say to him? That I loved him too? That being shackled to me wasn't worth it?

I rose from the tub, letting them know I was finished. When I stepped onto the wooden floor, I heard bones cracking and felt sticky tar under my foot. *It's not real. It's not real.*

Flora helped pat me dry, being extra cautious around my thigh. "What did you do back in your coven?"

"I did whatever I was told." My voice was flat, but I didn't care.

"Hmm. My uncle sold me to a man like that. I did what I was told to survive. But I always knew in my heart I wanted to be a scribe."

I was shocked at the way Flora shared her trauma without hesitation. My hardened heart softened, as I realized she had shared it to help me know I wasn't alone.

Throwen was a great listener and empathized with me. But this witch understood on a personal level. She was a survivor, just like me.

Babette laughed and pulled her hair into a large bun atop her head.

"Oh, hush!" Flora waved a hand. "She thinks I'm *lame* because I always dreamed of being a scribe."

Malik had a scribe for a few years before he killed him in an outburst of rage, claiming he didn't say half the things the scribe had recorded.

All those little things I had ignored. I wanted to punch a wall thinking about how fucking ignorant and naïve I was. *Your people blame you for not seeing his abuse. Sitting idly by while they suffer.*

"What did you dream of becoming?" Aiming her question at me, Flora squeezed the ends of my hair with a towel.

"A healer, but I'm starting to think that's impossible. I carry my pain around with me like an infection that spreads to anyone I touch."

Flora interpreted as Babette paused her work on my wounds. She was unnaturally fast, my thigh already coated in some sweet-smelling mixture and wrapped, and she'd been working her way up. I admired her skills and wished I could learn all that she knew.

"She asks if you think healers who experienced no pain would be very good at their jobs?" Flora smiled knowingly at her friend.

"I guess not." My pain helped me recognize it in others, but it felt like a curse not a gift. These witches were wise and lovely, but I was feeling anxious without Throwen near me.

Flora let me use her shoulder for balance while Babette tugged a long, rust-colored skirt over my hips. "Your wounds seem to be healing fast."

"They do that. Goddess blood or something like that." I shrugged, uncertain of what else to say.

Babette signed at the ceiling, and I recognized her thank you.

"What did she say?" I asked.

Flora's brows rose, and she helped me pull on a sunset orange top that lazily hung across my shoulders, exposing the bruises along my clavicle. The sleeves were thin and flared out around my wrists.

"She said... *thank the Goddess* for sending her daughter." Flora shuffled, scurrying away to tend to something in the far corner of the room. Babette, however, looked at me with wide, adoring eyes.

I stared back, wishing I could be the uncorrupted daughter of the Goddess she believed I was.

I PASSED THE time waiting for Throwen to appear by helping Flora and Babette in their apothecary. We entered through the back door connected to their home through a small alleyway. It was quaint and easy, and I was jealous of their lifestyle. What I would have given to have just one truly loyal friend in that suffocating castle.

The front of their tiny store had a counter with a window that propped open. Witches merely had to stroll up instead of coming inside.

There was a large crowd across from the apothecary where witches gathered around a mossy stage made up of differing sizes and colors of wood. Some lovers sat in small rowboats along the edges of the docks, nuzzling into each other as the music whisked them away.

I had been assisting the girls for what seemed like ages. We fell into a rhythm of grabbing what Babette handed me and then giving it to Flora. Each time, Flora would name the herb and give the customers instructions on how to use them.

But trying to concentrate on Flora's teaching was impossible. Babette began to weave flowers into my braid, and I kept scanning the crowd, squinting around the floating boats and into the darkness of hidden alleyways. I swore I could feel his eyes on me.

Flora merrily chatted with a witch looking for some nausea relief for his pregnant wife.

"Ginger root?" I looked to Flora for approval and her face lit up.

"Yes! Look at you, well on your way to becoming a healer." She winked, but I couldn't enjoy her praise.

There was only one witch's attention I longed for right now. I puffed up my cheeks, forcing out some air as I looked at the musicians. They were playing a sensuous melody while witches belly danced around them, and others cheered for their skillful entertainment.

Babette halted weaving bright red cardinal flowers into my left braid. I understood these pauses now and looked at Flora, who was laughing.

"What?" I turned to see Babette, who was already off giggling and mixing up some dark paint that reminded me of squashed tomatoes.

"She says not to fret, that your *sexy* bard will make a grand appearance, as usual."

My mouth fell open, and I adjusted my top nervously. I smoothed my skirt, hoping I didn't look as terrible as I felt. "Is it that obvious?"

"I mean, maybe a little." Flora scrunched up her long, thin nose apologetically. Babette sat beside us and looked out over her glasses while signing.

"She says, I'd say that's more than a little obvious."

Straightening, I took a shaky breath, and my stomach dropped. I could feel his eyes on me again, and I turned to see him leaning against a wooden wall beside the stage.

He took a deep drag of a joint and gradually blew the smoke up into the air. Smirking, he handed it back to another musician.

My core heated like the hot smoke rising from his lungs. He wore a rust-colored silk shirt with red flowers strewn across it in a stunning pattern. It was open down to the last two buttons, revealing his beaten and bruised chest before tucking into a pair of black pants held up by a thin brown belt.

"You do make quite the exquisite pair." Flora rested her pointed chin in her hands like a hopeless romantic.

My head was swimming. I had to tell him how I felt. Had to figure out how to put these impossibly disorganized emotions into words. But love seemed too diminutive to describe everything brewing within me.

Our longing stares were interrupted by a witch hugging Throwen tightly and patting him on the back. He lifted a pair of beads up and over Throwen's head, followed by another witch who repeated the sentiment.

"What are they doing?"

"The weight of the beads is to remind the grieving of the support they have all around them." Flora removed some beads from around her neck and placed them over my head. "A tangible thing they can touch to know its truth."

"That's beautiful." I thought of Oxvein and their arches as I rolled the beads between my fingers. The way Theldeans treated death was becoming yet another morbid fixation, and I wanted to learn how each and every coven grieved the dead.

Babette signed between dipping her pinky into the paint and drawing something onto my forehead underneath my wound.

"Hmm, you are wise, my friend." Flora smiled, taking advantage of the break in customers to tie a bright red scarf around the top of my head. "Death doesn't have to be ugly."

She held up a reflective tincture bottle and showed me the crescent moon Babette painted.

Death had always been repulsive, the threat of not making it into Malik's Ether a looming fear. But as I watched witch after witch layer beads around Throwen's neck, I understood the validity in Babette's insight.

Throwen appeased the line of witches and raised his hands, backing away and pulling his lute to his chest. He had fixed the broken strings, and I supposed that's why he took so *Goddess-damned* long. Striding up the steps to the stage, he then pivoted and gave me an odd look. I tilted my head in question.

"*Oh. My. Goddess.*" Flora gasped and turned to face us. "He's nervous."

Babette bounded to her feet, rushing over to the counter to investigate her friend's claim.

I could have sworn I glimpsed his cheeks bloom before he turned away from their scrutiny. He was conversing with the musicians, and they all nodded and smiled.

"No. He doesn't get nervous. *Does he?* Maybe it's because he doesn't have his picks." But even I could feel my pulse quickening as the musicians left Throwen standing alone on the raised platform.

The crowd hushed and lanterns flickered, bouncing light off the water surrounding us.

When he spoke, his voice cracked, "This—" He coughed, shaking out his hands before returning them to his lute. "This is a song I've been working on."

Babette jumped up onto the counter, focusing on a tall witch signing below the stage, their hands moving with Throwen's words.

Throwen looked at me the way he had when he told me how he felt. "I hope you like it."

Flora squealed and helped me up onto the counter with them, our legs dangling over the side. His warm baritone wrapped me in comfort as he began strumming a rhythmic pattern.

"When an enchanting witch
Fell into the snow"

Sacred Ether… this song was about me.

"The adventure was sure to be rich
I readied my lute and my bow"

A ridiculous grin tugged at the corner of my lips, growing more prominent with every note he played. Something massive bloomed in my chest, and I covered my mouth with my hands.

I was the witch from my fantasies, being serenaded by her lover. I was like a giddy nineteen-year-old, eager to hang onto his every word. My reaction seemed to bolster his resolve, and he thrust himself into the performance.

"When we first did meet
My charm she ignored"

He playfully acted wounded, eliciting a laugh from the crowd.

"But my heart changed its beat
Twas her darkness I first adored"

His words rang true, his numerous acceptances of the worst parts of me running through my mind. As he shifted into the chorus, the whole of Drybourne swayed as one and he plucked the strings into the most pleasing of melodies.

"Darling, you only know what it's like to survive
You think there's only darkness but I see your light"

Tears welled at his words. I took a deep breath, realizing I was ready to open that box with him and ready to accept that what happened to me was wrong. Malik's abduction, grief for a childhood lost, all the murder and trauma I had ever been through. It happened. And I could deny its wickedness no longer.

Throwen's face softened, holding my teary gaze.

"Don't worry I promise to help you thrive
You are my muse now and I'll help you fight"

I sniffed and Babette offered me a cloth as he finished up the chorus. I wasn't sure I would make it through the entire song without melting onto the floor.

"This is the most romantic thing I have ever witnessed." Flora reached for my hand at the same time Babette rested hers on my shoulder to avoid my splint. Strangers that became friends and supporters. I had no idea friendships could evolve so rapidly.

"Shadows wrapped around her
And I offered her my hand

Her acceptance was an honor
Like that, I was in her command

She was beauty itself
Both a woman and a storm
reading books from all shelves
her golden glow kept me warm"

Laughing, I sat taller, feeling confident in his assessments for once. There was a raging storm within me that only he could coerce into momentary peace. My mark shone brightly, and Babette and Flora gasped, lowering their heads in respect.

He paced the edge of the stage, singing to the crowd as he went through the chorus again. My lovable bard. He was eating up their love and attention and I pressed my shaking fingers to my upper lip, trying to settle myself.

Theldea was marvelous, full of extraordinary places and people. But none of those things came close to the thrill I got from seeing him happy. I would do anything within my power to keep that sappy, charming smile on his face. The spirits danced around him, and I could tell he was struggling to keep them from becoming unruly.

"Now she has become my moon
And I long to be her sun"

Babette sighed dreamily at the prose, poking the moon on my forehead with a wink.

"Who knew that I could swoon?"

The coven erupted into laughter, and I joined in. I loved that fucking charisma.

"Life without you would never be fun"

I closed my eyes for a moment, picturing our journey and all the adventures I shared with him. The music slowed and grew muted as he crooned the last lines of his ballad.

"A partnership of protection"

He sang them to me like a vow and once again he transported us to somewhere in between this crowd, somewhere all we saw and heard were each other.

"Dare to touch her, you'll be torn"

Leveling his gaze, he dared the entirety of Theldea to try it just so he could rip them apart. Any sane woman would find it repulsive, but that type of commitment had me crossing my legs to relieve the ache building between them.

Luckily, I was never a sane woman to begin with. Feeling the same protectiveness, I knew I would tear down any witch who stood between us. Especially Malik.

"I'll worship her with affection"

He placed his hand across the neck of his lute, silencing all sound as the spirits whipped throughout the coven, dousing all the flames, leaving behind nothing but the glow of the moon and fireflies. After a short pause, he smiled and sweetly sang the last line, playing the notes as if these words were a revelation to him as well.

"I fell in love with the Goddess-born"

The entire coven gasped and turned to look at me. Murmurs broke through the silence, and I stood on their apothecary counter, stupefied.

He hadn't just professed his love to me privately, but to the entirety of Theldea. Until that last line, that song could have been about any witch. I didn't care about the extra attention or the deafening beating of my heart; he was the only one I saw.

I looked around and panicked, grabbing onto Babette. Asking her my question, she pressed her forehead to mine and smiled before showing me.

Following her instructions, I created an 'L' shape with my thumb and index finger while holding up my little finger. My middle and ring fingers curled down, touching my palm.

I victoriously punched my hand high into the air at Throwen, standing on my tiptoes to make sure he could see it. Recognition and exhilaration rushed through his worried expression, and he hooted and hollered with the other revelers.

"She loves me! That Goddess fucking loves me!" He pointed at me proudly, jumping up and down. I laughed, lowering myself to the ground and walking through the crowd toward him. Our love didn't need words or overthinking. It simply existed, like its own entity, a creation of the Goddess.

I'd always desired to heal others on the deepest levels, but here he was making me want to start healing myself, too. The crowd parted, bowing low as I passed, my mark illuminating their joyous faces.

When I reached him, he was throwing his lute over his back. I stood a few steps away, unsure of what to do next. His mustache tilted with his smile.

"So, you liked it?" His eyes were ravenous, and they trailed down from my face to my nipples hardening beneath my thin shirt.

I laughed and wrapped my arms around his neck. He winced, and I tried to move away, but he gripped my hips against him.

"Throwen, I *loved* it." Lifting onto my toes, I pressed my lips to his. Electricity shot through me, and he deepened our kiss. Our tongues danced as we claimed each other.

He finally broke the kiss and laughed through a small sob. "Thank you."

The crowd pressed in; the noise was too loud for us to talk. Everyone wanted to congratulate us. I stiffened, the adrenaline of the moment seeping from my body with the looming threat of more attention and socialization.

Throwen bent down to whisper in my ear, "You look beautiful tonight, darling."

"Thanks, you look pretty too." I pressed my palm flat against his hot chest, curling my fingers tightly into his chest hair. My anxiety was making all my muscles tense, and my thigh throbbed.

"Thank you all! We need to rest now! Thank you!" He bowed low and everyone clapped as the musicians started back up and the attention was drawn away from us.

Throwen led me by the elbow to wherever it was we were sleeping. I looked to where Babette and Flora waved and offered me a thumbs up.

I signed a thank you back and Throwen chuckled. "You're a quick learner."

"I'm just glad you knew the sign for I love you." I froze. It was the first time I said it aloud, my words forming it into fact. I was completely overwhelmed with emotion. "I love you, Throwen."

His eyes shifted into a deeper purple. We strolled to a secluded hut a few yards off the main dock. Then he said five words I longed to hear my entire life, "I love you too, Octavia."

Chapter 29

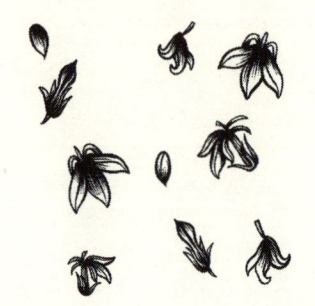

THROWEN

Octavia walked over to the kitchen area, shooing me to a chair sitting next to a small wooden table. "Sit."

My insides were charged, and my skin vibrated with joy. The spirits tickled along my veins.

"This is my love, I can't share this with you. *She's mine.*" They brushed my cheek sweetly before flitting away.

Octavia strode over with a warm cloth and some medical supplies she found in the cupboards. She gingerly took off her splint.

"Let me help you," I said and went to move toward her—

She propelled me back down into my chair with a blast of air and pulled her own chair up beside me. "Babette and Flora took care of me. It's my turn to take care of you. I believe your song said something about a partnership of protection?"

Her cheeks turned as red as the flowers woven into her braids. She pulled off the scarf and the top of her head was an adorable, frizzy mess.

I was at a loss for words, but giddiness riled within me. I needed to kiss her, hold her, sing to her, and whisper sweet nothings. But above all that, I seriously needed to be inside of her.

She was fucking devastating in her bright clothes, and she no longer flinched when her mark's glow changed with the phases of her moods. The more she embraced herself, the more attracted I became. I wanted to know everything about her.

She patted her hands dry after washing them. "This is Flora's creation. It's a lot like Whynnie's but less thick."

She frowned, inspecting my knuckles where the blade had sliced. I wished it had gone through my hand instead of Lucky's side. "Curse you and your musical charms. You broke your knuckles open playing." Her lips pressed together, trying but failing to conceal her smile.

"Oh I see, you *want* to be mad at me but you can't because you loooove me."

"Shut up. You loved me first." She flicked my nose with the sticky mixture before tending to my hands. "It's weird how you can barely tell you're bleeding against your skin. The blood blends right in." She smeared it around, inspecting as she went.

To anyone else, this would be gross, but seeing her curiosities, however random or weird, was uplifting. I was worried Kallan and Calliope's deaths would be the nail in her coffin.

"I—" I wove our fingers together, needing support from the whiplash of emotions.

"It's okay." She kissed my cheek and finished wrapping my knuckles. It was slightly too tight, but I was too proud of her to say anything.

"I miss Lucky." My chin trembled, my sweet muse pulling on my heartstrings merely by seeing the needs I ignored. I hadn't been taken care of in this way since I was a child with Whynnie.

"Me too. I hope she gets a whole field full of carrots in the Ether. How long did you have her?"

"Ten years. Whynnie, Kallan, and Echo all chipped in to get her for my twenty-first Name Day." I smiled, remembering how happy they all looked when I first rode her in circles around the hovel.

"I'm happy I got to meet her." Her smile wavered, and I pulled myself together to help her.

"I know it's going to be hard and probably impossible. But we can't blame ourselves. I've failed before. I've lost witches I was trying to save. We aren't perfect. I *hate* that I couldn't save my brother, but it's impossible to save everyone." I said it knowing that we would both fall in and out of guilt over Kallan, but we could hold each other up through it.

"One tragic, humiliating accident." She huffed.

I grabbed onto her shoulders and searched her eyes, worried about where her thoughts were taking her. "What?"

Raising her chin to the ceiling, her limbs went slack. "That's what I told myself. Back in the Coven of the Grave. I would find myself in situations fantasizing about the different ways I could end it. The first time you saw me—" She froze.

I cradled her face. "There is nothing you could say or do that would tarnish the way I see you, darling."

She took a steadying breath, lowering to the floor to focus on the gashes left from the rocks I had peeled out of my shins. As she applied the mixture, her tongue poked out adorably.

"All the shit. Okay." She kept her focus on my mangled shins. "That night you saw me in the mirror, I wasn't just trying to flee. My world had gotten too small and all I had to do to be free was…"

She swallowed hard. "All I had to do was jump out my window, step off that ledge into the unknown because anything had to be better than the life I was living."

"And you jumped? Without your broom?"

Rising to her knees, she winced, pulling away the cloth from my thigh that my healing burn had soaked through.

"I jumped without my broom." She finished wrapping my shins. "It was cowardly and selfish, but then I was stopped by this golden wall. I think it was my broom or the Goddess or something. I have no idea." She scowled at the unanswered question.

The news of her suicide attempt and some type of miracle saving her wasn't shocking, but it did scare me. Would she leave this world, leave me, given the chance?

"Wait, was your broom sentient?"

"I don't know. It acted like a pet. This endearingly pesky thing that I adored."

I smirked. "Either way, it sounds like a miracle."

She didn't appreciate the irony. It was a miracle, no matter how much her nose scrunched in distaste for the idea. The Goddess intervened somehow, keeping her alive for me to find.

"Maybe…" Trailing off, she finished re-wrapping the burn.

I didn't know what to say. I would not put pressure on her again by making her promise to never leave me. So, I gave her the most honest response I could think of. "I'm sorry you have to deal with extra voices in your head. The thought of losing you like that terrifies me."

"Does it help if I tell you that you're the only witch who has ever made me want to stay alive?" The way she was looking up at me stole my breath.

"It does. Octavia, before you, I fended for myself. I would help Kallan and Echo from time to time, but we could handle our own shit. I thought I was content and maybe I was until you, but even in the few brief moments I wasn't next to you, I was left with this lonely feeling in the pit of my stomach."

I pressed my palm to my erratic heart. "This love thing is new for me. I've never felt like this before. Thank you for taking care of me, too."

Her smile reached her eyes, and she rested her chin on my uninjured thigh.

I gave her a teasing grin. "I'm going to make it my mission to get a smile out of you at least once a day."

The way her smile shifted so quickly into the deepest frown in all Theldea continued to amaze me.

"Ha. Ha." Sarcasm laced her pretty, little lips, and blood rushed to my cock.

"So, after all of this is over, you will move in with Babette and Flora, I assume? You fit right in behind their counter, helping people." Pride swelled my chest.

"Hmm..." She rose, gathering the dirty water and supplies, and wandered over to the sink to wash her hands. "That does sound tempting."

"You would be excellent. You're kind and passionate about everything you do."

She walked slowly back to me, patting her hands dry with a towel. The way she strutted toward me one foot crossing over the other, her hips popping back and forth was deliberate. She undid her braids as waves cascaded over her bare shoulder and flowers fell beneath her feet. "So, what you're saying is you like my passion?"

I swallowed, "Yes, but, Octavia, you're injured."

"I told you already, bard." She lowered to her knees in front of me, "It's my turn to take care of you."

"Octavia—"

She reached out, rubbing her palm hard against my throbbing cock, the friction pulling a needy groan from my chest.

"Shhh," she purred as she pulled my cock free, licking it from base to tip. I threw my head back as vibrations ran down my spine.

"*Fuck.*" *Sacred Ether*, this woman was going to destroy me.

She made eye contact with me as she licked the pre-cum off the tip, flicking her tongue at the end. "You taste better than I imagined." Wrapping her small hand firmly around the base, she leaned over to put me in her mouth, moaning against me.

"Goddess Octavia."

Expertly, she started pumping up and down with her lips wrapped around me. Everything was warm and wet, and her black and blue wrist rested on my hip, avoiding my injured thigh.

How did this beautiful Goddess end up on her knees for me? It was a heady feeling I didn't want to end.

As she looked seductively at me, we both knew exactly what she was doing. She wanted so badly to push me over that edge, but it was too soon. I wanted her jaw to ache tomorrow at the memory of my cock in her mouth. To remind her that not only was I hers, but she was mine, too.

I gathered her hair at the base of her neck around my fist, pulling her off me, and her tongue darted out, wetting her lips. I yanked hard, forcing her head down so her enchanting eyes couldn't tempt me into completion. "You know the word, my love."

As she gripped onto my hip with her uninjured hand, I pressed her head up and down, painfully slow, exactly how I needed it. She wanted to please me and take care of me, and I would let her. I used my other hand to trace around the glowing spiral of her mark. She shivered and moaned, and the vibrations made me pick up speed. I pushed her head further down, eliciting a small gag. "You're doing such a good job for me."

A delicious warmth spread through my limbs, all the blood flowing to my cock. "Are you ready?"

She whimpered, opening her jaw wide, and sliding her tongue against me.

My palms pressed against the back of her head, using her to draw out my pleasure. After a few more hard thrusts, my control snapped. My cock pumped warmth, and she swallowed. "Fuck, yes, Octavia!"

I slumped, panting, as she cleaned us up. When I fell from the euphoria, I found her looking up at me with a shit-eating grin.

"Fine." I tucked a strand of hair behind her ear. "You can take care of me sometimes, too."

She laughed, wrapping her arms around me in a tight embrace. "Thank you for finding me. For seeing all the parts of me and loving them. I want to know everything about you, Throwen. I might not be able to put it in a song, but I'm equally as enchanted as you."

It was an acceptance I never asked for but somehow needed. Like my unsettled insecurity was satiated for the time being.

"I love you." The words were easy.

"I love you too. Now I don't know about you, but I can't wait to jump into those fluffy blankets. They look like moss." She ran over to touch them. "*Oh, my Goddess*, they're even softer than they look."

She squealed, stripping down to her underwear. A lacey red creation that had me wanting to go for another round. But before I could properly get a good look at her ass, she hopped under the covers wiggling around like a worm.

Walking over, I followed her lead, shedding my extra clothes. I crawled beside her and kissed her on her forehead gently.

She wrapped her hand around my neck. "I want to hold you tonight."

Did she just say she wants to hold me? "Oh, um."

She studied my reaction with those *Goddess-damned* large expectant eyes.

"Okay." I rolled over with my back facing her. Never in my life had I been held after sex.

Octavia curled around me like a small warm backpack, tightening her grip around my chest and squeezing her legs against me. She played mindlessly with my chest hair, and after a moment, I started to laugh.

She gave a gentle squeeze and giggled along. "See? It feels good, doesn't it? That's how you make me feel when you hold me."

I snuggled into my pillow, accepting her comfort.

Chapter 30

OCTAVIA

Furothia unfurled as we rode on the horse Simulie lent us. As we trotted around the coven of Fearmore, I admired the luminous lanterns that witches had lit outside their homes and shops. Most of the houses here looked cozy, were one-level, and spread out.

The trees were thin and white, creating dizzying vertical lines that seemed to go on forever as they spread out far and wide beyond the coven. Their markings looked like eyes and once within the forest's depths, I couldn't help but feel watched. Instead of finding it creepy, I thought of it as a mysterious puzzle to solve.

Our horse was named Pepper and had a captivating coat that seemed to shift from deep brown to a smoky black as the sun descended.

My body was unfamiliar with the shape of Pepper's back, and I kept shifting to get comfortable. Lucky had been vocal, but Pepper doled out infrequent responses about how she felt.

"There's so much open space." I ran my fingers through Pepper's thick mane and her hooves padded against the dirt path. It was an uncomfortable juxtaposition to the clip-clop sounds Lucky's hooves had made in Graygarde.

"It's one of the things I love about Furothia. Overpopulation isn't an issue here." Throwen took a deep breath of fresh air through his nose, releasing it slowly through his mouth.

That sounded like the type of place I imagined living. The Coven of the Grave was always crowded, bursting with new recruits. It wasn't exactly easy to expand into the unlivable Ombra Lurra.

"I must say, darling, you look intoxicatingly dangerous." He rubbed his hand along my thigh.

We ditched our Drybourne attire as soon as we entered Fearmore. I wore thick black leather that acted more like armor and felt like a second skin. The top resembled the pleated bone armor the scouts wore, and the collar covered my neck.

Stretching my legs and arms, the unique leather was near-silent as it shifted.

Throwen reached for my chin, turning my gaze to him. "You're going to be very distracting."

He looked deadly in a matching outfit that clung to his rippling muscles. I wanted to run my hands all over him, find all the spots where he was hiding his weapons, and pluck them from him so he was completely vulnerable.

Pressing a gentle kiss to my lips, he released my chin. As I faced forward, he pulled me closer, and I sunk into his hold.

I smiled and unsheathed my knife. "Look at what Flora gave me." It was beautiful, with cardinal flowers carved into the wooden hilt. It reminded me of Kallan's sword, and I twirled the point around my fingertip, tempting the skin to split and release a drop of my Goddess-born blood in atonement.

"It's gorgeous, but if you aren't careful, you're going to need the jars of ointment Babette gave you, too." He chuckled, and I elbowed him gently.

My new friends from Drybourne had made me promise to return as soon as I could, and I feared it was a promise I wouldn't be able to keep.

With a frown, I slipped the knife back into its sheath. It was a comfort since losing my dagger in the battle.

He directed Pepper down a path leading to a run-down tavern. "We're here."

Once Throwen learned of witches escaping the battle, he knew exactly where to gain intel on what was happening with the necromancers before going to Whynnie.

I tilted my head at the broken sign hanging by one chain at a diagonal. "The Fox's Den. This is nothing like the taverns where we entered Fearmore." I shook my head in disbelief that this was even the same coven.

"Poverty has always been a concern in Furothia. Their main sources of income come from crops and livestock, which can be unpredictable from year to year."

"Many of the witches in our coven were from Furothia." I thought of those who came to us dirty and too malnourished to work.

Throwen dismounted and helped me to the ground. Music leaked through the broken shutters and witches stood outside, peeing on the side of the building.

While Throwen tied up Pepper, I bent my knees, my wounds more of a nagging ache than a sharp stabbing pain. My hands shook, unsure if I was ready for this type of work. *Throwen's type of work.*

"Stick to the back. Follow my lead." He tied on a red cape, covering most of his leathers. He pulled up my hood and tugged at the sides, pulling me close for a kiss. "You're going to be great. Are you ready?"

I bit my lip and smiled up at him, trying to ignore the fear of what we might find in there. "Ready."

With a wink, he spun, his cape billowing around him, and I followed him through the door.

Patrons and barmaids alike stomped their feet and banged their fists to the beat of the music. It was dark and dirty. Broken glass sporadically rested on the sticky floor.

We separated and Throwen took the stage while I stayed in the shadows at the back.

"Ladies and Gents! Throwen!" a tall witch announced, and the crowd erupted into applause.

He bowed and started working his magic, his voice a cool balm over my anxious thoughts. Watching him in his element as he sang and danced was illuminating.

Before long, the lewd song was finished and witches were holding their bellies, laughing and cheering. Glass clinked as they thrust their mugs together, spilling ale everywhere.

"Booooo!" A noisy shout of protest rang out and Throwen found the witch making it, like a hawk about to dive on its prey. This witch had to have been insane or drunk to take on Throwen.

He sauntered over to the table, saying something I couldn't hear with a flourish, making the witch sneer. I slinked along the wall, sticking to the shadows with my hood drawn and facemask pulled up, leaving my eyes as the only visible feature.

"I'm thrilled you appreciated my masterful performance. I didn't catch your name." Throwen always sounded so *Goddess-damned* friendly despite the lethal man that lay in wait.

The witch burped. "Donald."

Throwen offered his hand and Donald pushed it away.

"You're supposed to be, *hic*..." Donald swayed in his seat. "Distracting us from our problems with yer pretty little voice, bard. Do yer fucking job."

Throwen rested his lute beside him.

The crowd quieted and Throwen tapped his fingers against the table.

"One more for my new friend, Donald," he called to a worker who scurried away, and the crowd resumed their usual antics.

"Oh, fuuck off! I'm not yer fucking friend." Donald's accent was thick, and his hair fell into his face as he rested his head on the table. "I had friends once. But they're gone now. Turned their backs on me."

"Do you have any family?" The drink was delivered and Throwen slid it over to the already inebriated witch.

"Nope." Donald licked his lips, and his glazed eyes admired the foam pouring out over the mug. "They hate me."

I thought of the Oxvein memorial amongst the arches. Surely there had to be someone who still cared, who would write his name amongst the missing.

"So, you ended up here, nowhere to go?" Throwen flicked his gaze to me.

"Yuuuup." He popped the 'p' at the end of his words and took a long swig, slamming the mug on the table so hard it splashed everywhere.

"Well, there is somewhere I could go."

"Oh?" Throwen leaned closer. "That's great. Where is it?"

A crow cawed outside, and the sun fell below the tree line in the distance.

Donald raised his head, suddenly very aware of his environment. "Fuck. What time is it? I have to go. Thanks for the drink, bard. Ye were flat during that last song, by the way." Chuckling, he wrapped his gray cloak around himself and bolted unsteadily for the door.

Throwen's fingers twitched, purple tendrils running along them. We slipped out the door, following a stumbling Donald as we headed toward the forest.

"Are you sure you want to do this?" Throwen spoke in a hushed whisper.

"In Malik's eyes, I'm already a traitor. I saw what necromancy did to Calliope and Malik has been using it for years. We have to stop the lies and violence."

Rationalizing my anger into sympathy was impossible. I could only hope that in the beginning his intentions were noble. But even if that man existed at one time, he was gone now and what was left behind had to be destroyed.

As we neared the edge of the forest, the sounds of the coven faded. They were replaced by rustling leaves and twigs snapping under Donald's feet. I walked delicately, just like I used to do around my coven.

"He's veering off the path. Stay low," Throwen instructed, and we crouched behind a small hill.

Donald brought a flame to his fingertip, looking around to make sure nobody was watching.

"Now what?" I asked.

"We follow him. It will be easier in the forest. I don't think he'll wander too far; these forests are full of bears."

"What?" I poked him but was met with the hard surface of his chest. "You didn't mention bears."

He licked his lips. "I know you like the added element of danger."

I huffed because he was right. This was thrilling. I felt like a child shadowing their caregiver at work.

The trees creaked eerily as we followed Donald for what felt like ages. I kept hearing the low growls of a bear, my mind playing tricks on me and my heart beat faster the deeper we traveled into the woods.

It's all in your head. Calm down.

I reached for Throwen's arm and squeezed.

"It's ok, I see light up ahead," he reassured me.

"Look who came back!" a loud voice bellowed over the soft chatter coming from the camp. Donald shook a large scout's hand hesitantly.

"Observe and assess." Shivers ran down my spine as Throwen whispered commands in my ear. He pressed into my back, shoving me against the thick tree we hid behind.

Donald ran his fingers through his messy blonde waves. "Yeah, um.

Listen, Sully, I have no money and nowhere else to go. I know I declined, but please let me come with ye."

Sully laughed, patting Donald roughly on the shoulder.

"It's hard to concentrate when you're so close." I squirmed. "Also, it's too dark. How in the Abyss am I supposed to assess?"

Throwen chuckled. "If you want to adopt this lifestyle, you have to get used to working nights. Learn how to work under any condition, even if that condition is a devilishly handsome bard pressing you against a tree under moonlit skies." He squeezed my ass tightly through the leathers. "Next time we are in this position I'll be fucking you, so for now focus."

I grit my teeth and took a deep breath.

"Welcome to the family, Donald. Malik would be honored to have you join his army." Sully looked a little unhinged with his bulging eyes and mussed hair. "You're just in time. We received a crow from Malik this morning."

My heart palpitated, and shivers ran down my spine.

Donald sat on a log by the fire, defeated, hunching his shoulders. "What did it say?"

A witch sitting next to Donald answered, "Malik is calling it the transformation of Theldea. We are expanding!" The witch was understandably excited but naïve. The thought of expanding into the rest of Theldea would have thrilled me too after being stuck in Ombra Lurra.

Throwen pulled me closer and my body shook. "It's okay, Octavia. I'm here. We need more information."

"So ye aren't taking me to the Coven of the Grave?" Clutching a crystal hanging around his neck, Donald rubbed it with shaking fingers.

The girl started to answer, but Sully interrupted, gaining back his dominance over the conversation. "No need. Malik is on his way, and we will meet him on the southern coast. He is bringing an entire fleet full of scouts and coven members. It will be a great honor for you to serve Malik in battle so soon. Most of us have to go through training first."

Donald paled, unable to answer.

An entire fleet? I didn't even know Malik had boats built. The catacombs must have extended to the coast somewhere and if that was true, they were much more extensive than I thought. I gagged on the bile rising in my throat.

"Count the scouts for me, darling."

I knew it was a distraction to keep me busy while he gathered pertinent information, but I didn't care. I welcomed it. I counted slowly, blocking out the sounds around me.

"There's at least ten, maybe more in the tents." There were too many of them. I didn't mean to start a war. I just wanted to feel the fresh air on my skin and experience the rest of the world.

"Isn't he worried about the Goddess-born?" One of the other scout's questions demanded my attention and the hairs on the back of my neck lifted. Throwen's protective grip on me tightened.

Sully laughed and continued, "Nah, Malik isn't scared."

"He should be." The camp quieted, and a necromancer covered in bandages whittled a piece of wood. "Our Lady is far worse than the Angel of Death. The things I witnessed her do were worse than death." His stare was vacant, like he had shut off after seeing too much.

I curled my nails into the bark of the tree. He was one of the scouts who escaped. I hadn't recognized him without his armor on. Sully glared at him and the scout stood up with a grunt and limped back to his tent.

Sully returned his attention to Donald with a shaky laugh. "Malik's magic is much stronger than any Goddess's magic. I told you, his Ether is the true Ether. Don't worry, you're safe now."

Utter nonsense. A delusional opinion stated as fact. I saw the tactics now. Infiltrating covens, luring witches who thought they had nowhere else to turn, and ultimately trapping them within the Coven of the Grave. Scouts weren't saviors, they were poachers. The knowledge bolstered my resolve.

"How did she escape, anyway?" a witch twirling some meat over the fire asked.

Sully scoffed. "It was our librarian's fault."

"*No.*" I spoke softly into the bark of the tree.

"He worked together with a rogue scout. Delivered her right to the enemy. Malik is punishing them properly for their treason. Don't worry."

Fucking liar! He was using my escape to fuel his insane mission, claiming to be spreading the gift of his Ether to everyone, but it was all so he could have total control.

Badru must have risked his life to sneak me that book and now he was paying the price. My head ached from the guilt, and I pressed against my temple.

A group of scouts exited a tent. My eyes roamed from one jagged and stained bone weapon to the next. Axes, swords, daggers, arrows, and maces.

I allowed myself to look at their faces even as the guilt clawed its way up my throat. "This can't be right. Scouts go through months of training to learn how to wield their powers."

It felt like the more I learned about the reality of the cult I grew up in, the more confusion it caused. Then a flash of Indigo's little red eyes and dead body danced across my vision.

"He is building an army; he won't care about proper training." Throwen pulled me along, leading us closer to the group. These witches had no idea what they were getting themselves into.

I grabbed onto Throwen's arm. There had to be a way to stop this. "Malik is just going to kill them all and use their bodies. We could tell them the truth. Save them from this war."

"We can't, Octavia. We are outnumbered and injured."

I knew it was true, but that didn't make it any less painful. Donald didn't know they always showered new recruits with praise and attention until they didn't. Even if he made it inside our coven boundary, it would only take a few months to slowly be deprived of meaningful connections and fall into an inescapable and dangerous isolation.

"When will he be here? I-I can't wait to meet him." Donald was stuttering and shaking and his Adam's apple bobbed in his throat.

A tiny girl with holes in her shoes who couldn't be older than thirteen said, "Soon! And then we get to see Theldea! I've never been to the southern part of Furothia, but I hear the trees are so tall they reach the clouds!" She reached her arms to the sky.

Donald forced a smile, shifting his focus to the dancing flames of the fire.

"Let's get back. I'll send Whynnie a bird and then we'll head to Goldhaven to prepare." Throwen set out the plan before me, but my chest felt like it was being ripped apart. I cried for the girl with dreams as big as my own. She would die if this war happened.

Taking a last look at the girl, we crept back through the forest to gather our supplies and Pepper.

My blood boiled. Malik's heartlessness, lies, and manipulation fanning the flames.

I will not let him use me anymore. I wasn't his pet and now that my leash was off, he would feel the anguish of my bite.

Chapter 31

THROWEN

Dark gray clouds greeted us as we entered through Goldhaven's gates in the middle of the night. Everything ached after a day of non-stop travel. Octavia couldn't see much but she expressed how the open space and sporadic houses were similar to Fearmore.

Anxiety radiated from her, accompanying her uncharacteristic silence, and I hoped my room would provide a safe place for her to unleash all of her fears and questions.

As we trotted by Rosewood, the tavern that I called home, the spirits reached out, slithering around the windows and sounds of merriment. They swiftly vanished, sulking at the loss of a good time as we rounded the corner to the back of the building.

"Here we are." My muscles twitched and my stomach quivered as I hopped off Pepper.

Even after professing my love, I still worried about what she might think of the parts of me she hadn't seen yet. It felt ridiculous to think of my room as an extension of myself, especially since I spent most of my nights away from it. But what if she didn't like it? What if it didn't make her feel safe and comforted?

"What's that smell?" Tilting her chin in the air, she breathed in deeply, exhaling with a moan. Strong notes of smoked bacon accompanied a creamy cheddar aroma.

I laughed, helping her off Pepper, and her legs wobbled. "It's cheesy potato soup. Rosewood's specialty. They put the soup in a large loaf of bread, which acts as the bowl."

"That sounds amazing." Octavia moaned, clutching her stomach. We had been grazing on nuts and berries all day, and I felt ashamed for having to neglect her appetite.

With the goal of getting her warm and fed in my mind, I led Pepper toward the stables a few yards away.

"Parker!" I hollered to the witch, who was using his magic to focus a strong stream of water to clean a mare's hooves.

"Throwen!" He threw his other tools off his lap and ran to meet us. "We've missed you."

Gasping, he gazed dreamily at Octavia, who was poking her head out from behind me like a shy child.

"Hello, my name is Parker. Any friend of Throwen is a friend of mine."

He held out his hand, and Octavia shook it happily. "I'm Octavia."

I held back a growl as he appreciated all my muse's assets that were fully on display in her tight leathers. Uncertainty laced her posture, and she scooted away from me.

There would be none of that. Wrapping my arm around her waist, I pulled her in so tightly it would obliterate any notions she might still hold that I didn't want everyone to know I loved her. "She's *mine*."

"Throwen." She swatted my chest. But her face bloomed and her pupils dilated, her tits pressing into me.

Parker's jaw dropped and his eyes darted between us, eyebrows drawn together as if we were an unsolvable puzzle.

I had never brought a witch back to my room, and it was becoming increasingly apparent as Parker tried to talk but only succeeded at opening and closing his mouth like a fucking fish. Even in the height of my sexual escapades, I always sought one-night stands at any tavern except Rosewood.

Octavia smiled with realization and my embarrassment pushed me to change the subject before I was humiliated. "Parker, have two bread bowls sent up, please. And some *juicy* strawber—" Octavia elbowed me in the ribs. "Oof!"

A confused and uncomfortable Parker locked Pepper in her stall and rushed toward the kitchen entrance.

"You're an ass," Octavia chastised. "That poor man thinks you will pluck out his eyes if he looks at me again."

"Maybe I will." I shrugged, and she scoffed, her frown fighting hard against the smile that wanted to be set free.

"I'm *trying* to be frustrated with you. You're lucky all I can think about is that soup."

I laughed, taking her hand gently. It was healing faster now, no longer needing the splint.

The nervousness and anticipation blended into my favorite intoxicating sensation. A heady feeling only she could bring out of me as we entered yet another new experience together.

"This way, darling."

Grabbing our bags, I led us up a private staircase at the back right corner of the building. After four flights, we reached the top. I searched my songbook pouch for the crystal I had taken off the day I gave Octavia my leather strap.

My palms were sweating, and my fingers fumbled until they found my crystal key. I rubbed gently over the smooth surface, letting it ground me. Slipping it into the lock, I then twisted roughly until I heard the soft click.

The door creaked from lack of use, and Octavia inhaled as earthy smells enveloped us. I flicked flames into the lanterns hung high on the walls.

My room was narrow but long and covered in floor-to-ceiling windows. They were separated by pleasing beams of smooth wood so dark one might construe it as black at first glance. Plants covered every shelf and window ledge, and Octavia gazed from one fern to the next.

"I thought we would just be in another stuffy room," she said with wonder. "This is amazing."

"Thanks." I rubbed at the base of my neck. "Echo decorated it for me. They say it's good for my mental health, being surrounded by plants."

"As usual, I completely agree with them." She moved slowly, her posture stronger than normal.

"Of course you do." I laughed, and the spirits spread out to enjoy all the curiosity flowing from her.

"I'm serious," she whispered, as if being too loud would disturb the room. "I feel like I can really breathe in here."

Praise the Goddess.

"I love it here, but I can never stay long."

I couldn't help but stare at Octavia and watch her wonder as she took in pieces of me. She ran her hand along one of the smooth beams, and my heart raced. Even in her exhausted state, she looked radiant.

I dropped our things near the bureau that sat across from my large square bed and walked over to stroke her cheek. Her demeanor remained still as she observed, and I could tell she had a thousand questions.

"Who takes care of it while you're gone?" She spun in a circle, staring up through the windows in the ceiling, and frowned at the pitch-black sky.

I felt it too, the complete darkness like an omen of what was yet to come. The fear of losing her was unlike anything I ever felt. I pulled her against me, her back warming my chest. I swayed us gently.

"The tavern owner Briar and his wife foster kids all the time. They teach them the ins and outs of running a tavern. The kids take turns caring for the plants and keeping the room clean. Their cute little faces always trick me into tipping too much, though."

Octavia laughed, and I twirled us around to face the other direction.

"Is that a piano?" She squirmed against me.

On the other side of the room, right next to the main door leading to the tavern, was my small beat-up piano, the same dark wood as the rest of the interior. I stiffened at the memory of Kallan helping me lug the heavy beast up four flights of stairs.

"You didn't think I only played the lute?"

She shrugged, and I pulled away, holding my heart as if she had grievously wounded me. "Oh darling, what kind of a bard would I be if I only knew how to play one instrument?"

Confidently, I strode over to the piano and started playing. It was a somber yet sweet melody that I often played for the grieving. It felt more potent now that I was the one experiencing such a great loss. The spirits curled around my ankles and serpentined through my knuckles like tiny garden snakes. Their purple glow paired with my dark fingers against the ivory keys drew Octavia's attention.

She sat next to me on the dark green velvet bench, curling her toes into the soft rug beneath our feet. Resting her head on my shoulder, she listened to me play.

I wished we could stay in this room, in this moment, forever. We could sing and dance. *Cursed Abyss*, I was even excited to eat soup together. But the threats looming over us were too great to ignore, and our bubble would burst soon enough.

As I finished the song, she wrapped her arms around me, nuzzling into my neck. "I'm scared." Her soft admission was spoken like a prayer for help and stability.

Kallan's loss was already too much, and I didn't know what I would do if I lost anyone else. "Me too."

She shifted on the seat, and her eyes flicked to the bed. When she looked back at me, I smiled and she frowned, her lips pouty.

"What?"

"You want to feel my blankets, don't you?" I taunted.

She bit her lip. "They look *so* fuzzy."

She moved to go to the bed, but I stopped her, pulling her into a warm embrace and kissing the top of her head. "Let's wash up first, our soup should be here soon."

I guided her to the bathroom with a pile of clothes and a large towel. Taking care of her was now my greatest source of joy and the spirits danced around the room merrily, happy to be home.

I busied myself with putting away our things while Octavia quickly showered. Our cold night in the caves of Oxvein seemed so far away now. As my mind wandered, I remembered the feel of her against me as she held my bow for the first time. How tightly my cock had been throbbing against my pants. Letting her use my bow had been the most natural thing, despite being so protective of it.

I was imagining the feel of her soft skin when she emerged in one of my black shirts, her hair tied up into a pile on the top of her head resembling a bird's nest. Ignoring me completely, she tiptoed to the bookshelf, reaching high to grab one. The shirt rose, revealing her black lace panties with a bow at the top. I swallowed thickly.

As I watched her crawl into my bed and wrap herself in a blanket, it felt like everything in my life had led me to this. I took it all in, committing this version of her to memory. She looked like a fox, burrowed in a pile of snow with only her face poking out. She was my little creature of comfort, and I would do everything within my power to keep her this way. Happy, safe, and free.

The spirits swathed around her like a second blanket, relishing in her comfort and joy.

"I'll be right back."

"Okay." She didn't move, never lifting her eyes from the page.

Purple tendrils followed me, and I closed the bathroom door to assess the damage.

"*Sacred Ether.*" Yellowing bruises and cuts littered my skin, and I was well overdue for a shave. That could all wait. I needed to spend every moment I could with her.

I quickly scrubbed and threw on a steely blue shirt with some baggy pants that cinched at the waist.

Just as I threw my towel into the hamper, a soft knock tapped against the wooden door. When I opened it, my gut clenched at the sight of my only remaining sibling.

"I have your soup." Echo thrust one plate at me and took the other to Octavia.

They wore their baggy brown and salmon striped pants with a sleeveless cream top and no makeup. The red puffiness around their eyes looked wrong, their usual spunk snuffed out.

"It must be bad if you're in your lazy clothes." I closed the door and locked it.

"It's worse than bad. Malik's bringing a fucking army." Echo flopped onto the bed, curling up into a fetal position. Before I could comfort them, Octavia rubbed their back.

"We heard. How did you know about the army? Did you tell Whynnie?" I asked.

"Fennix sent a bird. He heard about a fleet seen off the east coast and confirmed it with Toffdank's coven leader. Whynnie says she's planning, but I don't see how she finds time between meltdowns." Echo's tone was too level when they mentioned Fennix and Whynnie, like they had no room left for emotions. "Is it selfish that all I can think about is Kallan? How am I supposed to plan for a battle like this?"

I froze, unsure how to comfort them. Luckily, Octavia stepped in. She looked like she was in pain, soaking up Echo's like an emotional sponge. "Grief comes for us all at some point, Echo."

"I know. But I've never experienced it like this before." Echo sniffed.

I joined them on the bed, bringing Kallan's pack with me, and spoke freely. "My mind can't wrap around the reality of it all. I keep thinking I see him coming around the corner or swear I hear his low laugh."

Echo's jaw dropped; I assumed from my newfound ability to share emotions. Sitting up, they wrapped an extra blanket around their shoulders. Everything about Echo was bleak as they spoke, "Whynnie is a mess."

We sat comfortably on the bed as Octavia and I ate our soup, listening to what Echo had to say. I smiled, watching Octavia suppress a moan with each bite in favor of being an active listener.

Echo continued, "She goes from being numb and unmoving to bouts of rage. I had to hide all her favorite teacups."

Octavia flinched, as if guilt wrapped its claws around her.

"I'm trying my best to be strong for her, but without Kallan, life is unbearable. I'm struggling to help her. I feel like my being there is just making it harder for her. Will I just become this constant reminder of the child she lost?" Echo's voice was hoarse.

We sat in silence, unsure what to say or do as lavender threads wrapped around us, pulling us together.

"I—" I coughed, trying to clear the lump forming in my throat. "I have some of his things." I opened the pack, grabbing the items one at a time and laying them on the bed.

Echo seized the chocolate-covered cherries with a smile. They were their favorite, and Kallan always had some for them. "He was the most thoughtful witch. His meticulous planning always included the needs of those around him."

Laughing, I snatched up the rolling papers. "He never smoked with me, but there was never any judgment. His perfectionism produced the best joints I've ever had." I carried the papers to a box on my dresser, pulling out some cannabis and rolling a joint.

"Beloved things are meant to be used…" Mumbling, I had to remind myself that he wouldn't want me to shove these in a drawer to collect dust. He wasn't in these items. He was in my heart, my memories. Even in death, he would live on through us.

I walked back to the bed, lighting the joint and offering it to Echo. They took a long drag, blowing the smoke out in rings before passing it to Octavia.

"Who will knit me a scarf now?" Echo stared at the tiny, half-knitted scarf.

"I will." Octavia reacted boldly to Echo's dismay and scooped up the knitting supplies. "I mean—" She clutched the items to her chest. "I don't know how to knit, but I'll learn. If-if that's ok with you both?"

Echo patted Octavia on the top of her head. "Thank you, Octavia."

I watched my sibling's strength falter, and they began to cry. It broke something in me, unleashing memories of their blades piercing through Kallan's heart. This was my brave sibling who rarely cried, and I could not imagine the pain they were in.

Echo and I stared blankly at the cards that poked out of the open metal case, hoping his hands would reach out and start shuffling, creating the soft swishing sound we all associated with his presence.

Echo broke the silence. "I think we should give these to Whynnie."

Octavia rested her hand on my knee, and I forced the sob back down.

"We can try." Echo clutched the blanket around them. "She's not herself right now. You should see the hovel, Throwen. Everything is already falling apart without him." Rocking back and forth, they chewed their fingernails.

This was unfamiliar territory and Echo was used to overcoming any problem quickly. Kallan's death could not be solved or fixed. It was something we had to endure but at least we could do it together.

I reached confidently for the cards, recalling the weeks it took Kallan to teach me to shuffle. "Do you remember when he got this deck?" I did the only thing I knew, soothe with stories.

Echo still fidgeted, but a small smile arched into their round cheeks. "Of course I do. He was so happy that he squealed."

Echo looked at Octavia, who laughed. They both looked at me expectantly, and I would do my part to walk them through their grief.

"It was his nineteenth Name Day, and he was pissed that we lured him into Whynnie's under false pretenses. But when Echo opened the door and we all yelled surprise, his anger morphed into the purest gratitude." I paused, taking a moment to picture that day. "He smelled like mint and pine needles. His hair was loose, and his beard was long. He had to put on a ridiculous red sweater that Whynnie got him."

Echo snorted. "He looked like a sack of potatoes packed way too tight. And the giant white heart in the middle. *Oh, my Goddess*, I laughed so hard that day that I'm pretty sure I pulled a muscle."

I gladly listened to my sibling's laugh and Octavia's joining in. My eyes filled with fresh tears. After Kallan's death, I wasn't sure I would ever hear their laughter again.

His screams and final moments replayed, forcing out the pleasant memory I was trying to grab onto.

"Throwen?" Octavia rubbed my thigh and Echo moved over to rub my back.

I let the tears fall and the sobs wrack my body. More than anything,

I wanted to be strong for them, but I couldn't. They cried with me, and I shuffled the cards with shaking hands, clinging to the sound, as if it would help me reach into the Abyss where he was.

When I prayed to the Goddess now, it always circled to the same plea, to rip the decay from my grieving soul, to somehow bring him back to us. "We can't let his death be this sinister ending. I can't live with the memory of his death."

"When we were in the library, he told me his favorite series was the Almondgrove Chronicles." Octavia retrieved the book she had been reading.

I laughed, knowing he had put it there. He always filled my empty shelves with his extra books, and as I scanned the colorful bindings around my room, I was glad.

"It's a book about found family." Octavia flipped through the pages.

Echo and I snorted. "A bit on the nose, don't you think?" I poked her nose, and she smiled.

"It's about Elaina Almondgrove, she is a fairy princess who fled her home after the shadow fairies decimated her family's castle leading to her parents' death. She finds a dwarf, shifter, and mermaid along the way." She summarized.

"You're sure he said this one was his favorite?" I rubbed my chest, an ache filling the cavity of my ribs. How could I not know his favorite book or what it was about? Within a short time, Octavia had dug her way into my brother's heart and mind in ways I had never thought to try.

"It's not about the fantasy. It's about the subtext. Can I read you this part? It's right after the shadow king captures her and promises he will kill her."

I shifted uncomfortably, unsure if I was ready to hear it.

"Does it spoil anything? Because I'm obviously going to read that book the first chance I get." Echo crossed their arms, unsuccessfully hiding the fact that they were hugging themself.

"No spoilers. We start with Elaina's inner thoughts." Sensing Echo and I weren't strong enough to decide for ourselves, Octavia cleared her throat before grabbing onto my hand and reading.

"What is family? Witches birthing children? Long lines of ancestors?" I gripped her hand tighter, reaching out for Echo's as well. "Is the blood coursing through my veins truly the strongest connection I was capable of and now that it's gone, will I ever know?" Octavia thrust her grief into her iterations.

We let our tears fall freely and the spirits wrapped around us.

"No." Octavia sniffed before continuing, "I found my family. The circumstances of us finding each other didn't matter, and neither did our blood. Our shared experiences helped us grow into what we were and who's to say that wasn't just as strong?"

A sob wracked through Octavia. "Then Elaina speaks to the shadow king."

She took in a few ragged breaths before sitting up as straight as she could manage.

"Cut my wrists, let it pour because they are the ones I would gladly spill it for."

Chapter 32

THROWEN

Morning light streamed in stunning streaks of gold as we hiked a winding path through the towering sequoia trees, a looming reminder of how small we were. Even as *special* as my powers were, I was just another speck, like every other witch within the expanse of Theldea.

The tops of the trees stretched their arms as high into the sky as possible. They seemed to be saying, 'pick me up.' *The Goddess's creations reaching for their mother.*

Octavia tripped over a root, but I swiftly caught her, hoisting her up by her armpits. She didn't appreciate my soft chuckle.

Echo twirled a teal strand around their finger, a nervous tic they weren't aware of, as we veered off the path up a steep hill. "Don't be embarrassed, visitors always trip. The trees call us to raise our eyes to soak in their majesty before putting us in our place, reminding us they aren't just above, but also below."

Echo winced, still healing from their injuries. I felt nauseous seeing them in such a state, knowing that they took the brunt of the burden. Our family's grief over the loss of Kallan was about to combine into a potent mourning.

Octavia assessed me, pausing at each of my injuries as if going through an inventory. Smiling softly, I hoped it would reassure her that I was fine. I'd shaved and trimmed my mustache, making my chin and jaw more pronounced. I imagined her licking along the smooth skin and briefly wished I had some time alone with her this morning. But I was happy to be there for Echo too.

"How are they so big?" Octavia asked.

Big was an understatement. The trees here were at least three hundred feet tall. I picked up one of the blue-green leaves that had fallen, tracing a finger along the slender veins.

"They protect themselves," Echo answered, then popped a chocolate-covered cherry into their mouth, trudging forward with determination.

The way Octavia was biting her lip suggested Echo's answer wasn't satisfactory, so I filled in the blanks. "What Echo means is that they survive thousands of years. They can't be blown over in the wind and their bark is dense and healthy."

I uttered a silent prayer to the Goddess. *Help me be as strong as these trees for my family.*

Octavia froze when we crested the top of the hill, then took a step back. I reached for her hand and squeezed, forever a watchman over her.

The large opening was full of gray saplings surrounded by one massive cinnamon-brown tree. Indigo fabric flowed in the breeze as wailing and crashing sounds leaked from the opening. *Our home.*

"Ahh!" Whynnie's scratchy scream and the sound of glass breaking pierced my ears as she continued to wail.

"Fuck." Echo and I spoke in unison and sprinted for the hovel.

"Wait!" Octavia sprinted behind us.

The spirits followed beside me, reaching out as we burst through the doorway. One tendril caught the teacup Whynnie was hurtling at the wall. The rest cocooned her, and I pulled out my lute, strumming her favorite lullaby.

Her screams shifted into soft whimpers, and the spirits placed her gently on the floor. Echo rushed over, falling to their knees and wrapping her in a tight embrace. My strength faltered at the sight of them, and I dropped my lute, unable to breathe, let alone strum.

The spirits flickered out, and I hurried to them, falling on my knees to join their embrace. We sat on the floor and held the shattered remains of our family together. After a few minutes, our sobs subsided, and a small cough from the door reminded me of my purpose.

I took Whynnie's hand in mine. "Are you okay?"

"No. But I can be for now. Thank you, Little Miracle."

Echo helped Whynnie stand, and I rose, striding over to Octavia. She looked like a child with the worst case of stage fright I'd ever seen.

"It's okay, darling. I'm here," I whispered before turning back to Whynnie. "Whynnie, this is Octavia. Octavia, this is Whynnie."

Octavia stepped forward and waved awkwardly. "Hello."

"It's so good to see you." Whynnie's lip quivered, and she fidgeted.

Silence lingered as Echo and I gaped between them like we were watching a play unfold.

Whynnie coughed, releasing herself from the ephemeral trance. "I hope Throwen wasn't too much trouble."

"I guess that depends on your definition of trouble," Octavia joked dryly, scratching at her neck.

Whynnie laughed, never taking her eyes off Octavia.

"Well, I know you all must have a lot of questions, especially you, Octavia." Whynnie's gaze lowered to the floor and Octavia took a shaky breath. Whynnie clasped her hands together. "It will be easiest to present everything down in the archives, I've got everything set up and ready to explain."

I looked at Echo who was already staring between me and Whynnie, eyes wide.

"*We* get to go to the archives?" Echo flung their arms in the air. "All these years you never let us in there. It was the *one* rule not to break."

I scoffed. "*Apparently*, all we needed was a Goddess-born for a key." Sarcasm laced my tone, but Whynnie leveled us with that motherly gaze and we shut up.

"Excuse my children." Whynnie led the way, and Echo and I grumbled.

We scrambled after her toward the stairs that spiraled into the ground beneath the tree. I'd fantasized about walking down these stairs for years.

Octavia followed behind me and I reached for her on the poorly lit staircase. She leaned forward, whispering in my ear, "I'm scared."

"If at any point you want to leave, I will take you back to my room." I gave her hand a squeeze.

We reached the bottom and Whynnie panted as she skillfully shot flames into some lanterns.

"*Sacred Ether*, Whynnie! This place is way bigger than I imagined," Echo exclaimed.

Books were piled high, some making pyramids to the ceiling, which consisted of twisting roots. As I moved swiftly to the center of a recessed oval surrounded by white workbenches, I glimpsed down the rows of shelves that branched out in spokes like sunbeams that seemed to go on forever.

Leather bindings of varying hues progressed in an enchanting, scattered rainbow. This entire archive was like a kaleidoscope of Goddess-born knowledge. The spirits tickled the back of my neck, living vicariously through my delight.

"Does it always look like this?" I gestured to a huge pyramid of books and turned to Whynnie, hoping to get some answers. Not only for me, but for Octavia.

"No!" Whynnie hustled forward, flicking her wrists as she carefully walked down the steps to me. "I usually organize by the author, but I um..."

She stared at the back of her hands, tracing the protruding veins, keeping her eyes locked on them. "Octavia, I've prepared for you. If you decide you want to learn, that is. I laid them out in chronological order of how I planned to mentor you, so there's a couple years' worth of studying."

She backed clumsily into a stack of books that had a cup of tea precariously placed upon it. I lurched forward, using air to cradle the cup before it could hit the tiled floor.

"I'd like to know what happened to me first." Octavia rubbed her mark.

I had never seen Whynnie quite this shaken before, and I couldn't imagine how she must be feeling. A son ripped away, and a daughter returned. How would one even reconcile with that?

She wrung her hands together, and I pulled up a chair for her to sit in. Then the three of us sat on the floor around her, eager and wary of what she had to say.

Whynnie coughed, reaching for a nearby cup of tea and reheating it. "The Goddess brought Octavia to me when I was thirty-seven years old."

Octavia tensed beside me. "She brought me? You've seen her?"

"No, it doesn't work like that. She leaves us somewhere our predecessor will find. My mentor, Lumin, found me near a waterfall on one of his trips to Ozuria." Whynnie's face softened as she looked at Octavia. "I found you in a big pile of dirt."

Scoffing, Octavia muttered, "Sounds about right."

"No! It was beautiful." Whynnie leaned forward, resting her arms on the chair. "Most Goddess-born find their mentees in their twenties. I was terrified the Goddess thought me unwise or unworthy to teach another of our magic. I had waited for you for *so long*."

Octavia squirmed uncomfortably and Whynnie handed Octavia an open grimoire from the table next to her, "I can remember it like it was yesterday."

Octavia ran her finger along the sketch of her as a baby, nestled in a pile of dirt.

"I was scavenging through the forest collecting herbs when I heard your cries." Whynnie's milky eyes met the ceiling as if reliving this memory for the first time in years. "It had just rained and petrichor rose from the soil and leaves. The moon was full that night and when I found you there, wrapped in a gold blanket. You shone brighter than any star I'd ever seen."

"Can we skip to the part with Malik?" Octavia's tone was matter of fact as she slammed the book shut and shifted into the woman I had found on that snowy mountain top. Hearing about her past was more painful than she let on.

Whynnie rubbed at her creaky knees. "I lost Lumin when I was only twenty-two. He was attacked on his way to Graygarde, shot through with arrows."

I glanced at Echo who shook their head, confirming that neither of us knew this part of the story.

"I brought his body home for a proper burial. Life after that was nearly impossible. Even with friends and allies in every coven I visited, it was a lonely existence, being the only Goddess-born in Theldea."

Octavia swallowed loudly. "I thought I was the only Goddess-born in Theldea until Throwen told me about you."

Whynnie's fingers curled tightly into the wood of the chair. "Malik was my closest friend."

"What?" Echo asked, clutching their head, and Whynnie's limbs went limp.

"Patience, Peacock, or I'm never going to get through this story." Whynnie dealt with them gently and Echo fidgeted with their pants, trying to contain their shock.

"Malik was much younger than me." Whynnie rocked as she spoke.

"He was charismatic and could always make me laugh. I needed his spontaneity, and he needed my practicality."

That fucker is dead. He had a pension for hurting the ones I held most dear, and I would destroy him if given the chance. My need for vengeance mixed with the feeling of betrayal Whynnie had just dealt us. *Why did she keep this from us?*

"So, what happened?" Echo's arms were crossed and their cheeks were red, perhaps feeling the same sting of duplicity as me.

Whynnie hunched further, crumpling under our scrutiny. "He was there for me through Lumin's loss. I know at the beginning he grieved for Lumin, too. He stayed with me and helped me make sense of Lumin's extensive plans on how to help Theldea grow and prosper. What we do has always been too much for even a Goddess-born to manage. Our purpose is meant to be supported by those around us. I thought I needed him."

The spirits returned, reaching out with sympathy as they wrapped around Whynnie. But my sympathy felt limited, like this omission of truth had the power to tear our trust apart if we let it.

She sat up straighter and the spirits worked to lower her pulse. "Lumin's passing only solidified my beliefs in our creator and the Ether. I was at peace with his death. Malik was not. As the years passed by, he started questioning the Goddess's power and sovereignty."

That's *exactly* what Malik did. Poison the lost with his lies.

Whynnie took a shaky sip of her tea before continuing, "Once Octavia joined us, he worked to twist my grief into hatred. He would casually bring up the Goddess's cruelty in making me wait so long for Octavia. Sometimes he would point out how unfortunate it was that Lumin would never meet her."

Tears rolled down her cheeks, and the spirits wiped them away, my intention now flowing through them.

Octavia sat just out of reach. I could feel the heat pouring off of her, and I fought to connect with her mind the way she had when she used my magic. Desperation to know her thoughts, to know how to comfort her in this moment, consumed me.

"Goddess! Hearing myself say it out loud now it seems so obvious. But he was my most trusted friend. I didn't think he would—" She sobbed.

I knew Whynnie's slump in posture well, Octavia had it too every time she unburdened herself of heavy secrets. Whynnie was like a flower that had laid dormant for years and Octavia was the light coaxing her to open.

Moving closer, Octavia's empathy pushed her into action, taking Whynnie's shriveling hand in her own. "It's okay. We are here to help you carry the weight."

My chest swelled with pride.

With Octavia's support, Whynnie continued, "Captain Sterling Fennix—"

"*Goddess's tits*! Of course, Julian's father made it into this." Echo flung themselves to the floor, staring at the ceiling like a starfish.

Whynnie pinched the bridge of her nose. "About a year before Malik took Octavia, Sterling found a book. The only worthwhile thing that man taught his son was finding treasure."

Echo grunted, and I was about to burst out of my skin. My fingers twitched but didn't reach out for Octavia's, especially with Whynnie's eyes on us. Her opinion of my love for Octavia held the most significance.

"It seemed like fiction. Something claimed to be written by a Goddess-born centuries ago, something predating all our written histories." Whynnie gestured to the tomes.

"How many of us were there?" Octavia asked as she settled back in beside me, crossing her legs.

"Nobody knows. But as far as we can tell, thousands. The Goddess created the witches to inhabit Theldea, and she created us to help them."

The answer seemed too simple, and I knew Octavia wasn't truly satisfied with it as she crossed her arms.

Whynnie pushed on, straining to relay the story. "The book speculated a direct connection to the Abyss somewhere in Ombra Lurra that should be avoided at all costs. I didn't think it was even possible, nor did I want to explore it. I thought Malik had dropped it after I told him that."

"But how didn't your sight see his betrayal coming?" I asked.

Whynnie focused on Octavia, switching her tone of voice to that of a teacher. "My gift from the Goddess is sight. I can sometimes see bits and pieces of future events. For instance, in the past, I've been able to prevent wildfires, rockslides, gang activity, and human trafficking. But the sight is subject to change, since witches still have free will and their decisions could alter things."

Octavia gave a slow nod. Whynnie's sight was fickle and there were times she sent us on missions we couldn't complete because the event never came to pass.

"I don't know why I couldn't see it coming. I've asked myself that question every day for years," Whynnie admitted with a deep frown.

"When did he take me from you?" Octavia asked in a monotone voice, but I saw her tiny fists, not wanting to hear the next part but needing to.

Whynnie's chin trembled, and she fought through tears. "Octavia and I were out in the woods. You practically lived outside and slept outside any chance you got. You said you liked to fall asleep talking with the moon."

Octavia stroked the phases on her neck.

Whynnie clung to the arms of the chair. "I stepped away to gather some mushrooms while you were spreading clover seeds. My basket was almost full when I heard the screams of our people."

My blood boiled, and I wasn't sure I could endure hearing this story.

"Goldhaven wasn't always our home. We once lived in Starpass."

Whynnie handed Octavia another grimoire with the words Starpass embossed in silver on the cover. Octavia opened the book, looking at the map with a frown.

An uncomfortable silence permeated the room. I blanched, realizing this was much bigger than the child abduction we thought it to be.

"Our maps weren't very accurate. Where is Starpass?" Octavia asked as the room seemed to grow hotter.

"It's gone." My voice held a sharp edge as my veins throbbed and my entire body tensed like a snake ready to lash out.

Echo began to clarify for Octavia who was struggling to grasp the significance of Starpass. "Scholars theorized it was a fatal disaster that killed everyone instantly and sank the coven as if the moon itself fell atop it. There was nothing left but a crater." Echo sat up, curling their arms around themselves in a hug.

Octavia shook her head, trying to sort through the maelstrom of information.

Whynnie massaged the back of her neck. "It was Malik and his followers who set off the initial explosions. I was shocked at how many of our people he had swayed. I was so busy looking for threats in the future that I was blind to the one sitting next to me every day."

"No." Octavia shot up, tossing the book to the floor, and shaking her hands at her sides. When her wrist popped, I could contain myself no more. I stood up and pulled her into a tight embrace as she lost herself in an effort to cope.

"*No. No. No.*" Shoving her face into my chest, she repeated the words like a mantra that would come true if she believed it hard enough.

Whynnie spoke just above a whisper, "I flew around the treetops on my broom searching for you and I found you near the Furothia border heading into Stranata. You were surrounded by the empty husks of our people. Trying to drown out the horrid sounds they made when Malik and his necromancers bound them was impossible. I had never seen such a thing. I remember the smell of sulfur was *so* strong."

Octavia was shaking and the spirits and I kept her wrapped tightly as I smoothed her hair. Malik hadn't simply abducted Octavia, but destroyed an entire coven while doing so. I threw up an air shield around us.

"Darling?" I grabbed her by her shoulders, trying to get her skittering eyes to find mine. I held her steady, but she just kept chanting denials.

"Octavia. Look at me, my muse." Tilting her chin revealed tear-stained cheeks and a face contorted in pain. The spirits pressed against her chest in circles.

"I-I thought he loved me. In his own way. But he was *always* a monster."

"You didn't know what love was. But you do now. Right?"

She blinked away fresh tears. Wrapping her arms around my shoulders, she embraced me as hard as she could. "Yes."

"You're the strongest witch I know, Octavia. Are you ready to hear the rest? I'm right here and if at any point you need a break, you just say the word and I'll take us back to Rosewood."

"No. I need to know."

"Okay." Pressing my forehead to hers, I let go of the shield. Apprehension made my fingers twitch, and it felt wrong without my picks to soothe me. Everything felt so fucked up.

Whynnie's breath hitched as we turned back to her, hand in hand. She squinted at Echo, who shrugged and pressed their lips together as if to say this wasn't their secret to tell. Whynnie breathed heavily in and out, her body fatigued from reliving so much trauma. Echo lurched forward, wrapping her in a hug.

She continued, "I flew down to face him, but when I tried to reason with him, he attacked me brutally. I think he left me alive on purpose, so I had to live with the loss and pain. By the time I awoke in Simului's hut, I couldn't sense Octavia anymore."

"But didn't anyone see them passing by on their way to Ombra Lurra?" Echo picked through the account, searching for any holes.

"They didn't follow any paths, but some witches did see a few undead pass by. Over the years, the narratives became exaggerated, witches assigning it whatever meanings suited them. It became a scary necromancer story parents told their children to keep them from straying too far from their covens."

"Why didn't you ask for help?" Disappointment laced my tone and Echo pulled away from Whynnie.

Whynnie's brow was damp with sweat. "I did at first. But most of the coven leaders at the time didn't respect me, especially when they found out about Malik's cult. They knew we were friends, but they didn't know the extent of my role in his choices. Some of the surrounding covens sent volunteers to help me rebuild, but I couldn't rebuild on the ashes of Starpass. Instead, we moved north and built Goldhaven."

"But Simulie had to know. She found you." Echo toyed mindlessly with their empty candy wrapper.

"Simulie knew, but she promised not to tell anyone, *especially* her mother. She never did tell my secret." Whynnie almost smiled at the notion of having a genuine friend, but her expression quickly turned sour. "Shortly after building our home, I locked up the archives. If Malik could steal a book that created such chaos, so could others."

When nobody spoke, Whynnie looked between Echo and me. We now stood a few feet back. Echo's arms were crossed, and their jaw ticked. I avoided making eye contact with anyone. Whynnie's secrets were potent, and I wasn't sure how to work past the concealed truths.

My heart sank at the worried expression on her face, as if wondering if we would give her our forgiveness. "I'd like some time alone with Octavia, please. If everyone is comfortable with that."

"Shouldn't we make a plan? Malik is coming." I looked around, but nobody seemed inclined to agree. *Fuck.* I wasn't trying to be insensitive. I was just terrified of losing Octavia.

Whynnie sat taller. "As soon as Echo arrived back, I notified every coven leader, detailing the story I just told you and the position we have found ourselves in."

Sacred Ether. She didn't just reveal her secrets to us, she told everyone. The strength and wisdom Whynnie possessed was surreal, and I stared at her with pride.

"I told them to share it freely with their people and let them choose for themselves what they wanted to do. I've received a handful of replies. Witches are on their way as we speak."

Witches who wanted to aid us in this fight. Whether they fought for justice, vengeance, or protection for their loved ones didn't matter. The entirety of Theldea wanted to see Malik's tyranny come to an end, and I hoped it would be enough.

"How many?" I hated that my instinct was to question Whynnie's answer, a part of me still hurt and was hesitant to trust.

She was stoic as she stared at me. "I don't know."

Spinning, I looked down at Octavia. "Your choice, darling."

"I think I would like some time with Whynnie. I have a few questions."

"A few?" My mustache tickled as it curled with my smile, and I pressed warmth into her hand.

She grinned back, and it was like a gift.

I turned to speak to Whynnie, "Good luck, once she asks one question, it doesn't stop."

I walked up to Whynnie, hugging her. Echo came in from the other side, squishing us together. There was a gaping hole where Kallan should have been.

"Thank you," Whynnie said with sincerity as she wiped her tears. "Echo, can you make us some food?"

"Of course I can, but we are going to need *a lot* of ale after that."

"I couldn't agree more," I said and gave Octavia a final embrace. "Octavia is also going to need about five pounds of chocolate." I laughed at her frown, happy it was one of annoyance instead of pain.

"Throwen can you clean?" Whynnie asked, but I didn't take my eyes off Octavia.

"Yes." I reluctantly released Octavia and linked arms with my sibling. We mumbled curses about being kicked out again and trudged toward the steps.

"Whynnie knows you're in *loooove*." Echo sang tauntingly up the stairs.

I enjoyed the taunt because it meant my sibling was still in there under all the horror and anguish. I laughed because love didn't even come close to describing how I felt about my sexy little muse. She was my fucking everything and *nobody* was going to take her away from me. I would hold onto her in this life and into the next.

Chapter 33

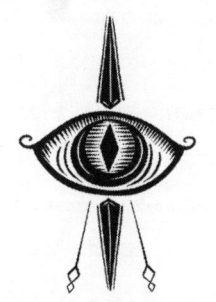

OCTAVIA

An unnerving energy worked its way between Whynnie and me once Throwen and Echo's voices faded. She was stooped and plump and her hair was made up of dark silver waves that spilled over her shoulders. Her skin was olive like mine but leaned warmer where I shifted cooler.

The humming of our marks was the only sound, and I fought a gasp as our unique connection refused to be ignored any longer. My flesh pebbled and I could practically see the invisible strand the Goddess had woven between us.

I didn't know if I could cope with the changes shuffling rapidly through my life like Kallan shuffling his cards. Because of me, Whynnie lost a son and she might think I seduced her other. The memories of Kallan's unnatural sounds after being bound rattled me but I kept my face neutral.

Whynnie seemed content to just keep staring at me like I was a fucking oil painting for who knows how long.

"So… Have you ever seen a book entitled 'The History of Broom Making?'" I asked. She started at her beginning and I supposed the book was mine, the catalyst that changed the course of my life.

She shook her head, as if broken from her trance. "Oh, yes, follow me."

Whynnie invoked a flame, her wrinkles deepening with the harsh shadows. The lines mocked me, representing the thousands of hours with her that were stolen. Whynnie was my rightful mentor, the witch the Goddess brought me to. *What the fuck am I even supposed to think or do?*

She shuffled up the steps and led us down a row of books. "I believe that one is in Graygarde currently. If a book is harmless, I allow it out in the world. Goddess-born are the only ones who can ride brooms."

"I think my friend Badru snuck that grimoire into my room with the help of a scout." I prayed to the Goddess that Badru was ok, that I could somehow still save him.

"They both deserve a special place in the Ether for their actions," Whynnie said, her voice raspy and I wondered if it was always that way or if it was intensified because of the screaming and crying.

The first shrieks from Whynnie had sent chills down my spine. My mark heated uncomfortably, and I could hear my own screams echoing in my mind. If nothing else, I discerned Whynnie was prone to outbursts like me, letting her unregulated emotions flow up her throat and out through her strained vocal cords.

"Sometimes I loan certain grimoires to trusted scholars and museums. It wouldn't surprise me if Mayson was too chicken shit to report that one was stolen."

I was starting to see what Throwen and Kallan had spoken of on our journey. This woman was very frank. Not someone I would quickly dismiss.

"I saw you riding your broom," she said.

An emptiness I thought I had forgotten about made itself known. My face heated, and I rubbed the back of my neck. "Oh. So, you saw me fall?"

She chuckled. "I did. But for not having a proper teacher, I'd say you did pretty damn good."

The praise passed through me like a phantom. I didn't know how to accept it.

"Tell me about your broom," she said.

I looked at my feet, shuffling them along the long orange rug that was fitting against the navy tile. "She was very precious to me. It's how I breached our barrier."

"Barrier? Is that why I couldn't see you?" Whynnie paused and turned to look at me, as if hoping this was the answer to a question she had asked all of her life.

I swallowed hard. "It was a kind of concealment spell. Malik used my blood and his connection to his Eth—" I stuttered, realizing just how deep his brainwashing went. "To the Abyss."

"*Fucker*," Whynnie spat as she continued in more of a stomp than a shuffle.

"He told us it protected us from the horrors of Theldea. I grew up thinking I was safe when in reality I was nothing more than an oblivious, chained mut."

Glass shattered. I felt something wet and hot across my knuckles. When I looked down, I was back in my room at the coven, my knuckles torn apart from punching my mirror because I coveted physical pain over emotional pain.

It's not real. It's not real.

I blinked rapidly and the smell of black tea acted like oil in water, pushing out the hallucination to dig through the ashes of my memories of this woman. It seemed familiar, but not.

Concentrating on the glowing and humming of Whynnie's mark, I asked, "Can you tell me about the marks?"

Well, cutting it off didn't work. Let's try burning next.

I grit my teeth against Malik's unwelcome voice in my mind. How could I let him hold such power over me? I wanted to obliterate that cruel part of him, just like he tried to erase the parts of me that were from the Goddess. He detested her, and he would always despise that part of me, too. Malik could never truly love me.

Whynnie reached back, pulling her hair aside so that I could see her mark fully. "Echo used to say I had eyes on the back of my head." She chuckled.

A gold glowing eye stared at me. It was elegant and had two spokes shooting out from the top and bottom like a compass. There were two lines beside the bottom spoke that crossed into diamonds.

"What do they mean?" I had lost count years ago of the many nights I would stare at a reflection of my moons and spiral.

"Each Goddess-born has their own mark. It usually connects to our unique powers and who we are at our core. Mine is pretty obvious with the eye and my power of sight, but there's much more to it than that." She turned and winked.

"So your eyes were always…"

"White?" She smirked. "Born this way. I can see fine, though. Well, as well as any old woman sees." She snorted. "The Goddess has a very *interesting* sense of humor."

I liked the idea that I got my dark sense of humor from my creator. I didn't want to live in ignorance and fear anymore. "Any idea what mine might mean?"

It was imperative that I learned how to use my abilities, whatever they were. I had a short time to wrap my head around Goddess-born magic. Malik was coming and as it stood, I was more of a liability than an asset.

"I wish I could tell you, but that's something extremely personal. That's between you and the Goddess. We don't write down what we think the meanings of our marks are. It's meant to be something no witch can ever take from you."

The sentiment was lovely. The moon had always comforted me, letting me know I wasn't the only one stuck repeating my many phases over and over.

My thoughts were interrupted as we entered an open area. Grimoires were spread across three workbenches and bright green moss grew up the sides of the walls. I walked over and ran my finger along its spongy texture. I moved to examine the tomes, caressing their soft pages. "This place is like a dream."

Whynnie shuffled to where two tangerine chairs sat. She flicked a spark to light the candle that was melted right onto the tiny wooden table that sat between the chairs.

I focused back on the book, skimming some of the pages. They reminded me of the book I used to create my broom, filled with detailed accounts and beautiful illustrations. That book gave me the tools to obtain my freedom.

The pages were too overwhelming, and I turned to take the seat beside Whynnie. A deep purple book rested on the table between us that both called to me and sent chills down my spine.

I fidgeted in the chair, pulling the pillow tightly against my chest and squeezing. Stroking the silky fabric, I attempted to calm my nerves. There were too many questions buzzing around my skull, and I wasn't sure which were the most pertinent. "How does it usually work? If I wasn't taken from you, what would life have been like?"

"I would have been your mentor. So would Lumin if he would have still been with us. It's like parenthood."

My ribs felt too tight, and I could feel my Name Day corset pressing into them. A phantom of discomfort. But I'd always dreamed of having a mother. "But it's not parenthood? The Goddess brings us to Theldea herself?"

Whynnie tapped her chin. "Yes, she brings us. The babies are always wrapped in a golden blanket and their marks glow so brightly you'd think it was a star. When I found you, it was like there was a wick inside me all along and you sparked it to life. Family is too weak a word, there is no word to describe it. The bond is on a spiritual level and while Lumin was like a father to me, we were also always equals."

I pressed my finger to the tip of my nose, digesting the information as best I could. The sorrow over years lost was evident in her hushed tone. She lost years with Lumin and me, forced to be the only known Goddess-born in Theldea. These bonds sounded vital, and she had gone most of her life with those ties severed.

"Malik spoke often of a mentor who never understood him. He also claimed the Goddess was deceitful and selfish. It's what he based his entire belief system on."

Whynnie rubbed a hand over her face. "I suppose that could be Lumin. They did butt heads occasionally when Lumin caught him in falsehoods. Lumin struggled to reign in his overzealous tendencies to run into things headfirst. But... maybe he meant me..." Whynnie placed a hand against her heart, trying to keep the regret from bleeding out.

"What was he like? Before the cult?"

"He was a good friend. At least I thought that at the time. Thinking back now, I can see the warning signs. They were small, things a normal witch wouldn't think twice about."

I knew exactly what she meant, but I needed to hear her say it. I needed to confirm that underneath it all, his heart and mind were always stained. "Like what?"

Whynnie wrapped her arms around her torso. "He would minimize my feelings."

Stop overreacting, Lady. We are the faces of this coven.

"He would try to use the Goddess's love against me, claiming she loved the Goddess-born more than the rest of Theldea."

Do you think you're special because of the blood that runs through your veins?

"He would constantly ask me if I was confused, and I started doubting myself and my abilities. If he would have stayed with us, I think over time, he would have warped me into an entirely different witch."

Do you need rest, Lady? I think the sun is making you hysterical.

Are you sure you want to wear that? It doesn't exactly look flattering, does it?

You want to be a scout? Are you confused about how things work in this coven?

I blinked, letting a tear splash against the pillow I clung to. The memories of Malik's words and my coven's responding laughter played through my mind like a nightmare.

Whynnie sniffed as tears streamed down her face. "You shouldn't have had to endure him, Octavia. I wish I could have mentored you. You have to be witty if you can put Throwen in his place."

She attempted to lighten the mood, but another witch in my life who could hold such sway over me was not what I sought.

"I don't want another mentor," I said dryly as I found her gaze, my mask begging to settle into place. Defeat hunched Whynnie's shoulders as I winced against the bitter memories of Malik's words I would rather forget. I could see from the hundreds of grimoires laid out that Whynnie valued me, and I would give her something better than what she thought she had missed out on. "But I could use another friend."

Whynnie laughed and beamed, shaking her head and wiping her tears. "Well then, how can I ease your mind, friend?"

"I remember that first night." I closed my eyes, trying to tap into my senses. "I was being led through an underground tunnel, and the gurgling sounds scared me, so I covered my ears."

Don't worry, those are the sounds of victory.

Malik had forced me to listen. I recalled the smell of sulfur and burning wood, and I clung to the pinky finger of someone I trusted as we fled. The memory was always my most precious because it proved that, despite his cruelty, Malik cared enough to save me.

Whynnie ran her fingers through her hair. "That night I was forced to watch witches I loved die, cursed to never see them again. And now Kallan is amongst them because of my mistake."

"That was my fault. I—"

Whynnie firmly raised her hand. I pressed my lips together.

"When I landed," Whynnie continued, "I made a mistake. I sought to reason with Malik. In the process of trying to save him, I lost you." Her haunted expression sought me out. "He flung me against a tree with a laugh when I asked him to come back and assured him that we could still fix this."

Unsure how to respond, my leg bounced.

Whynnie took a shaky breath. "You were unreachable, and it was agony."

Guilt etched itself into my skin like a tattoo.

"But then, I sensed you and saw you in that mirror and it was like my entire world exploded again. Then I found out about Kallan and..." Her stare grew distant, as if she was realizing just how much she had been through.

How had I forgotten about Whynnie? I was too young... too impressionable. Years of being told I was the only Goddess-born had washed her away. *Sacred Ether,* I wished I could remember that little girl who lived in Starpass.

A sob broke free from Whynnie, and I rushed to her. Taking her palms, I pressed warmth into them.

So many witches in Theldea grieved the same way, even if it looked different. Togetherness. Support. Community. All things I thought I knew the meaning of, but was just starting to truly comprehend.

"No matter what happens, or how much time we have together, Octavia, I want you to know how precious you are to me. I missed you."

As I gazed up at her, a piece of silver hair falling over her aged cheek, I knew I was loved. The way she looked at me was better than I imagined. I always dreamed of Malik looking at me like she was. "And thanks for bringing Throwen home." She patted my head. Her gaze shifted to the purple book between us and back to me. Grimacing, she released my hands. "I have one final thing to tell you."

My stomach dropped, and I moved back into my seat. With trembling hands, she offered me the book. Reading the title made me dizzy, hairs rising on the back of my neck and arms. I spoke over the massive lump forming in my throat. "The history of Death Witches."

My nails dug into the firm binding and my body tensed. I opened the book slowly, wary of what I might find on its pages. Inside was an illustration of a woman with death-touched arms and hands, just like Throwen's. She stood next to a cheerful witch with a thick beard.

I slapped a hand over my mouth. She had that same look as Throwen, one of joy and purpose, with her arm wrapped around his shoulders.

I flipped to the front of the book and read the first sentence: *The purpose of the death witch is to protect their Goddess-born with their life.*

"Throwen said he didn't know why the Goddess brought him back." I snapped my head up, and Whynnie averted her gaze. "You've shown him this book, right? Why would he say he didn't know?"

Today was supposed to be one of horrible truths for myself, not Throwen. My mouth went dry, and the room started to spin.

"I chose not to tell him about the others. But I did tell him the truth. The Goddess did send him back for a purpose."

I shot up and started pacing. "And you *knew* that purpose! Why would you keep this from him?" I was shouting and my knuckles were growing white as I contemplated chucking the book at her.

"Death witches are extremely rare. The histories we do have all fit inside that book." It wasn't thick, maybe five to six hundred pages. "The accounts all claim that the Goddess creates a death witch in times of great need to protect the Goddess-born currently living. It has been *decades* since one has been recorded."

"I don't care about the histories right now. Why didn't you tell Throwen the truth? That there were others like him? Do you comprehend how alone he must have felt?"

"*Do I comprehend it?*" Whynnie's face turned red. "Who do you think held him as he cried when the other kids made fun of how he looked? Who do you think took care of his wounds when he came back from training with Kallan month after month until he could hold his own? I watched Throwen evade personal relationships for years because they meant nothing to him compared to the bond his soul was yearning for. I am his *mother*. I more than comprehended it. I fucking lived it."

"Then why?" Resentment threatened to take hold as I glared. Whynnie could easily become another Malik, and lies through omission were still lies. I plopped back into the comfort of the chair, exhausted, defeated, and confused.

Whynnie let out a long sigh. "I was scared. At first, I thought the Goddess sent him for me. I was in a very dark place after you were taken, and I thought he was sent to pull me out of it. But it became increasingly apparent he wasn't sent for me. I could see with my sight as he grew that he wasn't made to protect me."

"You saw him protecting me?"

"Only very brief glimpses and I was never sure it was you, the image was always blurry. For a long time, I thought the Goddess would deliver another Goddess-born to protect, but as the years went by, I lost hope. I thought it was another one of her cruelties. Octavia, I never even got close to finding you. But Throwen never faltered in his belief that the Goddess would show him his purpose. I kept it from him because I was certain it would never be fulfilled."

"*And* you would've had to tell him the truth about me. About Malik and Starpass." I tapped my foot.

"Yes. And if there was even a chance that you were still out there where he couldn't reach you... It would have killed him. It would have driven him mad."

I opened my mouth to retaliate, but we both knew Throwen at his core. Her assessment was accurate. He would have killed himself trying to get to me. I understood the loss of hope and being driven to madness, and I wouldn't wish that on anyone, especially Throwen.

Laughing, I threw the grimoire onto the floor, clutching my chest and trying not to vomit. "I knew it was too fucking good to be true."

I dug the palm of my good hand into an eye socket to alleviate the building pressure. Curling my knees up to my chest, I rocked back and forth. I threw my thoughts out into the air because there was no fucking way they were staying inside.

"So, this whole time our feelings for each other were bullshit? He was forced to leave the Ether to be chained to me?" I believed in soul mates the way one believes in mermaids. It was just fantasy. I might have been naïve to true love, but I knew it couldn't be real if it was forced.

Whynnie rushed over, pulling me into a tight embrace. "Hush, little Sprout."

The use of the nickname was jarring at first, but quickly changed into a different sense of comfort that I wasn't prepared for. I wept into her shawl, gasping for breath.

Our love existing as something other than what I thought it was felt like a fate worse than death.

Whynnie spoke softly, "He is fated to protect. Not to love. There were other pairings before you that were platonic."

I pulled away from her and grabbed the pillow sitting on the chair, screaming into it.

"There you go. Scream as much as you want, that's what I do." She patted my head until I crumpled further into the chair, letting my legs and head sag over the arms.

"I didn't expect him to fall in love with you, Octavia. I was going to tell him if we ever got you back, but I no longer feel like it's my place."

I snapped my head to where she was retreating to her chair. "Excuse me? You want *me* to tell him?"

She retrieved the book from the floor, giving it back to me. I cradled it against my chest, letting its weight soothe me.

"I wasn't even supposed to read it. There's a clear note at the beginning that says it is for the death witch and paired Goddess-born's eyes only. The bond you have is sacred." *The bond we have wasn't Throwen's choice.*

Echo's voice called loudly from the end of the row, "I hate to interrupt, but Throwen is going fucking insane about what you two might be talking about down here. *Please* don't leave me alone with him anymore. I can't cater to him and cook at the same time!"

Whynnie snorted. "We're coming, Peacock!"

"*Praise the Goddess!*" they shouted and stomped back up the stairs.

Whynnie pulled out a satchel and handed it to me. I slipped the death witch grimoire in. She added a few others for me to start with, including a more detailed broom guide.

I pulled the bag over my shoulder and recalled watching Throwen's reaction to the archives. His smile had been wide as he crossed his arms, spinning slowly in a circle, his senses devouring this newly uncovered secret.

Seeing his pure excitement had me curling my toes. He craved life the way I craved death and it fascinated me.

Whynnie looked at me apologetically as we reached the steps. I understood why I had to be the one to tell him. It was my fault he wasn't in paradise with the Goddess and instead was now stuck with me. Our time left with each other had a deadline and I would spend every spare moment drowning myself in his praise until I found the courage to tell him the truth.

Chapter 34

OCTAVIA

Wiping the sweat from my brow, I welcomed the cool breeze as I dropped my hands to my knees. I was trying to determine my magic, something Goddess-born spent years practicing but I had mere days to learn.

"You can do this, Octavia," Whynnie said, offering useless encouragement. "You have to locate that connection. For me, it's like a bright thread that I have to reach out and unravel. You aren't focusing."

All my life, I'd learned through observation and I wasn't used to having a teacher. Exhaustion forced out my next unkind words. "I am fucking focusing! You dragged me into the middle of nowhere." Spinning in a circle, I gestured to the trees surrounding us. "The only other thing I could focus on is you, and I'm starting to tune you out, honestly. You say the *same* thing every time. I can't find the fucking thread! There is no thread!"

Huffing, I gathered my disheveled hair into a ponytail, sweat holding back any flyaways.

Whynnie paced, as if unable to stay still. "I'm sorry, I'm not used to instructing someone remarkable like you. My only intention is to guide you to what the Goddess endowed you. It takes time."

"We don't have time. I have to get this now if I'm to be of any help. I've been making progress with Throwen and the bow, but without the help of the spirits, my aim is shit." I hadn't been able to tap into Throwen's magic since Calliope. "Echo says I'm getting better with my daggers, but I know they're sugarcoating it. I won't be able to rely on anyone else when Malik attacks."

Unlike Whynnie, my brain could only conjure fucked up fantasies instead of helpful realities.

"Once you work through some of the grimoires I gave you, you can find other examples of how our ancestors made their connections. But I doubt you're doing much *studying* in your free time." She smirked.

I coughed. "I've worked my way through some of Lumin's records. His abilities were especially interesting. Could he really tell when someone was lying?"

"Not all the time, but enough that I had to work hard to sneak out at night."

Chuckling, I pictured a youthful Whynnie trying to evade her mentor. According to the stories so far, she was pretty wild before her isolation.

I started pacing. "I don't know what I'm doing wrong."

"You need to connect with something other than..." she shouted, "the *assassin* hiding in the treetops!"

There was a rustling of leaves and a loud thump somewhere nearby.

Whynnie shook her head. "Throwen, if you don't go home and help Echo you aren't getting any of the chocolate cake I'm making for Octavia tonight!"

The thought of celebrating with them in honor of all the Name Days we missed warmed my chest, stretching out to my limbs, making me feel almost weightless. I was hesitant at first, but it was Echo's idea, and I couldn't say no to them.

A thrilling electricity shot up my spine, leaving heat across my cheeks.

We heard no sound of Throwen leaving and the thought of him watching me without my knowledge was like an aphrodisiac. The past two days we had fucked any chance we got. Fear that each time might be our last compelled us to devour each other. It was a dizzying euphoria of pleasure that I never wanted to end.

"*Good Goddess*, girl, it can't be *that* good." Whynnie rolled her eyes.

I was at a loss for words as she handed me my broom and I gaped at her bluntness.

We had spent the entire night in the archives as she guided me through constructing my broom with the proper intent. The next morning, we had wandered back toward Fearmore through the forest until I found the wood that called to me.

Whynnie had helped me treat the peeling papery wood, so it was now a smooth solid thing. Bright orange leaves hung around her twigs that made up the bristles. Whynnie had given me instructions on how to preserve the leaves and make them strong so they wouldn't fall off.

I ran my thumb over the soft grip of my broom composed of strands of variegated purple leather that reminded me of Throwen and the spirits.

"*Goddess's tits*, I haven't done this in ages." Whynnie tapped the short branches that created a sphere on top of her broom where the bristles would usually be.

It was ingenious, the way she created it to double as a walking stick. She wrapped her aged hands around the thick sycamore bark. A grip wrapped in deep purple, teal, and white fabric was at the front; at the tip, a carving of a tiny sprout.

I looked back one more time to see if I could spot him.

"You complement Throwen well. It's as if he was *made* for you or something."

I snorted at her joke, realizing the ridiculousness of the situation.

He was made for me. I couldn't determine if that was a good thing. Part of me wanted to take the knowledge and let it flourish within me like this great forest. But my demon purred against my conscience. *If you tell him, he will resent you in the end.*

I pulled the fabric of my shirt collar up over my face and Whynnie did the same. A face covering was considered a flying necessity because, as Lumin's grimoire so eloquently put it, 'windburn was a bitch.'

As I learned more about Lumin, I saw the sass and stubbornness that was passed onto Whynnie, and I allowed myself a hidden smile. She sat sidesaddle on her broom, motioning for me to do the same. "Remember, let your broom know where you want to go. Intent. Then allow her to guide you. Let go of controlling her. Trust her."

Octavia. Intent.

"My favorite words," I mumbled and wrapped my fingers around the silvery bark of my new broom, swatting Malik's voice to the back of my mind, where it belonged. "Where are we going?"

She sat taller. "Starpass."

I tilted my head, trying to work out her reasoning, but she shot me a look that said 'don't even try'.

The dark gray knots in the wood reminded me of my mark. I sent my intent through the swirls. *To Starpass.* A faint golden glow pulsed once, and we lifted off the ground.

Looking once more to the woods behind us, I searched for my bard, but he was nowhere to be seen.

Flying had this way of ripping time away. Up here above it all, I could just be. The chill was stronger the closer we got to the sea and Whynnie pulled a knitted cap over her ears, wiping a tear away from her eye. Kallan must have made it for her.

Closing my eyes, I let the weightlessness soothe the grief as I arched my back, and the air whipped my ponytail around as it pleased. The sun warmed my face, and I felt that same strong connection I experienced in Drybourne. As if I could feel the Goddess blowing the clouds as they floated by. Flying was thoughtless when I wasn't fighting the Goddess, as easy as walking and as natural as curling up with my favorite book.

I laughed to myself, remembering my first broom and how much of my shit she had to put up with. Lumin's grimoire detailed that brooms were exactly like pets. I missed her iridescent paint and her sturdy black twine.

Opening my eyes, I stroked my new broom that had started humming beneath me. "Oh, hush. I don't pick favorites."

The humming lulled, and as I registered what loomed in the distance, my gut clenched. The yellow leaves were behind us now, fading into orange. And further ahead, I could see the start of a deep red that prompted flashes of Kallan's blood pouring from his neck.

My jaw ticked, and I thought about the chaos and harm I had caused.

How far had I truly come since leaving my coven? I left bloodshed, hoping that spilling my own would be the answer. Then Throwen happened. All the witches I met along the way, good and bad, happened. But here I was, hurtling right back into more bloodshed.

Malik was a viper, eating his own tail, forcing us all into his unending delusion.

"We are going to land just over that ridge." Whynnie's finger was pressed to her throat, amplifying her voice over the wind. I gave her a thumbs up and moved from a sidesaddle position into a straddle, keeping my chin tucked as we barreled toward the large crater where all life seemed to stop.

"First one to land gets to lick the batter!" Whynnie hooted and picked up speed.

Reveling in a challenge that wasn't meant to stretch my magic abilities was exactly what I needed. I cackled, lifting my ass in the air as I sped past her.

No funny business. My broom pulsed in response, and I knew her ambition to win was as strong as mine. I had built my natural competitiveness into her.

We hurtled toward the dirt and my breath was taken away as we nearly crashed before she pulled up and leveled out. I hopped off just as Whynnie landed.

I licked my lips. "I fucking *love* batter."

"Hah! I know. You used to eat more batter than cake, no matter how badly your stomach hurt the next day. Malik might have stolen you away, but he didn't destroy who you are at your core."

I sat beside her on the ground, stretching my legs out and crossing my ankles. The emptiness of this place was overwhelming. No flora of any kind. Only dirt, miles of dirt. *This would have been my home.*

"What was Starpass like?" I squinted at the hollowness of it. "How did it get like this?"

"After setting off the explosions, the necromancers burned everything."

I scanned the entirety of the crater's rim and my mind played its tricks as I saw necromancers lining it, surrounding us.

"Honestly, it was a lot like Goldhaven." Whynnie interrupted the hallucination, but I kept my eyes fixed on the necromancers my mind conjured, just in case.

"You've been to Goldhaven? Throwen said you never leave your hovel." I pressed my lips together, realizing my slip-up. But Whynnie looked equally caught.

"Don't tell him, but when he first moved out, I *might* have taken a few nighttime flights to make sure he was settling in okay."

"That's very sweet," I said, and she scoffed in response.

"He wouldn't think so. He would say I'm *creepy.*"

As we laughed, I looked over the dead expanse where Whynnie's other loved ones used to dwell alongside her. Something in the air shifted as the energy around us changed. "It must have been hard to retell that story to all of Theldea. But your transparency will bring us the help we need. I'm sure of it."

She brushed off the compliment. "This is where he will come once they dock. Pull out your grimoire. I want you to draw as accurate a map as you can for the others."

Happily unbuckling the deep teal grimoire from my strap, I started drawing with a piece of charcoal. I hadn't drawn for years because Malik had taken my art supplies. I'd forgotten how restorative it was.

Art is for the idle.

I hummed, getting used to letting Malik's voice come and go. Whynnie sat on the ground, pulling soil into her fist and watching it fall like ash.

"How do you know that this is where he will come? Why not Goldhaven?" As I swept the charcoal across the page in long strokes, I pictured the homes, people, and businesses that used to be here. What they must have looked like before they were obliterated.

"Because I've seen it."

"Have you seen anything else? Anything to give us an advantage?"

She sighed heavily. "I've seen many outcomes, but it changes like the winds. There are just too many moving components."

I looked to the skies, hoping for an answer.

"I do know that you and Throwen are both integral if we are to succeed. That is the one common component in all of this." She pressed her hand flat against the ground.

A flash of Malik's whip around Throwen's neck assaulted me as I unsuccessfully attempted to focus.

"Malik makes power moves," she continued. "He will think that by making me face him here, it will dig up memories that will make me prone to mistakes. He was always very intelligent. It's a shame it poisoned his soul."

"Will it make you prone to mistakes? Being here with him?" Putting the final touches on the sketch, I started adding notes at the bottom. I marked the side facing the sea where Malik would emerge and the quickest paths to get the injured out and back to Goldhaven for treatment.

"No. Maybe a few years ago, but when I come here now, I think of all the good times we had in Starpass. He bound those who weren't already dead, but I know I'll see at least a few of them again. It's morbid, I know, but it's how I get through it."

After returning my grimoire to its straps, I pulled some soil into my hand, breathing in its earthy scent. It was cool from the chill in the air as the sun fell below the high crater wall. I could tell there was light just out of sight, a deep orange glow lining the top of the wall like salt on the rim of a glass.

We were trapped in a pocket of darkness but as I pinched the soil between my fingers, slowly letting it fall, I thought for a moment that I felt a connection of some kind, but it quickly faded.

Seeing the state of Starpass made me want to wrap my arms around it and pull it up from where it had fallen. "I like morbid."

Whynnie barked out an unexpected laugh. "You don't have to tell me, I remember. You used to make little graves out of twigs for the worms because you thought when they went underground, they died. You would say 'bye bye, wormies.'"

I was exhausted and shifted onto my back to stare into the cloudy gray sky. After spending an entire lifetime trying to make deep connections that were impossible, it made the task of using any Goddess-born skills challenging.

We lay there in a meditative silence until the waning crescent made her debut. "Let's go home, Sprout. I need to make you that cake."

I stood first, helping her up. The way she called me Sprout was like those years between us changed everything and nothing at all. I was still that little girl, enjoying helping worms pass on to what I thought was next.

"Thank you, Whynnie. For everything. I want you to know without a doubt that I'm on your side in this."

She smiled warmly before wrapping me in a tight hug. It was a hug that lasted, and for the first time in my life, it was as if I had a mother. When I was with Whynnie, she gave me the freedom to be the child I never got to be.

Kallan, Echo, Whynnie, and Throwen had this uncanny ability to pull me into a present where I wanted to be. Maybe that's what love did, helped witches endure the ups and downs of life.

My concept of love was just as confined as I had been in Ombra Lurra and I knew setting it free was our only hope. My intent when I made my first broom was still the same.

I lowered to my knees, focused on the massacre that had happened here. The catalyst that started it all. I looked to the moon. She passed through her phases effortlessly, with dignity and grace. I admired her. I wanted to *be* her.

Something powerful tingled and pulsed through my body with my mark as the epicenter. My decision was resolute. Malik was a scourge to this world, and I wouldn't let him feed on it anymore.

With faith I didn't know I possessed, I dropped my palm to the hard soil, speaking freely to my creator the way I would have as a child, without fear. "I, Octavia, blessed Goddess-born, intend to help witches throughout the entirety of Theldea." But there was more at stake now, so I ripped the final stones from the wall I had built up around the Goddess, asking freely. "Please help us."

A gold strand left my palm. It looked like a worm burrowing into the ground, and Whynnie hummed in approval.

"What the fuck was that?" I whirled on her, worried I had some sort of Goddess-born parasite.

"Every Goddess-born has their own unique magic. We are not the Goddess, but there is a remnant of her power in each of us." She cupped my face. "Sometimes we have to wait for the answers to our biggest questions."

WHYNNIE'S HOVEL WAS painted in a kaleidoscope of deep purples and teals, due to the oddly shaped windows carved into the tree filled with beautiful stained glass.

The floor creaked as I perused Whynnie's fiction shelves. Echo poured us some cider while Throwen and Whynnie discussed the terms of the game they were playing.

I pulled a book from the row and started to read somewhere around the middle. I pressed my lips together as I read about a monster with a tail that presumably served multiple purposes. Fighting a blush, I slipped the book back, making a note of the title for later.

I slid onto the sofa beside Echo, holding a cracked but repaired mug, heating the cider in my palms. Whynnie and Throwen started laying cards down at a fast pace and hurled playful taunts at one another.

"I had no idea life could be like this." I rested my head on the fox inked across Echo's bicep. They wore a sleeveless black top and a fitted pair of black pants, showing off their generous curves that I always admired, as if they were carved skillfully from marble.

"What does the fox mean?"

"Oh, *that one*." Echo hummed, resting their head on top of mine. "Foxes are clever and quick-thinking. Just like me."

"It's beautiful."

Snorting, Echo nudged me upright. "I'm fucking with you. I got it because it looked cool. Art doesn't always have to mean something."

I supposed they were right, but I preferred for things to have meaning.

Throwen yelped as Whynnie slapped his hand hard and laughter had them both holding their stomachs.

"What are they playing?"

Echo snickered. "It's called slaps. It's how you introduce children to card games. You slap when you both lay the same card and whoever hits first keeps the stack. Whoever has all the cards at the end wins."

It was one of the things I loved about Throwen. He was just a grown child himself, easily connecting with their unique type of joy.

Gasping, I fought the urge to clutch my head, and I froze. The thought of all those children in the library and all the children in Oxvein flashed through my mind.

Echo recognized the shift and pulled me up. I had told them about the hallucinations yesterday at training when I had started swinging at a scout who wasn't actually there.

"We are going to get some air." Two messy teal buns popped out of the head hole in their sweater as they pulled it swiftly over their head.

"What's wrong?" Throwen moved to come help, but Whynnie grabbed his arm.

"If you leave the table you lose."

Before he could make a choice, Echo made it for him, pulling me out the door and down the path toward Goldhaven.

My knees buckled and my mind conjured images of the Rosewood's foster children loaded up in the caravans being killed and bound to their tiny bodies. Their red eyes were erratic, staring at me as if I had bound them myself.

"They're getting more frequent." Echo rubbed my back until the hallucination subsided.

"I know." I rubbed my temples and panted. "It's because of *him*. The closer Malik gets, the less control I have over them. Stress has always made them more vivid." More vivid was an understatement. Sometimes I couldn't even tell if they were real.

"He triggers you." Echo locked elbows with me and kept walking as if this was normal and my mind didn't just create an entire gruesome scene out of thin air.

"Triggers me?" Catching my breath, I focused on the towering trees lining the path like columns holding up the inky black sky.

"It's like when something that would ordinarily elicit no response instead induces an unexpected reaction. For example, when you think of Malik, you immediately feel uncomfortable," they said. "Your mind just takes it further. Conjures images. When I'm triggered, I lash out defensively. For you, it's a state of panic."

"It makes me feel like I'm broken. Like somehow, the Goddess made a mistake when creating me because I can't fucking regulate my emotions like a normal witch."

I could hear the sounds of Goldhaven in the distance. Most of the witches who weren't fighting had evacuated. But more witches arrived every hour to fight or volunteer, but instead of hope, it filled me with guilt. The coven would soon be full of victims of this war as volunteers clamored to keep up with the injuries.

"I hate to break it to you, but you aren't a normal witch, Octavia. Your environment growing up was bad. Plus, you're Goddess-born."

"Yeah, a lot of good that's doing me. All I can do is make creepy gold worms."

They gagged and grabbed me gently by the shoulders. "I'm going to pretend I didn't hear that because that's fucking *gross*."

I snorted, and my eyes burned with unshed tears. "I'm not special

Echo. I'm fractured beyond repair. Malik tore out so much of who I was, and my beliefs keep changing. How am I supposed to fix this? To heal everyone *and* myself?"

Echo rested their hand atop my head, pressing a comforting warmth into my scalp. "Have you seen how many teacups Whynnie has glued back together? They're still fractured, but they're so special she takes the time to fix them and put them back on the shelf."

"I don't *want* to be a broken teacup. I want to be a sexy, mentally stable one." I laughed through a sob as Echo pulled me into a tight embrace. The pressure of their embrace helped relieve my overtaxed mind.

"None of us want to be broken." Echo looped us back around towards Whynnie's. "Now, tell me what you believe."

I stopped walking, the question taking me by surprise. "I don't know."

They lifted a painted eyebrow. "Maybe take a second to think about it."

I didn't want to think about it. But maybe that was the problem. If you don't look at the broken teacup, you can't fix it.

"I believe every witch deserves to be loved. I believe the Goddess made me..." I tried to sort through what I had been taught and what I knew now, but the two refused to untangle.

"Great start. Let's do one more," Echo encouraged.

"Oh! I believe that chocolate is the most precious gift the Goddess has given Theldea."

"Wow, our beliefs align so well, should we be friends?" Echo grabbed my hand, and we laughed.

I could see the glow of stained glass as Throwen's music leaked through the open windows. I looked at the night sky, unsure how to do what I had to. He deserved the truth, no matter what that meant for us.

"The first time I met you, I knew you were special." Echo smiled down at me and I frowned in return.

"I know, I know my aura—"

"No. Not your aura, smartass." They playfully tugged on a strand of my windblown hair. "It was when I knew Throwen loved you. Which took about two seconds, by the way."

"Hey!" I felt lighter with Echo and as we laughed, I searched to pinpoint this feeling. It wasn't the same lightness as when witches shared in grief. This was a placid, internal understanding that I could hold a conversation with them. Something I could never do with the witches in my coven.

"I'm serious. Octavia. Do you know *how long* I've waited to see Throwen look at someone the way he looks at you?"

I blushed and tilted my chin down.

"Hey!" Throwen emerged from the entrance, looking fuckable as ever as he mindlessly strummed his lute.

I knew exactly what those fingers could do, and I needed them. Once they were inside of me, thinking was no longer an option, throwing me into only pleasant sensations.

"I have to take Octavia home to sleep. Whynnie expects you at sunrise for training." He winced as my face soured. Despite all the rigid hours in my coven, I had never been a morning person.

"Sleep. Yeah. Okay." Echo flicked their wrist and strode toward the hovel calling out behind them, "Night. Night. Love you!"

Throwen grumbled but reciprocated, "Night. Night. Love you too."

"That's cute." I moved to twist his nipple, and he caught my wrist, rubbing his calloused thumb gently over my steadily increasing pulse.

"Does this mean you're choosing to be a brat tonight?" His smile was wicked.

"Always," I taunted, pressing my body against his.

He hummed in approval as he lifted my chin, pulling me into a punishing kiss.

Chapter 35

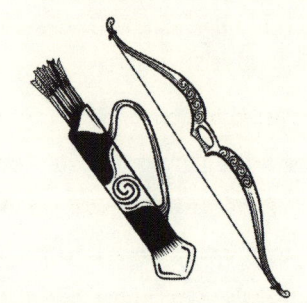

OCTAVIA

Fidgeting with my necklace, I rubbed the pink stone I now relied on for something to do with my hands. I reached an arm across my chest, trying to stretch out my muscles that were screaming for a break. There wasn't time to feel pain, so I stretched the other arm and fought a wince.

The spirits wrapped around my ankles from where Throwen sat and strummed lazily behind me.

"No," I said. "I have to be able to do this without you." Even though I was fatigued, I didn't want to be coddled, and I kicked them away.

They withdrew slowly like a sulky child. Throwen chuckled, and I ignored him and the spirits.

Whynnie was right. He was a distraction. We had been at this for hours and I had yet to hit a fucking apple. It had been two days since our visit to Starpass and since then, my powers were unreachable. I hadn't been able to connect with Throwen's magic either, and had to rely on what Throwen could teach me without it.

Sighing, I tightened the brown leather bracers Echo gifted me. They all had given such thoughtful and practical gifts. Whynnie gave me a matching leather vest that I was still breaking in. It was comfortable, but thick for protection. But Throwen's gift was now my most prized possession besides my broom.

It was a dark wooden bow, much smaller than his. The matching quiver was breathtaking. I wasn't sure how he found a witch to craft something so perfect in such a short time. They were both adorned with artfully drawn versions of my mark.

He was helping me learn not to loathe my mark entirely, caressing it any chance he got. It was the best Name Day I could remember, other than having to do my sprints through a stomachache the next morning from eating too much cake.

I had pulled half of my hair up into a bun with a new leather strap from Throwen. He had given me an entire box full of them in every color imaginable, claiming I was bound to lose this one, too. Reaching up, I tightened the strap, making sure no hair would fall into my field of vision.

The smooth texture of my bow's grip filled me with determination as I shifted into my stance. I wiggled around, trying to get my footing just right.

Throwen hummed from behind. "Take your time, darling."

I could feel him watching my ass as it wobbled with me, my tight gray pants leaving little to the imagination. "Shut. Up."

Such a fucking tempting distraction. I kept my legs spread in the shooting position and notched an arrow. My arms shook and I pulled back as far as I could.

I. Could. Do. *This!* I loosed the arrow and held my breath as it flew toward the apple. It landed in the ground a few inches away from its target.

"Fuuuuck!" I lashed out, shooting it with a ball of fire instead. "Fuck you, apple!"

I raised my middle fingers at it as Throwen coughed, obviously trying to conceal his amusement at my outburst. "It's okay, darling. Archery isn't something you learn in a few days."

"Well, that's all I have!" There was too much inside of me that couldn't break free and as I pivoted, I marked him as my target. "How are you so calm? *Malik is coming.* With an army."

Setting his lute aside, Throwen walked over, taking my bow and quiver and resting them on the ground. "Do you see that tree over there?" He pointed to an entire forest full of trees.

"Oh yeah. That one there." I gestured sarcastically to all the spectators witnessing my pathetic strength and shitty aim.

"Come on, you feisty little thing."

"No. I have to train." I dug in my heels, unwilling to let him pull me into that space where only we existed. "I have to be ready."

"*Goddess's tits*, you're so fucking stubborn. War isn't something that anyone can ever truly be prepared for. *Trust me.*"

I hated when he said that because he knew I trusted him explicitly. I exhaled. "Fine. Show me this stupid tree that will somehow magically make me a better shot."

"The tree isn't stupid." He frowned, appearing hurt. I pressed my lips together. He turned, pulling me around a tree that seemed to wind on forever. I rested my finger on the tip of my nose as we neared a part that appeared freshly burned.

"What is this?" I knelt and pressed my hand to the blackened grass first. It was cool to the touch, and I worked my way up the black roots and onto the rough bark. My fingertips tingled as I walked them up the bark, closing my eyes and reaching to feel the pulse of the tree. "Is she dying?"

"No. This is where Whynnie found me."

Something within my consciousness clicked into place, as I knew that the energy that ran through this tree was different. It bore the marks of a life taken and then, against the laws of nature, given back. *Given back to protect me.*

"About Whynnie…" He rubbed his chest. "I wanted to thank you, I've *never* seen so much life in her. You're healing her just like you're going to heal the rest of us."

He expected too much of me. Here I was, keeping something important from him while he put all his faith and trust in me. Nausea climbed up my throat, and I stared into the death-touched spot, hoping it would swallow me whole.

A vision of a tiny Throwen played out before me. Wearing nothing but an oversized shirt, he was curled up in a fetal position against the tree. His teeth chattered as he hummed to himself in an effort to fight off the bitter cold. Then he went still, growing pale and then blue, as a misty fog fell from his lips one last time. It was a final shuddering breath of life, but one unlike I'd ever experienced before.

I'd never stopped to think about the Throwen that had existed before. The pain and suffering he must've endured to be left alone in the woods so young. I watched his petite limbs grow pitch-black as if the Goddess was splashing them with ink, rewriting his story for him.

"*Don't* thank me." It came out bitter and cold as the vision fizzled out. My feelings and desires were being shaken to the point of explosion. I wanted to end Malik's terror, but the guilt, shame, and sorrow were holding me back. Strung out was an understatement. I was ripping at the seams.

"Octavia—" He reached out to help me and I pushed it away. I bit my cheek hard; knowing my tears were about to make an unwelcome appearance.

"I can't save any of us. I can't... I can't even shoot a bow or feed off your power like a fucking parasite. That's all I am. I can't find my *special* power no matter how hard I try to connect with the Goddess. I don't know how. I told you Throwen, she made me wrong."

He lowered himself to the ground, leaning against the tree and pulling me into his lap despite my grunts of protest. "You're not just struggling to connect with the Goddess right now, you're struggling to connect with me. I can feel it. What's going on?"

I hated how he could see right through me and the way he looked at me like I was the only thing that mattered pushed me over the edge.

"Whynnie told me something." My body ached, and I was happy for it. I deserved it.

"Okay..." Grabbing my hand, he gave it a reassuring squeeze.

"It's something about you. About us."

"*Fuck.* What was it about? My early twenties were a *really* weird time for me."

"No. It's—" My fear grew, and tears tagged along.

"You're a death witch," I whispered, but the demon inside spoke. *He will hate you.*

"I know that." His thick brows pulled together.

"No, not like, Angel of Death... a death witch. There were others before you." I pulled away as he smoothed his mustache, considering the information.

"How does this affect us?"

I stared at him, trying to decipher what exactly he was feeling but I couldn't tell. "Throwen, I just told you there were others like you and all you care about is how it affects us?"

Plastering on that charming smile, he shrugged. "What we have is more important than those that came before me."

I scoffed and threw my face into my palms.

"Octavia, *it's okay.*" He rubbed gentle circles on my back.

"It's not okay! Whynnie told me the first night. I kept it from you because I'm weak and selfish and—"

Throwen grabbed onto my chin forcefully. "You are *neither* of those things."

I helped him up, steering us back to our bags. I grabbed the book and walked us over to a fallen log that was so large it was more of a tiny moss-covered bridge.

We climbed up the rock leading to the log and as we made it to the center; I took a deep breath, the earthy smells grounding me. We sat, the soft moss becoming our cushions as our feet dangled.

"This is yours." I handed him the book.

He took it reverently, not opening it but setting it on the moss, the dark purple pairing nicely with the deep greens. "I don't want to read about it. I want you to tell me."

"Goddess, Throwen, I knew you didn't like to read but… wait, can you not read?" I taunted, and he barked a laugh.

"I can read, but why would I when those pretty lips could tell me instead?"

There was a knot in my throat for multiple reasons now.

"The Goddess brought you back because of me. You were recreated to protect me." The words came out rushed and disdain filled my tone as a small smile spread across his face. "Why the fuck are you smiling about this? This isn't funny."

Trying to stop a brewing laugh, he ran a hand over his head. "I mean, it's a little funny."

I was going to kill him and his constant positivity. What would it take to break through that wall of contentment he displayed? "I've been wrestling with this for *days*."

"It's funny because I already knew something was up when Whynnie didn't absolutely annihilate me. Kallan would be pissed there were no repercussions for fucking you."

"*Sacred Ether*, Throwen!" I pushed his chest forcefully, eliciting the frown I was expecting when I told him about this. It was satisfying somehow, making him react in the way I had prepared for. "Our love isn't real. You were forced to be with me."

His frown shifted into something lethal, and I braced myself for his response. "I *dare* you to tell me that again. Look into my eyes and tell me that our love isn't real."

I whimpered, fighting a sob as he pressed my back flat against the log and straddled me. "I already knew that my soul was connected to yours, Octavia. I didn't need proof that you were meant to consume every iota of my purpose in this life that was gifted to me. But I *am* thankful for it."

This didn't make any sense. This was supposed to give him pause. To make him question what and who we were. But if anything, it was pushing him even deeper into his affections.

"Why?"

We were pressed close as deep chuckles vibrated against my tender breasts and I arched into him further. I could feel his racing heart and hard cock as my breathing hitched.

"Because it means beyond a shadow of a doubt that you're *mine*." He grabbed onto the back of my neck, pulling me into a passionate kiss. Our tongues chased each other as I let myself accept our connection. He kissed along my neck, whispering in my ear, "You've been working hard for hours. Why don't I help you take a much-needed break from those incessant deep thoughts of yours?"

My pulse quickened as he pulled us to our feet. My need to talk about us flickered in and out as he blew out the flames of analysis and replaced them with ones of passion.

"What did you have in mind?" I licked my lips, hoping he was about to throw me to the ground and ravish me.

"Run."

I looked into the unending depth of the forest, the trees looming above like giants. "Excuse me?"

"I said run, sexy little muse. I need some inspiration and I think hunting you and fucking all the thoughts from your mind will do the trick.

Consider it part of your training."

Fuck. Me.

"You can't be serious." *I hope he is.*

"Ten." He took a step closer, and I thought about the last time he gave me a countdown. How good it felt to come all over his firm thigh.

"Throwen." The adrenaline did nothing to help as heat moved from my face down to my abdomen and lower, making my clit ache. For a moment, I was mesmerized by his hunger for me, wishing I could see what I looked like right now through his eyes.

"Nine."

I hopped off the log, landing with my knees bent before sprinting through the trees.

"Five!"

The sounds of crunching leaves and snapping twigs beneath my boots seemed twice as loud.

Stick to the shadows. Throwen's instructions replayed in my mind. I looked around, seeing plenty of shadows and thanking the moon for her phase of darkness. I slowed, slinking into some underbrush.

"Three!"

Stay low to the ground. I laid flat on my stomach, pulling some tangled hair free of twigs as I threw up an air shield and worked to control my breathing.

"One!"

Everything fell quiet except for a light rustling from the breeze. I knew I couldn't stay in one place, he would find me. My pulse was racing, my competitive nature mixing with my lust. It was thrilling in the most salacious way.

Dropping the shield, I listened, attuning myself to the sounds of the surrounding forest. Filling my lungs as full as possible, I let all of it in. These majestic trees created a uniquely sweet scent.

A crisp breeze tickled the sweat at the back of my neck, sending shivers down my spine. I had to gain some ground. Staying crouched, I moved toward a tree surrounded by large bushes.

Only move about thirty to fifty yards at a time. I followed his smooth voice in my mind as if he were watching because a part of me knew he had to be.

Some movement caught in my periphery as I slowly lowered all the way to the ground, but as I did, a twig snapped loudly like a bone breaking.

Tsking came from somewhere above me in the tops of the trees. "*Oh, you were so close, darling.*" *When the fuck did he have time to climb a tree?*

"*Shit.*" I started sprinting but, in the darkness, I had gotten all spun around with no concept of what direction I had come from.

"Wrong way." He popped out from behind a tree, reaching for my waist, but I ducked as he fell forward.

"Oof!" He landed with a thump, and I laughed, sprinting away, knowing I didn't stand a chance. I just wanted to make it as difficult for him as possible.

"Oh, I see." His voice was getting closer, but I pumped my arms, enjoying the bite of the wind across my face and the large trees passing by me in a blur. *This is freedom. This is what I craved.*

"Ah!" I screamed and laughed as he caught me around my waist.

"You like being chased."

I went limp, trying to pull him down with me. Grunting, he lifted and flipped me around.

"You like making it hard for me." He seized my hand, rubbing my palm roughly against his hardened cock that was straining against the laces of his pants.

"And Octavia." He leaned in as I rubbed him harder, his whisper tickling. "You *want* to be mine. Don't you?"

I shuddered, moving my arms around his neck, and pressed my body against his in answer. I *needed* friction. There was too much space between us.

He bit my neck hard and sucked the skin between his teeth. I hissed.

When he released, he soothed the tender spot with a kiss. "Use your words."

"Yes." I panted, reaching for the hem of his shirt and pulling it over his head. He was perfect. His chest was firm with just the right amount of hair.

I twirled some between my fingers, fighting the urge to pull it as hard as I could. It was dark against his pale skin. My eyes lingered on his arms; veins should not be that enticing.

"Yes, what?" He took off my bracers, then my vest and shirt. It was cold, but it did nothing to the heat rising from my skin. I was going to go properly insane if he didn't fuck me right now.

Groaning, I fumbled for his pants. "Yes, Throwen. I *want* to be yours. I want *you* to be mine."

He curled his fingers into the waistband of my pants, pulling me against him. "Good girl."

He pulled my pants down, discarding them on the ground before wrapping an arm under me and lifting. I squealed and then moaned as his forearm pressed hard against my core, but before I had a chance to start grinding, I was lowered and thrust against a tree, the bark pressing into my skin.

He massaged my breast roughly, fingers digging into the pebbled skin as his other hand molded to my hip. I grabbed onto his biceps, tilting my chin to the sky above.

"Eyes on me, my muse."

My eyelashes fluttered as he worked the tender tissue of my breasts with both hands. I was staring into a moving painting. An artist sat within his pupil, splashing out shades of lavender, plum, and violet.

He grabbed onto my chin and drew me into a kiss. Everything reached that point of wet and warm that had my legs shaking. When he moved away, he held my face, stroking the corner of my lip with his thumb. "This is the most real thing I've ever experienced."

He pressed two fingers to my lips and slowly pushed them into my mouth. I kept my eyes on him and sucked on them, swirling my tongue around them how I would if it were his cock. In answer to my challenge, he pressed his fingers in further, eliciting a gag before he pulled them free.

"Every. Inch. Of you. Is mine." He trailed his wet fingers slowly down between my breasts and over my abdomen.

"Throwen, *please*."

He thrust both fingers into me at once, my soaking pussy welcoming the abrupt shock followed by pleasure. He hissed as he slowly pumped his fingers in and out, realizing just how ready for him I truly was.

"*Fuck*. You're dripping, Octavia." Lowering to his knees, he then pressed his tongue flat against my clit while he expertly moved his fingers and added even more pressure.

"*Sacred Ether!* Throwen!"

He bit my clit, pulling it between his teeth. All thought left me and I ground against his mouth and fingers. He curled them, hitting the most sensitive spot as I cried out.

"Don't. Stop." I panted as my musician continued a steady rhythm. I was his instrument, and he was playing my strings to the point of breaking. He moaned into me and the vibration pushed me over that edge. My legs shook as he squeezed tightly onto my ass and licked my cum. He flicked his tongue playfully as I rode out the last shudders of my orgasm.

A euphoric daze fell over me as he gently lowered me to the ground and removed the rest of his clothing. The leaves were soft and when he climbed on top of me, I could smell cannabis and campfire smoke.

He kissed me from my toes, up my legs, over my hip, across my abdomen. It was making me see stars in a cloudy sky that had none. Little bursts of pleasure radiating out from each hot kiss. When he reached my mouth, I could still taste myself on his tongue.

He lined himself up, and as he slid in, my pussy clenched around him. After a few languid thrusts in and out, his other hand rubbed along the opening he already filled. He eased his finger inside, making it even tighter.

I cried out. I couldn't remember ever feeling this full.

"You can take it." He picked up speed and, without warning, slid in another finger.

"Fuck! Throwen. I can't—"

"You know the word to make me stop. But you and I both know you take me so well."

We both glanced down to where his cock and hand worked together. I clawed at his chest. He knew me better than I knew myself when it came to pleasure and mixing it perfectly with pain.

I was writhing beneath him, chasing another release. I bit my lip hard, trying to keep in the primal sounds that wanted to break free. Throwen's chuckle was dark and full of promise as he released his fingers and moved his hand to my throat.

"Don't fight it. You *will* sing for me." He flipped me over onto my stomach, wrapping one hand tightly around the hair at the base of my neck. Leaning over me, he licked circles around each of the moons adorning my skin.

"Does this feel real? Can you feel our connection?" His wet cock slid against my ass.

I gasped as he slid a hand over my ass before teasing me with a finger.

"Oh, Goddess. Yes." I wanted him to fill every part of me.

"Louder. I want the entire forest to know you're fucking *mine*." He abandoned his teasing and gripped onto both my hips roughly. Entering me again, his thrusts became punishing, pushing so deep within me that I knew my organs were feeling him, too.

"Throwen! Fuck!" It took me a moment to realize the guttural sounds were coming from me. This was more than fucking. This was primal, something engraved deeply into who we were.

"You feel so fucking tight. *Shit.* I love it when you sing for me." Slowly his hand moved from the base of my tailbone, along my spine, ending with his fingers gripped around the sides of my neck. He squeezed just enough to bring that lightheaded sensation and as I floated away from myself and into us, I launched over that edge.

"I'm coming!" I cried out and with a few more thrusts, he pulled out, covering my back with hot cum, and I fell flat onto the ground.

Throwen dabbed the head of his cock against my back and panted. He had marked me as his many times over, but this felt different, like I had accepted his unconditional love without my brain twisting it into something it wasn't.

"I love you, Throwen. I am yours and you are mine."

)))) ⊙ (((

AFTER CLEANING UP in a nearby stream, we returned to the tree where Throwen had been reborn. He set up a romantic little area with candles and heaps of blankets and pillows. Even Pepper enjoyed laying on one of them. My thoughts were clearer, as if he fucked the negativity right out of me for the time being.

Blowing out a puff of smoke, Throwen passed the joint to me. "How are you feeling?"

I breathed it in and took an extra breath, being sure to fill my lungs. As I blew it out, I struggled to decipher what was going on inside of me.

"I feel scared." I handed the joint back and curled against him, resting my head on his chest so I could listen to the beat of his heart. How much longer would I be blessed to feel the steady thump against my ear?

"I know what you meant now. That your family was your home," I continued, "When you told me, I couldn't comprehend how a person could be a home, but I feel it now. I feel it and it terrifies me."

He chuckled and smoothed my hair. I couldn't lose my new family this soon. I barely had any time with them at all.

"That's what love is. Sending your heart out with them as they go about their lives. It is terrifying, but worth the reward of watching them grow."

"Hmm." I liked that idea, but it did nothing to squelch the fear. Who knew if we would even have the time to watch each other grow beyond that battlefield?

My eyelids felt heavy, and my body was succumbing to the strain I had put on it.

"You have part of the Goddess in you, right?"

The sudden change in topic had me lifting my head. "I guess so, yeah."

"So, I've *actually* touched a piece of the Goddess." He wiggled his fingers playfully.

"Gross!" I pushed at his chest but frowned at his bare fingers. Guilt spilled like acid in my stomach. He had time to have the perfect bow and quiver made for me, and I couldn't return the favor. "I'm sorry you lost your picks."

The look he gave me was sinful. "Does your pussy miss them, too?"

I couldn't help the stupid grin that spread across my face. "Shut up." Laughing, I settled back into his comfort.

"Octavia, I was so bored before you. It was like Theldea was becoming this painting that started bright and colorful, but over the years the paint

453

built up into a muddy monotonous mess. You make my life better. You make it exciting and fun."

"I don't think I've ever been described as exciting or fun before." I pulled the blanket up under my chin. Soon I would be described as the war-bringer, the Lady of the Grave who killed countless.

This war was coming and nights like this were almost out of reach. I wasn't ready for it to end. I wanted more time with my friends. Wanted the Goddess to give me back the time that was stolen from us.

Throwen continued, "You are that, and so much more. Don't think that this passion has a timeline because it doesn't. You will forever be my source of purpose and joy."

The spirits danced around our toes and tickled at Peppers's hooves. The solace was too much, and I wanted to listen to his praises all night.

"Will you tell me a story?"

The laughter that rumbled his chest reminded me of thunder. "Once, there was a witch who was brave and strong. She grew up having to hide and lost herself along the way. But then she broke free and spread her kindness far and wide."

I hummed in approval, tracing his veins and memorizing their patterns, following the path his blood took to pump that kind, generous, selfless heart.

Chapter 36

THROWEN

Shadowed skies loomed and even though we couldn't hear the necromancers, we knew they were there. I could feel it as my need to protect Octavia grew unbearable. A wasteland lay between us and every part of me wanted to traverse it and destroy Malik myself.

We arrived just before sunset and through the trees we could see the small entrances into Starpass we would use tomorrow. Taking a deep breath, I concentrated on the wind blowing toward the sea.

The atmosphere around the campfire was sullen. Octavia sat nestled under a blanket, resting her feet on my lap while I rubbed out the aches that three days of marching with a small army brought with it.

Echo sat across from us, polishing their blades with such intensity that I knew they were thinking of Kallan, of piercing their own brother's heart.

"*Goddess's tits!* You're all acting as if we've already lost." Whynnie threw little bursts of air at us, striding toward a fallen log and plopped down.

"Ah, the curse of youth. They're holdin' onta' the years they think they have left," Simulie joked.

"And you don't?" I smirked.

Simulie took her place beside Whynnie and offered her a cup of tea as they both laughed. "No, Angel. *We're old.* We've both been livin' like it might be our last day for a few years now. Isn't that right, ya' old crone?"

She bumped into Whynnie and I could picture it. Whynnie spilling her secrets to her best friend and teaching her the path of healing, just two troublemakers trying to make Theldea a better place and having fun doing it together.

"You're correct, you leathery old croc." Whynnie lifted her pinky as she drank.

They giggled and sipped their tea as if the years Whynnie chose to isolate herself didn't matter. The two had always kept correspondence through their letters; Whynnie had boxes full of them. It made Whynnie's joy a tangible thing, and the spirits slithered around their ankles.

"How do you do that? Live without fear of death? Of leaving your loved ones behind?" Echo asked, taking their place beside Whynnie on the edge of the log.

They had become increasingly existential as the days passed. Thankfully, Octavia was more than happy to engage in the heady conversations I wanted no part of.

It was an odd way to heal, to claw as deeply as they could into the meaning of it all. For me, it was different. I accepted this was the reality without having to question its meaning. As long as they were by my side, there would still be joy despite the scar on my heart.

"Well, Peacock, you first have to accept that some things are out of our control. The best we can do is wake up, thank the Goddess for another day, and try to do better than the last."

Flora hopped onto the blanket beside Octavia. "Plus, if we all die, then you won't technically be leaving anyone behind."

"Flora! What are you doing here?" Octavia's momentary joy shifted into wrath, but Flora tapped her nose playfully.

"Don't fret those gorgeous brows. I could probably defeat your lovesick assassin over there. I'm *classically trained*." She moved into a mocking curtsey.

"You wish, swamp witch," I taunted, and Flora flicked me off, placing her exquisite weapon on the ground with reverence.

"Is that yours?" Octavia's mouth remained parted.

Smiling, Flora unsheathed her curved, single-edged blade. The pink grip was long so that she could use two hands when wielding it. I'd seen Flora train before, and she was a fierce competitor. I was grateful for her willingness to help us.

"It's the first thing I bought with my money after I got away from my uncle." Flora's freckles stretched with her smile, and she shrugged. "At least the pervert gave me a decent education."

Octavia scowled at the mention of Flora's uncle and held the weapon reverently. Curious honey eyes inspected the blade before giving it back to Flora. She sheathed it and moved to Octavia's back, sectioning off pieces of her hair to braid.

Fennix marched across the circle with a bowl of cherries and seized a spot beside Echo. He was dressed casually in black leathers, with a white button-up rolled to his elbows. The pirate was covered in ink and when he sat beside Echo, their tattoos complimented each other in a way that you could only notice if you were looking closely.

Echo ignored him with a scowl, pushing their frustration into sharpening their blades. He just sat there, cherry bowl resting on his lap, staring into the fire while he waited for Echo to acknowledge him. The patience that man had was baffling.

Fingers twitching, I reached for my lute, sliding my finger along her ebony body. She was covered in knicks and scratches from our journey. I was able to patch her up, but I would have to commission a new one if we got through this. Even she couldn't escape the pain and hurt that came with a life like ours.

Chatter continued around the fire, and I played some lazy chords.

Whynnie and Simulie laughed with their arms wrapped around each other, and Flora and Octavia compared their blades excitedly, slashing them through the air to test their weight. Flora had braided her hair into a halo on her head.

Echo and Fennix were in a heated debate as he fed them the cherries between admonishments. I wasn't sure if it was anger or passion. Honestly, I'd rather not know.

This wasn't just about losing Octavia. *These were my people.*

They were Octavia's now too, but they hadn't always been.

My strumming faltered. Octavia may have been victimized by Malik but so had her people. They were just on the other side of Starpass, scared and oppressed. Malik tore apart Theldean families, brainwashing witches to convince them they were alone and his coven was the only option. But those witches weren't alone.

As I pressed my palm flat against the strings muting the sound, the spirits vanished and everyone looked to where I sat, frowning.

Leaning over, Octavia rubbed circles on my back, her comfort and kindness urging me on. "Throwen?"

I stood. "Malik's army is large. We know that from Fennix's correspondence with the covens along the southeast coast."

Octavia glanced around at the others, her brows pulling together.

"Those are Octavia's people. They're *Theldea's* people." Leaves rustled overhead and a contemplative silence fell upon the group.

Despite our differences, we were all here to end necromancy. We had that in common, the hurt they had caused every coven. But how many of them were like Octavia? Born and raised in an isolated world, who knew nothing else.

Octavia rose and addressed her friends, "Some of them love Malik and they support him. Many of the scouts think he is a god. But some of my people are scared. I saw it in their eyes every time they had to ask for a new piece of clothing or report an injury. I saw it in the children as they were reassigned to another family across the coven where they were 'better suited'. I saw it in myself every time I made myself small so Malik could be big."

Tears rolled down her cheeks, and I fought the urge to whisk them away. This was her moment. She was the leader of her people, whether or not they knew it. She would be the one to free them and speak on their behalf.

Pride made my chest swell, and I swore doves would fly from my mouth at any moment.

"I know many will die, and I feel a great deal of responsibility for *all* of this. But if we make it through, if we can stop him…" She reached a hand back to where I stood behind her and I accepted it.

I was the only one able to see the glowing spiral of her mark as it radiated out to the other moons. *This is where I belong.* She was the little Goddess, and I was merely here to protect and encourage her while enjoying the pleasures that came with knowing her.

"My people have seen things no witch should. Have endured treatment that will forever leave them scarred. I know because I too, have these scars. Some are engraved in my skin, but many of them are gouged into my brain and I'm still not sure they can ever truly be healed. They will need not only our help but our empathy."

I wanted to scoop her up in my arms.

Whynnie stood and hobbled over, wrapping her in a tight embrace. "I'm so proud of you, Sprout. You've grown into the most beautiful sequoia."

Octavia huffed a laugh, and I closed in around her. Echo sprinted over, enveloping Whynnie from behind. Flora squealed, jumping as she joined in with Simulie who was cackling.

"Julian!" Echo chided, and he grunted as he stood.

"Fine." He strode over with a smirk, his gold tooth glistening, and snaked his disgusting arms around my sibling. "There. Now we are all hugging. How precious."

"You're just jealous you didn't get to press against me," Whynnie taunted across the circle of friends and we all whined and separated at the image.

Simulie whispered something into Whynnie's ear, coaxing out a rosy tint to paint her cheeks.

Everyone fell back into place with more purpose than before, and we worked to make sure our weapons and minds were ready.

"Angel, a word." Fennix stood and beckoned me over to his tent and I reluctantly followed, leaving Octavia to learn how to sharpen her knives from Flora and Echo.

Once I entered the tent, my stomach dropped. He had a cacophony of items strewn about, including a map with battle plans that he glared at like an enemy.

"What is this?" Black and red markers were set up around Starpass.

"Battle strategies." He scratched his beard. "I keep trying to go through each option. Figure out what's most viable."

"I had no idea you even knew what a strategy was. Aren't you more the kill first ask questions later type?"

He smiled, accepting the taunt like a compliment. "Usually yes. But when Echo is involved, I make damn sure I'm prepared." He shifted into the Fennix I knew and grinned with shining teeth. "Plus, I can't maintain my lifestyle with necromancers running Theldea."

"We have our plan, Fennix." I crossed my arms. "We wait once they emerge, staying out of any arrows' reach. We let Octavia offer mercy. If that doesn't work, Whynnie and Octavia will be our eyes in the sky. I'll lead the most experienced in the front."

"No."

"Excuse me?" I clenched my fist, fighting the urge to throw a punch at his audacity. How many times had we asked for his help? How many times did he deny us, only caring about himself?

"I'll lead them. If I fall, it's of no consequence. But if we lose you, Throwen..." He shook his head, and I had a hard time not letting my mouth fall open in shock. Never had he addressed me by my true name.

"Your powers are needed if we stand any chance. I've gone over this for days." There were bags under his eyes, the state of his hair looking like he had pulled on it too much.

"So what do you suggest, Julian?"

Mercy. It's what we all longed for, and he had shown up so I would give him mine.

His face softened into the man I'm sure Echo loved, the one who was genuine to himself instead of his upbringing. "Have you ever been in a battle? How many have you taken on at once?"

His questions weren't condescending, he needed this information to form his plan.

"Thirty, maybe forty. But Kallan was there, and you know how he fought."

Fennix dropped his focus to the map. Starpass was a giant pit waiting to swallow us all. "A battle is different. You aren't playing the long game anymore. There will be a winner and it's the most hostile of situations you'll ever find yourself in."

He turned, opening a crate and digging through the straw packing it.

"You've seen battle?" I knew his father had died in a battle between covens when he was a youth, but had he been there?

Sighing heavily, he pulled something out of the crate and offered it to me. Time stopped and my ears rang loudly.

Brother, please!

Sounds of defeat played through my mind and my chest burst as a lump caught in my throat at the sight of Kallan's cutlass.

"Throwen, I don't know what to do with this. I don't know if I should give it to you or Echo or Whynnie. When I heard of the attack and how distraught Echo was in their letter, I had to see for myself."

My eyes welled with tears as I traced the intricate sage and dahlia carvings. "I think, for now, we let it rest." My body shook as I handed it back and he returned it to the crate.

"Nobody should have had to endure what you did in that clearing. I saw Throwen. *I saw*. Battle is ten times worse. It's ruthless and vindictive and I beg of you to let me on the frontline. Not only to protect Echo, but to protect you and the rest of your family."

I had to focus on something else or my anger would drive me to irrational actions. "What's the rest of the plan?"

Fennix perked up, as if ready to unleash what his mind had been stewing over. "I take the front."

"You know Echo is going to kill me for agreeing to this?"

He waved me off. Apparently, he handled Echo's wrath better than anyone. "When we charge, we form our lines seven witches deep so that when the witches in front burnout—" He knocked over one of the frontline witches. "The second witch fills their place, filling the gap."

Moving the pieces around, he continued. "We cycle through." I frowned, but he raised a hand covered in rings. "I know how callous that sounds, but most of them aren't trained properly and many of them will need to regain their strength."

"So, that's your whole plan?" I raised my eyebrows.

"Everything else is as planned except you work from behind the front lines and use your bow and spirits. If we need to retreat, Octavia and

Whynnie will lead us out. There aren't many exits on our end, so it will be like trying to shove a parrot into a bottle."

I grimaced at the horrid image.

He shrugged. "Pirate humor."

Smoothing my mustache, I thought through his plan. "*Fuck*, I hate it when you're right." I smiled up at him and he laughed.

It was as if a sense of peace fell over him when his shoulders relaxed and I knew he was thinking about Echo.

"But if Echo becomes a distraction—"

"They won't. If I've learned anything about Echo, it's that they can take care of themselves. I'm merely there for support if they want it."

I envied his strength. Terror filled me at the thought of Octavia flying around on her own with necromancers everywhere.

Standing taller, I arched my back, stretching out the tension. "Okay. Let's tell the others."

"The rumors only mentioned you chopping off a hand, not that she was fucking Goddess-born." He smiled, his shiny teeth glinting against the lantern light. "You've been holding out on me."

I scoffed. "It wasn't a hand, it was only a finger."

"I'm glad you found her." He gave me a nod. "Thank you, Throwen."

Biting the inside of my cheek, I nodded back. I strode toward the exit, unable to be in the same room with Kallan's blade.

The plan brought with it a new sense of purpose. I would stand behind those witches who chose to help us when they could have just stayed away. The Goddess would use me as her conduit of vengeance, and I would save as many as I could from both sides.

"Oh, and Throwen." As I opened the tent, I turned to appraise the man I held an entirely new respect for. "I hope you've prepared a war song. Malik will hate that shit."

"We just need to find a drummer." I winked, and he followed me to inform our friends and family of the changes in our plan and spend what little time we had left with them.

Chapter 37

OCTAVIA

Our day had begun by taking to the cloudy skies before the sun could even think about rising. As Whynnie and I hovered on our brooms, we had seen the necromancers already in place.

My jaw ached when I had found Malik decked out in the best armor necromancers had to offer. His crown sat atop his silver hair, and I had wanted to shoot it off. There was no warmth left for him in my heart. Anyone could have seen there were too many of them. There were groups of families, and I had swallowed back the bile burning my throat.

He truly did see this battle as an expansion of his territory. It was no longer just about me fleeing; it was about him gaining control over all of Theldea.

For a moment, I believed I could've avoided this by staying in the Coven of the Grave, but I knew that wasn't the reality. He would've committed to taking over at some point.

Fog twisted around our feet where we now walked the tunnel leading into Starpass. It drew me back to the present. Light poured through the opening a few yards away. I tamped down my doubts and channeled the unyielding confidence I had always strived to mimic.

Rolling my shoulders and puffing out my chest, I cataloged the weapons attached to various areas of my outfit to appease the terror. My stomach felt like someone had force fed me a pile of rocks.

My gaze unfocused and I held my broom at my side where Whynnie hovered on hers. Echo and Fennix followed close behind and Flora led another group through one of the other tunnels. *Fuck, I feel like I might pass out.*

As soon as we were herded through the small space, the air from my lungs had been stolen and I worried I would never breathe a full breath again. Fennix pounded a steady beat on his drum while Throwen played deep, eerie chords and our army marched steadily to the rhythm. He was on my right, but I kept my eyes forward, fearful that one furtive glance might be the last.

Enoch made quick work of my flight suit. It was a special blend of thick gray and charcoal fibers that were lightweight and gave me full mobility while remaining breathable to keep me cool. Whynnie had a matching brown outfit.

I paused just before crossing the precipice into a battle I never wanted but was ready to die for. I whispered, "Goddess, protect us. Protect them. Protect *him*."

As I strode out into the open, I reached for the right words to ground me. *Feel Octavia. It's not your weakness. It's your strength.*

Despite seeing Malik a great distance away, it was Throwen's voice in my mind. I would not let Malik hold any power over me here and maybe if he died, so would his voice inside my mind. *Or we will all die.*

After a few minutes, our army was in place and Throwen's war song ceased. The lack of noise from the necromancers unsettled me, and I reached for Throwen, needing some stability.

Usually, Malik liked to make a spectacle, but not one bone weapon was being smacked against the ground. I held my chin high, never taking my gaze off Malik. A smile fell across my face as he fidgeted. He was waiting for me to speak so he could silence me, but I could wait him out for as long as needed.

It didn't take long for him to cave, and he pressed a finger to his throat, bellowing confidently, "Lady. Come with us now and none of your precious new friends have to die."

Of course, the first words out of his mouth were a blatant lie. If he didn't kill my friends now, he would the moment he got me back within those suffocating walls of his.

I gave my broom to Throwen, leaning in to kiss him. He wrapped a hand around the back of my neck. I could picture the vein in Malik's neck pulsing with the need to rip me away from these witches and isolate me.

I let that fuel me, I would not be caged again. I lazily pressed a finger against my throat, baring my teeth.

"Malik," I said it so plainly that I could have been talking to any witch, not the feared leader of our coven. "If you're going to address me using my title, at least say it properly."

His posture shifted into a predatory stance, his hand moving to his whip. Purple spirits flicked irritably in my periphery.

I decided as soon as I awoke from a restless sleep that I would embrace the title for my people. I no longer hated it. After this was over, I would save witches from an early grave, healing everyone I could. I would be their Lady, a proper leader. Or I would die and if that was the case, at least I would go out with a fight.

"I am the Lady of the Grave, and those are *my* people you're oppressing." I harnessed my knowledge of captivating a crowd using my voice from Malik, combining it with the way Throwen animated his performances as I paced back and forth. Throwing my whole body into it, not to entertain or command, but to reach out with a genuine desire to guide them to safety. Gradually, I pointed from one end of his army to the next, wishing I could make eye contact with each imprisoned witch.

Some of the scouts near him looked at each other, uncertainty pulling them from their perfect posture. Malik was pacing, fury bringing with it red smoke.

"*Your* people?" He gripped onto his whip and cracked it, the sound piercing the air like lightning as I fought back a flinch. "Let me show you, and *them*, what happens to anyone who claims to be a supporter of you and your treasured Goddess!"

A scout threw a witch onto the ground. The mass didn't move, but a sob caught in my throat. I would recognize that plum coat anywhere.

"Badru?" It was a whisper and plea as I lowered my finger, silenced by his cruelty. Nausea threatened to overwhelm me and I started to sweat profusely.

"This *heretic* aided our Lady to help her abandon us for this Theldean *filth!*"

Loud shouts of protest rang out and the scouts nearby hurled rocks at Badru's body with their magic. His hand lifted in an attempt to block the onslaught, but his air shield only lasted a few seconds. I was now fixated on Badru's crumbling body, my vision tunneling around him.

"Stop! Please!" I screamed, but it was no use. Malik had broken me already, so quickly seeped through my pores and into my bloodstream. I had been begging him all my life, a cycle I still couldn't break as I helplessly watched my friend be abused for helping me.

"Oh Goddess, Throwen." I held my stomach.

He rushed to me, wrapping me in his arms and the spirits. I covered my mouth to suppress the screams. Malik wrapped his whip around Badru's neck and snapped it like a twig, and my control was close to follow.

"No!" I didn't care about appearances anymore. I screamed and wailed as I fell to my knees. I wanted them to see this. The pain Malik was putting me through by killing my friend. I wanted them to see because I *cared* about Badru, about all of them. That is something Malik would never offer.

Pain wasn't a stranger, and I wore it like armor.

As I shakily rose to my feet, Malik bound Badru's soul. I grit my teeth, unwilling to let him play with me any longer, and returned my finger to my burning throat.

"You stole their lives!" My voice was hoarse, my insides thoroughly tearing apart piece by piece. "You stole *my* life!"

Malik's laugh was evil, and he lifted Baru's undead corpse and tossed it aside to one of the scouts. "You've always been a selfish cunt!"

Throwen shifted his stance, his entire being fighting to suppress a reaction. He would never give Malik the satisfaction.

"I stole nothing." Malik continued. "Those Theldean pieces of shit following you aren't worth the air they consume. Their feeble minds will be much more suited for transformation. *Can't you see?*" He spun in a deliberate circle with his free hand raised high in the sky. "We are ushering in the transformation of Theldea. This is what I was made for. I am their God, and I will punish the Goddess and her *spawns* for their audacity to claim power over me!"

An uncontrollable shudder wracked my body. I attempted to make sense of what was happening. He was insane, and I was helpless to talk any reason into him.

Throwen held my full weight. My mind had fled, and I was just a body until Whynnie linked her arm around mine. Our connection hummed and brought me back, strengthening my legs and my resolve.

"Do you know why you will never be a God, Malik?" He froze at the sound of Whynnie's low scratchy voice scraping at his chest.

My lungs expanded with pride. Whynnie had no fear. *But I do.*

"A God doesn't take away free will. A God doesn't isolate their creation. And a God doesn't need to prove they are a God."

He roared, and the unnatural sound of it made me know without a doubt that this was it.

"When this is over, you'll be asking yourself if this childish tantrum was worth all these lives. Any blood spilled today is on *your* hands, Octavia!"

The earth shook and vibrated the bottoms of my boots as our armies stormed toward each other. I didn't have time to think, and Throwen pulled me into a punishing kiss. "I love you." I held onto him tightly, unwilling to let go.

"I love you too." My response wasn't enough. I needed him with me. Without him by my side, I didn't feel whole. He kissed my forehead and clung to me.

"You have to let me go, Octavia."

Tears streamed down my cheeks, and I gasped for air. He took my fingers that were clutched tightly around his back and removed them. "You can do this. You're the strongest witch I know."

"I can't do this without you." I reached for him, but he stepped back.

"Octavia, you never needed me to be who you were meant to be. *You* can do this."

As he took a few more steps back, I saw the pain it caused him. His chest heaved as his love for me radiated from him like an aura. We needed each other, but Theldea needed us too.

He wiped fresh tears from his lavender eyes and turned away, running and hopping onto Pepper's back.

I stood dumbfounded, unsure how to do this without him. I took a deep breath, pulling my black leather goggles over my wet eyes, praying the heat wouldn't fog them.

As I watched him race toward the front lines, our memories flashed before my eyes. Normally my visions were rancid, but this… this was something entirely more potent than fear.

I saw his smugness on the mountaintop and his devastation at the arches. His wanderlust and enthusiasm as he showed me his world. His constant support and tenderness as he discovered my scars and endeavored to help me heal.

I let the love we had for each other fill my empty lungs as I took to the skies, holding back my sobs.

Once in the sky, I stretched out my arms and rolled my shoulders back. I needed to be attuned to keep us alive.

It was like watching two landmasses collide as magic exploded between the armies. The fire, earth, water, and air combined like ropes that pulled them closer together. The sound it made when they met was gut-wrenching and the screams were ever present.

Find the patterns. Fill the gaps.

Fennix's words echoed in my pounding skull. He was a surprisingly good teacher when it came to battle, and I followed the lines he had shown me on his map. We wouldn't know if his plan would work until our witches started to burn out.

I rounded the far east curve of the crater and shivered at the sight. I could see Throwen's magic, but it was only a splatter on the growing red canvas. It was as if the Abyss held red ink above Starpass, letting it drip down sporadically as necromancers bound the fallen.

Witches carried out a throne made of bones for Malik to sit on at the back of his army. A thick wall of his most elite scouts surrounded him. *Coward.*

My flight maneuvers were sharp and stiff, but I reined in my bitterness.

Focus Octavia!

I berated myself and angled flat against my broom, gliding back toward the middle of our army. Loud shouts fell in and out of earshot from our commanders as I spiraled, dodging fire and rocks. I could see Whynnie, serpentining around obstacles too.

An arrow whooshed past me and I pulled up on my broom just in time to dodge it. We were holding our ground as our skilled frontline witches fought against the necromancers. Our archers seemed especially adept, and with each arrow that hit its mark came hope.

Whynnie circled me. "Let's go again, it's too soon to assess." She directed us and I was thankful for it as my control wavered. We flew side by side to the back of our army before separating to repeat our pattern.

She rounded one side of the crater, and I took on the other. As I neared the edge of the eastern front lines, I spotted a flash of white encircled by red.

Flora.

Reacting on instinct alone, I sped toward where she stood, surrounded by necromancers and the undead. She laughed while expertly spinning her sword, seemingly unphased by the surrounding danger.

Standing up on my broom, I shot fire and rock toward the necromancers so Flora could target the undead. I bounded from my broom to the hard ground, leaving it to hover out of harm's way. Landing in a crouch, I smiled up at Flora.

"Hah! Nice goggles! Babette is going to *love* them." Flora somehow teased in the middle of the chaos. That's one reason I loved her. She had this way of calming me in the most stressful of situations.

"I'm here to help you!" I threw up an air shield and debris showered over us.

"Who said I need help?" She swiftly broke through the shield and stabbed through one undead's heart after another, collecting them on her long sword like an offensive kabob.

The sulfuric smell threatened to pull me back to the field with Calliope, where we lost Kallan but I concentrated on the hypnotic movement of Flora's high white ponytail instead.

As the enemy pressed closer, they walked through the pools of black blood mixing with red. The battle was a painting of harsh contrast. One, that if observed for too long, could drive any witch mad and I feared I was already falling into it.

"Okay, fine! I could use some help." She slashed as quickly as she could, strategically hitting arteries and areas that were quick to kill while also targeting the pulsating hearts of the undead. Her lethal movements reminded me of illustrations of jungle cats pouncing on their prey.

"I'll get the undead. The scouts are yours." Flora instructed, and moved quickly. Once she narrowed her focus, she ceased their gurgles and gnashing, unleashing one red orb after another.

I unsheathed a dagger, aiming it at a scout who was sprinting straight at me. Taking a steadying breath like Throwen had taught me, I waited until he got closer. When I knew I could hit my mark, I flung it into his neck.

"Fuck!" I pivoted to the side, and he stumbled past me, but his jagged bone rapier slashed into my stomach.

Wincing, I pressed my hand against the wound.

"Octavia! Are you okay?" Flora called out as I witnessed witches from Volgsump surge through the hole we made in the scouts' circle. They wore a ceremonial white, just like Flora that was now covered in gore, another unfortunate canvas of war.

"I'm fine!" Reaching up, I waited until I felt the smooth shaft of my broom in my palm and pulled myself up with a cry of pain as she carried me up and away from the battle.

I pressed my palm to my stomach, feeling the hot, sticky blood. It wasn't too deep, and I looked at the mayhem, trying to see any areas of weakness.

They were corroding our lines, breaking through them like dripping acid. The largest openings were toward the west, where Whynnie buzzed around like a bat, trying to direct the frantic witches.

Suddenly, I couldn't feel my injury as terror thrashed within me.

I searched for the lavender strands and pressed a hand to my heart as I found them in the middle of the throng. Throwen was too far away to help.

I raced toward Whynnie, doing my best to ignore the screams and growls. I couldn't help them all and with every passing witch, I let the numbness overtake me because without it, I wouldn't survive.

A red feather drew my eye, and I saw Fennix and Echo expertly working together. Fennix slashed at the undead, mindfully using his skill with his cutlass. He was rationing his magic. Echo crossed their arms, piercing two scouts' throats at once. They were decimating their opponents, a long line of bodies as evidence behind them.

I pressed my finger to my throat. "Fennix!" He kept fighting as I continued, "They're breaking through the west side! Throwen is further east!"

He looked west after driving his sword straight through a scout, catching Whynnie swooping in and out of the line of fire. Her attempts to help the witches below were proving futile.

"Tell them to cycle! And get Throwen to head west to help!" He launched at his opponent, and I heard the sharp clang of his metal against a necromancer's bone blade.

I projected my voice as loudly as possible to the witches below, "Cycle! Cycle!"

Slowly, those in front were ushered to the back, and a new line of witches moved forward. They were fierce in battle, but their magic could only stretch so far.

My heart thrashed violently against my chest, reminding me how little time we had left. I flew straight up and looped around toward Throwen and the spirits, thankful I could hear his voice and be in their presence again.

Chapter 38

OCTAVIA

Muddy piles of blood squished under my boots, and I careened toward Throwen. He was fighting alongside witches who were screaming with terror, some of them shaking as they clashed against the undead spraying black saliva all over their shields.

"Fennix says to head west."

Throwen threw up an air shield around us before yanking my mask down to kiss me. The blood on his lips was salty, and I pulled away with a gasp. I held his face in my hands looking past the dirt and chunks of tarry undead flesh for any wounds. "Are you hurt?"

"Not badly. I'll head that way. *You* stay safe. You're precious cargo." He rested his forehead on mine briefly. Sticky blood and sweat be damned. I leaned into the horror of it all, thankful he was still with me.

Lowering his shield, he vaulted up onto Pepper's back. As he readied his bow, the spirits burst out around him like tentacles, his bright arrow glowing against his weapon.

I flew over him, aiming fireballs at the necromancers surrounding his targets while dodging arrows and debris the enemy hurled at me.

Pepper ran hard along the back of the front lines and Thrown stood up straight in the stirrups. His posture was exquisite, and he shot arrow after arrow, taking out as many undead as he could. He moved along the west side of the battlefield and lowered, resting his entire body on Pepper's neck. *His magic is draining him.*

"Throwen!" I swooped down low, hopping to the ground beside Pepper and throwing up a shield. Arrows bounced off it and I gave her some reassuring pats and rubbed Throwen's leg. He panted and pushed himself up. His chest rose and fell heavily, and he seemed too fragile.

"Tell me how I can keep you safe too!" I screamed as fresh tears stung my windburned face.

He smirked down at me with a soft expression. "Don't worry, darling, that bruise on your ass from our first meeting will be worse than any of this."

A joke. He gestured to his beaten body. It was somehow the last thing and the only thing I needed from my charming bard. He was my constant, caught in a life of uncertainty. But I knew my time with him was over for now, as a disturbance of some kind drew my attention toward the necromancer lines.

"I love you." I proclaimed, allowing myself one more look at him.

I sprinted away from the other half of my soul, crouching low to the ground and bursting into the air just as my broom fell under my feet. Pain shot through my ankle and when I looked down, an undead held on firmly. They squeezed tighter.

My broom sped up and did several loops and twists as I kicked with my other foot. Finally, the bastard fell to the ground. Hopefully, the impact would rip his heart from his chest.

My broom hummed, pleased to be putting all the skills we had practiced to use.

"Good girl." She carried me higher and higher so I could see the entire battlefield as if it were Fennix's map.

"*What is that?*" I swore my broom shivered in response and the realization hit me.

Malik was working his way through his own army, surrounded by the most highly trained scouts. They were killing anyone they passed, necromancer or not.

"Octavia!" Whynnie's voice shook me from my stupor, and she pulled her broom up beside me. We were too high now for anyone to attack.

She looked frightened and fatigued, and the rocks that already dwelt within my gut piled higher, threatening to roll from my throat and out over my tongue until I suffocated. As I flew closer, I saw a large burn across Whynnie's back and several scrapes on her cheek. She lifted her goggles to the top of her head and I did the same.

Red smoke oozed from Malik, eating up everything around him. I was reminded of the concealment ceremony, our people surrounding us in wide circles. Except this time, our people were bound. *Gone. Forever.*

Before long, he would reach what was left of our army. Retreat was imminent.

"The last time I let him go, he stole you from me. He stole our life together. His necromancers killed and *bound* my son. It is his fault I will never see him again. Not to mention that it is my Goddess-born duty to protect Theldea from witches like him. I will *not* repeat my mistake." There was fire in her eyes as she ripped open old wounds and new.

"We have to try." My words fell flat amongst the sounds of anguish below.

"If things go poorly, get out of there and find Throwen. It's imperative you keep each other safe."

As my gaze darted from Malik to Whynnie, my mouth went dry. I was hyperventilating, and she ran her hand over the top of my head and cupped my chin.

Her milky eyes softened, and a smile fell across her face, wrinkles doubling as she did so. "I'm proud of you, Sprout. Let's end this."

Nodding, I sped after her, spiraling toward an overly eager Malik.

Adjusting his crown, silver strands of hair fell onto his sweaty forehead. He tightened his grip on his whip. His sneer came into focus as Whynnie and I landed. I crouched on the ground, throwing up an air shield around us. Scouts started to pummel us with elements. Nature was working against us, and it felt so wrong that my already weary heart faltered.

"Stop! They're mine!" Malik roared.

Mine. So funny how the word could feel like home or a cage depending on the context. The scouts ceased, creating a ring around us.

"*You.* This is all because of you!" Malik pointed at Whynnie before gesturing to the battle that was slowly fading away behind a thick wall of burned maroon smoke. Soon it would only be us in here, the armies blotted out.

Whynnie dropped her broom and yelled "What did I do to deserve this? I treasured you as my friend, and I trusted you!"

A sob caught in her throat and my arms shook as I fought with my exhaustion. He wasn't attacking, but I knew better than to let my guard down in front of him. I slid a hand to my thigh, wrapping it around a dagger.

Malik paced angrily and for a moment, I was back in our coven about to be branded.

Fear drove me to speak quietly so only she would hear. "Whynnie, we need to fly away." My ribs burned against the memory of him losing control as I pleaded for her to come with me. I groaned and my air shield broke.

Malik advanced on us quickly. "Off to find your fuck buddy bard so soon, Lady? You always were a whore."

I bit my cheek hard, reveling in the taste of blood running over my teeth, eager to spill Malik's. Keeping on the mask I created because of him, I gave him absolutely nothing now. No emotion. No reaction. He didn't deserve them.

Malik laughed, flicking out his whip and raising his arms high above his head.

Undead witches spilled through the wall of smoke, knocking us both to the ground.

Dropping my dagger, I shrieked and thrashed as I was hauled up by my ankles. The undead holding me had an arrow through his cheeks and gurgled as he carried me to Malik.

I aimed fire at his heart, but before I could unleash it, he delivered a hard punch to my gut. The air was stolen from me as I writhed.

"Did you actually think you stood a chance?" Malik circled around me and four scouts held onto each of Whynnie's limbs, pulling her taut until she cried out. She was reaching for her magic too, but only small blue flames flickered in her palms. The pain was too much for her.

"If you touch her, I promise by the Goddess that I will fucking kill you, Malik!" Spit flung from my mouth, and I wiggled my fingers.

"Who said I was going to touch her first? You're the one who deserves punishment for leaving. Thledea is *mine*! I have no use for your rancid blood anymore. I am done hiding. I'll get to the old hag once she watches you die." His eyes were glowing red, and he flicked his whip into the air.

I strained desperately to connect with the Goddess and my abilities. *Please help me!*

"You're a coward!" Whynnie's voice taunted in a blatant attempt to draw his attention away from me. All the blood was rushing to my head, and I felt dizzy.

"*Fine.*" His head snapped to Whynnie. "You asked why you deserve this other than being a Goddess-born piece of shit. Well, I'd *love* to tell you." He was eerily calm as he strode over to her.

"Malik! Don't!" I fought against my assailant, who flipped me upright, slapping me hard across the face before wrapping two large hands around the sides of my head, forcing me to watch.

I was happy for the stabilization, my head swimming. Bright bursts of light popped in and out of my vision.

"You always thought you were better than me." Malik straddled her, and she coughed as he put his full weight on her heaving chest. My magic was silent, and I couldn't even conjure a flame.

He grabbed her chin roughly.

"No." I wheezed, my voice nearly gone.

"You decided to keep things from me."

Does he hear himself? He accused Whynnie of the very things he spent years doing to me.

"Hypocrite!" I hurled the word at him like a weapon, hoping it would draw his attention, but he was fixated.

"You kept this knowledge from me." Flicking his whip, it wrapped around the nearest scout's neck, snapping it as the others jumped back. He raised an arm in the air, twisting his wrist and effortlessly bound the spirit within seconds. "You kept this *power* from me!"

"I kept this from you because I knew if this connection was real *this* is what you would turn into." Whynnie leaned into his hold. "A monster doesn't deserve power. *You are undeserving.*"

"Whynnie, don't!" Tears streamed down my aching jaw. I reached for my Goddess-born powers, needing them in this moment. Needing to save her.

Flames burst from my hands, and I aimed them at Malik's head, but his scout easily blocked my attacks with an air shield. The undead punched my abdomen harder this time, and I coughed and sputtered for air.

"At the end of the day, it was these *eyes.*" Malik sounded almost wistful as he brushed a thumb gently over her eyelid. "Always watching me, the Goddess taunting me through that disgusting white film."

"I wasn't created to taunt anyone," Whynnie said, her voice calm.

Communicating it as a fact only infuriated him more. "I was created to help."

"I see you in there, you cunt! You may have created me, but that doesn't make me yours!" His demeanor shifted and his spit splattered against Whynnie's face.

I screamed as he pressed his thumbs harder into Whynnie's eyes.

"I. Don't. Need. You!" He was panting and wheezing, no longer a man, but something else entirely.

Even over her ear-shattering wail, I heard her eyes pop. He circled her eye sockets roughly with his thumbs and continued to reach deeper, as if trying to locate her brain.

"Malik, you've won. Please stop." I gagged, and the bile launched its way up my throat and splashed across the ground.

Whynnie's body twitched, and she gradually bled out through her eye sockets.

I screamed like a feral cat, and a loud rumble of thunder consumed the skies above. Rain poured over us, the Goddess mourning the loss of her child.

My mark burned as Whynnie's faded. Rage pulled at the roots of my hair and deep within my pores. It was all-consuming and I let myself feel it. I thrashed against the hold on me, allowing the rain to soak me to the point of slipping free.

Once my knees hit the hard ground below, I spun in a circle and snagged my dagger from the ground, thrusting it deep into the undead's heart. He wailed and fell with a loud thud as the spirit fled his body to join the others searching for an empty husk.

As I turned back to face Malik, he lifted his chin high, standing and puffing out his heaving chest. Holding a dripping hand over Whynnie, he prepared to bind her.

"See? The Goddess can be killed. I am their God now!"

"Fuck! You!" I reached for a dagger and hurled it toward his chest so quickly that he had no time to block. It embedded deep into his shoulder.

"You bitch!"

I grabbed the dagger I kept tucked in my sleeve and launched it. He pivoted just as the blade caught the side of his face, slicing through his right eyebrow, blood pouring into his eye.

Whynnie's soul was a golden orb that slowly floated toward the sky.

"No! She's *mine!*" Malik pushed his magic, trying to grasp it. The smoke was dissipating with his sole intent on binding her, and scouts were closing in with their undead.

I raised a hand into the air.

"Stop her!" Malik cried, but it was too late. I was already hopping onto my broom, squeezing tightly. She shared the weight of it all and I clung to her, circling high above Malik.

No witch would see me through the haze of the battle. I followed Whynnie's soul as far as I could until the air was too thin, and the cold was too much. I wished I could follow her to the stars and the moon.

Hurtling back down, my body trembled. I was coming apart at the seams, but she was free. *She is free.*

Once I found Malik, I hovered. He was searching the skies for me.

Placing a finger to my throat, I spoke to Malik from the clouds like the Goddess-born I was intended to be, "I see you for what you are up here. Tell me, how does it feel? When I'm *just* out of your reach?"

He roared, shooting fire into the sky.

"*You're so small.* Puny really," I spat my disdain.

The wind shifted, and it carried with it screams of the injured and dying. I was whisked back to the loss of Lucky as sounds of wounded horses filled the air. The current state of our armies sent my heart up into my throat.

Vultures circled, waiting to feast on the many piles of mutilated witches.

Red orbs flew around erratically, clamoring for bodies they could inhabit. Our defenses had been torn to pieces and witches scrambled aimlessly with seemingly no direction.

Malik roared and stormed forward through his scouts toward what was left of our army.

Keep each other safe.

Whynnie's words played through my mind on a loop.

I couldn't breathe and my heart pounded mercilessly against my ribcage. *Where is he?* I unearthed the minuscule purple tendrils to the west side of where our lines used to be. They were so faint I almost missed them.

"Throwen." I flew faster than ever, ignoring the rain pelting my face and forcing Malik and my need for revenge to the back of my mind.

Chapter 39

THROWEN

Dagger clutched tightly in hand, I forced it into the undead's heart, tearing down through its burned ribs. Gurgling sputters emanated from where the red-orbed spirit had fled, a loud thump signifying its defeat.

The sounds and sights should have chilled me to my core, but I lost count of how many I had killed. The rain enhanced the smells of burning flesh, waste, and rot.

"Throwen!" Octavia's voice sounded wrong and as I turned to see her barreling toward me, I shuddered.

Nausea threatened to force the bile twisting in my stomach out into the air. *Something is wrong.* A disturbance to our realm I couldn't quite place.

"Octavia, where have you been? We need to know what's happening."

She sprang off her broom, driving her dagger into an oncoming scout's heart straight through his armor with a wail.

She rushed toward me with a slight limp, and she held her bleeding stomach. "Are you okay? I could barely see the spirits. I thought you were dying."

I was seething with rage at whoever spilled her precious blood and broke her perfect body.

Rubbing the blood and sweat from my eyes, I assessed the area, spinning in a circle. Any witch who witnessed the aftermath of my powers would know the Angel of Death was responsible. I had unknowingly been piling up bodies and a wall of fallen had formed around me, closing me in.

"Malik—" She moved her goggles to the top of her head and stumbled, her entire body unsteady.

I frowned at the already purpling bruises around her red, puffy eyes. With a hand clutching her chest, she fell to her knees, gasping for air.

I rushed over, shooting a scout who had breached the carcass mound with a lavender arrow. "I'm okay. Are you? Darling, talk to me."

Fuck! I hated pushing her like this, but there was so much blood and I had no idea how much of it was hers or what was going on beyond the hazy skies.

"Whynnie." The world halted and a loud sob broke free from her, thunder rattling the clouds. After Oxvein and the arches, I never wanted to hear that type of pain from her again. Octavia threw herself to the ground, pounding her fists into the dirt as her dry throat attempted to scream.

No. No. No.

"He killed her?" I didn't recognize the monotone voice coming from my mouth. Grip tightening on my bow, I stood.

"He didn't just kill her, Throwen. He fucking *mutilated* her. I couldn't stop it..." Her eyes might as well have been flames with the disgust and hatred roiling through their honey depths.

"I'll be back." I strode up to the mound of bodies, climbing them like a pile of wet stones. I grabbed onto a limp arm and almost slipped. Reaching for a severed string of muscle, I hoisted myself. Protruding bones became my footholds. But I didn't care, didn't truly see any of it.

My mom is gone.

"Wait!" Wrapping her arms around my waist, Octavia strained to tug me back down. "I couldn't save her body, but I did protect her soul. She's with the Goddess."

"He killed my fucking mom, Octavia!"

She cringed and stepped away.

Mom.

I had never said it aloud, always been afraid that if I took that step, it would somehow make me a target, make my family a target.

"I know. But Whynnie said we *have* to keep each other safe. Throwen, it's up to us," she said. "What do we do?"

She looked so small beneath me, and it felt unnatural. I was here to lift her up and protect her and I would do what I could to help her.

"Can you find Fennix?" I asked and her gaze lifted to the skies as she blinked against the rain like she saw something in them that I couldn't.

"I'll try." Running to her broom, she flew straight back into the hazy sky.

I sat in a bloody puddle, taking out the occasional scout and undead who surmounted the wall of bodies. Soon they would pile so high they would topple over, burying me in death and decay.

Sitting still was unbearable, but I needed to regain my stamina.

Octavia landed and limped to me, pulling me to my feet. She had a fresh wound on her arm where an arrow must have grazed her.

Panting, she relayed the information she gathered. "Fennix isn't far, but he is surrounded. Echo got separated from him, I can't see them anywhere. Can you follow me? Pepper is just there over the…" She hesitated. "Bodies."

"Let's go," I responded and started climbing.

Find Fennix. Make a plan. Find Fennix. Make a plan.

I recited it like a prayer because if I gave one more iota of thought to Whynnie it would swallow me and any rationality I had left. Pepper was young and strong, and we zigzagged through the chaos well, but a necromancer's knife grazed my calf.

The spirits lashed out, wrapping around his limbs and pulling him until his bones popped and he cried out from the pain. Taking it out on him did nothing to squelch the malevolence taking over my every thought.

I flicked my eyes to Octavia, flying overhead, ensuring we were going in the correct direction. Arrows and red orbs aimed to slow her down, but she weaved between them as if she belonged on that broom. I could argue it was what was keeping her alive as she hovered over the battle.

She stopped, throwing a flimsy shield around herself and pointing directly below her, just a few yards away. As I neared, I yelled, not wanting to use any more magic than I had to.

"Fennix!" When I found him in the mass of bodies, he was limping, slashing out at the undead closing in. I fired arrows into all their hearts and Fennix turned.

His usually honed expression was full of panic and his bicep was cut through like a thick slab of meat. I shook my head, a signal to let him know our people could not survive this.

"Parrot in a bottle!" Yelling over the sounds of the dying, he motioned toward the five exits. It seemed like days since we had entered through them as time distorted, an unwelcome effect of the shock radiating through my shaking muscles.

Nodding, I hollered to where Octavia hovered above us. "Octavia, lead them out! Retreat! Fly!"

She summoned bright flames to her palms, and her chest heaved, flying over our confused army. "Follow me!"

At first, only a few followed, but before long, she was leading them like a flock of sheep.

The bright leaves on the back of her broom faded into the distance. It felt eerily like the first time I saw her in the mirror. *This will likely be my last glimpse of the woman I love more than life itself.*

Whynnie said we have to keep each other safe. Octavia would never be safe if Malik still drew breath.

Striding away from the exit, I marched through the wet mud toward Malik's army when a hand gripped my arm. Pushing the assailant away roughly, I raised my dagger above my head.

"Throwen!" Fennix's voice caused me to falter. "You can't do this."

I blinked to make sure he was real before I pulled him close by his collar so he could hear me. "You can't stop me, Fennix. He killed Kallan. He killed Whynnie. I won't let him take anyone else from me."

I flung him back, and he fell to the ground. Turning, I strode toward a wall of undead, but ran into an air shield. Growling, I whirled on Fennix.

"Think of Echo. Think of Octavia." He was back on his feet, clutching his injured arm.

"I *am* thinking of them!" I whistled and Pepper ran up, stopping beside me. "Tell them I love them."

"Tell them yourself!" Rain trickled along his blade, but it did nothing to wash away the gore coating it.

I would if I could. We galloped away, Pepper's hooves splashing red stained mud everywhere.

Standing in the stirrups, I shot my way through Malik's army, and Fennix's screams of protest withered into nothing. I threw out fire and rock as I went, saving the spirits for when I needed them.

Making as much noise as possible, I dared to draw Malik's attention. "Where are you fucker?"

Protect her! Protect her! Protect her!

The force propelling me was more than revenge. This need to protect was in my soul, pulling me toward the threat.

Taking a deep breath, I scanned over the heads of those still standing. I couldn't decipher between the erratic red orbs and the smoke through the thick rain. "Goddess, show me where he is. Help me fulfill my purpose."

I steered Pepper forward, her hooves pounding the ground and squishing into the blood-soaked earth. Then I heard it, the tip of his whip cracking. "Thank you."

Blood pumped loudly in my ears as I neared the thick wall of red smoke and hopped off Pepper. I aimed her toward the exit and gave her a firm pat, pushing her in that direction. "Go to Octavia."

I stepped through the smoke, and it wrapped around me uncomfortably, purple tendrils whipping against it, furious to be enveloped. As I emerged, Malik stood, laughing, kicking something that made a wet thwack. He was distracted; the scouts surrounding him were unable to look away from what he was doing.

They were as white as the bones they wore. One covered his ears. Another vomited and the scout next to them fainted. Then it caught my eye, a strand of bright silver hair somehow still untouched by the gore.

No! You can feel later.

I slipped back into the smoke. My skin itched, and I fought against my nausea. The spirits spasmed, eager to eliminate the threat. "You'll have your chance soon."

His laughter grew more deafening, and I rounded the space, placing his back right in front of me through the dark red haze. I *was* the Angel of Death, and I was more than ready to deliver his.

Kill him.

The spirits shot out, wrapping around his eyes like a blindfold. I plunged my dagger toward him but he pulled away at the last moment. He lifted a hand, red smoke snuffing out where the spirits had curtained his vision.

We circled each other. "We haven't properly met. I'm Throwen."

Roaring, he snapped his whip toward my neck. I dodged, rolling on the ground and right back to my feet. As he pulled his whip back, ready to strike again, I invaded his space, tackling him to the ground.

I groaned against the pain of my injuries and unsheathed a dagger, aiming it for his heart. His palms caught the blade, and he cried out as it sliced through.

"You imprisoned the woman I love!"

His mouth foamed black, and he called on his necromancer magic. Red tendrils wrapped around the blade, pushing it back in my direction. He sneered, false victory already in his eyes.

"Your necromancers killed my brother!" Purple tendrils wrapped around the hilt, pushing back. They lashed against the red like fighting cobras.

"No!" he spat, squirming against my firm hold, still keeping his hands on the blade.

"You killed my *mom*!" I allowed myself to look at what was left of Whynnie's body as the spirits pressed harder, the blade nearing his chest. Words couldn't explain the state of it, and I fought the sob wanting to break free from my throat.

"What are you doing? Kill him!" Malik ordered his scouts but most of them were in a state of shock from his unhinged violence. The others did nothing, staring at me with hope in their watery eyes.

"You have no real power. Your people fear you, they don't love you." Small tendrils curled around my fingers and licked at the blade, eager to enact their revenge.

But I was almost completely drained of my magic, and I had to hurry. Malik's momentary fear morphed into something sinister. I detected the footsteps too late.

I was knocked over, hitting my head painfully against the ground as a massive undead drove its knee into my chest. He pinned me roughly, and I panted, overstretching for my magic. Wisps of lavender caressed my face before fading into nothing.

Malik's eyes glowed a deep red, and I couldn't tell if he was fully human anymore. Had the Abyss turned him into this, or did he commit so many atrocities that it changed him?

He lowered to the ground, crawling toward me on all fours like a rabid dog.

"I think I'll cut out your windpipe first." He hovered over me, dragging a knife down my throat to my sternum, just enough to pierce through the skin as he went. Blood matted into my chest hair, and I bit into my lip hard, refusing to give him what he wanted.

"That is a bard's most prized possession, no? Or maybe it's your cock. Do you think it's somehow special now that you've had it buried inside a Goddess-born?"

Octavia. I have to save her. I have to get out of this.

"I'm going to kill you for what you did to her!" I spit in his face, and he smiled as he wiped it away before wrapping his hands around my skull. He pressed his face close to mine, and I gagged from the acrid smell pouring from his lips.

"I think I'll take your eyes." He dragged his knife from my temple down along my jaw. I couldn't help the screams that fell from my lips. "Whynnie made such satisfying screams when I took hers. Let's see if that annoying voice of yours is any good. It *has* to be better than your other skills because tracking you was easy, and *this* was pathetic."

"Fuck you!" I lashed out, trying to bite him, but the undead punched my face as Malik laughed. I kicked my legs wildly, but they only dug us deeper into the mud.

This wasn't right. This couldn't be the will of the Goddess. He killed my mom and my brother. Tortured and manipulated Octavia and his entire fucked up cult. *He* was the one who should have died, not them. Not my family.

As he brushed his thumbs against my eyes, I failed to shake my head free, the undead now held it steady for him. My body felt like it was on fire as I screamed.

"You should be thanking me. Being killed by a God is an honor." His thumbs began to curl into my eye sockets, and that's when I heard it.

Her voice was clear in my mind. It reminded me of nights alone in the caves when I would sing, and my voice bounced back to me. She threw my own words back in my face.

I will never let you die.

Lightning struck the ground beside us as a banshee-like scream pierced the air, forcing Malik to roll off me to deflect and cover his head from the threat.

No. Not lightning.

Gradually, I took in the miracle before me as my jaw fell. Golden strands intertwined with the purple spirits that were somehow being tugged from me. There was no pain. I was simply a vessel now.

Octavia stood effortlessly as she hovered over us on her broom. She was a beacon, the brightest star in the dark sky, unleashing her fury like a storm. The rain came harder now, and the purple strands split, wrapping around Malik's chest while the gold ones coiled around his neck like a viper.

"Goodbye, Malik." Her words echoed so loudly I was sure our fleeing armies heard.

As his neck snapped, the spirits flooded through his body. His skin bubbled and boiled as Octavia called on her necromancy for a final time, binding him to the Abyss forever.

Chapter 40

THROWEN

3 months later

"Once you walked through those catacombs, there was no escape. Traveling through Ombra Lurra was a death sentence... and my son... he tried anyway. If the wildlife didn't slaughter him, the scouts did. I wish I could have stopped him."

As I strummed gently, the spirits languidly moved around the circle of witches sitting near the fire. Tents were erected all around and the foundations of new buildings lingered in the distance.

"I remember Percy." Octavia sat across from me, leading a session with survivors who wished to participate. She wore a turquoise pleated top and matching pants that Enoch had crafted. The neckline plunged below her breasts with a braided tie cinching the bottom tight around her ribs. Her brand could be seen by all but it was just another way they knew that she endured the same treatment they did.

Once Malik fell, the witches handled it in confusing riffs. Some fled while others wailed, slitting their throats and falling on their swords. Malik's lies were so powerfully ingrained in their minds that they thought death was the only choice.

Others raised their arms high and fell in surrender. A large group even surged toward Octavia, falling at her feet in worship.

"You do?" Percy's mother lifted her face from her hands, black tears dripping from her kohl-lined eyes. Her accent was gone, but you could still tell she hailed from Luftor.

"I used to sneak to the gardens, and I remember hearing his jokes. He had a fabulous sense of humor."

The mother choked on a laugh. My playing helped to calm their anxieties enough to speak their truths, but Octavia's ability to take on other's emotions as her own made her extremely adept at helping the grieving and traumatized.

Shortly after the battle, my muse took any willing witches back to the Coven of the Grave. After we collected anything of use or value, she led us to the tree.

She was the first to take an axe to its thick, black bark. I'd recognized the tree from her first broom, but seeing the rest of it left a chasm in the pit of my stomach. She'd offered the axe to another coven member who stepped up and took their anger and grief out on the monstrosity.

One by one, they had taken their turns, thwacks were followed by grunts, screams, and tears. Coming together as a community, they had torn down the evil they had lived with for so long.

I had helped them pull out the stump and burn it to ash before we said our final goodbyes to the prison portrayed as paradise.

Octavia stood, and I pressed my palm flat against the strings, ensuring she had the group's full attention.

"Life is difficult right now. But I will fight to make things better. Everything you're feeling is valid." She moved her head slowly, drifting from one witch's gaze to the next. "Your pain, anger, guilt, even numbness are valid. It's real. I know because I feel it too." A tear streamed down her cheek as she pressed her hand over her heart, and I felt it, too.

My grief over Kallan and Whynnie had simmered into something else. I could feel my usual peace and contentedness while I picked up the shards of my life and created a new mosaic. The only way to get through it was to keep going.

"If there is anything you need, please don't hesitate to ask us." Her golden stare fell on me, the hope in her eyes drawing me in. She reached out a hand to Percy's mother. "We chose this to be our home. So, let's make it that. You aren't alone here."

What was left of the coven had voted on a spot about a day's ride from Goldhaven toward the sea, toward Starpass.

Once all the buildings were complete, they would vote on a name. But for now, Octavia lovingly referred to it as Almondgrove, the fantastical land from Kallan's favorite books.

"Now, let's eat! I'm *starving*." As she clapped her hands together, everyone laughed and stood, meandering to the line forming near the pop-up kitchen where volunteers ladled out cheesy potato soup that the Rosewood donated.

Swinging my new lute over my back, I made my way to her. A few witches had gathered, and she was holding a little girl's hand, crouching to hear her whispers.

"I've got just the thing to help with those nightmares." Octavia searched her pack, pulling out a knitted wolf and giving it to the girl.

My satisfied grin was followed by a deep breath that filled my lungs completely. *I am so fucking proud of her.*

Sometimes, when she couldn't sleep, I would hear the clicking of Kallan's needles beside me. She would let out tiny grunts of frustration as she taught herself along the way. Echo now had scarves in every color combination imaginable.

"A doggy!" The little girl's adorable voice kept Octavia's smile in place as she held the gift tightly to her chest.

"Not just any doggy, Aria. *A wolf.* They talk to each other like this. Owwwww!" Octavia howled unabashedly into the clear night sky and some of the more jovial witches throughout the camp joined in, howling at the full moon.

Aria giggled and bounced up and down, howling along with them. "Thank you, Lady!" She sprinted to her father and showed him the stuffed animal.

"How did you know that would help her?" I asked.

Octavia shrugged. "Because it's what I would have wanted at her age."

"You know that's who you're becoming, right? The person little Octavia needed."

She pressed a finger to her nose. "That's a pretty deep thought, bard," she teased.

"Yeah, I have them from time to time." I wrapped my arms around her waist, pulling her close, "I know something else that gets pretty deep." I spanked her hard, eliciting a yelp. The velvety pants clung tightly to her ass and thighs, just waiting to be groped.

"*Goddesses's tits!*" Spikes dangled from her silver ear cuff, swinging wildly with her movements.

"You like it." I rubbed the spot, massaging the muscle in her glutes. She trained with me whenever possible and was getting stronger every day.

Resting her forehead against my chest, she curled her fingers under the hem of my collar. "Yes. But the whole camp doesn't need to know that."

She glanced up just as a cloud shifted, revealing the full moon. As if greeting a friend, her eyes softened. Her hair was longer now, and I brushed a piece away from her face, slipping it behind her ear.

"*Sacred Ether* you get more captivating every day." I swayed us back and forth to the music in my head, humming it in her ear. Expressing how

I felt about her was becoming another honed skill in my arsenal. She loved the praise, and I was more than willing to give it to her.

"Oh! I got you something!" She ducked out of my hold, racing to her bag and returning with a crimson pouch.

"When did you have time to get me a gift?"

She had been working non-stop to make sure her people had a safe place to call home and studying the grimoires Whynnie had left her every spare moment. Shifting uncomfortably, I watched her search for the right words.

"I didn't know exactly what you might like. I figured a break from the gold might be nice..." She handed me the pouch and I guessed at what the jingling sounds could be.

She held her breath as I emptied the contents onto my palm. I traced my fingers tenderly over each silver pick.

"That one is engraved." Octavia lifted up and down on her heels, impatiently awaiting my response.

For my charming bard.

Sliding them onto my fingertips made me realize just how incomplete I felt without them. Like always, Octavia found ways to make me feel alive and whole.

I held my hand up, admiring their shine against my death-touched skin. All my doubts about protecting her faded. It wasn't all on me anymore, I knew she could handle herself. "Octavia, they're perfect."

"Are you sure? Because I can ask them to make a gold pair—"

I silenced her uncertainty, grabbing onto her face and sliding my tongue into her mouth as she moaned. When I pulled away, I held her chin.

She looked different. Her expression was filled with purpose and passion. Her body was strong and healthy.

"I love them. But not nearly as much as I love you. Thank you." Expressing my own emotions was still a struggle, but I was learning.

"I can think of a few ways you can repay my kindness." She pressed against me, and it took all of my self-control not to throw her over my shoulder and carry her back to our tent so I could rip that top off and run my thumbs over her peaked nipples.

"Throwen! Play us a song!" Aria rushed up with her wolf, hugging my leg. Octavia smiled sweetly at her before returning a hungry gaze to me.

"Duty calls, bard." She leaned in, kissing my nose and lacing her fingers in mine. "We can finish this discussion later."

With a wink, she strode over to help serve food to her people. As she pulled her hair up into a high ponytail, her glowing mark stole my breath. I would never get used to seeing it. She took my life, which was turning stale, and added so much spice that I would never again fear being bored.

I praised my creator because she was mine, and I was hers. And I couldn't wait to tell the entirety of Theldea about how and why I fell in love with the Goddess-born.

Chapter 41

OCTAVIA

One year after The Battle of Starpass

"I'm not sure I'm ready." I ran my hands over my white blouse, failing to ease the tension in my bare shoulders. Enoch made sure the black cincher gave me plenty of room to breathe, but I still left it slightly open in case panic overtook me.

"This isn't like the ceremonies your brain and body are used to. It's okay to feel trepidation," Throwen reassured me.

The uneven hem of my silver skirt flew out into four points as he twirled me in a circle, pulling me back in to sway to the beating of his heart.

Without the threat of Malik and necromancy, I gradually grew into myself. I was indeed the sprout Whynnie had so wisely nicknamed me. After being stunted all my life, I finally had room to spread my branches, but the fear of rejection and failure was still strong.

"I know. It just feels weird. My skin is itchy and I'm sweating *a lot*. Can you tell?"

He chuckled as I raised my arms high above my head, smelling myself. Reaching out a hand, he hauled me into a tight embrace. The pressure of his hug relieved some of the energy that had been building in me for days.

"We can take a bath as soon as we get back home."

Home. It was something I had now. But it wasn't just Almondgrove, it was the entirety of Theldea. I felt most comfortable in Throwen's room at the Rosewood, but we were welcomed into every coven we visited.

I had spent hours in the archives studying the grimoires Whynnie had left. I followed her layout and had barely made a dent in the education she would have offered me. As I read through them, it was almost like she was still here with me, guiding me through the words of Goddess-born past.

Once word spread that a new Goddess-born saved them from necromancy, every coven leader was lining up to meet with me. Some of them were genuine, like Nova and Simulie, wanting only to help their covens thrive.

Mayson pretended to want what was best for Graygarde but he favored the elite. This seemed to be true for most of the Luftor covens, but they still claimed to be taking Echo's advice at our meetings.

The Stranata coven leaders were next on my list to deal with, and I had been putting them off, hoping Fennix would ease the tension beforehand.

Though they all managed me and the situation in different ways, they always had a look of awe and fear when speaking with me directly. I didn't blame them; they had every right to be cautious. Many had learned of what happened with Calliope. Fennix's men had loose lips and word traveled fast in Theldea.

"What if they hate me?" I worried my lip between my teeth. I read the death witch grimoire over and over and still had no answers as to what exactly happened when I unleashed myself to kill Malik.

The magic I used was desperate, frantic, and dangerously unstable. The kind of magic that makes you throw away your morals because your love is more potent than any of them. A unique hybrid born of my bond with Throwen and my own powers. I'd refused to reach for that much power since.

"Octavia. Just for tonight, give yourself a little slack. You've helped as many as were willing. You've healed not only the witches of Theldea, but the very land we tread."

I knew in my mind he was right, but it was rioting against any form of positivity. "Throwen…"

Like clockwork, I searched for his comfort as my mind conjured visions. They weren't like they used to be. Hallucinations that used to consist of scouts and Malik morphed into my new nightmares, usually horrific scenes of my loved ones dying.

I blinked, knowing that the lifeless Throwen before me wasn't real and soon the vision would subside. My demon still purred in my mind on the hardest nights, guilt wanting me to finish what I started when I jumped out of that window.

Hallucinations seemed to be a part of who I was, not just a type of trauma. It was something about how my brain functioned, or maybe it was how the blood flowed through it. There was no true way to tell, but it was easier now that I always had a hand to hold. I waited it out, squeezing until I could see the deep plum and lavender dancing around his pupils.

"I know stress makes them worse. If you need to sit this out that's okay." He pressed a warm palm to my cheek, and I leaned into it.

"No. I want to do this. They need to see my magic, so they don't fear it." I scrunched up my nose at his choice of outfit. "Speaking of scaring people, did you have to wear that?"

Throwen was dressed in all-black leather with a matching cloak. Daggers were strapped across his firm chest and his songbook was buckled at his side.

My charming bard with the mind of an assassin.

"Yup. Death witch. My entire purpose is to protect you. Plus, you think it's hot."

"Ugh! Stop." I protested with a huge smile and was thankful for his ability to always make me laugh.

Horns sounded loudly and my momentary joy shifted as we followed their call hand in hand. I paused at the entrance and turned to Throwen. He gently placed the crown I had retrieved from the Coven of the Grave upon my head and knelt before me. I placed my hand atop his head.

Malik no longer defined my title. I was the Lady of the Grave, and I was a healer. The crown was part of me, and I prayed when the witches of Theldea saw it, they would experience hope instead of fear. It was time to give it a new meaning, a new purpose.

I lowered to his level, kissing him one last time before we stood and walked through the entrance to Starpass.

I fought the urge to throw on my mask of apathy. Instead, I looked at my feet, my silver flats contrasting against the dark soil.

"Goddess, O, you look magnificent!" Echo's voice warmed my chest, and I lifted my gaze. They were in a flowing white dress with sleeves that grazed the ground. Kallan's cutlass was strapped to their side. When I saw the teal scarf I had knit around their neck, my eyes burned with unshed tears.

Fennix stood to their left, wearing his matching crimson scarf with an embarrassed grimace. They had been treasure hunting, attempting to unite the Stranatan covens along the way. His skin was so tanned he looked like he was made of leather.

His wounds from the battle were on display, the worst one a large scar from where a sword cut straight through his bicep. I couldn't speak but instead rushed over, hugging them both. "Thank you."

When I turned to face Throwen he had his horribly disproportional violet scarf on, the first one I ever made. "Oh, my Goddess. You're all going to embarrass me, aren't you?"

"Yup!" Echo flicked their scarf dramatically over their shoulder, falling behind us. The other eyes on me registered as I took in the thousands of witches lining the path to the center of Starpass.

I moved slowly, taking deep breaths. Rumors of my powers on the battlefield had spread and many of them were greatly exaggerated. My true powers were not destructive. My magic was connected to nature, and I could grow and mend the land itself.

I helped rebuild the ice bridge between Miren and Oxvein that was melting, but it took two months of using my powers daily. Eventually, the ice reformed, stronger than before.

But Starpass was my place to push the limits of my powers. I had been able to grow a grove of trees on the west and east sides. The middle I reserved for fields of wildflowers. I flew on my broom whenever I could, sprinkling seeds over the soil before pressing my magic into the land.

Now witches from all over Theldea stood near the stone markers I had lined the path with. Each one was inscribed with the name of a fallen witch. Families found their loved ones' stones and stood at the markers.

"Thank ye, Lady," one witch spoke up from my left. I bowed in response as more and more thanked me as we walked the long path. As we neared the center, my mark hummed and glowed.

I knelt with my family before Whynnie's and Kallan's stone markers. Echo touched Kallan's and Throwen pressed a hand to Whynnie's.

Their markers were the same size as the rest. Atop Kallan's sat a deck of worn playing cards inside a glass jar with sprigs of sage and deep maroon dahlias. A matching glass jar sat atop Whynnie's with her favorite teacup, one Echo, Throwen, and Kallan had painted her when they were kids.

I took a deep breath, turning to address the crowd. Flora, Babette, Nova, and Petwa stood beside Fennix, Enoch, and Finian in front of the crowd. They smiled at me encouragingly. I had practiced my speech with my friends and family many times, but my nerves still made my knees shake.

The crowd stood in a ring around me, but instead of the dread ceremonies like this usually evoked, I felt empowered. Pressing a finger to my throat, I ensured even the back of the crowd could hear me.

"For a year, I have been asking myself if freedom is worth the cost."

The only sound was a soft breeze carrying the first fallen leaves with it.

"Whynnie taught me that sometimes we have to wait for the answers to our biggest questions. I may not give you an answer to that question, but I can give you this."

I lowered to the ground, mimicking my actions from the first time I stepped foot in Starpass with Whynnie. My voice echoed in the cavernous graveyard as witches from all over Theldea listened.

"I, Octavia, Lady of the Grave and blessed Goddess-born, intend to heal Theldea's lands and the witches who inhabit them to the best of my ability. My intentions are not a vie for power. I love this land and the witches in it. I want to see this world and these people thrive." A lump caught in my throat at just how far I had come.

Instead of using my words, I pressed my palm to the ground beside Whynnie and Kallan's stones. As I sent my intent into the soil, gold strands burst out from around me, pulsing through the entire ground beneath the monuments like excited inchworms.

Lush clover sprouted around their feet. Witches gasped and murmured as they got to see my distinctive magic for themselves. Witches could manipulate elements that were already there. But I could create life from nothing. It seemed the Goddess intended for me to be a creator as well.

I might never truly be comfortable in my skin. But maybe that's because a piece of our deity flowed through me. Maybe what was inside of me wasn't meant to be shoved into a physical body.

But for now, I would endure the discomfort for all of them. Throwen lifted me up, and I panted from using so much magic. He pulled me close, taking some of the weight.

The crowd erupted into cheers and applause.

"I'm proud of you, little muse," Throwen whispered in my ear, and I hummed happily, soaking in his warmth.

"I'm proud of myself, too."

Epilogue

In the groves of Starpass, Octavia walks barefoot, gathering honey from the bee boxes she and Echo splattered with vibrant colors.

She sings softly, "How could the raven befriend the crow? I don't know... I don't—"

The ground rumbles under her feet and soon after, a baby's cry can be heard not far off. A beaming smile lights up her face.

Grabbing her broom, she sits side-saddle and glides toward the sounds, though she is sure she already knows where they are coming from. The golden mark on her neck glows brightly as autumn leaves whip around her long chestnut hair.

She often comes here to read when her bard forces her to take a day off. Sometimes Throwen accompanies her, singing her sweet songs as they remember Whynnie and Kallan.

The baby is nestled next to their memorials. His full head of thick black hair is dark as night. He cries as the chill reaches his arms that he wriggled free of the golden fabric he is wrapped in.

Octavia quickly scoops him up into her arms. "Hush now, I'm right here. You aren't alone. It's going to be just fine."

She offers her finger and as the baby squeezes, he calms.

"There you go little Raven, hold on as tightly as you need. I was wondering when you were going to show up." She rocks the baby in her arms, lightly tracing the tiny golden key on the back of his neck. "I can't wait to see the doors of new possibilities you will open."

He giggles in response, drool dripping down his round chin. His eyes are slate gray and around each iris is a thin band of a blue so deep Octavia isn't sure she's ever seen the shade before.

"Throwen and Echo are going to be very cross you showed up when they weren't here. But don't worry, I'll protect you from their dramatics."

He squeezes harder and Octavia hums with delight. "So strong already! That reminds me, I made you something" She reaches into her bag and hands the baby a tiny knit teddy bear. "Kallan would have loved you."

A bitter wind sweeps through the wildflower field, and the baby cries. Soon the bees will stay in their hives.

"It's okay, I'll keep you warm." She swaddles the baby in the golden fabric and wraps him against her chest with the scarf she wore. Rubbing the top of his soft head makes his eyes start to close, weary from his journey and being hand-delivered by the Goddess. She watches from a parallel plane, smiling at her special creations.

As Octavia flies them back home, she holds firmly to who she is now. The past no longer controls her. Her mind throws tantrums that she's learned to handle, sometimes with help.

She knows she will never be completely free of her demons, but even in her darkness, she's loved and free. Things she vows to pass onto the baby sleeping and drooling on her shirt.

"Welcome to the family, little Raven. We have so much to teach you."

Acknowledgements

Ben, you earned the dedication but deserve to be at the end of this book too. (Try not to let it go to your head.) Thank you for your support, reassurance, and inspiration. The world could use more people like you and Throwen.

I want to thank my dad for instilling in me a love of all things fantasy. Mom, your support means the world to me. To my sister, thank you for inspiring me to write, always giving me the books you no longer want, and sharing your audiobooks. Aunt Gina this book wouldn't have a pronunciation guide without you so thank you for sounding out these nonsensical places with me.

To my editor, Brit, I want to say thank you for your patience.

Emily, who would have thought we would go from life drawing to lifelong friends? The cover of this book means so much more because you made it. The map is remarkable. Thank you for dealing with my many, many changes throughout this process.

Tess, Aspen, Kat, Rikka, JALS, and Heather: thank you for trudging through this thick girl ten chapters at a time while I figured everything out. Your tactful comments helped me mold the manuscript from nothing but a pile of clay.

Kelsey, Katie, Mira, Freya, Chelsea: thank you for hyping me up and pointing out the things I somehow still missed after five drafts. Your love of my world and characters kept me going through the doubt and fear.

Tess, you were a phenomenal proofreader, and I sincerely hope you can proofread my next book.

To my Discord friends, there aren't words. You have become my closest companions and confidants. Thank you for answering my questions, walking the path with me as I pursue my passions, and being there when I have nobody else to talk to.

This book would not exist without the incredible indie community I tripped and fell into. Readers, thank you for your excitement. Authors thank you for inspiring and supporting me.

I want to thank the girl who went through many things that helped write Octavia's mental illness and trauma. I want to thank the young adult who attempted to leave but found a reason to stay. I want to thank the woman who found herself and finished writing this book. In the words of Octavia, "I'm proud of myself, too."

About the Author

F.S. Autumn writes stirring fantasy infused with tension. She enjoys the oddities of life, especially the morbid side of things. Diagnosed with bipolar disorder in 2018, she is an advocate for mental health and suicide awareness and prevention. When not consumed by writing down the stories that live rent-free in her mind, she spends quality time with her husband and child (who she lovingly refers to as her baby bat), or enjoys her other passions, which include creating art for other indie authors, reading, and binge-watching the latest shows.

Made in the USA
Columbia, SC
09 April 2025